The PATH of ANGER

ANTOINE ROUAUD

Translated from the French by Tom Clegg

GOLLANCZ

LONDON

First published in Great Britain in 2013 by Gollancz
An imprint of the Orion Publishing Group
Orion House, 5 Upper St Martin's Lane, London WC2H 9EA
An Hachette UK Company

A CIP catalogue record for this book is available
from the British Library

ISBN 978 0 575 13080 7 (Cased)
ISBN 978 0 575 13081 4 (Trade Paperback)

1 3 5 7 9 10 8 6 4 2

Typeset by Input Data Services Ltd, Bridgwater, Somerset

Printed and bound by CPI Group (UK) Ltd, Croydon, CR0 4YY

The Orion Publishing Group's policy is to use papers
that are natural, renewable and recyclable products and made from
wood grown in sustainable forests. The logging and manufacturing
processes are expected to conform to the environmental
regulations of the country of origin.

www.orionbooks.co.uk
www.gollancz.co.uk

To Greg, my friend, my brother,
whose unfailing support and friendship,
despite the distances between us, let me keep writing.

PART I

A SCENT OF LAVENDER

There comes a day in every life,
A meeting point of what we were,
What we are and what we will be.
At that moment,
As all things draw to a close,
We decide our fate.
Proud or ashamed of the road travelled ...

Es it allae, Es it alle en, Es it allarae.

What you were, what you are, what you shall be. It was the port city's motto. Its true meaning mattered little when even the humblest traveller knew the saying without ever visiting the city. Here, in the South of the former Kingdoms, Masalia had always been the city where all things were possible.

Possible because, positioned far from the Imperial capital, at the end of the world, it represented the last outpost of civilisation before the so-far-unexplored expanse of the Western Ocean. Large numbers of trading ships ventured from its port, sailing to the Sudies Islands or following the coastline to the cities of the North. And possible because Masalia had been conquered so many times, by so many Kingdoms, that it no longer possessed an architecture it could call its own. Each neighbourhood bore the traces of its successive rulers, from the tall square towers of the Aztene period, with their characteristic dragonhorn crowns, to the proud mansions of the Caglieri dynasty and their flower-filled balconies, not to mention the three cathedrals of the Fangolin faith, two of which had been built on the still-smoking remains of pagan temples. In this city it mattered little where you came from, who you were, or what you might become. Masalia was the product of the history of all the former Kingdoms. As the saying went: 'Rich or poor, weak or powerful, you who are fleeing from other parts of the world, rest assured that here, at the crossroads of peoples, you shall find what you are seeking.'

Nothing could dampen the hopes and dreams evoked by the mere mention of Masalia. Not the heavy rain pouring down upon the red tiled rooftops. Not the mud it carried along the gutters in the narrow alleys. And not even the worn stone façade of this particular tavern, from whose open windows came the muffled sounds of men drinking.

'Are you sure this is the place?' asked a hoarse voice.

From beneath her ample hood, Viola peered at the tavern door. A few raindrops slid slowly down her round spectacles, blurring the brightly lit windows. She nodded, stepped forward and her boots sank into the mud with an unpleasant squelch. Her slender shadow, which fell across the wooden door, was suddenly engulfed by the much larger one of the person walking behind her. She hesitated, her hand poised over the heavy iron door handle. Trickles of rain ran over the black metal flecked with rust ...

'You who are fleeing from other parts of the world ...'

There was no going back now. Her mouth was terribly dry but there was no question of giving up at this stage. The sound of her companion clearing his throat drew her out of her reverie. With a brusque gesture, she seized the handle and pressed down.

'Rest assured that here you shall find what you are seeking.'

The fresh air they brought in with them dissipated quickly in the coils of acrid smoke which rose up to the ceiling, while the rhythmic drumming of the raindrops on the ground outside almost vanished beneath the hubbub of loud voices, bursts of laughter and the clinking of tankards. A bolt of lightning briefly silhouetted the massive shoulders and bald skull of the man with her. He closed the door behind him before following in Viola's footsteps and emerging into the light cast by the oil lamps. A serving wench came to a sudden halt, almost dropping her tray as she saw the tattoos covering his olive skin. They snaked their way gracefully over the most minute features of his face. For an instant he locked eyes with her before she ducked away to serve a table nearby. The drab, elderly merchants seated there applauded her arrival.

Times had changed and the Nâaga were no longer such frightening figures. It was becoming less surprising to see a *savage* here, in the city, and still less in a dive like this. While the Empire had included only civilised folk, the Republic prided itself on opening its doors to anyone ... or anything.

The Nâaga took in the room with a wary eye. Most of those present were traders from the small towns of the West, here in Masalia on business, but there were also travellers of a very different sort. When he saw Viola was already forging through the crowd without waiting for him, he let out a groan. He knew the kind of brigands who tended to hide in a place like this, where even a simple glance taken the wrong way led to trouble.

She had already reached the counter when he caught up with her and she was holding a wrinkled piece of paper out to a round-faced man. As he smoothed it out on the countertop to decipher it, the tavern keeper ran a hand over his balding, sweat-beaded head. His mouth fell open as he puzzled over it, revealing his three remaining teeth.

'Dun ... Dun ...' he said out loud. 'Ah yes, that must be pronounced like "Deune"! He's a fellow from the West? Yes, yes. That's why I didn't understand ... Written Dun, but pronounced Deune. Typical of the Westies, that is. Go figure, they're not like us.'

'This Dun ... is he here?' asked Viola.

The tavern keeper raised an eyebrow and gave both the young woman and the Nâaga leaning against the counter to her right an appraising look. The dark face with the black serpents dancing across the smooth skin made him feel uncomfortable and he patted down a tangled tuft of pepper-and-salt hair sticking out over one ear. The woman was still hooded and shadow masked the upper part of her face. He only caught the gleam of a pair of spectacles reflecting the lamplight.

'And who are you, exactly?' he grumbled, peering at the protruding handle of the mace which the giant carried on his back. 'I don't want any trouble here.'

'We don't intend to cause any,' Viola assured him. 'Rogant here is merely my ... protector,' she added as she slowly lowered her hood, her lips curled in a slight smile.

The tavern keeper's recalcitrance vanished as to he took in the delicate features of her face. Behind the small round lenses of her

5

spectacles two deep green, almond-shaped eyes gazed back at him. Above her cheeks, freckles dotted her milky-white skin, accentuated by bright red hair which was gathered into a chignon, two stray locks dangling before her ears.

'As you might imagine, without him, in these neighbourhoods, I'd be the one risking trouble.'

She was beautiful, and barely twenty years of age. Easy prey for any cutthroat lurking in the shadowy alleyways outside. A fine golden pattern had been carefully stitched on the hem of her shoulder cape. If she wasn't a noblewoman who'd survived the purges after the fall of the Empire, then she must belong to the new breed of Republican upstarts.

'Dun's just an old man,' explained the tavern keeper wiping his damp hands with a dirty rag. 'He's a bit touched in the head, but he's never hurt anyone.'

'I told you, we're not here to cause any trouble . . .'

'All right then. He was once a soldier as he tells it, but he's not dangerous, you know.'

'I simply wish to speak with him,' insisted Viola, carefully enunciating each word in a soft voice.

'I remember the last time, about five years ago, somebody "simply" wanted to speak to a fellow like Dun,' retorted the tavern keeper with a hard expression. 'And you know what? The next day he was hanged in the square, in front of a cheering crowd.'

'The purges are over,' the young woman assured him in a tight voice.

The tavern keeper exchanged a glance with the Nâaga. The latter's black eyes gave no indication of deceit.

'So it seems,' the man muttered.

He mopped his brow, as if weighing the consequences of pointing out the man they sought. As if he were wondering if lying would help matters. When he lifted his head again he wore a rueful expression. He had already given the old man away by alluding to his past.

'You're from Emeris, I'd stake my head on it.'

'We don't chop off heads,' replied Viola, holding back a smile. 'Nor do we hang people any more without a trial.'

'But there are some Imperials still being hunted . . .' the tavern keeper said cagily.

'That's right,' she acknowledged in a tone intended to be soothing. 'There are some. But as it happens, that isn't what brings me here. I don't believe Dun committed any crimes other than following orders. I simply wish to speak with him. So just tell us if he's here, and you won't be bothered further, I swear to you.'

'No problems, hmm ...?' said the tavern keeper, glancing pointedly at Rogant.

'Just speak with him,' Viola repeated.

The tavern keeper flung his rag over his shoulder and hunted for a familiar figure among his customers. When he caught sight of the man, sitting at a table, he pointed him out with a swift nod of the head. Viola turned and spent several seconds trying to ascertain which man he was indicating. She exchanged glances with the Nâaga, but he was of no assistance. Rogant limited himself to keeping a watchful eye on the movements and actions of those present. She dismissed the tavern keeper with a wave of her hand and plunged back into the crowd, braving the men who stared wide-eyed at her and whistled in her wake. Serving wenches were rushing to and fro around her, carrying jugs in either hand. Raucous laughter rose from the seated merchants. The odour of sweat mixed with the pall of smoke hanging over the entire taproom. It grew sharper as she reached Dun's table.

'Just a few coppers, Dun ... I'll pay ya back double,' begged a small man, holding an upturned hat in his hands.

'An' I told you, I don't want to see yer ugly mug again,' groused the old man.

His grey hair was spattered with filth and there was a black smudge on the back of his neck. If his shirt had once been white, only the sleeves preserved any evidence of that, here and there beneath a layer of grey grime and brown spots. His leather vest was so worn that thin cracks ran across the back.

'I can win it all back, there's four of 'em come from Serray. They don't know nothin' 'bout playin' fraps. Ya know me, I can beat 'em two ta one.'

'If you hadn't spoken to me that way, I might've advanced you a stake. Never speak to me like that. Never.'

He jabbed an accusing finger and, with a sweep of the arm which caused the small man to stumble, pointed to another table where four lively fellows wearing broad purple cloaks were singing at the top of their lungs.

'Go speak to yer mates from Serray the way you spoke to me,' he growled. 'And you'll get yer head stuffed up yer arse. Maybe then you'll see what a generous sod I am. Now get away ...'

Head bowed, the small man turned on his heel and scuttled into the crowd of customers. Viola sensed Rogant at her back. She turned her head slightly and caught his eye over her shoulder. The Nâaga nodded. She lost no time in moving around the table to stand in front of the old man. His hands gripping a large tankard, he raised an eyebrow to peer at her. His face was weathered and stubble surrounded his chapped lips, while a ridged scar traced a curve beneath his right eye. He fit the description she had.

'Dun?'

He gave no reply.

'May I?' she asked, placing a hand on the back of the chair.

Still no response.

'I won't take up too much of your time.'

He took a swallow from his tankard as she sat down, but almost choked when he saw the Nâaga taking a seat to his right.

'What's this savage doing at my table?' he growled, giving Viola a black look.

'Rogant is a Nâaga,' she told him curtly. 'Not a savage. Most of them are sedentary now, you know. Just like you and me.'

She pushed her spectacles up with the tip of her index finger before adding:

'And he's with me.'

'So this tattooed creature is sedentary now, is he?' the old man snapped. 'And how does that excuse his sitting at my table without being invited?'

Viola withstood the soldier's glare with such a determined air that he finally turned away to glance at the Nâaga. He had fought the Nâaga so many times that he found the Republic's tolerance of them unbearable. These uncouth barbarians had burnt cities ... and were now settling down in them without anyone objecting. They were working their way in, just like the serpents they venerated. And one of them was sitting next to him. He balled his fist.

'It's said, here and there, that you served in the Empire's army.'

'Plenty of things are said in Masalia,' muttered Dun before emptying his tankard.

'I'm not from Masalia,' replied Viola.

A serving girl came over to replace his jug and deposited two tankards in front of Rogant and Viola before disappearing into the milling crowd.

'No ... to be sure,' said Dun, still glaring at her. 'Your clothing is fine, carefully made, but covered with a thin layer of dust. So you've been travelling ... and you're well-born.'

'There is no such thing as "well-born" since the end of the Empire,' Viola corrected him sharply.

'Oh, that's right!' sneered the old man. 'Blood doesn't count in the Republic. Anyone with the necessary drive can rise to the top ... I've heard all that—' he took a gulp '—drivel before,' he concluded with a snort.

Viola exchanged a weary gaze with her companion. A faint smile played beneath Rogant's tattoos.

'My name is Viola. I am a historian working at the Great College of Emeris.'

'What of it?' Dun leaned towards her with a mocking expression. 'You could at least wait until I'm dead and buried before studying me like some relic. In my day people were less impatient.'

'It's not *you* I've come here to study.' Viola scowled.

Dun wagged his head, eyebrows raised. The girl was pretty, although a little too young for his taste. But her academic's spectacles and her blood-red hair with the two stray locks trailing down over her ivory skin were appealing to the eye. Moreover, she carried a faint, delicious scent of lavender which awoke gentler memories. His drunken state overrode his good sense and for an instant he wanted to charm her. He let his guard slip.

'I'm searching for something and I believe you can help me find it,' Viola explained. 'I have crossed the former Kingdoms and spoken with many traders and travellers ... and one of them mentioned an old soldier he met in Masalia.'

The old man let out a sigh, both hands gripping his tankard, with a glassy look in his eye. But when he turned his head towards the Nâaga his face grew rigid again. Rogant was so discreet he'd almost forgotten the barbarian's presence.

'And?' hissed Dun.

'And he said this soldier told the most astonishing story,' she continued. 'That during the final hours of the Empire, when you were posted in Emeris, you fled the Imperial capital ...'

She drew in a breath and lowered her eyes, as if searching for the right words. Dun stared at her as he took another gulp.

'... and that you took the Emperor's sword with you.'

The old man remained still, tankard concealing the lower part of his face, the wine trickling gently through his lips. There was a fleeting glimpse of something like sadness in his eyes. The hubbub within the tavern seemed to fade away, replaced by the tumult of a battle echoing in his head. The bustling surroundings drew him back to here and now, but his heart beat more quickly and more forcefully. He felt a sharp stab of pain in his chest and breathed deeply as he lowered his tankard to the table, his gaze drifting over the grainy wooden surface.

'You're seeking Eraëd—'

'We're seeking Eraëd,' agreed Viola.

'And you think I have it,' said Dun with a wry smile.

'No.'

She shook her head, lifting one of her locks with a gloved hand. Then she took hold of the jug and started to fill the tankards the serving girl had left them. The red wine poured into the ochre tankards like blood upon the ground. Dun ran his hand through his beard, his eyes vague.

'But you know where you hid it—'

'And what if I were lying that evening; boasting to make myself seem more important?' suggested Dun, scratching his chin.

'I don't think so,' Viola replied.

'You don't know that.'

'I am certain of it. I was told you spoke of the Eastern territories, beyond the Vershan mountains. That's where you hid it, didn't you?'

'Even admitting I ever had Eraëd in my possession, why would it be of interest to the Republic?'

'The sword served the Imperial family for years, and before that, the royal dynasties of the Caglieri, the Perthuis, the Majoranes ... I can go back even further if you like.'

'I've never been fond of history lessons.'

'I didn't think so.'

Dun looked away, not sure what to make of her.

'That sword represents everything your Republic hates,' he said, meeting Viola's eyes once more.

'That sword is reputed to be magical. It has been wielded by many heroes ... it has even fought dragons. It's part of the history of this world, regardless of whether an Empire or a Republic currently determines its destiny.'

Dun's eyes narrowed and his lips began to twitch. He leaned back and gave a thunderous roar of laughter which drew attention from the neighbouring tables. A plump woman sitting on the lap of an old merchant who looked as fragile as a dry twig, visibly pricked up her ears. But one baleful gaze from the Nâaga quickly discouraged her from eavesdropping.

'Heroes?' Dun guffawed. 'Dragons? Listen to yourself. There's nothing easier than being a hero. Or slaying dragons. Do you know what a dragon is? Have you ever come across one?'

Viola hesitated before shaking her head, looking ill at ease. The old soldier's sneering tone did not sit well with her. But she would have to put up with it. She'd been forewarned, after all.

'They're just lizards,' Dun continued. 'Big stupid lizards like the ones your guard dog here venerates.'

He tilted his head towards Rogant.

'Now, let me guess. You and your friend here are going to ask me to accompany you to the Eastern territories in search of Eraëd. And what dangers shall we face along the way?' His tone wavered between mockery and contempt. 'Fighting monsters no one has ever heard of, saving besieged castles, slaying dragons? Ha! You're young. And you remind me of someone else I knew who was always dreaming, always believing in great deeds, always imagining a *destiny*. That's exactly what you've got with your ... Republic. The world belongs to you, eh? You have nothing to fear, you can just forge ahead. But in the end you know nothing about the world that surrounds you ... and when reality comes rushing in—'

He clapped his hands suddenly and gritted his teeth.

'It will crush you like a bug. You believe all the legends and waste your energy trying to write your own. You think you can succeed at anything, at the dawn of your life, because you possess *the truth*. Well, here's some truth for you.'

With a wave of his hand, he beckoned Viola to draw closer. And leaning forward, he whispered:

'You don't get to choose. No, no. You're not that important. You've convinced yourself that your destiny belongs to you, that you just have to create the right opportunities. Well, know this: men's destiny has never been anything but the murmur of the gods.'

Keeping his gaze locked on Viola's he straightened up, nodding.

'Nothing but a murmur … The gods sealed our fates when they created this world. But you, with all your grand ideas, have forgotten that, haven't you? You don't believe in anything. I'm surprised you haven't burnt all the churches.'

'The Order of Fangol is respected, despite what you may think.'

'You don't know the meaning of the word respect,' Dun scoffed, shaking his head in contempt. 'You've forsaken the Book, renounced it.'

'Each individual may choose to believe or not. It's a new world.'

'It's not mine,' the old man said with a grimace, glancing at the Nâaga.

Viola did not doubt for a single instant that he was the man she'd been looking for. But perhaps she needed a different strategy to find a way to prod him into giving up his secrets.

'Who's speaking now? The soldier skulking far behind the battle lines, or the drunk old man?' she asked. 'Both, perhaps? I have trouble telling them apart, they're so alike in their cowardice.'

The old man's face stiffened.

'You insult me,' he muttered.

'Really, Dun? What do I know about you, apart from the fact that you fled Emeris after stealing Eraëd?'

Dun wasn't drunk enough to succumb to his anger, but nor was he lucid enough to consider the consequences of his next act. He stretched out his hand towards the jug and, without his fingers touching it, it began to slide across the table towards him. Viola was speechless, her eyes widening in astonishment. She slowly pushed her spectacles up to the bridge of her nose with the tip of her index finger as if to reassure herself that she was seeing clearly. His arms crossed, Rogant grew very still.

The *animus*. Only the great knights of the Empire knew how to use it. And since the Empire's fall, there were few left who could have given such a demonstration. The gift had been lost.

The carousing in the tavern had become a distant buzz, the customers no more than ghostly silhouettes. Viola and Rogant only had eyes for the jug before them. It had well and truly moved and Dun suddenly realised what his simple gesture, born of annoyance, would cost him. Here, where he had always acted the part of an ordinary soldier, he had revealed his true face to a chit of a girl just graduated from the Great College of Emeris. She had barely known the Empire. How would she judge him? As one of the butchers of the former Kingdoms, an enemy of the Republic she served? How could she, escorted by a barbarian, an enemy from his previous life, possibly understand him?

'You're n-not simply a s-soldier,' stammered Viola. 'You're a knight.'

'Bah!' said Dun dismissively, looking away. 'The Knighthood died along with the Empire ...'

Dun. She repeated the name to herself, trying to recall as much as possible from her history classes. *Dun* ... the name was familiar to her.

'Dun-Cadal,' she whispered.

The old man's eyes shone with sadness.

'You're Dun-Cadal, General Dun-Cadal of the House of Daermon,' Viola continued. 'Dun-Cadal, the commander at the battle of the Saltmarsh, you—'

'And was I cowering far behind the battle lines, then?' the old man interrupted her.

Viola was at a loss for words. The battle of the Saltmarsh was noteworthy in history for its consequences, but above all for its terrible violence. Few had survived. Dun-Cadal had been trapped in enemy territory for months before he managed to slip through the lines and return to Emeris. He'd accomplished his fair share of great deeds, but, of them all, his escape was the feat that stuck in people's memories.

'The sword is in the Eastern territories. Go and look for it there and stop pestering me. Go ahead, take what's left of the Empire and expose it for all to see.'

'So you admit you carried it—'

13

Dun looked distracted, his gaze lost in the distance, his eyelids beginning to droop.

'I say many things when I've been drinking,' he fumed. 'You'll spill your venom on that blade and its guard will seem quite dull compared to your arrogance,' he added in a low mutter.

He wanted nothing to do with her, or with the Nâaga, or with what he had once been. Here, he was simply Dun and that was enough. Viola observed him closely, noting the details of his time-worn face, the brown wrinkles marking his cheeks. Dun-Cadal, the glorious general, now gone to ground in the slums of Masalia. He had not come here looking to make a new life for himself, but in search of death. She then noticed he was seated with his back to the door, so that any cutthroat could take him by surprise. If he was recounting, night after night, how he had been a soldier of the Empire, perhaps he hoped that someone seeking vengeance would finally put an end to his torment.

'You await death here,' Viola said.

'I await whatever is given to me. Another jug, for example?'

With a sad expression, he upturned the empty container on the table with a trembling hand and gave the Nâaga to his right a twisted scowl. As was his wont, Rogant did not react.

'Help us,' pleaded Viola. 'That sword is more important than you can imagine. I must find it.'

But amidst the raucous noise of the tavern her request seemed to go unheard. The smoke from the pipe of a fat man seated at an adjoining table drifted between the old general and herself.

'I beg you, Dun-Cadal ...'

He slowly waved away the cloud of smoke, lost in his thoughts. She was wasting her breath. He wasn't listening any more. Rogant leaned towards her and the look he gave her was eloquent enough to need no words. She swallowed and ran her gloved hands over her cape which had barely had time to dry. Then she stood up.

'Very well,' she declared. 'I suppose it's useless to plead with you.'

She slowly drew up her hood so that only the sparkle of her green eyes penetrated the darkness masking her face.

'I thought I was speaking to the great General Dun-Cadal but I'm forced to conclude I was mistaken. Look at you ... you're not even the shadow of what you once were. You're an empty husk without any dignity, only fit to raise a glass in bitterness. I can scarcely believe the legend of your deeds at the battle of the Saltmarsh can be true. Seeing you like this, I'm forced to doubt you ever had greatness in you.'

He did not once lift his eyes to hers while she spoke.

'Yes ... you came here to find death. You haven't understood: you're *already* dead. You can try to hide your true identity, to protect your reputation, but you're wasting your time. When the world learns what has become of Dun-Cadal Daermon ... the only tears shed will be of pity, not of sorrow.'

She disappeared into the crowd without waiting for a reply, followed by the Nâaga. As the fresher air in the alley cleared away the stale smell of sweat and alcohol, she was still asking herself if she had found the right words, and she slowed her stride as they walked through the pouring rain.

'Have faith,' Rogant advised.

Have faith? When she hadn't even been warned she'd be dealing with Dun-Cadal Daermon, not some ordinary soldier.

'I've known *him* longer than you have,' Rogant was saying. '*He* knows what he's doing.'

As if to confirm this statement, a voice called out from behind them.

'Hey!'

Viola turned round slowly. Dun-Cadal was an even more miserable sight standing on the tavern step than he had been seated at his table. The rain dripped down his face and it was possible there were tears mixed in with it.

'What do you know of Dun-Cadal?' he snarled with a quaver in his voice. 'You come *here*, you sit at my table and you spit all over what I was. What I am ... what I will still be ...' He balled his fists, tottering on his feet. 'But what do you know?' he raged. 'What has the Republic taught you?'

He took a few paces and then slumped against a wall. A flash of lightning illuminated his wrinkled face. He seemed so ... ravaged.

'What do you know of my story?' he asked, lifting his eyes to the sky. 'What I've seen, what I've done? What do you know about the battle of the Saltmarsh?'

Viola did not move a muscle. She simply looked at him leaning against the façade of a house, his boots covered in mud, his cracked leather vest, his wine-stained shirt sleeves soaking in the rain.

'So tell me.'

2

THE BATTLE OF THE SALTMARSH

My childhood ended
The day I hesitated,
For the first time ...

Fifteen years ago. The air had been fresh despite the overcast sky but there was a rumbling in the background. A dull roaring which continued to swell, sweeping over the tall grasses of the marshes. There were no signs of any storm, just heavy clouds of sparkling white, edged with hints of grey as if to better define their shapes. There was no need for direct sunlight to blind the men at their posts in the trench. The dazzling clouds alone achieved that effect.

There was no storm, or even anger, in the air, only a sense of fulfilling one's duty.

'You should step back, Dun-Cadal,' advised a voice.

A black shape came hurtling out of the sky in a perfect arc, followed by a sharp whistle. Even before the sound lowered in pitch, the ball of rock and tow, covered with burning grease, crashed to the ground right in front of the knight without his taking the slightest step to avoid it.

'You think so ...?' murmured Dun-Cadal as he stared at the horizon.

Before him stretched saltwater marshes and swamps, so long and wide that the most distant portions were blurred by haze. He could hardly make out the outline of the enemy camp. Lowering his eyes to the boiling crater at his feet, he observed the streams of smoke coming off the hot ball. He turned it over with a kick.

'Negus,' he said in a pensive tone. 'I'm getting the sense they're growing restless over there.' He spun round with a mocking smile on his lips. 'Shall we give them a rude awakening?'

The small round man, squeezed into his armour, raised his eyes to the sky before replying:

'If you are thinking up ways to get yourself killed before even crossing blades with them, then it would indeed be quite rude on your part.'

They had been waiting on the edge of the Saltmarsh for two weeks now without a single blow being struck. Just a few catapult shots that never managed to hit their targets. The Imperial Army had not even made use of its own artillery yet. The Saltmarsh revolt was, if possible, to be suppressed without bloodshed. Tucked up in the warmth of his palace in Emeris, the Emperor believed that the fear generated by his regiments would be enough to persuade the insurgents to lay down their weapons. But although no sword had been unsheathed during the last two weeks, neither had any been abandoned on the field of battle . . .

Dun-Cadal joined his brother-in-arms and patted his shoulder.

'Have no fear, Negus. I can always detect the smell of death. And here, except for salt, nothing has pricked my nostrils.'

He had short brown hair, which the wind barely ruffled. A small goatee surrounded his thin lips and his face, while still youthful in appearance, was marked by a life of combat. This was not his first battle and he was counting on it not being his last. He had just arrived and had insisted on assessing the situation himself before other generals could paint the picture for him in a more flattering light. He jumped down into the trench and waited for his friend to do the same before continuing his inspection.

He had lost count of the fights they had come through together, from small skirmishes to great fields of battle. Of all the Empire's generals. Negus had always been his closest friend, a kindred spirit who dismissed the rumours about Dun-Cadal and accepted his rough character. Dun-Cadal came from the House of Daermon, whose title of nobility only dated back a century. Negus's lineage, on the other hand, had been associated with the aristocracy, from the first Kingdoms right up to the Empire. Affable by nature, Anselme Nagolé Egos, more commonly known as Negus, had never seen their difference in social standing as reason to despise a man who had repeatedly saved his life in the midst of chaos. Their friendship, known to all, was unstinting, as deep as the rift valleys in the wild territories and as enduring as the stones from the Kapernevic mines. The dangers they had faced together only confirmed it and the bond between them resembled something like true brotherhood.

All along the dug-in line, soldiers were studying the horizon, spears at their side. As the two generals passed, they tried to look sharp despite being tense, saluting with a fist pressed against their chest. They all knew of Dun-Cadal and his bravery in combat. All of them felt a sincere admiration for him. Seeing him walk past at Negus's side might have been reassuring in other circumstances but, although it was heartening, the commanders' presence was not enough to dispel the prevailing mood. The troops were distressed by the waiting, and the situation was becoming unbearable – as witnessed by the excrement stagnating at the bottom of the trench and the terrible odour. It had been two weeks since they had arrived and already the camp was suffering from the poor conditions in the Saltmarsh. Mud and swamp combined to prevent the soldiers from disposing of their waste properly.

'They're terrified,' observed Negus.

'They don't look too frightened.'

'They dare not. They belong to Captain Azdeki's unit.'

'Azinn's nephew? That young good-for-nothing?' Dun-Cadal exclaimed in surprise.

'Didn't they warn you at the border? He's been in charge of the region for the past two years. He's the one who's held it since the revolt began.'

'Held it?!' scoffed Dun-Cadal. 'That idiot can't even keep a hold on himself.'

'There hasn't been a battle up until now,' retorted Negus as he climbed a makeshift ladder leading to the edge of the camp, 'so one might argue he has held it.'

Really? Etienne Azdeki, nephew of Baron Azinn Azdeki of the East Vershan baronies, was not known for his level-headedness and still less for his ability as a strategist. The fact that the Emperor had placed him in charge of the Saltmarsh region could pass for a mere mistake, but now that war had come to these lands he was supposed to control he became a risky proposition. Etienne Azdeki had been appointed captain without any experience of combat. Acting as he *should* never entered his mind. Acting as he *pleased*, on the other hand, was his sole rule of conduct.

'No matter,' Dun-Cadal said aloud. 'The Emperor sent me here to coordinate the troops. Azdeki will have to content himself with following my orders.'

'Cocky as always, Daermon?' said Negus with a smile.

'Out here I feel like I'm in a courtesan's arms!' Dun-Cadal replied with a wide grin. 'In love as in war, in war as in love!'

Tens of thousands of dark green tents stretched across the marshes, standing among the reeds and the tall grasses. Here and there, knights were training in single combat, surrounded by circles of attentive spectators. The waiting was an even more serious risk than battle itself. Boredom blunted the soldiers' readiness. It gave them too much time to contemplate the dangers they faced. It robbed them of any spontaneity once combat was engaged. Two weeks was not much in the course of a war, but was far too long without even a skirmish to break the enforced idleness. Dun-Cadal feared the Saltmarsh rebels were counting on this lethargy to impose their own rhythm on the forthcoming battle.

But as soon as he drew aside the flaps of the command tent erected at the centre of the camp, he knew it was too late to deal with the revolt swiftly.

'They're massing most of their forces here ...'

Bent over a large model representing the Saltmarsh, a knight in black armour pointed to a line along the edge of a small forest. Facing him, a thirty-year-old man with a gaunt face and an aquiline nose jutting over thin pinched lips was listening attentively, his hands clasped behind his back. His silver breastplate depicted a proud eagle holding a serpent in its talons. It was the emblem of the Azdeki family, an heirloom of their rise to glory during the great battles between the civilised forces of the Empire and the nomadic Nâaga, before the latter were finally subjugated.

'Our scouts have tried to get as close as possible, to accurately determine the number of their catapults, but they've been spotted every time. Two of them did not return.'

There were five knights surrounding this small-scale model of the battlefield, all of them wearing family colours which identified them as members of the provincial nobility. Their families had sworn allegiance to the Emperor and sent their sons off to the military academy in order to serve with honour in the Imperial Army. Only the most experienced among them ever reached the rank of general, but owing to his appointment as captain of Uster county, Etienne Azdeki had authority over those present. They were merely reinforcements and, despite their superior military rank, were bound to comply with his commands.

All of them except Dun-Cadal. Upon catching sight of him, the young nobleman stiffened.

'You'd better count on there being twice as many catapults as you saw when you controlled this situation, Azdeki,' said Dun-Cadal as he advanced towards them, not even acknowledging the soldiers' salutes with a glance.

'General Daermon,' Azdeki greeted him tersely.

He made a slight bow. Even that simple gesture seemed to be an effort.

'Azdeki,' Dun-Cadal replied with a smile, before addressing the entire group. 'What a pleasure to see you again, and so eager to kick peasant arses!'

'You didn't waste any time getting here,' the man in black armour observed gleefully.

'I came as quickly as I could, Tomlinn. Although I'm having trouble understanding why the situation has not evolved since the uprising began.'

Dun-Cadal caught a glimpse of Azdeki's lip curling in a bitter grimace The Emperor respected his general's judgement more than that of any other man. There were rumours about why this was so, but few could claim to know the truth behind them. The idea that there might be a bond of friendship between the Emperor and this provincial nobody, despite his promotion to the highest rank, was simply inconceivable to most aristocrats. But instead of feeling hurt by this, Dun-Cadal responded to their restrained contempt with an unstinting flow of withering comments. No one would dare complain.

For he was here at the request of His Imperial Majesty, to redress an extremely ... embarrassing situation.

'Now, explain what's going on,' requested Dun-Cadal.

His tone had become less stern. Although these generals might dislike him, he nevertheless had complete confidence in them. Two of them had even been his classmates during military training and he felt a certain affection for them. Although the feeling was not mutual, Dun-Cadal felt at ease in their company. He knew these men were gifted when it came to battle and that was really all that mattered to him. Tomlinn, the man in black armour with a bald head and a large scar across his face, began to speak as he walked around the model. He was one of the few on friendly terms with Daermon.

'The county of Uster has demanded its independence. The rest of the Saltmarsh region has rallied to its call.'

'I did what I had to do,' Azdeki immediately broke in to say.

A heavy silence fell, which his quavering voice tried to dispel.

'For two years, I've tried to keep hold of the region, but these peasants won't accept that the Count of Uster betrayed them. I was only applying the law!'

Azdeki may have been acting in accordance with the Emperor's orders, but Daermon could not have cared less. Nor was he interested in the reasons behind the revolt or the manner in which it had been dealt with. Only the consequences warranted his attention.

'These peasants have raised the army which stands before you and does not appear at all frightened by the might of the Empire,' observed Dun-Cadal.

'I deemed it preferable not to attack,' Azdeki replied. 'And the Emperor trusted my judgement. I'm not a warmonger.'

'That, I don't doubt for an instant,' the general replied scornfully.

'Daermon,' sighed Negus from behind him.

Azdeki was visibly seething, standing straight with his hands joined at his back. For a brief instant Dun-Cadal thought the man might dare to respond, but instead he drew in a deep breath and kept still.

'The strategy might still work,' conceded Negus. 'Once they realise we have more than a hundred thousand soldiers, plus a thousand knights capable of employing the *animus* . . . surely they will see that any combat would be in vain. And we'll keep the Empire intact without shedding even a drop of blood.'

'The Count of Uster was well-liked in these parts. Many doubt he betrayed the Empire,' Tomlinn interjected as he approached Dun-Cadal.

'They no longer trust us,' added a massively built man wearing blood-red armour.

Standing at Azdeki's side, he pushed forward a wooden block representing an Imperial legion.

'Rebellious sentiment has made them bold, but when they see exactly how many we are, they will recognise their error and order will be restored.'

'So you hope, but you're wrong. You should have attacked them from the very start,' declared Dun-Cadal, sweeping away the blocks of wood with his hand. 'You should have shown them, rather than waiting for them to see for themselves, General Kay. All this means nothing; they have been lulling you into a false sense of security. Believe me, I can sense this sort of thing.'

Kay took a step back, his head bowed. He had known Dun-Cadal for some time and was one of those who criticised the general. He was too sure of himself . . . too arrogant. And even when he was right, it did not excuse his lack of tact. The world was changing and it seemed Dun-Cadal was the only one not following the current; too rooted in his own certainties, too confident in the abilities which, thus far, had been the source of his strength and fame. All of those present here were of high lineages, unlike Daermon. Dun-Cadal was a conceited upstart . . . but for now it was better to be on his side than against him.

'The problem would have been resolved once and for all. But instead you dithered. You dithered and complicated matters . . . and everything would have been so simple if you had attacked first. It would have been child's play.'

'And if there were some other way to—' Kay objected.

'You're asking yourselves too many questions!' Dun-Cadal roared.

A whistling noise could be heard, growing louder and more strident, piercing their ears.

'No more dithering,' he muttered, before yelling: 'Down!'

The top of the tent ripped apart. All the officers dove to the ground, arms over their heads, their hearts pounding wildly. A fireball crashed down upon the model, splashing hungry flames against the walls of the shelter. It only took a few seconds for the whole tent to become a blazing inferno with flames running up the wooden poles in flickering waves. Lying on his belly, Dun-

Cadal tried to spit out the dirt he'd swallowed in his fall. With an abrupt movement, he turned over and calmly took stock of the trap which had ensnared them. To his right, he recognised Kay's red armour rising from the ground with a stagger.

'Kay! With me!' Dun-Cadal yelled as a thunderous roar came from outside.

Close by, obscured by the spreading black smoke, he glimpsed Negus' round silhouette helping Tomlinn and Azdeki to their feet. Dun-Cadal spat out another clod of earth, feeling a burning in his lungs.

'*Kay!*'

'I'm here,' Kay replied at last in a groggy voice.

Like Dun-Cadal, the general clasped his hands together and brought them down, inhaling deeply. Their lungs were burning, but they ignored the pain as they stretched their arms out in front of them, releasing as much air, and *animus*, as possible. A violent gust of air parted the flames, tearing away what was left of the tent and breaking the burning poles in two. The fire continued to spread over the remnants of their shelter, but already the pungent air of the salt marshes was dispersing the smoke. The entire camp was in upheaval. Soldiers were yelling and running towards the trenches, as knights with unsheathed swords pointed the way for them. And more flaming balls were still falling from the sky. This time, the Saltmarsh rebels' aim was true.

With Negus propping up Azdeki, both still dazed, Dun-Cadal passed before them, hand on the pommel of his sword.

'You should have attacked first,' he growled.

'Th-there aren't that many of them,' stammered Azdeki, his eyes reddened from the smoke.

Amidst the soldiers' cries there came a dull thudding sound, like a giant's footsteps.

'A rouarg!' Kay exclaimed in dismay, drawing his sword from its scabbard.

Not just a rouarg, but twenty of them, with bristles like dark pikes sprouting from their round backs, maws dripping with white slaver and long powerful forelegs ploughing through the swamps as they charged forward. Behind the furious beasts rose a wall of flames. The Saltmarsh rebels had smoked them out of their lairs and goaded them into a destructive rage. The peasants could not match the Imperial

Army's numbers ... but they had the resources of an entire region at their disposal.

'They stand a good three metres tall at the withers,' commented Negus as he pushed himself away from Azdeki. 'Six tons of anger.'

He also drew his sword and placed a firm hand on Dun-Cadal's shoulder.

'My friend, what exciting lives we lead!'

They exchanged a smile before joining the trenches at the edge of the camp. Once there, they endeavoured to organise the defensive lines. The rouargs were only a first taste of the onslaught to come; behind them the enemy troops were advancing. Some knights remained behind to coordinate the men charged with extinguishing the fires. The balls covered with flaming tow were still falling at a steady rate. Then, suddenly, there was only silence. A dark veil slipped beneath the white clouds, formed by streams of smoke rippling in the wind. It was soon punctured by swarms of arrows. Perched on the lip of the trenches, the Imperial archers quickly nocked new missiles on their bowstrings.

'Stand!' ordered Tomlinn, marching behind them, brandishing a sword. 'Loose!'

Whistles, roars, crackling ... no sound managed to stifle the thumping hearts of the soldiers at their posts, watching in horror as the huge rouargs charged towards them. They were too close now for the archers to arm their bows in time, and even if they could the creatures' skins were too thick to be pierced by a small metal point. Whistles, roars, crackling ... and then the screams which accompanied the deafening crash as the beasts leapt over the trenches, their maws twisted in rage. The black smoke dispersed in wavy ribbons. Between the rouargs, the white of the clouds was mixed with the grey of metal, sparkling body armour with the brown of surcoats. And then blood began to stain the earth red.

Off in the distance, the rebels' drums began to beat as their troops advanced.

A few of the rouargs did not manage to break through the Imperial lines, their bare bellies riddled with spears. But those that succeeded were free to rampage at will, the savage beasts thirsting for blood, biting, crushing, ripping apart anything that came within reach of their giant jaws. As he was tossed about in one monster's maw a soldier screamed until his vocal chords broke, before finally being flung into the air. He landed with a heavy thud a few feet away. No further sound came from his broken body. His pale face was marked by a trickle of bright red blood running from the corner of his mouth.

Although the rouargs wreaked mayhem in the Imperial ranks, they were guided only by their own fear of the flames behind them. The terrifying beasts were themselves terrified. Most of them managed to flee into the marshes, carrying off tattered tents snagged on their hind legs, broken carts ... and several limp bodies of Imperial soldiers.

'Get out of the way! Get out of its way!' ordered Dun-Cadal, as a lone rouarg found itself encircled.

It showed its fangs, with its wide, high turned-up nostrils quivering and black bristles standing erect on its round back. Its eyes narrowed for an instant and then the beast charged. Dun-Cadal just had time to sidestep, barely avoiding one of the forelegs. Three of his men were less fortunate and were thrown into the air like wisps of straw.

The circle immediately re-formed around the animal and Dun-Cadal chose its flank to deliver his attack. But his sword failed to leave even a scratch on its armoured hide. The Rouarg let out a howl, digging its claws into the ground before spinning round. The general took a leap backwards. Spears broke against the monster's thick furry side, enraging it further. It kicked out in all directions, breaking the circle. Some soldiers were trampled and others were torn to pieces by the sudden snaps of its jaws, before the beast reared up defiantly on its hind legs.

Through the smoke Dun-Cadal spotted its weak point. The belly. It was the only solution available to him. A well-placed sword stroke beneath the beast, where the thinner skin revealed the presence of some thick purple veins. He inhaled a gulp of air, held his breath and launched himself at the creature.

'*Feel the* animus, *be the* animus. *Feel it, Frog!*'

His heart was beating so slowly that he could barely hear it. Each gesture, each movement around him, seemed as slow as the progress of a snail across a leaf.

'*It's there, the magic. In every breath you exhale ...*'

The rouarg reared up again, its maw wide open.

'It's like music, Frog ... It's not enough to simply listen. Feel it ... legato ...'

In mid-dash, Dun-Cadal went down on his knees, sliding across the damp ground, flattening the tall grasses. Time stood still for him. Burning embers hung in the air, their red glow standing out against the immaculate white clouds.

'Staccato ...'

The embers whirled, the grasses sprang up again, the general's heartbeat accelerated. He felt everything, perceived every movement, anticipated every action. Bent backwards, his rear end almost touching the heels of his boots, he kept his eyes fixed on the beast's exposed belly. He expelled the air from his lungs, pointing his sword at the brown skin and its bulging veins.

'Feel the animus, Frog. Breathe as one life with it. Breathe in the same rhythm with it ... And strike!'

The rouarg lifted its maw to the sky, howling in pain as the blade perforated its body. Dun-Cadal rolled to the side to avoid being crushed. The monster collapsed with a harrowing death rattle.

'They're coming!'

'Resume your positions! Halberdiers! I want halberdiers here!'

'Hold fast!'

The orders could barely be heard over the drum rolls. On his knees in the mud, Dun-Cadal stared at the still-warm body of the rouarg. Before he could rise, an arrow landed just a few inches from his right foot.

'Dun-Cadal!' Negus called from somewhere behind him. 'Dun-Cadal!'

Once he stood up, the general went to join his friend by the trenches. Facing them, thousands of soldiers in mismatched kit were advancing to a drummer boy's beat. Behind them, the crisp snap of bowstrings resounded. A swarm of arrows rose, slicing through the clouds of smoke with a hiss. The first wave plunged down upon the rebel troops, piercing armour, riddling shields, planting themselves deep in the damp earth.

It was the opening blow of the battle of the Saltmarsh. The first confrontation between these two armies. It was brief but bloody. The Empire had the advantage of numbers, the rebels that of surprise. The stampeding rouargs had opened numerous breaches in the Imperial lines, the artillery barrage had set fires in the heart of the Imperial camp and the rebels made good use of the resulting chaos. It required all of the knights' discipline to reorganise their troops. Clamour, thunder, the clash of swords, bodies charging at one another, shouts … Clamour … thunder … and the *animus* … That was what the rebels lacked and they were well aware of the fact. When the Imperial generals deployed the *animus*, they beat a hasty retreat.

All in all, the first battle of the Saltmarsh lasted only ten minutes. Ten short minutes during which two thousand soldiers died. Standing at the lip of a trench, watching the fading sunlight wash over the still corpses in the broken tall grasses, Dun-Cadal cursed Azdeki's dithering. All the conditions needed to inflict a stinging blow against the Empire had been allowed to gather. Within the week, half of the Kingdoms would hear of the Saltmarsh revolt. About the peasants who had stood up to the greatest army in the world … People always took delight in stories like this. Just so long as they did not rally to the Saltmarsh cause. The effort to contain the revolt in this region had already been botched, but if other counties or baronies showed leanings towards independence, the situation would quickly become unmanageable. It would no longer be a simple rebellion, but a revolution.

Sitting on a corpse's broken armour, an enormous crow fluttered its wings as it plunged its beak into a seeping wound.

'The sky has turned red …'

Dun-Cadal nodded, letting his gaze drift out over the salt marshes. Beneath the grey clouds, the glow of the setting sun cast a curious coppery veil just above the tall grasses. Negus halted at the general's side, his thumbs hooked into his belt, bearing a wide raw cut on his round face.

'… as it often does the evening after a battle,' he continued with a sigh.

'What do they want?' Dun-Cadal suddenly asked. 'What are they seeking? War? For this is no longer merely a rebellion.'

'We've seen harder fighting than this. And they retreated in the end. In two months' time, we'll no longer speak of it.'

'No, my friend,' the general replied, shaking his head, an expression of disgust on his face. 'They've won.'

He caught the puzzled gaze of the small man encased in his mud-spattered armour.

'They know what they're doing, believe me. This is only the beginning. Everyone will remember the battle of the Saltmarsh, because they managed to bring the Empire to its knees.'

Behind them, the camp was still smoking, tents lay in tatters and soldiers hobbled about ... The whole place was a shambles.

In the days that followed, Dun-Cadal tried to regain control of the situation, collecting all available information about the opposing forces: Who? What? How? Once the Count of Uster had been executed, Etienne Azdeki had ordered the disbanding of the county guards throughout the Saltmarsh region. In view of this, and after seeing the enemy's strategy, Dun-Cadal supposed that the former county guard captain, Meurnau, was leading the revolt. But he had no hard proof of this. Over the next months, the Imperial forces suffered a series of lightning attacks and skirmishes which prevented them from advancing into the marshes. Several times, their enemies used the same tactic again: smoking out the rouargs' giant lairs and sending the frightened beasts against the Imperial outposts, before launching a lethal attack. Wandering through the tall grasses, the Imperial Army did its best; if not to advance, then at least not to retreat. Between the unfamiliar territory of the deep marshes, in which numerous men weighed down by armour drowned, the rouargs who delighted in chewing up their flesh and the constant harassment by enemy troops, the Saltmarsh soon earned a sad notoriety.

Hell was on earth ... and it burned in the marshlands.

General Kay lost his life along with fifty of his men trying to establish a bridge across the Seyman river. He was only the first of several generals to fall. In addition to fighting, they also had to contend with the diseases carried by mosquitoes and the putrid swamp water. And despite the sweat dripping from the soldiers' faces and their fixed, feverish eyes, they needed to remain alert.

'I want these catapults repaired at once!' ordered Captain Azdeki.

Facing him, three ill-looking soldiers were on the receiving end of this order. They had not slept for two days and despite their fever they were supposed to repair the two catapults damaged during the previous assault. Since the arrival of General Daermon, Azdeki had been seeking any means to reassert his authority. The soldiers weren't fooled.

'They need to be operational by this evening,' continued Azdeki, looking tense.

'Yes, Captain,' acknowledged one of the soldiers in a feeble voice.

'No rest breaks until you've finished—'

'Take three hours!'

Azdeki's head snapped around. Accompanied by Negus, Dun-Cadal passed behind him without even giving him a glance. He preferred to devote his entire attention to the tottering soldiers.

'You can barely stand on your feet,' observed the general. 'Go and get some rest. Azdeki, the catapults can wait. The men come first.'

The soldiers could not refrain from smiling in relief, which they barely managed to disguise when Azdeki shot them a black look.

'General Daermon!' he called.

But both Dun-Cadal and Negus walked away without paying him any heed.

'General Daermon!' Azdeki repeated as the two men entered a large violet tent decorated with the golden symbol of the Imperial general staff, a slender sword circled by a crown of laurels.

Fists clenched, the captain followed them inside. Sitting in a small armchair, Dun-Cadal was removing his mud-crusted boots, letting out a moan of relief. In the corner, Negus was filling two tankards with wine.

'General Daermon!' roared Azdeki. 'By what right do you—'

'Save your breath, Azdeki,' interrupted Dun-Cadal in a dreadfully calm voice. 'You're so red in the face it looks like your head will explode.'

'Explode? Explode?!' the captain said indignantly, spreading his arms wide. 'This time, you've really gone too far!'

'I remind you that you're under my command. You too, go and rest for three hours.'

In the shadows, Negus smiled faintly as he brought a tankard to his lips.

'I don't have time to rest! No one here has time to rest, Dun-Cadal. And I demand that in front of my men you address me by my rank. That's *Captain* Azdeki.'

He was seething. Like his troops, he had not slept, or only very little, for days now.

'You arrive by order of the Emperor, proud and arrogant. You demean me in front of my men, countermanding my orders for one reason or other—'

'Perhaps because they were bad orders,' Dun-Cadal suggested mildly as he scraped the mud from one of his boots.

'Oh, spare me that, please,' sighed the captain, pointing an accusing finger at the general. 'My family is close to the Emperor, too, and I know why and how you came to be promoted so quickly! Don't ever forget, Dun-Cadal! Don't ever forget where you came from or how you became a general. It was not due, in any way, to your sense of honour!'

Dun-Cadal did not raise an eyebrow, did not lift his head, and did not seem upset by the young officer's insinuations. He contented himself with removing the excess filth from the leather boot with his gauntleted hand. As he busied himself with this task he said in an ominously dry tone:

'Don't you forget that you are only a captain . . . Azdeki. And if we find ourselves in this situation, if so many men have perished, it is your fault. Don't forget that if your uncle had not dandled you on his knee, you would not even be in this tent speaking to me.'

He stopped rubbing his boot as soon as the tent flaps fell shut behind Azdeki's exit.

'You shouldn't have done that,' said Negus, bringing him a tankard of wine.

'His anger will pass soon enough,' Dun-Cadal grumbled.

'It's not a matter of anger, my friend . . .' Negus leaned forward with a sad expression. 'You've humiliated him.'

It was far worse than that. They already had more than enough trouble dealing with the rebels. Adding tensions within their own camp and, what's more, among their commanders, was suicidal. They might as well have accepted their defeat immediately.

'He's too sensitive,' said Dun-Cadal dismissively. 'The result of inbreeding, no doubt.'

Negus chose to ignore this comment and with a weary step went to sit down on an old chest, his gaze lost in his tankard. The quarrels between the ancient families of the East and those of the West, ennobled more recently, were common currency. But there was more

31

than that going on between Daermon and young Azdeki. Sooner or later, blood would be spilled.

'Does the fact that he was dubbed a knight by the Emperor himself still rankle you so much?' asked Negus in a hoarse voice.

Dun-Cadal waited a moment before replying, carefully removing his iron gauntlets. When he finished, he let out a sigh before turning to his friend, looking hurt.

'My grandfather started off as a captain, did you know that? Fighting against the Toule kingdom.' A strange smile stretched the corners of his lips as his gaze wandered around the tent's interior. 'He was the first soldier from the House of Daermon. Ah, those Toules! They put up a devil of a fight, the unbelievers ... It was a holy mission, capturing their kingdom. Bringing them to the light of the gods and the Sacred Book.'

He was seized by emotion as he pictured his ancestor taking up arms and waging war for a just cause. The Daermons had earned their nobility through sacrifice.

'He came across a gigantic library during the capture of Toule,' Dun-Cadal continued. 'They wrote books of their own, can you imagine that? They gave themselves that right! What—'

His voice suddenly choked up.

'He burnt the books,' he resumed, shaking his head. 'He burnt them all. And then the Toulish troops fell upon him and his men. He lost an arm there.'

'I know how much your grandfather gave the Empire, Dun-Cadal, you don't—'

'Yes I do!' Dun-Cadal cut him off brusquely. 'That's my whole point. The Azdekis have had great knights in their family, as well as great statesmen, but Etienne is not one of them. Has he even unsheathed his sword once, since he was given charge of the Saltmarsh? Has he displayed his courage? His family fought in the great Nâaga incursions, but he flees before his enemy. This is the type of man who will bring about the Empire's downfall, Negus. Not all nobles are knights, but all knights must earn their title.'

'He graduated from the academy,' objected Negus calmly. 'As we all did.'

He drank a sip of wine keeping his eyes fixed on Dun-Cadal, who remained with his head down and his jaws clenched.

'He earned his dubbing.'

'Men are dying under his command.'

'Many have died under your command as well.'

'Never so uselessly,' said Dun-Cadal with feeling. 'Would you put your life in the hands of Etienne Azdeki? In the midst of battle, would you entrust your life to him? Tell me truthfully, Negus …'

He looked into his friend's eyes. His anger had faded into his usual self-assurance, certain he'd won the argument.

'No …' Negus admitted weakly.

'No man would,' Dun-Cadal concluded. 'He lacks the charisma to persuade his troops to follow him. And when faced with danger, his decisions are always the wrong ones.'

It was only a few weeks later that Dun-Cadal realised how mistaken he was on Etienne Azdeki's account. Before he met the lad.

Although, Kay had been unable to build a bridge permitting them to cross the Seyman river and advance further into the Saltmarsh lands, they had not given up on the idea. A new expedition was sent with Tomlinn, Azdeki and Dun-Cadal at its head. If they were to have any hope of bringing the conflict to an end they needed to capture the town of Aëd's Watch. And it was located on the far side of the river.

Moving cautiously through the marshes, the expedition numbered sixty in all, with half the men hauling pre-built sections of the bridge. The three commanders went back and forth on horseback, urging their troops on. They rarely resorted to abuse, aware of the difficulty of the task. Weighed down by their armour and weapons, the soldiers also had to bear the burden of the wooden structures. And in addition to the physical effort, they had to put up with the pestilential odour of the sludge. In this area, the salt marshes blended with the swamps.

They were only an hour's march away from the river when Dun-Cadal's attention was drawn by something in the rushes. Pulling on his mount's reins to force it to turn round, he trotted back up to Tomlinn at the head of their column.

'We're being spied on.'

'I sense that, too,' Tomlinn agreed with a grim face. 'How many, do you reckon?'

'I don't know … a dozen maybe. Scouts,' he suggested in a low voice.

To the west, beneath the scarlet rays of the setting sun, the rushes moved strangely among the tall grasses, as though someone was parting them with extreme caution. There was only one way to make sure. Dun-Cadal threw Tomlinn an amused glance before he gave the flanks of his horse a nudge with his heels. He galloped over to Captain Azdeki at the other end of the column and just as he drew up he warned:

'There's movement to the west. Keep the formation close together but get the men ready to respond to an attack.'

'We're flanking the enemy, General Daermon. It's surely wild animals, not rebels. Going over there would be a waste of time.'

'That was an order,' murmured Dun-Cadal, clenching his jaw before hissing, 'Captain Azdeki.'

Although certain he was right, the young captain decided to obey and while the general rode back towards Tomlinn he alerted the soldiers who were advancing at a slow walk.

'Be on your guard. There's danger to the west,' he said. 'When the moment comes, be ready to act swiftly.'

Wild animals … or rebels. The idea that Azdeki might be right did not even occur to the general. The presumptuous young officer always made the wrong choices. Why would be it otherwise in this case? Seconded by Tomlinn, he moved away from the column. His horse shied as if aware of a danger close by. A reassuring pat on his neck induced it to move forward once more. Nothing in the tall grasses seemed threatening. A few mosquitoes buzzed by their ears and the smell of the sludge was almost unbearable. But there was no sign of any enemy.

The horses' hooves sank into the muck, hampering their progress. Another few yards and they would no longer be able to extricate themselves from the natural trap of the quagmire. Nevertheless, the two generals picked their way forward, the tall grasses springing up again behind them with a slight hiss. Soon the soldiers in the distance were only silhouettes beyond the rushes, growing faint in the haze from the heat.

The wind quickened, bending the wild grasses and forming ripples on the stagnant water. And along with the breeze there came a long snarl.

'Dun-Ca—'

A black shape sprang from the marsh, carrying Tomlinn off before he had time to react. Riderless, his horse reared and whinnied, before fleeing westward. There was a growl, then a second and a third, moving off through the reeds. Yanking his sword from its scabbard and holding the reins in a firm hand, Dun-Cadal felt his temples beating like drums.

He saw shadows rolling about in the grasses.

'Azdeki!' he yelled. *'Azdeki!'*

But his call went unanswered. With a sharp jerk on the reins, he forced his mount to make a hazardous about-turn. Its hooves sank further into the sludge.

'Azdeki!'

Off in the distance, the captain was ordering his men to advance.

'Blast it!' Dun-Cadal swore.

He could finally see the shapes more clearly: three rouargs with green fur and black spots. They uttered roars that sounded like a challenge.

'Tomlinn!' he called, sweeping the air with his sword. *'Tomlinn!'*

He heard a cry of pain a few feet away, beneath the heaving round back of one of the beasts. *'Azdeki!'*

The impact was so violent he could almost hear his ribs crack. The rouarg's jaws closed on his forearm guard, its fangs nearly piercing the metal before the beast carried him down in its fall. And with them came the horse, whinnying in terror, its eyes bulging, two black marbles surrounded by white.

An enormous jolt was followed by a sound like ripping cloth as the rouarg began to gut the fallen horse. There was a sharp snap and Dun-Cadal felt his leg break beneath the weight of his mount. Trapped, his head bathed in the loathsome sludge, he caught a glimpse of the tops of the tall grasses slowly dancing in the wind.

'Azdeki!'

All was quiet now, as the grunts of the feasting rouarg grew distant. Almost as quiet as the trickle of blood making a groove in the mud, mixing with the filthy marsh water until it looked like wine ...

'Frog ... I shall call you Frog ...'

A sharp, bitter wine with such peaceful little ripples in the tankard of an old knight lost in Masalia. Far, far away from the Saltmarsh.

'*Frog...*'

'Frog?' asked Viola.

His eyes gone vague, Dun-Cadal's head swayed as if he didn't know where to look. There were not many customers left in the tavern. How long had he been talking? Longer than he would have liked. Once again, he had been betrayed by his inebriated state. At their table, the merchants from Serray were humming now, close to sleep, their eyelids drooping and their jugs empty. The small man who had begged Dun-Cadal for a loan took advantage of their inattention to pick their pockets.

'What?'

'You were saying: "I called Azdeki with all my might, Azdeki, Azdeki",' recounted Viola, 'and then suddenly, out of the blue, you said "Frog".'

Although the tavern had emptied, a thick cloud of smoke still floated in the air.

'Ah,' Dun-Cadal sighed.

And then he added in a thick voice, with a sad smile playing at the corner of his mouth:

'Frog was the lad. The lad who saved my life.'

Was it the smoke that had made his eyes grow red? His expression immediately hardened. He has spoken too much, said too much, told too much.

'It's nothing, forget it,' he muttered with too much spit in his mouth.

'He's drunk too much,' declared the tavern keeper as he gathered up the empty jugs at the adjoining table. 'You should get him home.'

Surprised, Viola raised her eyebrows.

'Home? But where?'

'The courtesan Mildrel's house. It's two streets away from here. That's where we usually leave him when he's just a barrel on legs,' the tavern keeper explained before returning behind his counter with a weary, heavy step.

Dun-Cadal leaned dangerously forward, his nose falling into his tankard, his eyes half-closed.

'The lad...' said Viola thoughtfully.

And then, as though he had lost none of his vigour, the knight lifted his head, a strange gleam lighting up in his wide-open eyes like the sparkle of a tear.

'He was the greatest knight this world has ever known.'

3
WOUND

———

All wounds heal.
Although the scars remind us of them.
And if the pain is less keen,
It still cuts deep.

He had clearly slept for a long time, but the length of sleep didn't matter when one had succumbed to the weight of so many tankards. He sat up in the rumpled bed with a splitting headache, as if a blade had been driven into the back of his skull. The rays of the noontime sun shone through the brown curtains, forming luminous columns upon the waxed wooden floor, far too bright for his half-awake eyes. He raised a hand over his eyes to mask the light, muttering words even he could not understand. It was one thing to try to forget who you were in drink. It was another to be reminded of it with your head beaten like an anvil. He had shed his boots and his vest, but he was relieved to find he was still wearing the rest of his clothes, and then disappointed again when he recognised the chamber. A few feet from him, a basin stood beside a tall cheval glass. Slightly tilted on its pivots, the mirror reflected a pale image of the knight he had once been.

The door opened slowly to reveal a lady, still beautiful despite her age, her curly hair falling on bare shoulders. Her green dress clasped her waist and a corset delicately uplifted her bosom upon which lay a pendant in the shape of a sword. The few wrinkles which gently ran from the corners of her ocean blue eyes did not mar her beauty. She advanced to the window, setting the platter in her hands down on a table bathed in sunlight. His throat dry, Dun-Cadal sat on the edge of the bed and rubbed the back of his neck with numbed fingers, hoping his headache would go away. The scent of lavender drifted towards him, making him forget the pain for an instant.

'I suppose you don't remember a thing,' she said as she transferred a breadbasket, apples, a pitcher and a glass from the platter to the table top.

From the tone of her voice, it was certainly not shyness that made her stand with her back to the knight and her eyes on the platter. And it was not the first time he had woken here with no memory of reaching his bed.

'A young red-headed woman brought you back,' she said, filling the glass with fruit juice. 'Well, not her so much as the Nâaga. He had to carry you here since your legs were already asleep.'

The Nâaga ... Viola ... little by little, his memory returned. And as it did, the terrible taste of remorse filled his mouth.

'I talked ...' he murmured.

'Too much?'

She raised her head. Tilted slightly to one side, it looked as though the sun bestowed a golden kiss upon her cheek. It made her look twenty years younger. Dun-Cadal's weary heart raced and he realized that, with her, he would never feel so alive again.

'The Saltmarsh,' he replied.

'I know.'

She turned, her face rigid with contained anger. A single misplaced word on his part, one single mistake, and she would let it burst forth. From experience, Dun-Cadal knew that her wrath was best avoided.

'She asked you questions about *Frog*,' she said, her tone stinging. 'But don't worry, you were in no state to tell her anything.'

'Mildrel,' he whispered, as if seeking some excuse he could offer her.

She brought him the glass and held it out stiffly.

'Drink. It's Amauris berry juice.'

Without further prompting he swallowed a gulp and then, despite the drink's bitterness, drained the entire glass.

'I know, it tastes bad,' she observed, 'but it will prevent you from having a stomach ache. There's bread and some apples as well.'

'Mildrel,' he said, clutching her hand.

He raised his eyes to her and it was worse than taking a sword point in the heart. She remained still, her eyes staring at the wall and her lips pinched. There was no need for her to repeat the same old reproaches, nor would he have been able to answer them. They had known one another for so long that even their most simple gestures spoke volumes. Sniffing the air, Dun-Cadal ventured a faint, tired smile.

'Lavender,' he said with a smile. 'She smelled of lavender, just like you ...'

'She's born of the Republic. And you know what the Republic has done to generals who failed to rally to its side,' she said sadly. 'Why did you talk to her? What were you thinking? You've been willing enough to lie until now, and suddenly you've given yourself away!'

'What do I care about the Republic ... ? It means nothing to me.'

She snatched her hand from him and gave him a withering look, as if he were an unruly child who had done something naughty.

'She can have you arrested at any moment—'

'It doesn't matter,' he sighed as he rose to his feet.

He walked painfully over to the basin at the far side of the chamber and was glad to see that it was already filled with warm water. He carefully undid the top buttons of his shirt and then, with a mounting impatience, he pulled it off over his head.

'It matters to me,' Mildrel insisted.

She hadn't moved from her spot next to the unmade bed, her hands clutched together. Looking over his shoulder he saw her haloed by the sunlight, so beautiful, so dignified, in her controlled anger.

'I don't represent anything to anyone here,' he replied. 'Not any more. It's been too long ... What danger could I pose to them? The girl knows that all too well.'

He leaned over the basin, plunging his hands in and splashing his face. The warmth of the water soothed the worn skin of his face and he rubbed his eyelids, still sore from the effects of alcohol and the bright midday sun. His memories of the purges which had followed the fall of the Empire were as hazy as the steam rising from the water. So many knights had been judged by the Republic, so many proud, steadfast men had been sentenced, so much honour had been besmirched in public trials dictated by popular sentiment. He had survived it all, running before the heralds of the newborn Republic like a dog, even hiding out for two years in the forests of the North. And there Dun-Cadal Daermon and the others who had served the cursed Emperor were all finally forgotten ...

'That's true. The only person you're a danger to is yourself. And that's been the case for longer than you think; it wasn't the fall of the Empire that brought down the great Dun-Cadal Daermon.'

He froze, his arms resting on the edge of the basin and drops of water running down his face. The young boy's image haunted him, and every time it aroused the same feelings of pain and dismay. His memories were nothing but an open, festering wound.

'Losing Frog destroyed you.'

'You don't know what you're talking about.'

'Really?' She laughed, but it was a mocking, perfidious, disdainful sound. 'And do you know what you're talking about, with strange women? Did you even ask yourself what she wanted?'

Mildrel walked slowly towards the door, keeping her eyes on the old warrior's bare back. A large scar crossed one of his shoulder blades, the kiss of an axe, from the days when he'd defended his ideal of a glorious civilisation, heart and soul. How she had loved to feel that scar beneath her fingers ...

'She's a historian from Emeris,' Dun-Cadal said as he continued to wash. 'She wanted to speak to a soldier of the Empire.'

'And she stumbled across you by sheer accident,' she mocked him, opening the door. 'In case you've forgotten, it's foolish to be nostalgic for the old times in Masalia. Especially when so many councillors have been invited to celebrate Masque Night in the city.'

She waited for a reaction but Dun-Cadal was silent, his gaze lost in the steam from the basin. Since his arrival in Masalia he had paid no attention to anything but filling his tankard. Mildrel could bear it no longer. Only when she had shut the door behind her and her footsteps were no more than a distant echo did he straighten up.

He could not be angry with her, not for being worried about him. She had always worried. Worse still, she was always right. He had said too much to this Viola without knowing anything about her or her real intentions, if she were concealing any. It was the first time he had told anyone the truth during his alcoholic ramblings. If she were actually seeking Eraëd, would she accept his refusal to tell her where it was, or would she threaten to denounce him? And would the name Dun-Cadal Daermon be of any interest to the august councillors of the young Republic?

He was not even a shadow of his former self. The Knighthood had been dissolved along with the Empire. The *animus* had been forgotten. And still more serious in Dun-Cadal's eyes, it seemed people

41

no longer believed in the Book of Destiny and had little by little abandoned the old gods. Times were changing, as his aching body reminded him constantly. And, more forcefully, the sharp pains that ran down his right leg. He placed a trembling hand there as if hoping to calm them but it had no effect. He exchanged a glance with his reflection in the cheval glass.

'Azdeki!!! You filthy piece of shit! Come back!'

The pain was not merely physical. No, the real wound was located elsewhere, hidden deep inside.

'Azdeki!'

He bore a scar of the worst kind, one which could not be seen but would be felt, burning and sharp, as long as his heart was still beating.

'Azdeki! Tomlinn!'

'Azdeki!' he screamed as he lay in the swamp.

At that moment, the thought that Azdeki might abandon him to his fate was only a vague, farfetched hypothesis. Stunned by the fall and pinned by the weight of the horse crushing his leg, he wasn't capable of reason. He was lost, with his body pressed into the thick Saltmarsh mud. Attracted by his cries, the rouarg appeared above his horse's carcass, its maw smeared with blood and its large nostrils flaring in time with its heavy breathing.

'Come on …!' snarled Dun-Cadal, adrenaline masking any pain … adrenaline and a sudden fever. Standing on the horse's remains, the rouarg towered over the injured knight, its muscles bulging beneath skin covered with patches of long green-and-black fur. Keeping a wary eye on the beast, Dun-Cadal searched the mud for his sword. The rouarg's eyes narrowed, slowly opening its maw to release a putrid breath and a low growl. In the tall grasses, the knight heard the sound of two more monsters gradually approaching, drawn by his sweat and blood. His hand sank into the muck without finding any trace of his weapon.

'Godsfuck!' he cursed.

Pain shot up his broken leg, pinned and slowly crushed beneath the combined weight of the horse and the rouarg. The beast roared, stretching its neck in challenge towards its imprisoned prey. Any hope of locating his sword and slashing at its maw was vain. Only one solution remained before the suffering became unbearable and he fainted. Inhaling deeply, he drew in his arms, a grimace of pain twisting his sweat-and-mud-stained face. He needed to focus his entire being on listening to the world, feeling every vibration around him, rising above the pain and melting into the air, becoming one with everything around him ... He felt the *animus*, he became the *animus*. His leg awoke with agony, broken bones rending his flesh like razor blades.

The rouarg reared over him, ready to rip his head off with a swift snap of its teeth. Yet something prevented it. The monster stared at the trapped man with an air of disbelief; his hair was immersed in the stagnant water, his eyes half-closed, his features drawn with pain and fatigue. He stretched his hands forward, and the furious beast opened its jaws to reveal its steely fangs. The man had no means of reaching it and still less any hope of wounding it with his bare hands. And yet ... an overpowering force propelled the rouarg, and the horse's gutted carcass, far into the air.

At that instant, Dun-Cadal felt a sickening dropping sensation, every part of him jolting with the violent impact of a fall. He screamed to the point of dislocating his jaw, and when his cry finally faded he passed out.

In the distance, a snarling could be heard.

When he came to his senses for the first time, he saw a frog spying on him, its eyes blinking rapidly and its throat swelling in fits and starts.

When he opened his eyes again the frog had gone and he was alone with the tall grasses which seemed to be advancing across the marsh in slow waves. Raindrops formed craters in the black mud. The world was dark, but it was brighter than the blackness that engulfed him once more.

His eyelids fluttered slowly. The tall grasses were sparkling, bathed in blazing sunlight. And somehow he was ... dry?

'Bloody hell ...' he croaked, his voice terribly hoarse, his throat on fire.

He winced as he raised his head as far as he could. His neck was as stiff as an old piece of wood, but that was nothing compared to the rest of his body. He saw that he was stretched out on an old blanket, full of holes, spread over a patch of cracked earth at the edge of the marsh.

He was shaded by an old cart lying on its side, propped up by two big wooden logs. A makeshift splint made from branches and twisted grass supported his broken leg, wrapped in a blood-stained cloth. How had he got here? Who had brought him? And how long ago?

'Don't move too quickly,' a childlike voice said. 'Your leg is far from being knit back together. I did what I could, now only time will heal it.'

Seated beneath one corner of the cart, his legs folded under him, was a boy. Arms crossed on his knees, he stared at the knight with grey eyes and a solemn expression.

'Your leg was a really ugly mess,' he commented.

'As bad as that,' murmured Dun-Cadal.

'There were bones sticking out in places,' the boy said very calmly.

'And you ...' His head ached and he had trouble moving, his body numbed by days of inactivity. But little by little, he regained his senses. '*You* brought me here ...?'

The child nodded without revealing the lower part of his face, hidden behind his arms.

'The horse,' he said. 'With the help of a horse.'

He had a round face, just barely out of childhood, with tousled hair and a pale complexion. Dun-Cadal let himself fall back, short of breath. His head felt heavy and his vision was studded with tiny, fleeting stars. The blue sky rippled in his vision for an instant and then grew still.

'You need to go easy,' the boy continued. 'You've been lying there for eight days.'

'E-eight days ...' stammered the knight.

He tried to swallow but his throat was too dry. Seeing him so, with his head tilted back, gasping like a fish out of water, the boy seemed amused. He stood up and approached Dun-Cadal slowly.

'I left you something to drink, there,' he said, pointing to a small flask made from a sheep's stomach placed next to the knight. 'It's all I could find. There's more salt water than fresh hereabouts.'

Still eying his rescuer, Dun-Cadal sat up on his blanket with some difficulty, holding his injured ribs. He did not know what age to give the lad. Twelve, thirteen ... perhaps fourteen years old, but not more. He was wearing a plain beige shirt, open at the collar, worn-out black trousers and boots held together with pieces of string. Brown locks floated across his brow and his face was so smeared with

44

dirt he might have plunged headfirst into the mud.

'Thank you,' Dun-Cadal mumbled as he took the flask with a shaky hand.

He drank a gulp and almost spat it out immediately. It tasted foul but his thirst was so great he forced himself to swallow, grimacing. Out of the corner of his eye he saw his sword planted in the ground, not far from a pile of weathered crates half-covered with an old dark green cloth.

'You're a knight, aren't you? A knight of the Empire,' said the boy, his smile vanishing.

Dun-Cadal nodded carefully. His neck was too stiff to move it normally.

'And you are?' he asked.

The boy did not reply. He looked down at the dry earth where a slight breeze rolled bits of gravel across the ground between his boots. Dun-Cadal waited patiently but nothing broke the silence so he spent a moment scanning his surroundings in search of a landmark to indicate his position. The lad had evidently dragged him some distance to extract him from the marshes he had been mired in. In the distance he could see the oaks of the forest bordering the Seyman river. On the far bank lay only swamps bristling with tall grasses and rushes rustling in the wind. An odd heat haze shivered above their wind-blown tips. He wondered if Azdeki had managed to build the bridge and cross the river ... and then he remembered Azdeki abandoning him, and he felt his anger rising.

'The Empire crossed the Seyman four days ago,' the boy announced, as he rummaged through some crates lying at the rear of the cart.

So Azdeki had built the bridge.

'And we took Aëd's Watch,' Dun-Cadal sighed.

The revolt had been put down and Captain Azdeki was the hero of the battle of the Saltmarsh. He grimaced with his chapped lips. How ironic ...

'No,' replied the boy tersely, coming over with some sort of box in his hands.

He sat cross-legged beside the knight, the box nestled on his lap.

'They tried but they didn't succeed,' he said evasively, before adopting a bossy tone which did not suit him at all. 'Now give me that flask.'

45

'What do you mean, "they tried"?'

Seeing Dun-Cadal would not give him the flask if he did not answer, the boy reached out and snatched it, looking incensed.

'What are you going to—'

'I'm not going to poison you,' the boy said grumpily. 'It's something you need to drink to get better. Otherwise you'll never be back on your feet.'

Of course the boy wouldn't poison him. Dun-Cadal had seen his sword planted in the ground not far away. The lad had already had eight days to kill him if he wanted to. But the fact that he was going to such lengths to aid a likely enemy was intriguing. The entire region was at war … Dun-Cadal could not afford to forget that and place his trust in anyone. He had to be cautious.

'Are you from the Saltmarsh?' he asked.

'Yes.'

The boy slid the box lid open and his nimble fingers plunged inside. They emerged as a fist clutching a wriggling green shape. As he placed it over the flask, he added:

'But I saved you from the rouargs.'

'How?' asked the knight, disbelieving.

'It's a secret.'

Two long wriggling legs appeared from the boy's closed fist. He squeezed and a steaming yellow liquid ran into the neck of the flask. Dun-Cadal understood what the boy held in his fist and looked away in disgust, saying:

'Godsfuck … that's a frog … you're making a frog piss in the flask and I *drank* …'

'It's an *ashala machal*, a frog that lives in the rushes,' the boy said as if reciting a lesson. 'When they're frightened they urinate and it's very good for when you're ill.'

'It's revolting.'

'Maybe.' The boy smiled as he returned the frog to the box. 'But the whole time you were unconscious I made you drink it. If your fever broke, it's thanks to this. And I made an ointment from the mucus on their skin. The salt from the marshes was starting to eat away at the wound. But with the ointment, the pain was soothed. And their urine acts like a tonic so that you'll get better.'

Dun-Cadal swallowed. He'd drunk some nasty things in his time, but agreeing to gulp down *frog's piss* was asking a bit much.

'And you expect me to drink this—?'

'Do you want to die out here?'

They glared at one another while the boy held out the flask to him. No, of course he didn't want to die out here. No more than he wanted to linger here. In the lad's grey eyes he saw a determination that forced him to smile. The boy was willing to do anything to make him drink this concoction and, in his present state, trying to avoid it wasn't a very good idea. To be sure, he could resist. He could even kill the lad, despite his wound. He was an Imperial general after all, not some small fry ...

But there was something in the child's eyes, a longing and an anger that aroused Dun-Cadal's curiosity.

He drank a mouthful and it was now clear where the water's foul taste came from.

'Seriously,' he murmured, narrowing his eyes, 'who are you?'

The lad's gaze was lost in the distant mist as he gathered up some pebbles lying at his feet and began to pitch them distractedly into the weeds.

'You must have a name. What do they call you in these parts?'

'I have no name.'

'No name?' Dun-Cadal asked in surprise.

'Not any more. I lost it,' the boy sounded aggrieved and his pebble throwing became more vigorous.

'What about your family?'

'Dead. There's a war going on here, in case you didn't know,' he said sarcastically, scowling at Dun-Cadal. 'I escaped Aëd's Watch a long time ago ...'

'Why?'

The boy reflected for a moment. Recalling painful events? Or searching for an answer that would seem credible? The general reminded himself that his young saviour was a child of the Saltmarsh, probably a rebel sympathiser and possibly a traitor to the Empire. Not killing Dun-Cadal was one thing, but the lad might still be trying to gain his trust for some reason or another.

'Because of the war ... I was frightened.'

As he swallowed another mouthful of the doctored water Dun-Cadal watched the lad carefully.

'And the cart? Was it yours?'

'No ... it's old. It's my shelter. I was hiding out here and then one day I saw you lot going by. You were attacked by the rouargs … and now here you are.'

The boy stopped pitching stones but his eyes remained lost in the distance, as if his mind were elsewhere.

'There were three of them,' remembered Dun-Cadal. 'You fought off three rouargs all by yourself?'

'I told you, I have a secret.'

He sprang up suddenly.

'You need to rest. I'm going to try to find something for us to eat this evening. There are frogs as big as your fist, hive frogs we call them. They're a bit like chicken.'

As the boy went to the rear of the cart to look for a bag, Dun-Cadal called out to him:

'Lad! I appreciate your help, really I do, but I must rejoin my troops, they need— '

The boy turned round, passing the bag's bandolier over his shoulder.

'Not yet. You're still too weak.'

And then he disappeared behind the cart.

'Lad! Hey! Lad! Come back!' the knight called.

But shout as he might, there was no reply. He fell back wearily against his blanket and allowed his eyelids to droop, his head feeling incredibly heavy. He tried hard to think about what he should or could do to locate the Imperials' camp, but his fatigue overcame him and he slept.

When he awoke, the sun was setting behind the leaning cart and the boy was lighting a fire. Dun-Cadal struggled to rise up on an elbow. He felt as if his entire body had been trampled beneath the hooves of a furious horse. His wounded leg drew his attention in particular, wrapped in a bandage that was starting to smell like rotten meat. The boy saw he was awake but said nothing. Indeed, they exchanged no words at all until the boy brought him a small bowl filled with grilled frog legs. Witnessing the knight's disgust, he stifled a giggle.

'You find this funny, do you, lad?' the knight sighed. 'Seeing one of the invaders subjected to your … awful taste in food …'

'The Saltmarsh has always been part of the Empire,' replied the boy as he sat back down by the fire.

Dun-Cadal was surprised, almost letting go of the frog leg he was lifting to his mouth.

'Happy to hear you say that,' he said before biting off a piece of meat.

It did in fact taste like chicken. When he managed to forget the unpalatable appearance of the frog it came from, it wasn't too bad. Night had fallen and only the glow from the wavering flames lit the boy's face. His usual severe expression had softened.

'This is how I've survived out here,' he explained, pointing at the dish of frogs. 'There are fourteen species in the western part of the Saltmarsh alone. In the entire region, there must be ... thirty, forty different kinds of frog. They all have their uses. Some help to make poisons, others, remedies ... With their skin, their drool, their urine ...' He pointed at Dun-Cadal's bowl again. 'And some can be eaten ...'

'Is this what they teach at school in Aëd's Watch?' Dun-Cadal asked sarcastically as he chewed.

The boy bowed his head pensively as he slowly plunged the branch he was holding into the heart of the fire.

'So, lad ... tell me what happens next.'

'Next?'

'Yes, next. You saved me from the rouargs and then you cared for my wounds as best you could. And although you think the Salt-marsh has always been part of the Empire, you are and you remain a Saltmarsh lad. So what will you do next? It seems to me I'm your prisoner ...'

The boy let the burning piece of wood go and looked away.

'Your friend's horse is over there behind the cart.'

Dun-Cadal rose higher on his elbows, taking care not to move his broken leg, and saw the Tomlinn's mount's ears visible above the cart.

'True. So that's how you dragged me here ...' he recalled.

'I wound a rope around your waist,' explained the boy, miming how he had harnessed the knight. 'Then I passed it under your arms. I attached the ends to the horse ... and here you are ...'

'And here I am,' repeated Dun-Cadal.

He stared at the boy while he finished his frog legs. He wasn't very hungry, despite having gone eight days without eating, no doubt due to the pain. But as he swallowed the tender meat he slowly recovered his appetite.

49

'You're really something, lad,' he said.

For the rest of the evening, Dun-Cadal tried to get the boy to speak but it was like talking to a wall. As he was drifting off to sleep, his last thought was a terrible one ...

What if the lad turns me in to the rebels tomorrow?

That fear haunted him over the following days. His leg was still healing, the pain from his ribs burned him and every breath he took was torture. Whenever he tried to stand up, he thought he would faint. The boy changed his bandage three times and on each occasion he was able to take stock of the damage. The large, leaking wounds had been crudely sewn up in several places where the bones had broken and torn through the skin. It was not the work of one of the Empire's finest surgeons, but the lad had done the best he could.

Several times the knight had sought to draw him out about himself, but to little avail. Dun-Cadal was more skilled at wielding a sword than asking questions. And several times the boy left their improvised camp, riding away on Tomlinn's horse to some Saltmarsh village.

Dun-Cadal tried to wait patiently during his absence, going over every possible strategy available to him if the lad betrayed him. But why then would he go to so much trouble to treat his wounds? Worrying over the paradox bore a hole in his skull. He tried to find a solution, any logical sequence that would allow him to guess at the lad's real goal, until he finally decided to let matters take their course. Destiny was already written, he had no real control over the future. There was no fatalism or surrender in this idea, simply a quiet acceptance of events.

Days passed and no rebels showed up to arrest the wounded general. Although the lad said little, he continued to take care of his patient as best he could. Dun-Cadal contented himself with that. When he was strong enough to stand on his feet, using a plank from the cart as a crutch, the knight told himself he had spent more than enough time in the marshes.

'You look like a wading bird ...' a voice behind him said in a mocking tone.

Dun-Cadal tried to keep his balance with his good leg.

'You shouldn't be doing this,' the boy advised as the general struggled to harness the horse.

Each time his healing leg touched the ground, a fiery arrow raced up it and into his heart and his brow burst out in sweat. The horse had been quietly grazing behind the cart and did not seem to appreciate having a lame cripple trying to cinch a saddle upon its back.

'The war goes on without me. I've recovered enough to go and find my men, lad,' Dun-Cadal assured him.

But his perspiring face and his features drawn by pain contradicted his words.

'You won't be able to ride with that leg,' the boy warned. 'Waders don't belong on horseback. You look funny like that, trying to keep your balance, but you're going to fall over.'

'Oh, you think so, do you?' jested the knight as he finished buckling the girth beneath the horse's belly.

In fact, he almost fell as he stepped back, the plank digging into his armpit despite the chain mail protecting his upper body. He was anxious to be rid of it. He placed one hand on the pommel of the saddle and used the crutch to heave himself painfully onto his mount. He had to try several times before he succeeded in lifting his injured leg over the horse's rump. Then he let it slide across the saddle with a moan. His scabbard smacked against his unpolished armour and he thought he was going to pass out as his leg with its wooden brace knocked against the useless stirrup. But once he was settled in the saddle, his hands gripping the reins, he was able to catch his breath and wait for the pain to slowly subside.

'You think so,' he repeated in a murmur, staring into the distance. A heat haze covered the marshes and the sky was masked by the same white clouds that had greeted his arrival in the region. 'I must find my men.'

With a twitch of the reins, he urged the horse to a walk. Even this gentle movement made him grimace in pain, each time the splint tapped the saddle leather. If he was going to ride for hours with only one good leg, this was merely a foretaste of what he would have to endure.

'What about me?' the boy asked plaintively.

'You? Well, live long and happy with your frogs and avoid armed men whenever possible. All hell may break loose around here ... I still have a town to capture.'

'You mean Aëd's Watch?' The boy was walking up beside the

horse now, trying to catch the reins. 'You don't know what happened there—'

If the lad persisted in his efforts, he was going to stop the horse. Dun-Cadal gritted his teeth and kicked twice with his good heel to make the horse trot. The boy had to step aside to avoid being jostled. Seeing his frown, the knight gave him a mocking smile.

'I should think that idiot Azdeki was unable to take the town and had to retreat.'

He held back a laugh, however, as his ribs ached with the slightest jolt. The pain made him want to vomit up his guts, but he imposed his will upon his body. He had to find his troops, lead the fight to the end and stamp out the revolt.

'They lost,' the boy said, 'You said it yourself: the war went on without you.' Dun-Cadal tugged slightly on the reins. The horse slowed. 'The Empire lost the Saltmarsh four days ago.'

With one hand, the general turned the steed. A few feet from him, the lad was standing up straight, his balled fists close to his thighs. His face had reclaimed the angry expression he'd worn during the first few days and there was still a childish quality about it, as if he had just been punished and was about to throw a tantrum. Should Dun-Cadal believe him? He could accept that Azdeki had failed to capture the town, but the idea that he, a hundred thousand soldiers and a thousand knights using the *animus* had suffered a decisive defeat was quite simply unthinkable.

'Aëd's Watch was a trap. They held off your men and then launched a great attack,' the boy said mournfully. 'Your army was so surprised it couldn't react in time ... It was routed.'

'How could that be ...?' Dun-Cadal whispered, tight-faced and overwhelmed; the once proud and arrogant military leader suddenly an injured man reeling on top of a scrawny horse.

'You'll need to cross the enemy's lines to rejoin your men,' the boy said. 'You're lost out here, behind the rebels holding the borders of the Saltmarsh.'

Dun-Cadal leaned over the horse's neck, one hand gripping the saddle pommel, and stared at the lad. He was well and truly stuck out here, all on his own. No one even knew he was still alive.

'You should have told me sooner,' he snapped. 'Godsfuck, why didn't you tell me sooner?'

'How would knowing have changed anything?'

The insolent little imp gave him a strange smile that was at odds with his severe gaze.

'You're going to need me,' he added.

'For what? Now you want to help me escape the Saltmarsh as well as saving my life?'

Dun-Cadal's voice had risen in both anger and despair. He tried to think things through, searching for a solution, any way out. But his leg was incredibly painful, an agony which ran up his thigh and bored its way through his guts to strike at his heart. The lad was right; he was not yet fit enough to ride.

'You're a knight.'

He gave Dun-Cadal a determined look.

'Teach me to fight.'

'What?' exclaimed the general, startled.

'Teach me to fight and I'll help you escape from the Saltmarsh and find your troops.'

'Because you think the two of us will be able to cross the enemy lines, just like that?' Dun-Cadal asked in a mocking tone.

He placed a feverish hand on his damaged ribs. If he stayed on the horse any longer he was in danger of keeling over.

'It's possible,' the boy insisted. 'You have no idea what I'm capable of.'

'I don't know anything about you! I don't even know your name!'

'You can give me whatever name you like,' the boy said evasively. 'Teach me to fight. You won't be sorry.'

He didn't move an inch, his shoulders slightly hunched but his dark eyes looking up at the knight, standing his ground without a hint of fear.

'You, fight? At your age you want to take up arms?'

'I'll be a knight before you know it.'

'Such confidence! It takes a long time to become a knight, lad.'

'I can do it.'

'You won't be any use to me crossing enemy lines.'

'I can do it,' the boy insisted.

Each time the knight raised his tone, the boy answered in a low but firm voice.

'You're starting to annoy me!' bellowed Dun-Cadal as he drew on the reins. 'You're only a child! Stay in your place and stop dreaming

53

of ridiculous things. The situation is too complicated for me to train you now.'

'I'm not a child!' The boy pointed an accusing finger at the general. 'And you won't get far like that and you know it! But you'd rather go and tempt the demons out there than stay here and give your wounds time to heal. You could use all that time to teach me to fight, but no, you'd rather go and throw yourself into death's arms on your own. Who cares that I know where the rebels are located, how many there are and how to get past them! And the two of us, together we can do it!'

Out of breath, his mouth twisted in anger, he lowered his arm. He was on the edge of tears.

'And I'm not a child,' he repeated.

The horse snorted. It seemed tired too. Reluctantly, Dun-Cadal accepted the idea that he could not undertake the journey on his own.

'Do you even know how to wield a sword?' he asked.

The boy nodded and they went back to the cart. Dun-Cadal needed the lad's help to dismount and, one arm around the shoulders of his young rescuer, he hobbled back to his blanket. Only when he was finally lying down did the pain in his leg subside ... for the moment. He raised it with the help of an old crate to ensure the blood would drain better and not cause his foot to swell.

'Help me take off my boot,' he sighed.

He watched as the lad obeyed, searching his face for any signs that would tell him something more ... A scar, an expression, a detail he'd overlooked up until now, the slightest clue that would reveal a shred of this lad's past. Anything but this complete blank. Once the boy had removed the boot, he moved to the knight's side and took the frog from its box to extract more urine from it.

'If I'm staying then I'll have to give you a name,' said Dun-Cadal, lifting his chin.

'If you like,' the boy replied, shaking the flask to mix the water and urine together.

'Let's see ... you called me Wader didn't you? Why don't I return the favour? As you seem to like those wriggling beasties you will be ... Frog ... I shall call you Frog.'

He waited to see if the lad would take offense but he merely nodded before opening the flask and passing it to the general.

'It suits me,' the boy said with a wistful smile, 'Wader.'

Evidently, he was willing to put up with anything to achieve his goals, even a ridiculous nickname.

'Sir Frog the knight … Do you want to be known as Sir Frog?' Dun-Cadal asked jestingly as he took the flask.

But the glance the boy gave him made him to falter. In those grey eyes lay the force of an unbreakable will. The lad's next words were quiet but firm, a mere murmur which nonetheless carved itself into Dun-Cadal's memory, as powerful as any cry.

'One day you'll understand. Be certain of that. I shall be the greatest knight this world has ever known.'

4

THE ASSASSIN

'Attack someone from behind?
There's no honour in fighting like that!'
'There's no honour at all in killing someone, lad.
No matter how you strike.
There's no glory to be had in taking a life.'

Everything she knew of the world came from books. Her long years of study at the Great College of Emeris had made her impressively erudite, but all that knowledge consisted merely of words. Here, she was discovering their true meaning. She was finally seeing the living embodiment of those written works, copied and recopied down the centuries by the monks of the Order of Fangol. Until now these servants of the gods had been the sole masters of writing. Recording the voices of the gods themselves, set down in the Sacred Book. But the *Liaber Dest* vanished long ago, while the Empire had been overthrown and the rules had changed. Knowledge was no longer supposed to be the sole preserve of the elite. In the Republic, a young peasant girl like Viola could be taught the history of her world and how to relate its events with the help of a quill dipped in ink. But what had she really seen with her own eyes? The leafy paths of the village where she had been born, and later, the long and wide avenues of the Imperial city of Emeris. But what else? Nothing but words in books, describing the former Kingdoms in a poetic way.

So the simple act of walking along the cobbled streets of Masalia seemed to mark a new stage in her life. All along the street, traders exhorted passers-by to try their magnificent goods: vegetables, spices that pricked the nostrils, braided necklaces, lace-trimmed fabrics, dried meats, or the still bloody chops from a pig slaughtered right by the stalls ...

The noon sun at its zenith bathed the city in light and the heavy scent of musk and citrus fruit floated in the air. In the days of the Empire, Masalia had been the only city where someone who dreamt of something better might achieve their goal. Now that the Republic ruled the destinies of its peoples, the advantages of this city had spread like an unexpected wind of hope throughout the former Kingdoms. Viola was a perfect example of this, a blacksmith's daughter who had proved quite brilliant and completed her studies at the Great College, hitherto reserved for the nobility. What career lay ahead of her now? That of a historian, cooped up in a library with ancient tomes? Or that of an archaeologist, travelling the world in search of antique artefacts and idols? Who would she fall in love with? With whom would she raise a family? What was her place in this new chapter of the world, now everyone had the chance to choose their own future ...?

She pondered all these questions without really expecting to find any answers, and the possibility that there might be more than one pleased her. Her parents had not, at any point in their lives, had a chance to consider their futures. Her father had been a blacksmith like his father before him, while her mother barely knew how to write her name. The Fangolin monks had taught the skill of writing to some, but they ensured they alone mastered the art.

'Miss, try the flavours of the Sudies Islands! Spices like you've never tasted before!' hailed a smooth-faced man with an olive complexion. His round belly almost rested on his stall, its surface covered with bags of spices.

She gave him a brief smile and nodded disinterestedly before passing two men brawling in the middle of the street. No one paid them much attention, and she had other things to do than stroll about the city. She had been charged with a mission and was intent on carrying it out. Finding Eraëd, the Emperors' sword, was not a passing whim but rather a conscious effort on the part of some to honour the past. Eraëd ... the sword was much more than a symbol, it was a legendary object, said to have been forged at the beginning of time.

Leaving the market street, she spotted the dried-up fountain that stood at the centre of a small square paved in red and white cobblestones. There, among the tall, prosperous-looking houses with balconies bright with flowers and wide windows, was the townhouse where she had left Dun-Cadal the previous night. It was not hard to recognise in the light of day. It was the only house whose curtains remained drawn and there were young women with exposed shoulders parading in front of the door. Long skirts fell to their bare feet, and they wore fine, brightly coloured cloth that clung perfectly to their curves. They were selling their charms to the highest bidder, and they had come to the right address for proper training. It was murmured here and there that Mildrel had been one of the most prominent courtesans of the Empire, sharing bedchamber secrets as she distributed both her favours and her advice in the shadowy light of private salons.

Viola adjusted her spectacles before seating herself on the lip of the fountain. A stone cherub stood in the middle with its wings spread wide and one knee bent, as if about to take flight. She observed the passers-by: traders in Masalia on business, dirt-stained travellers wearily leading their mounts, and even some Nâaga swaggered past, staring all about them. Then, out of the corner of her eye, she finally spied the familiar figure of a badly-shaven old knight.

Dun-Cadal emerged from Mildrel's house, raising a hand to shade his face from the sun. In his other he held an apple and he lifted it to his mouth to take a bite. Two of the girls pacing before the door greeted him with broad smiles. The bright sunlight reflecting off the paving stones was dazzling. For someone whose eyelids already bore the weight of a hangover, the glare was almost unbearable.

'I was afraid you'd never come out of there,' a voice said behind him.

He threw a glance over his shoulder, munching on a piece of the apple. Viola approached with a light step, her hands clasped behind her back and two rebellious curls falling before her ears. So the young red-headed woman was not going to leave him alone. He examined her from head to toe with a frown.

'You again ...' he grumbled hoarsely.

'Did you miss me?' she asked with a smile, rocking on her feet like a child. 'As female company goes, I think you did rather well for yourself last night.'

Dun-Cadal walked away, grumbling as he went. Viola kept up with him.

'I see you're just as pleasant as you were yesterday,' she said in a jesting tone.

'Your savage isn't with you?' the knight groused. 'Too busy drawing more tacky things on his face?'

'Oh well, if you're missing him then don't worry, you'll see him soon enough.'

'I could easily manage without that ...'

He picked up his pace, eating his apple with an irritated air. To be pestered like this, so soon after waking, was intolerable. As was the hammer beating an anvil within his head. And it was compounded by all the sounds of Masalia; its street peddlers and hawkers ... even its seagulls gliding past in the cloudless sky. Dun-Cadal shouldered his way through the crowd with Viola still dogging his heels.

'Have you come back to threaten me?' he asked.

'Threaten you? With what?'

'Now that you know who I am—'

'I'm not about to put you on trial,' Viola interrupted as she moved up to his side.

A trader coming towards them with a cask in his arms almost ran into her. She sidestepped to avoid him and then swung back to follow in the knight's wake. The trader went on his way without missing a step, whistling as he went.

'I'm seeking something other than vengeance,' she added.

'I won't help you find the rapier.'

'That sword belongs to history!'

'And that history is long over.'

At the end of the street, they could see the swaying masts of the ships anchored in the port. Eager to leave all this frantic activity behind and spend a quiet moment in front of a full tankard, Dun-Cadal turned right. But a tattooed colossus stood at the mouth of the alley with his arms crossed, one corner of his mouth twisted into a strange smile. Their eyes met and, judging by the old general's scowl, there was nothing friendly in their glances.

'I said you'd see Rogant again,' Viola murmured behind him.

Dun-Cadal turned round and headed for the port. Viola hurried to catch up with him before he disappeared into the crowd.

'Dun! Wait, Dun!' she cried. 'Wait for me!'

'Why should I wait for you?' he asked firmly. 'The only thing I'm

59

waiting for is the moment when you lead the Republican Guards to me.'

'The civil war is over, General,' Viola replied. 'Get that through your skull. You really believe I'd turn you in on the faint hope that you'll talk to me from a gaol cell?'

'The thought occurred to me.'

'Be serious. I'd have to be an idiot to try something like that.'

'That occurred to me as well,' the knight said sarcastically.

A multitude of proud, tall ships lay moored in the harbour, rocking gently on the water. Some sort of escort party was disembarking from one of them, composed of guards dressed in red and sky-blue armour, holding halberds and wearing swords at their side. At their head, two less heavily-armed soldiers bore standards with the colours of the arriving dignitaries. The councillors ... so the rumours were true. He had known several of them in his previous life. He halted and felt Viola's slight body press up against his back.

'Why would I denounce you,' she murmured, 'when so many who prospered far more than you under the Empire, yet never even defended it, are now the elected representatives of the people?'

There were four of them here, mostly old and wrinkled, wearing rich red cloaks adorned with gold fleurs-de-lys and trimmed with cream fur. Of these four, Dun-Cadal recognised three of them. The Duke of Azbourt, a cruel man with a deeply creased faced, massively-built despite his advanced age, who had long ago retreated to his northern duchy and made no effort to seek the Emperor's favour. The Marquis of Enain-Cassart was a small man with a high-pitched voice, wearing a tightly curled powdered wig and a large smile on his face, who walked with the help of a cane. He had frequented the palace corridors in Emeris and proclaimed his loyalty to the Empire until the day it fell. What sort of deals had made him a candidate to represent his region in the Council? His personal wealth had certainly played a part. The third councillor in line was a personage unknown to the knight, much younger in age, with a thin scar beneath his right eye, but Dun-Cadal felt sure he had connections with the first two. As for the last man ... Dun-Cadal shook his head, gritting his teeth.

'I don't know if you ever met again after he abandoned you in the Saltmarsh,' Viola said, 'but Etienne Azdeki is now one of the Republic's most prominent councillors. Others will be arriving soon for Masque Night. If the people don't hold their pasts against them, why should they hold yours against you?'

She stood at his side, her gaze drifting over the crowd that had gathered around the officials and their escort. He had paid no heed to the Republic's affairs, trying to forget about the world and hoping the world would forget about him. Although he had once known the Emperor himself, he cared little about who governed now, choosing to dwell in a reality apart. But some had risen again from the ruins of the Empire.

'Congratulations, General, you've just realised that this world is neither black nor white, contrary to what you believed in the Empire's heyday ...'

Something wasn't right. He had a sense ... but it was still too vague for him to understand the mounting fear inside him. His distraction partly accounted for his stinging retort:

'Don't play this little game with me.'

'I can be sarcastic, too. Only I have a few advantages over you.'

'Those being ...?'

'I don't stink of sweat, and I'm much prettier than you.'

Dun-Cadal couldn't hold back his smile, although the air around him seemed heavier, as if foreboding some disaster. No, truly, something wasn't right. But the scent of lavender had beguiled him for an instant. She wasn't lying about her pretty face, either.

'I don't mean you any harm, General, rest assured about that.'

She gazed at him, her eyes so beautiful, so green, with fine long eyelashes. Their light was barely disguised by the glasses of her spectacles. How could he resist the quiet charm radiating from her, the resolute will contained in a velvet glove? He had the impression that she was stroking him, as if he were an old wolf she was trying to tame. And he found himself liking the experience. He had even daydreamt that she could have been Mildrel's daughter. The way the lavender scent clung so deliciously to both women's throats ... Without a word he bit hard into the apple, tearing off a chunk as if were meat on a bone, and looked away.

But the ominous feeling was more distinct now. It was so obvious to him; his warrior's senses telling him to remain on his guard.

'Don't move,' he ordered, watching as the procession left the docks and crossed the big square just behind them.

Before a wide building whose front steps were framed by tall white marble columns, four carriages awaited the new arrivals.

The motley crowd was still pressing around the councillors, excited and curious enough that only the honour guard formed up by the halberdiers prevented the most intrepid from accosting their Council representatives. Although Azdeki, Azbourt and the unnamed stranger showed little interest in the people who had come to greet them, Enain-Cassart seemed delighted by their warm welcome. He squinted in the glare of sunlight reflecting off the paving stones, but anyone observing him could see a gleam of joy peeping through the slit between his eyelids.

'General ...?' ventured Viola.

He raised a hand towards her, warning her to remain silent, and walked towards the square, hunting for anything unusual within the crowd. He could feel it, picture it ... death, was lurking somewhere nearby, ready to pounce. But on whom? In what form? He couldn't say, but he could sense it. And when he spotted the hunched figure hidden by an old patched cloak and a hood with rippling folds, he knew, even though it looked like an old man hobbling among the onlookers, gazing intently at the marquis.

Dun-Cadal finally reached the crowd, the cheers aggravating his still aching head. He took one last bite of the apple and let it fall to the ground. The core was quickly crushed by passing feet. The figure advanced. There were cries of joy, laughter, and then a commotion started a few feet away. Curses and insults were exchanged and several halberdiers left their formation to aid their companions. A fight had broken out at the edge of the procession, small but enough to distract the guards. And the closer Dun-Cadal came, the more his alarm grew. Whatever happened would happen soon.

The cloaked figure stumbled against a guard. The latter almost seemed to apologise to the old man, but his smile vanished as his legs gave way beneath his own weight.

Very soon ...

The old man held the soldier's body for a few seconds before letting it drop silently and creeping up behind the marquis' back. A short distance away the halberdiers were separating three sailors from what looked like a furious Nâaga.

Now.

The old man straightened up suddenly, but the movement seemed curiously slow to Dun-Cadal's eyes. With a twitch of his shoulders, he shed the patched cloak and hood, revealing a much younger man dressed in a green cape, with a thinner hood still masking his face in shadow. On his belt, two daggers sat next to the dull pommel of a sword. He wore leather bracers on his wrists and his relaxed stance was evidence of an extraordinary composure.

Dun-Cadal came to a sudden halt, his breath cut short. He had been trained to seek out, recognise and detect the approach of assassins. He had protected the Emperor by becoming his shadow, watching for the slightest sign of suspicious movement at the Imperial court. When the Marquis of Enain-Cassart slowly turned round, he knew it was already too late.

'Now then, young man—'

The councillor's beaming smile vanished as the blade pierced his throat. There was no cry, nor any word, just bubbles of blood that flowed into his mouth before trickling from the corners of his mouth.

Fast and precise. And without any sign of remorse and regret, or even satisfaction at a duty accomplished. But Dun-Cadal could guess what the man was feeling. He had done similar work for years. To defend the Empire it had sometimes been necessary to strike first ...

Enain-Cassart fell to one side without the time to realise that his life was ending, and the cheers died away in general astonishment. For a brief moment, lasting no longer than the space of a breath, there was only the distant sound of water lapping in the harbour. And the flapping of the assassin's green cape, caught in the wind, against his boots. The sound matched the beat of blood in Dun-Cadal's temples and hypnotised the general.

Killing. He'd done it himself, many times, in the same manner.

'You were an assassin, weren't you?'

That was before the Emperor had allowed him to train a successor and be promoted to the rank of general in reward for his services. He'd given his uniform to his student ...

To Dun-Cadal's right, a woman with dirty hair tied back in a ponytail and pink cheeks covered in tiny red veins stood gaping. When she finally recovered enough to speak, her voice rang out across the dumbstruck square.

'Assassin!' she screamed.

And the crowd finally began to stir, panicked citizens fleeing the scene while the halberdiers hastily escorted the three remaining councillors to their carriages. Alone, standing over the marquis' body, the assassin seemed to take a perverse pleasure in watching the stampede. He hardly moved when the guards surrounded him, spears and halberds levelled in his direction.

Dun-Cadal had forgotten about that uniform from the very moment another man had donned it in his place. He had left it behind, like a legacy. A simple green cape ... a ghost from his past. The general breathed heavily, darting brief glances at the handful of onlookers still lingering a few feet from the scene, as curious as they were frightened. For years he had tried to drown his memories in alcohol, and in the last few hours his entire past had resurfaced. From Eraëd to Frog . . . from Azdeki to the man who'd replaced him at the Emperor's side.

'Throw down your weapons!'

'On your knees! Get down on your knees!'

'Throw down your weapons!'

The soldiers' peremptory commands were barely audible above the general commotion. Their spears were still pointing at the assassin. He seemed to accept the situation, looking in turn at the face of each man threatening him. His closed lips did not tremble, in fact he was terribly calm. Why? Why was he behaving this way? Any other assassin would have committed his crime as stealthily as possible, using the crowd's movements to make good his escape.

Only when a soldier dared to move forward did he finally react, seizing the man's spear with a firm hand and giving it a sharp tug to bring it towards him. His hapless victim was unable to parry the dagger thrust into his chain mail with enough force to perforate the metal mesh before digging into the soldier's abdomen.

This was a message. A warning. A threat directed at all of the councillors. As he climbed into his coach, Azdeki turned back to watch the scene. The circle of soldiers around the assassin tightened. At its centre, two daggers slashed the air and the clatter of blades and armour filled the square. And then, before the astonished eyes of the old general standing a few yards away, the killer emerged from the ring. A dagger in each hand, he shoved two soldiers aside and nimbly bounded out into the square.

It was him ... Reyes' protector, his loyal assassin ... the *Hand of the Emperor* ... Why? How? Dun-Cadal was borne away on a floodtide of emotions and questions. But there were no answers, no comforting explanations. He had to know for sure ... He had to stop that man! He ran, following in the wake of the guards. Onlookers dispersed ahead of the fugitive, yelling in alarm. No man dared to stand in his path. But another squad of soldiers deployed in a street that ran into the square, positioned to intercept the criminal and looking confident. There was no possible escape, the old man kept repeating that to himself.

The assassin didn't even slow at the sight of the wall of spears blocking the street. He dodged right with a twist of his hips, sprang on top of a barrel at the bottom of a rusty drainpipe and took a flying leap towards the flower-laden balcony of a house across the way. The stunned soldiers halted in their tracks. Behind them, Dun-Cadal spotted an alley to his left and ran into it, coughing from his exertions. It had been a long time since he run this hard, but he paid little heed to his laboured breathing or to his still-pounding head. Looking up, he saw the assassin's silhouette. He was climbing a rooftop with ease.

'Stop him! *Stop him!*'

'He went that way!'

'We can't lose him!'

An alley, a street, and then another ... Several times, Dun-Cadal almost collided with startled passers-by. As he ran, he tracked the assassin, jumping from roof to roof. His shoulder slammed into a woman carrying a basket of laundry. Grimacing, he struggled to keep his balance, ignoring the woman's insults, and resumed his chase. After five minutes, however, a sharp stitch in his side forced him to come to a halt. His hand pressed over his heart he leaned against a wall, listening to the guards' distant shouts. Breathing heavily, his face and lungs on fire, he drew in air deeply as he gathered his wits. The days when he had fled over rooftops, taken bold leaps, employed the *animus*, were long gone. He had been one of the greatest knights. And now?

He was nothing but a crazy old fool, lost in Masalia, waiting and hoping for a violent death to find him in some dive in the city's slums. But it wasn't death that had found him, no. It was a young red-head, and she'd brought his entire past with her ... Closing his eyes, he heard a voice, a murmur from the past ...

'I'm ready ...'

His knees folded and he slid down the wall, his face covered in sweat . . .

'*I'm ready!*'

'*No. I won't change my mind, Frog.*'

The lad's words, so long ago, just before their destinies became linked. With unexpected aplomb, he had told Dun-Cadal he was ready to leave the Saltmarsh, to cross the rebels' lines, to fight and to kill other men. Heedless that it was an entirely different matter to their training with sticks, Frog had believed he was ready to commit irrevocable deeds. Because a life once taken could never be returned . . .

'Yesterday you said I'd made enormous progress!!!'

'For an armless man, learning to lift a sword with his feet constitutes enormous progress,' Dun-Cadal replied with a sly grin. 'That doesn't mean he's capable of defeating an army.'

With the help of his makeshift crutch, he hobbled back to the leaning cart. In the two months he had been here, this was the first day he had managed to remain standing for more than two hours without suffering for it.

'You're . . . *stupid*,' spat Frog, balling his fists with a fierce scowl.

Weary, the general slowly sat down on a crate and propped his crutch against the worm-eaten cart. The sun was setting in the distance, bathing the tall Saltmarsh grasses in a blood-red glow. He had become accustomed to the young boy's insolence and was almost amused by it. He even put up with being called Wader. No one had dared give him a nickname before and his acceptance of one now wasn't because he was separated from his army. The lad had come to represent a part of himself that might survive his own death; his knowledge, and . . . No, even more than that. Frog had become the son he had dreamt of so often and been unable to offer Mildrel. As he watched Frog, standing a few feet away from the campfire, his fists pressed hard against his thighs in a pose of sullen anger, he felt no regret about agreeing to teach him the art of war. The lad handled himself well and, more importantly, a raging desire to learn burned within him, to the point of consuming him. Dun-Cadal had felt the same when he was younger, but never to this extreme. The fire had to be dampened from time to time; Frog still had many things to learn. Among them, patience.

'Stupid for wanting to keep you alive? Yes, perhaps.'

'You don't understand anything …' the boy sighed before sitting down.

'I understand that you're in a hurry to leave here. Me too! You've been feeding us on whatever you can pilfer from Aëd's Watch. And it's crap … although it's a bit tastier than those frogs you hunt out here … Speaking of which,' he pointed at the boy, screwing up his face in disgust, 'your hive frogs, they sit heavily on my stomach. Try to find something else.'

'That's exactly my point! It's time to go!' Frog protested, rolling his eyes.

'Not yet. You're not ready and neither am I,' said Dun-Cadal, lowering his finger to indicate his outstretched leg.

It seemed sturdier now, enough that he had decided to remove the splint, but he had to build up the muscles before he could attempt anything at all. He would need another month before chancing a frantic escape across the enemy lines. He'd already reconciled himself to the idea, having no other real choice. And the one factor that had convinced him this plan was the lesser evil was Frog's determination. He had started to train the lad without much conviction until he noticed that, after nightfall when he believed his teacher was asleep, Frog continued his exercises. He saw the boy's silhouette brandishing the wooden stick that served as his training sword, and later, as the days and nights passed, using the knight's own sword. Frog only permitted himself a few hours of sleep but he never complained. He kept his efforts secret, but every night he practised his moves.

'Tomorrow … tomorrow, we'll try a different lesson,' said Dun-Cadal.

He picked up the flask lying at his feet and opened it slowly. Frog went to sit down under the far corner of the cart, swearing to himself.

'You know how to parry and you've learned some offensive thrusts. Tomorrow I'll show you how to attack someone from behind.'

'Attack someone from behind?' Frog asked in surprise as he drew up his legs. It was his favourite position, masking his lower face behind his knees, just as Dun-Cadal had seen him sitting the first time.

'There's no honour in fighting like that!' he protested.

Dun-Cadal forced himself to drink a mouthful of Frog's peculiar remedy. It had proved effective, but he had stop himself from gagging each time he swallowed any of the mixture, even a drop. He gulped some more before leaning towards the lad.

'There's no honour at all in killing someone, lad.' His voice was suddenly grim and subdued. 'No matter how you strike. There's no glory to be had in taking a life.'

The only sound was the crackling of the fire in the twilight. The pair stared at one another. Finally, Frog lowered his eyes to his knees.

'You haven't always been a knight, have you?'

Dun-Cadal set the flask down at his feet, cracked his knuckles and yawned.

'No.'

With the foot of his healing leg he scuffed the ground before him, pensive. The lad hadn't earned the right to learn more about him. If he opened up, it would change their relationship. Could he trust the boy with the truth? He was a child of the Saltmarsh ... an enemy who had saved his life and rebelled against his own kind, instead of holing up at Aëd's Watch. Would he be able to understand the course his mentor's life had taken?

'You were an assassin, weren't you?' asked Frog bluntly.

Surprised, Dun-Cadal raised his eyes.

'What's the difference between an assassin and a knight, do you think?'

Looking puzzled, Frog poked the fire.

'One kills for money and the other for duty?' he offered finally, not certain it was the right answer.

'That's a very simplistic view,' Dun-Cadal sighed. 'Believe me, lad, one day you'll understand.'

They ate soon after, relishing a rabbit that Frog had pinched the previous day from the Aëd's Watch market. It made a pleasant change from hive frogs. That evening, they exchanged a few simple words, almost enjoying one another's company, and fell asleep in a serene state of mind, far from the uproar of the revolt.

The month that followed was, by and large, similar to the preceding ones. Frog learned to wield a sword more effectively, including parries and stealthy attacks. And each night, when he believed his mentor had fallen asleep, he continued to practise the moves he had learned during the day. As Dun-Cadal's leg strengthened, dark rings grew under the lad's eyes. But the general didn't comment. He watched the boy suffer, endure, and become exhausted to the point of falling to his knees, his face lined by the ordeal of training. Each time it happened, Frog picked himself up without his mentor ordering him to do so. How far would he go? Dun-Cadal neither criticised nor praised him. He limited himself to teaching and kept his admiration to himself when he saw the lad start to combine the moves he had been taught, wincing from the pain in his muscles.

The general had come across more gifted pupils in his day, but none with this degree of dedication. It was close to madness: the lad compensated for his faults with an unbending determination. Frog was convinced he would become the greatest knight the world had ever known, and after three months together, Dun-Cadal was starting to believe he had every chance of succeeding.

'Arm straight. Straighten your arm!'

In the middle of the tall grasses, the boy was pointing the general's sword before him, his face expressionless. The sun was playing hide-and-seek with the heavy grey-edged white clouds. The day before, a patrol from Aëd's Watch had passed close by their camp. The noose was tightening around them.

'Straighter,' said Dun-Cadal, raising his pupil's arm with a nudge of his stick.

Frog glared at him from of the corner of his eye but immediately focused on the sword before him.

'Now parry!'

With a brusque movement, he stretched one leg behind him, bent the other and brought the sword up towards his head.

'Cut!'

He turned the blade to strike at an imaginary enemy on his flank.

'Your feet, lad, pay attention to your feet.'

'I am paying attention,' Frog objected, abandoning his pose to relax his aching muscles.

He had been slashing the air with the blade for five hours now without a single break, and this was the first time he had made any complaint. Dun-Cadal had been waiting for this moment when his pupil finally showed signs of impatience. He knew the lad was over-confident, too sure of himself, too ready to throw himself into the wolf's jaws. The enemy's lines had not advanced, the Empire was no longer retreating. And the two of them were still barely surviving out here, in the heart of the marshes.

'Really?' said Dun-Cadal with a smile, wielding his stick like a sword.

He traced circles in the air with the point before slowly walking over to place himself in front of the boy.

'Resume your position,' he ordered.

Letting out a sigh, Frog obeyed.

'Parry!' shouted the general as he brandished his stick.

Frog parried the blow, but felt a sharp stab in his hand as the general struck.

'Thrust!'

He hadn't had time to finish the move before Dun-Cadal sidestepped, lunging to strike the boy's extended leg. Frog bent his knee, stifling a cry of pain. The stick whipped at the back of his head and then hard against his shoulder. Overbalanced, he fell hard to one side.

The lad cursed, lying with half his face plunged in the mud, and then breathed heavily.

'Your leg is stretched out too far. If a blade doesn't cut it, a club will break it,' Dun-Cadal said in a calm voice. 'Get up.'

Frog stood up with a scowl. Anger was visibly rising within the boy. For the first time, it was strong enough to burst through his patience.

'Keep your arm held very straight—'

'What good does it do?' the boy raged. 'If my arm is straight? If I have my feet here or there? Well? You're doing this to stop us leaving. Because you're scared. You're no great knight. I saved your life for *nothing*!'

He flung the sword down in disgust.

'I should have let the rouargs eat you,' he snapped, turning away.

'So that's why ...'

Dun-Cadal's features shifted, a thin smile appearing on his lips. The lad was still a mystery to him and he'd made little progress in learning more. A new side was revealing itself at last. To his surprise, he realised he was moved by the fact.

'So that's why you saved me.' Frog had his back to the knight, hands on his hips, staring at the marshes in the distance. 'To teach you to fight, help you escape from the Saltmarsh ... and after that?'

Dun-Cadal spoke quietly, his gaze fixed on the boy who had saved his life out of self-interest. He had kept his guard up for so long, done everything he could to remain aloof, but as the days passed he had grown fond of Frog. What was the lad fleeing, for him to pin so much hope on becoming a knight of the Empire?

'What will you do, Frog ... after that?'

'After what?' the boy snapped, exasperated.

'After we cross the lines and rejoin my army.'

Frog turned slowly, his gaze still furious but his face gradually softening.

'I told you I would help you get through the lines.'

'That's not why you asked me train you.'

The lad looked troubled.

'Why?' insisted the general. 'What are you running away from?'

The boy fidgeted and his expression grew suddenly sad.

'Frog—'

'There's nothing left for me here,' the boy finally said. 'Nothing at all.'

Dun-Cadal let the silence stretch, hoping the lad would break it with a confession. But there was no sound except the rustling of the wind in the tall grasses.

'You want to fight in order to kill people, is that it?' Frog did not react. 'Well, I'm teaching you how to stay alive. You made a distinction between being an assassin and being a knight, but in the end what you want, going about it like this, is to become an assassin.'

'No, that's not it, Wader, it's—'

'I've been teaching you to stay alive from the beginning because tomorrow, when we try to cross the lines, I don't want to lose you.'

'You don't understand, it's—'

Frog stopped, surprised.

'What did you just say?' he asked, excited. 'You said—'

'You saved my life. And you rarely complain. You're enduring these exercises as few knights have managed before you.'

'You just said—'

'I have respect for that, lad. But if you don't listen to me, you're going to die in combat. And I would never forgive myself for that.'

Frog finally held his tongue. He was listening this time. And seeing him listen, Dun-Cadal knew that he found the right words to make him reflect a little.

'Tomorrow. You're ready,' he said simply, before turning on his heel.

But Frog's voice stopped him.

'No.' The general spun around and was surprised to see the lad, sword in hand, arm outstretched. 'Show me more.'

The wind in the tall grasses, the sun slipping between the clouds, the croaking of frogs in the distance ... The life of the Saltmarsh went around them, heedless of the man and the lad lost in its midst. It took no notice of the fact that a bond had just grown between them which would change the world.

'Teach me ... I'm not ready.'

5

BLOOD-STAINED GLOVES

If there was one hero
In the Saltmarsh,
Just remember his name:
Dun-Cadal Daermon.

The hand tightened on the stick to test the grip, making sure it would not slip from a closed fist or break upon striking. With a movement of the wrist, he traced circles in the air before briskly halting the movement. The wood vibrated as if it had struck something. The knight brought the stick up towards his tarnished armour and placed his palm against the whittled point. The weapon was sharp enough to pierce the hide of an ox. Satisfied, he removed his hand as his gaze fell upon the reflection in a stagnant puddle: a tired-looking man. His features were etched by the salt, his face burnished by the sun. His beard bore witness to the many months he had spent in the Saltmarsh. Sitting there at the edge of the marshes he was almost unable to recognise himself.

'That won't be able to pierce armour,' Frog whined from behind his back.

'That's not the idea,' Dun-Cadal replied calmly.

He stood up, stifling a groan when he felt a pain run through his barely healed leg, like a dagger scraping against the femur. But it would withstand the ordeal ahead; he wasn't an old man yet. He was a general and had lived through other battles, other wars. His bones would not break this time.

Standing next to the horse, Frog stared at the ground, looking nervous. He held the reins loosely and gave the impression that he'd rather be anywhere but here. A few hours earlier, however, he'd been more enthusiastic as they left their camp. Dun-Cadal deduced from his change of mood that he was just anxious to see action. The lad was boiling with impatience and then closed up like a clam when confronted with the slightest obstacle. Although real clams never complained.

'We need to hurry, we can't stay here all day.'

'We'll wait for nightfall before trying anything,' Dun-Cadal replied as he went to join him.

He tossed the wooden sword to the boy without warning. Frog caught it in mid-air without difficulty. He was keen. Anxious but keen. That was good.

'The woods are only an hour's march away!' Frog pleaded. 'And in two hours, we could put this whole region behind us! There are very few soldiers in this area, I told you. It will be child's play.'

Dun-Cadal moved forward to face him. He expected him to lower his eyes again, but the lad was determined to be heard. Smiling faintly, the general spoke in a soft voice.

'When children play, they rarely plant a spear in a man's back.'

'But—'

'Nightfall,' Dun-Cadal insisted, before hoisting himself onto the horse's saddle.

The beast had lost all its sheen, its bones sticking out beneath its brown coat, the hooves as dry as old sticks. Even so, it had survived the past few months in the Saltmarsh, transporting Frog to Aëd's Watch on numerous occasions. During these trips, the lad had not merely stolen food, but also gathered crucial information about the development of the revolt. He had even been able to learn the precise disposition of the enemy's forces. Once, he'd laid out their lines beneath the shelter of the cart with the help of twigs and pebbles, he left the strategy to the knight's better judgement.

Dun-Cadal had taken stock of the situation and instantly saw where to strike. But to have the best chance of success, they would need the cover of darkness. Having pushed Azdeki and his men back, the insurgents had spread their forces across the whole northern boundary of the Saltmarsh, forming a wall of camps which stretched for miles. There might only be a few thousand seasoned warriors in the entire ragtag army, but the ordinary people who had taken up arms remained formidable. Their numbers meant Dun-Cadal couldn't hope for a discreet crossing. He had felt a distinct relief when he spotted a possible breach in the alignment marking out the front. It was obvious once he saw it, at the very spot where they kept their catapults. Standing slightly apart from the camps and not protected very closely, it offered an ideal crossing point.

'We'll stop here,' Dun-Cadal ordered.

They had finally reached the edge of the woods. Coils of grey smoke rose into the air above the tree tops; the rebels had poked up their campfires as soon as the blue sky began to darken. A few stars sparkled in the twilight, barely veiled by the thin clouds that slowly slid before them. The soft rustle of the evening wind was accompanied by the hooting of waking owls.

Dun-Cadal dismounted and began to unsaddle the horse.

'They're just on the other side of these woods,' Frog affirmed, darting nervous little glances all around.

He was afraid a patrol would discover them. Dun-Cadal was amused by this. The lad still needed to learn patience and to use the last peaceful moments remaining to calm his nerves. Otherwise they risked paralysing him when the hour for combat arrived.

'I know,' he murmured.

He threw the saddle down at the foot of the tree, removed the horse's bridle and gave it a slap on the rump with the flat of his hand. When the animal was no more than a silhouette galloping towards the darkness of the marshes, Frog approached his mentor.

'Did you like him?'

'He was just an old nag,' Dun-Cadal replied with a smile.

'No ... not the horse.'

The general's smile vanished as the image of Tomlinn being snatched up by the rouarg came back to him. He studied the horizon with a gaze as dark as his thoughts.

'He was a good general and a noble knight.' He turned round abruptly and then, placing a heavy hand on the boy's shoulder, he added: 'And, above all, he was my friend.' With a slow step, he climbed a small hillock that extended into the woods. Frog followed him. 'But we knew the risks. I'd just always believed he would die under a rain of arrows rather than be torn apart in the jaws of some nasty beast.'

As he leaned back against a tree to catch his breath he noticed the worried expression on his pupil's face. Tucked into the boy's belt, the sharpened stick hung like a sword. A wooden stick … against armour. He glanced down at his own weapon, the pommel gleaming at his waist. Could they really escape the Saltmarsh like this? Did he truly believe that? A limping knight and a … a lad from the marshes with a wooden sword?

'Do you know what's in store for you over there?' he asked in a hoarse voice.

'I … yes, we're going to fight—' 'No,' interrupted the knight with a shake of his head. 'Are you ready to inflict death?' There was a fraught silence, so fraught that Frog turned his gaze away. 'There's nothing worse than watching someone pass away, Frog. Nothing worse. The last breath, the last gleam in the eye looking at you. It's not a game. There's nothing innocent about it.'

'I'm ready.'

'It's not just them you're going to kill. Whatever the reason for your acts, whether you can justify them or not, there will never be any excuse for taking someone's life.'

'I'm ready,' repeated Frog, with insistence.

'Listen to me!' Dun-Cadal growled, coming off the tree he was leaning against. The boy retreated abruptly, surprised by the glow of anger in the knight's gaze. 'You're still just a lad. Once you've plunged that stick into the flesh of a man, what will happen? Will you break down like some little girl?'

'Never,' Frog hissed the word between his teeth.

'It's your own innocence you'll kill over there, lad. And believe me, I'm the first to regret that.'

The boy nodded, finally averting his eyes.

'But you said we can do this and I'm crazy enough to believe you.'

With a closed fist, Dun-Cadal punched the trunk of a young ash tree. He was not assailed by any sudden doubts before their mad attack, but fear was nevertheless slowly tightening its grip on his guts. He had seen men barely older than this boy march proudly into battle, only to find them later, kneeling in tears in the middle of the fighting. What would happen to his pupil? He was only a lad … just a mere lad.

'There's nothing left for me here,' Frog declared. His voice was quiet but his tone was firm. 'I'm no longer anyone … not here.'

Dun-Cadal looked at him, pensive. The opportunity was too good to let pass by.

'And who were you, before this?'

Frog glanced briefly at the marshes bathed in the falling night.

'Not much of anything interesting,' he confided as if talking about the weather. 'A child who wasn't much good at anything. I've never been very gifted.'

'And now? What are you?'

The lad gave him a look that would make the bravest man tremble. Determined, passionate, feverish ... no one would be able to stop him.

'At least I'm trying to do my best.'

What more can anyone ask of him? the knight said to himself. An owl glided over their heads and the wind strengthened, bending the short grass at their feet. The lapping of the water in the marshes seemed no more than a distant murmur. The lands of the former Kingdoms were spread behind these woods. Only the insurgents' front line separated them from friendly territory. Dun-Cadal sat down at the foot of the closest ash tree and raised his eyes towards the sky.

'We'll wait here and attack in the middle of the night when their sentries will be somewhat ... sleepy.'

He smiled faintly as Frog approached him. The lad hesitated as if waiting for his master to grant him permission to sit down. But Dun-Cadal looked away, plucking up a blade of grass and placing it in his mouth. As he chewed on the end, he let his gaze drift over the shadows growing at the edge of the woods. Frog settled down to his right, looking distracted, until the hoot of an owl broke the silence.

'Do you remember what I taught you?' Dun-Cadal asked suddenly, without a single glance at the boy.

'Yes,' Frog replied sullenly.

'What I asked you to do?'

'Yes.'

And with his left hand he pretended to seize something, while the right mimed striking a blow.

'As soon as I attack the guard, from behind, I block him with my arm and strike him, just once, below the shoulder blade.'

'And your hand?'

'My hand goes over his mouth to stifle the cry. All of these actions, at the same time.'

'Good,' Dun-Cadal sighed. 'Nothing else, just that, no direct confrontation ...' From the corner of his eye he saw the lad sitting with his head bowed, casually pulling at tufts of grass between his outstretched legs. 'You don't like that very much, do you?'

He waited a moment for a reply. When none came, the knight continued:

'You'd prefer something more grandiose. That's the picture you have of knights, am I wrong? Courageous, brave ... is that it? Facing the enemy head-on, like death itself ...'

'I'll do what you told me to do,' the boy murmured.

'Good,' said Dun-Cadal, satisfied.

He contemplated the stars that were coming out one by one in the darkening sky.

'Do you see these gloves?' And without turning his eyes away from the celestial spectacle, he held out his iron gauntlets to Frog, certain that curiosity would force the lad to look at them. 'They may not look it, but they're covered with blood. From battles and other combats, but not just those.'

'There's no blood on them,' noted Frog quietly.

'Oh no? That's because it can't be seen anymore. But me, I can sense it. And that's what matters in the end. Never try to avoid the responsibility; always face up to what you've done.'

'So you weren't only a knight, were you?'

The lad had already asked him the question. And truth be told, this time it was more like a statement than a real question.

'No. Before I became a knight, I was what you don't want to become.'

He turned his head towards the lad, curious to see his reaction.

'I was an assassin,' he admitted.

Frog didn't even blink. He bore Dun-Cadal's scrutiny, frowning slightly, waiting for the rest.

'I don't see much difference between the acts I committed as an assassin and the ones I committed as a knight of the Empire. In both cases, victory or success, call it what you will, requires the deaths of others. Of people who surely had a family, friends ... duties of their own.'

His voice had grown harsh, his tone more serious ... and his gaze more evasive.

'So killing people from in front or from behind, what difference does it make? As long as it's done quickly and done well. Without them suffering before they go off to the heavens ... Strike quickly and strike well, Frog.'

He stared at the lad for a long moment.

'Strike quickly and strike well,' he repeated.

'I shall,' Frog promised.

Without taking his eyes off his mentor he put on a pair of darned woollen gloves, which he had stolen from a trader at Aëd's Watch a few days earlier.

The lad's feigned calm did not fool a seasoned warrior like Dun-Cadal. How many times had he seen young soldiers – although older than Frog – similarly stiff, hoping to disguise the fear inside? No, the general wasn't taken in, especially not when he saw the boy rubbing his woollen-gloved hands together. He wasn't wearing them because of the cold. Frog was doing his best to build up his nerve, the general knew. Just as he knew the real reason the lad had stolen these gloves: to stop his hands being stained with blood.

What a vain hope.

The hours that followed seemed like days. When Dun-Cadal finally stood up again, a bright swathe crossed the sky, as if to lead men from one end of the earth to the other. Not a single cloud masked the twinkling of the stars. The wind slowly lifted the foliage. There was a sharp crackling sound. Dun-Cadal glanced over his shoulder to see Frog standing frozen, one foot poised over the twig he had just snapped.

'Be careful where you tread. We can't afford any mistakes.'

He turned his head slightly, his chin brushing his shoulder, eyes half-closed.

'I won't wait for you,' he breathed, before drawing his sword.

Dun-Cadal moved off into the woods without making any noise. He had just signalled their departure without any preamble or comforting speech, but only the advice: *'Be careful where you tread'*. One false step meant certain death. He'd insisted on that. Their plan had been studied, rehearsed and memorised over the past few weeks, and they had gone over it again the previous day. Frog had given the knight full information as to the enemy's numbers, its positions and when the sentries were relieved. Too many troops passing through Aëd's Watch had been talkative around a tavern table. Why burden this moment with futile words? The lad was already anxious enough. He'd seen Frog train hard, watched him grow up in a very short space of time. Any encouragement now would be a waste: the lad's pride would suffice. Although Dun-Cadal continued to call him 'lad' out of affection, he'd started to consider Frog a soldier. And unlike boys, men of war did not need to be coddled.

There was only the wind in the boughs, which helped to disguise the brush of his clothing against low-lying branches. No one could have heard them coming. An owl flapped its wings nervously before taking flight. After sneaking through the woods for almost half an hour they reached the far edge. Dun-Cadal knelt and with a sharp sign of his hand ordered Frog to get down. A few feet away, at the base of a last beech tree, was the beginning of a row of patched grey tents. To the right and to the left, the enemy camp stretched long and wide, dotted with a thousand fires. Silhouettes armed with spears marched slowly down the lanes between the tents. Were there really so many of them? How was that possible? They couldn't all be from the Saltmarsh ... Or else all of its inhabitants – children, adults, old people – had risen up against the Empire. Dun-Cadal brushed the grass with his fingertips. This was the last moment in which they could retreat, change their minds, or postpone this act of folly until tomorrow ...

Here, at this moment, the future was decided.

Before him stood some fifty catapults. He could only see four guards, armed with crudely made spears, but the major part of the camp lay just a few yards away . Others were on watch from the shelter of their illuminated tents. Luckily, the career soldiers, those who had real combat experience, were not to be found in the vicinity. The troops manning these catapults were green. And they were fools.

In the light from the tall torches, Dun-Cadal was astonished to see that the catapults arms were cocked and their buckets loaded with grease-smeared balls of rock. His entire body tensed as he looked carefully at the aligned weapons and the torches by them. The stupid buggers ... each catapult was ready to fire! This was the only way out for him and for Frog, and here he may have found the means of making good their escape.

The general advanced very slowly, bending forward as he went. The first guard didn't see him approaching and barely felt the blade slide into his back as a heavy hand fell across his mouth to suppress his cry of surprise. The knight carefully lowered the body and, keeping his eyes on the other two guards at the foot of a catapult, he beckoned Frog to join him. When the lad drew near he indicated the last soldier, who was urinating on the post of a tall torch. Then with an imperious finger he pointed to the corral at the edge of the camp. On this cloudless night, the curved shapes of the horses grazing inside could be clearly seen. Everything was proceeding better than expected. Dun-Cadal would take care of the two guards next to the catapults while the boy disposed of the fourth man, now whistling as he struggled to buckle his belt.

Like a predator stealthily approaching his prey, he slowly crouched forward with his back and knees bent. Behind him, Frog adopted the same posture and was headed for the guard at the foot of the torch. Just a few more steps. Out of the corner of his eye, Dun-Cadal saw the lad gripping the wooden stick with all his might. His other hand was trembling. He hoped the lad would remember all the moves they had rehearsed, over and over, down to the tiniest detail. The arm across the neck to choke his opponent, then a quick jab below the shoulder blade, rising towards the heart. Swift. Precise. Discreet. *Don't flinch. Don't retreat. Don't hesitate.* The general would not be there to protect the boy. He began to inch away from Frog.

The knight's silhouette slipped over to the tall wheels of the catapults. His shadow broke across the massive timber frame and the torchlight brought a fleeting gleam from the tip of his sword. Dun-Cadal immediately looked down. The wheels had dug a furrow in the earth, as if they had been recently turned. Arming the catapults for immediate use was one thing, but positioning them like this, so that none were even aiming at the front, was an enormous mistake.

He halted for a moment, looking over the camp with an eye trained to spot the slightest suspect movement, then glanced over at his apprentice just in time to see Frog almost stumble over a root.

Focus, stay focused, and watch where you put your feet! Dun-Cadal silently yelled. Just a few feet from the boy, the guard picked up a spear that had been leaning against the post he had pissed on.

Don't falther, lad. Don't retreat, the general repeated to himself, as

81

if hoping Frog might be influenced by his thoughts. Now the lad would prove his mettle. His worth would be decided the moment he plunged the sharpened wood into—

'Hey!'

Dun-Cadal froze next to a large wooden wheel, in the shadow of the catapult. He had just started to make his move, about to pounce on the soldiers, when he saw Frog fall to one side, burying his head in the grass. The general had to restrain himself from intervening, his hand twitching at the pommel of his sword.

'Is this how you were taught to stand guard?' a voice bellowed.

The lad had disappeared in the grass, a good thing with two rebel soldiers now standing over the very spot where he had been.

'What? I was just havin' a piss . . .'

They were close, so very close to Frog. Yet they hadn't seen the outline of his body on the ground in the darkness. The general could guess where the boy was hiding, however, and tried to consider all the possibilities. His trapped apprentice might attempt a rash assault, or else remain in place, petrified with fear. Whatever happened, Dun-Cadal needed to be ready to act. He was squeezing his sword hilt so tightly he could no longer feel his fingertips.

'Don't ever leave your post without warning the others,' the new-comer growled.

'We only arrived yesterday,' the soldier said in an insolent tone. 'Us lot, we don't know what's up yet, do we? They just told us, line up the catapults.'

'Where do you come from?'

'Avrai Wood, Cap'n. There're fifteen of us.'

Even from a distance, the general could see the shine of clean if somewhat worn boots. The officer wearing them must have been a member of late Count of Uster's guard. Dun-Cadal was certain of it. He leaned against the catapult and carefully observed the robust man bearing a large sword reprimanding the new recruit. Fomenting a rebellion with the support of the local rabble was one thing. Maintaining order in the ranks with people who had neither the vocation nor the sense of duty to be proper soldiers was another.

He looked back at the catapult, at the distraction firing it would offer, and in his mind's eye pictured the trajectory the ball would follow. His smile returned, now tinged with a degree of savageness. They were pointed directly at the rebels' camp . . .

'You should always be—' the officer was saying before his voice strangled as he noticed the catapults' odd alignment. 'What on earth have you done?'

'We lined up the catapults, didn't we?'

The officer advanced a pace. One single pace. And in the dim light, his experienced eye spotted the outline of a prone body. At the sound of his sword being unsheathed, Dun-Cadal's apprentice finally reacted. Was it out of courage or fear? Either way, he rolled to one side, snatched something up and then quickly stood.

Come on, lad . . . come on . . .

'You?' the man gasped. 'How?'

Sword in hand, he was ready to lunge at the intruder, but instead he just stood there, astonished. He had wide shoulders, a bald head and a split lip. A scar ran from his right eye to the corner of his mouth. Frog was shaking as if his legs were going to give way at any second.

Now! pleaded Dun-Cadal silently, as he crept along the catapult without taking his eyes off Frog. *Either do it now, or flee!*

'What are you—'

The wood perforated the man's throat with such force that neither the victim nor his comrade in arms had time to react. Frog screamed and, moved by a wild rage, let go of the wounded man before shoving him away with a kick. Frantically fumbling with his hands, the officer sought to yank out the wooden stick lodged in his neck. He spat blood and tilted his head back with a grimace before falling to the ground in convulsions at the feet of the stunned soldier. The man responded clumsily, pointing his spear at the boy with shaking hands. His gaze seemed lost. Sweat dripped from beneath his dented helmet, tracing crooked lines down the olive skin of his brow. Sweat . . . just like the tears that spilling from Frog's brimming eyes.

Dun-Cadal could no longer wait. He took a deep breath, grimacing from the pain stabbing his chest, and pictured the torch by the catapult breaking in two. The flaming tip fell upon the grease-covered ball resting within the bucket.

In the corral, the horses were growing restless. The captain lay still upon the ground, his eyes now glassy.

'Sound the al—' a voice started to say in the distance.

The rest of the sentence was covered by a sharp twang, followed

83

by a whistling sound. A ball of fire rose into the air in a perfect arc before plunging down towards the tents pitched a hundred yards away. Flames blossomed upwards and with them came screams. A shadow ran behind the line of tall torches, which toppled in succession at its approach. As the torches fell, their flames set light to the balls waiting in the weapons' buckets.

The horses whinnied.

Dun-Cadal controlled his breathing as best he could, pulling on an invisible thread as if he were snatching the torches down, using the *animus* to pull them over, then he disappeared into the darkness like a ghost and, without drawing his sword, severed the rope restraining the loaded arm of each catapult. When he felt he had caused enough chaos in the heart of the camp, he leapt on top of a wheel of one of the devices. Below him, the two remaining guards were gaping at the boy, who was confronting one of their own in the light of the flames spreading through the camp. They had no time to comprehend what came plunging down on them. A sword pierced the armpit of the first, in the space between his light armour and his arm, before whipping around in a circular motion and a spray of blood to slash deeply into the other man's throat.

'Lad!' the general shouted.

A few yards away, near the edge of the camp, Frog was still in a muddle. Facing him, the soldier didn't look like much of a challenge, hesitating with the spear trembling in his hand. The man attempted a jab. Frog backed up too fast and fell on his rear end. Against the grey tents being devoured by red and yellow flames he could see the dark and blurry silhouettes of more soldiers running in their direction. The moment of surprise was gone.

'Lad!' Dun-Cadal roared as he rushed towards the boy.

The guard saw a dark mass charging at him from out of the night.

'We ... we ...' he stammered, 'we're under attack!'

That was it; his own fear made him turn and flee. He dropped the spear without paying heed to the boy and disappeared among the tents. The sound of voices grew louder in the distance. Men were approaching and the clatter of swords against their armour rang like chimes. When he reached his pupil, Dun-Cadal had to stop himself from wheezing out loud, one hand on his leg. He had overtaxed himself, both his muscles and his bones reminding him how far they still were from being fully recovered. Kneeling down, he took hold of the boy's arm and the pair of them regained their feet, stumbling.

'Come on,' urged the general. 'Come on, let's go!'

In just a few steps, they reached the corral. An arrow sped past their ears.

'Mount up! Quickly, lad!'

He opened the gate and pushed Frog towards the horses. Another arrow landed at the knight's feet. Glancing up, he saw an archer near the tents nocking an arrow, his slender figure haloed by the flames. And more soldiers were arriving, still mere silhouettes, shadows detaching themselves from the blazing camp. Frog grabbed a horse around the neck and hoisted himself onto its back, almost falling back down when the animal whinnied and reared.

'Ride!' ordered Dun-Cadal, looking grim.

'But you ...' the boy mumbled in protest.

'Ride!' the general yelled in rage.

There's a legend that tells ...'

With a firm hand, he slapped the rump of Frog's horse and the beast went off at a gallop.

'It's no legend. Me, I was there in the Saltmarsh, I saw it!'

In the night, horse and rider was soon no more than an indistinct shape. Dun-Cadal spun round.

'I was there too, and he was all alone.'

There were at least twenty of them running in his direction as he limped towards the catapults. With a flick of his sword, he deflected an arrow, groaning from the effort.

'Months ... months, I've been out here and you think, right now, right here, that I'll give up ...' he muttered.

'There's a legend that tells of a man who stood alone at the Saltmarsh and set fire to our army.'

'I am Dun-Cadal Daermon, of the House of Daermon! Remember that name!' he cried as the shadows threw themselves at him.

Without moving a foot, he parried a blow from the left, then a blow from the right. His breathing became slower, quieter, as cool as the wind caressing the grass. He felt the life all around him, each sprig, each tree, each heart beating in those surrounding him. He blocked the blows aimed at him and struck in his turn, hacking and slashing with his sharp blade, punching with the pommel of his sword. There were always more opponents, still more coming for him, and in the distance, the shadows of the archers lifting their bows to take aim.

His heart slowed, his vision became clearer and it was as if he were everywhere at once, hearing each of their breaths, feeling the blood run from their wounds. He was ready.

'It's no legend, I fought him … and I fled before him like the others.'

He knelt and struck the ground with his sword's hilt, one single blow. And a powerful blast spread from it, like the wave caused by a pebble thrown in a river. His assailants were flung backwards a dozen yards. The arrows turned on their archers, the flames grew larger, the tents swayed, the catapults collapsed on their sides.

'He caused more damage than the assault on Aëd's Watch by ten thousand of his men! Him, we feared … because he was no mere general …'

Over in the grass, soldiers lay moaning. Some of them were only dazed. The general used up his last remaining strength reaching the corral.

'If there was one hero in the Saltmarsh, just remember his name …'

He set off at a gallop, dashing into the night like a phantom, leaving a landscape of devouring flames and limp bodies behind him. When reinforcements reached this section of the camp, the survivors with their livid faces and trembling hands could only utter the name:

'Dun-Cadal Daermon.'

6

A SON

How ironic:
I was always so good at sowing death.
But I was never able to sow life ...

'Words are like knots around a package, you know ...'

His wrinkled old hands surrounded a tankard filled with wine. His gaze was lost in the blood-red liquid as if he was hoping to drown his memories there, those fleeting but sharp-edged images, those figures he had hated, loved, despised, protected ...

'Many things are said, many things told. Words can be a far cry from the truth.'

There was a scraping sound as Viola pulled her chair towards her before sitting down. It had been easy for her to find him again, sitting in the same tavern where they had spoken the night before. After chasing the assassin, Dun-Cadal had given up, shaking all over. Right here he'd found the means of quelling his mental as well as physical pains ... or at least put them to sleep. He was already working on his second jug of wine. Apart from the young woman and himself, the only other customer was some poor old man seated at a table by the big window, silently laying down cards from a tarot deck.

'Words dress everything up.'

Slouched forward, he looked up and his features softened when his gaze met the young woman's placid green eyes. She was so calm, beautiful and sweet, her cheekbones sprinkled with small freckles. Although her pink lips were half-opened, she did not utter a single word. She simply listened, to him, the relic from a glorious bygone era, as useless as a blunt sword.

'I heard it told,' he said with an embarrassed laugh, 'that I fought

87

no less than three hundred men when I fled from the Saltmarsh.'

He lowered his eyes, pensive, and shook his head.

'I counted them, you know. I've always been able to take a quick count ...'

His voice was muffled, as if he were no longer addressing anyone but himself.

'There were fifteen of them. Fifteen boys, barely twenty years old. No combat training. Fifteen boys, two of whom hung back to shoot at me.'

Once again, his gaze met Viola's serene eyes.

'And it was as if I had become a legend ... without winning any battles. Just putting the devil of all fears into them. The story spread from mouth to mouth, village to village. Like a tumble of snow becoming an avalanche. Words dress everything up. A mere trifle becomes a ... a titanic deed ...'

He paused and raised the tankard to his mouth. He grimaced as the edge of the drinking vessel caught on his chapped lips.

'So here is your historic figure, Viola I-don't-know-who from the Republican city of Emeris ...'

He emptied the tankard in a single gulp and placed it back on the table with a thump. Everything inside him seemed to be breaking up and his body was so dry he couldn't even shed tears over his fate.

'*Teach me ... I'm not ready.*'

His thoughts wandered aimlessly through a past that had been torn apart, in pieces ... and still bloody.

'A councillor was killed in plain daylight,' Viola said at last. 'A man of the Republic was assassinated.'

'And he won't be the last,' Dun-Cadal snarled.

'The Republican Guards are looking for the assassin.'

'And they'll still be hunting for him tomorrow ...'

Delicately, she placed her hands on the table and blinked as if she were trying to soothe some sort of annoyance.

'You know who he is, don't you?' she surmised.

'The councillor?'

'The killer.'

He leaned back in his chair, perplexed. This was something far removed from the concerns of a historian. Had she developed a new-found passion for justice?

'And if that were the case, what would it change?'

'There's a connection somewhere with your personal history, isn't there?'

Her lips were pinched and there was a gleam of mischief in her eye.

'And I am a ... historian,' she added.

'What about the rapier?'

'You'll give it to me. I can be persuasive,' she said, leaning forward slightly. 'But your story interests me too.'

He picked up the jug on the table and filled his tankard with a sigh.

'And what makes you think I have any desire to tell you my story?

'Because you've already started the telling ...'

He put the jug back down with a faraway look in his eyes. She was right. Painfully right. Her lavender scent had bewitched him; he felt the urge to confide in her with no thought at all as to the consequences. Mildrel had warned him against it but he didn't care. Something about Viola made him trust her. Or perhaps he really wanted to confess it all, drain away everything that was weighing him down inside and preventing him from moving on. She looked at her now joined hands with a pensive air and took her time, as if measuring each of her words before uttering it. Dun-Cadal saw her hesitate and was curious. At last she said:

'People still believe in the *Liaber Dest*. As for me, I've never been able to decide if I should believe in it or not. Being a daughter of the Republic and all ...' She gave him an embarrassed smile. 'But ever since I left my village, I've met people who referred to the Sacred Book. It always seemed strange to me ... that they believed in something they had no proof even existed. And it's still more complicated for me, now that I am a historian. The Order of Fangol does not like the idea that we might re-examine history, which previously they alone had the right to recount. They even said that we wanted to – how did they put it? – oh yes, that we "dared to rewrite history" ...'

She stifled a nervous giggle. Dun-Cadal listened to her patiently, unsure where she was heading. He watched her search for the right words and felt no pleasure doing it. He simply waited, feeling somewhat dazed.

'In short ... all I mean to say is that I really have no opinion about the *Liaber Dest*, or about your beliefs,' she continued. 'Even though I know very well that someone like yourself has always kept the old faith. So if what they say about the *Liaber Dest* is true, if the destiny of men is inscribed there, then everything has already been played out in advance, am I right? So it was written that the great Dun-Cad-al would end up here, at death's door.'

'You think I'm at death's door?' he asked mockingly.

Her glance at his full tankard gave her answer. And then she seemed to abandon her reticence.

'You have the keys, at least,' she said simply. 'All these years, since the fall of the Empire and during your wanderings, haven't you dreamt of someone like me? Haven't you ever hoped someone would take an interest in you? In what you did? You were important! If the moment came, when someone was ready to listen to the whole story, would you really let the occasion pass by? Don't you think it was written that one day General Daermon would tell his true tale?'

He looked away. She had an answer for everything and how could he refute that? For years he had tried to forget what he had been, and what he was becoming. She demanded he lead her to that ancient sword, to the emblem of a fallen empire. Nevertheless, if the rapier was her main goal, she was also interested in the man. He would have denied it if anyone asked, but her interest touched him deeply. No one, except Mildrel, worried about his fate and, worse still, no one in Masalia cared about the ordeals he had endured in the course of his long life.

'So you want me to tell my tale, hmm?' he sighed. 'Where do I start . . . ?'

'Why not begin with Frog?'

Suddenly it seemed her green eyes were all he could see. The tavern had disappeared, his blood ran hotly in his veins, and his entire body felt like it was enveloped in cotton. Only that shining gaze seemed to keep him afloat, like a lighthouse guiding a lost mariner.

'Frog . . .' he agreed slowly.

And he told her.

He told her of meeting the lad in the marshes, of the months spent in the Saltmarsh waiting for his injured leg to heal before their mad escape one starry night. He told of the escape itself without dwelling on details he judged to be of minor import, and narrated how he found Frog waiting for him out on the plain that spread beyond the forest. His memory of events returned as if they had happened yesterday. He saw the face of his young apprentice again clearly, twisted in pain. It was not a physical kind of suffering, not at all. The lad had killed a man and could not forget his stunned expression, fixed forever by the point of a wooden sword planted in his neck. It had torn into the flesh, allowing a continuing flow of red to spill forth, a steaming and sticky stream. The general had known full well that the image of the blood running from the body, and with it a man's life, would mark the boy's mind forever. He used only a few words to retrace their journey to Emeris, passing quickly over their stay in Garmaret where the Imperial Army had taken up position after it had been expelled from the Saltmarsh.

No, only their arrival in Emeris really mattered ...

'How big is it?' asked Frog.

'How big?' his mentor laughed.

It had just been a year since they first met. Riding along a track lined with oak trees they looked like two weary travellers, their large black cloaks stained with mud. The young boy's frail figure had filled out and one could see the makings of a man; the child had been left behind in the Saltmarsh, with the body of a bald captain. Beneath his hood, the gaze was still dark but the features of his face had been subtly reshaped.

Dun-Cadal, too, had changed. The cheeks hollowed by months of hunger in the marshes had recovered their original form. The new beard on his face bore witness to their recently rejoining the road, after a halt during which he had enjoyed the comforts of food, a warm bath, a good shave and a soft bed ...

Two months had passed since their escape, and a month since their stay in the fort at Garmaret. These past few weeks they had crossed the former Kingdoms and were discovering that the rebellion had spread like gangrene, reaching all four corners of a badly shaken Empire.

They'd taken part in some of the fighting. They'd confronted many dangers ... but only their arrival in Emeris mattered to them. And during their journey, he and the lad had come to understand one another.

Day after day, Frog made progress. Day after day, he drew a little closer to what he had sworn to become. And, day after day, Dun-Cadal felt a pride he disguised behind a gruff exterior. He gave no praise or encouragement, limiting himself to a few satisfied nods of the head. The lad displayed no anger over this.

'Is it twice as big as Aëd's Watch?' Frog asked.

Dun-Cadal gave him a wry smile over his shoulder.

'Three times as big? Ten times?' the boy suggested in growing wonder.

'That's up to you to say when you see it, lad.'

Between the trees, drawn up like an honour guard, the path vanished before them. But, as they advanced, the sinuous track re-appeared, descending a wooded hill like a serpent slithering through the oaks. Down below, bordering a cliff from which a misty torrent cascaded, an immense city rose, shining and proud, with high silvery towers overlooking circle upon circle of tall buildings. The radiance of the noon sun sparkled off the summit of the highest tower. Frog's jaw dropped in silence. Since their escape from the Saltmarsh, he'd had the chance to see cities in the West which were twice as big as Aëd's Watch, his town of birth being his sole reference point for comparison. But this ... this exceeded anything he could have im-agined. Water from the falls foamed at the feet of the capital and flocks of birds with wide-stretched wings followed the course of the river before they swooped down to its surface. Then they climbed back up into the sky to fly over the great forest which spread for miles until it reached the mountains.

'Well?' asked Dun-Cadal in mock surprise. 'Have you lost your tongue, Frog? Or are you trying to figure out how many Aëd's Watch-es it would take to contain that city over there?'

Chuckling to himself, he urged his horse into a trot with a dig of his heels, moving away down the track. When Frog finally tore his eyes from Emeris, the knight was already descending the hill, zigzag-ging between the trees. As Dun-Cadal expected, the lad was quick to catch up, arriving out of breath.

'It's ... it's huge,' he stammered as he approached his master's side.

'There's another word to describe it,' Dun-Cadal replied.

He was remembering the first time he had crossed the bridge over the torrent. He would never forget the dizziness that overcame him when he had advanced beneath the great gate in the white walls sur-rounding the city. He had been about the same age as Frog ... and he had left the Daermon family home in the West behind, never to return.

'What word is that?' his pupil immediately asked.

'Imperial …' murmured Dun-Cadal in a surprisingly grave and respectful tone.

Yes, he could understand what the lad must be feeling, since he'd discovered the city in somewhat similar circumstances. His uncle had sent him to the military academy, fulfilling his nephew's desire to leave the West. Just like Frog, he had fled a life that did not suit him, that of a minor and unimpressive lord ruling a small feudal holding of no importance, surrounded by people lacking any ambition. The House of Daermon was relatively recent; its history only dated back to his grandfather and its interests depended on maintaining a sort of humility which Dun-Cadal considered to be craven. The less the House of Daermon was spoken of, the less it risked attracting the wrath of the Imperial family. As a child, he had seen his dreams of glory diminished until he could bear it no longer, and when the opportunity finally presented itself to serve the Empire in a worthy manner, he sought his uncle's consent to send him to the right school. That opened up a glorious road for him that he decided to stride with self-confidence and ostentation, shrugging off the habitual diffidence of the other members of his house. His destiny had started at Emeris, the symbol of success, for it was here the fate of the world was decided … It was the head and the heart of an immortal Empire.

They trotted through the muddy streets of the poorer neighbourhoods whose thatched houses formed a ring at the outskirts of the city. When their horses' hooves struck paving stones, the buildings became more grandiose, their windows much bigger. Frog remained silent. Yet, although he did not utter a word, his attitude said much. When they entered the palace, he seemed less serene. There, in the large rooms with their wide windows, standing among the generals his mentor greeted, he became stiff, his head bowed and his eyes furtive but always darting around as if he were seeking someone. Dun-Cadal introduced him to the others briefly, thereby avoiding further questioning from his brothers-in-arms.

Dun-Cadal's adventures in the Saltmarsh had caused quite a stir. The Imperial Knighthood evinced a mixture of pride and jealousy regarding his exploits. Everywhere people were saying he'd defeated the rebel army singlehandedly. Although he appeared not to be paying any attention, the knight kept an eye on his apprentice. It was not so much the lad's behaviour that concerned him, but what he might be feeling. What was he saying to himself as he clasped so many hands, met so many people, walked down hallways broader than he had ever seen before?

He must be feeling dizzy too...

To a child of the provinces, arriving among all these warriors in their brightly coloured armour, sporting the ancient symbols of their houses, was intimidating enough. Penetrating the lair of the Knighthood, seeing the coats-of-arms as well as the armour, the famous old blades hung on the walls like venerable souvenirs, was exhilarating. The relics of the Reyes dynasty's greatest defenders were gathered here, with the helms of the bravest combatants sitting proudly on display. Armour had grown lighter over the centuries, swords more refined. Daermon had no doubt in his mind that Frog would be able to follow in the footsteps of their illustrious predecessors. But first he would have to overcome his nerves.

Everything, from the milky white walls of the palace to the stained glass decorating the halls, from the guards in golden helmets, the tips of their spears gleaming in the sun, to the respectful silence of the ladies in their satin gowns, was new to someone who had lived in the marshes. Here the scent of roses and freshly cut grass was mixed with the most bewitching perfumes.

'This is your first visit, isn't it?' asked a man wearing a white robe with a red fabric draped over one shoulder.

They were following him down a long hallway lined with mirrors. Dun-Cadal had introduced the man as a steward to the Emperor. The latter, on hearing of their arrival, had summoned them immediately. Among all these generals, these captains, these counts and barons glimpsed since they had entered the palace, Frog was visibly becoming bewildered. He who had been so insolent, on more than one occasion, was now timid and reserved. To that was added an obvious nervousness. His master observed the effects as they approached a wide pair of varnished doors with gilded frames. The young man's skin was beaded with sweat, his gestures grew jerky and his breathing muffled.

'Are you mute, then, having said nothing until now?' asked the steward. 'I've heard of you, you know. You're Frog, am I right?'

'Yes.'

'Frog ...' said Dun-Cadal reproachfully.

'Yes, my lord,' the boy rectified.

'Your devotion to the Empire has caught our attention … as well as our respect, young man.'

'Thank you, my lord,' he replied in a suddenly sharp tone.

Dun-Cadal knew very well what was bothering his apprentice. He recalled the way he had behaved upon arriving here for the first time and meeting Asham's father, disguising his apprehension with a false cockiness. But Frog was still too young to be conceited.

The steward pushed open the two great doors with a slow loud creak. Beyond, in a large room with a black-streaked marble floor, dozens of smooth columns ascended to the ceiling. There was no furniture, not a seat or even a throne. Just a thin red curtain that stretched out near a balcony overlooking rustling tree tops. A strange, imposing shadow seemed to be seated in a wide tub from which curls of steam were rising into the air. Feminine-looking silhouettes were pouring buckets of water into the bath.

Frog froze.

'Advance,' ordered Dun-Cadal, pressing him in the back. 'And don't speak until he addresses you.'

Behind the cloth, the shadow bent over like a sick child. With a sign of his hand, the steward beckoned them to follow him.

'Your Imperial Majesty,' he announced in a loud voice. 'General Daermon, returned from the Saltmarsh, and his young … protégé.'

'Have you returned with a son?' a voice jeered. 'Is that what took you so long?'

As they approached, Dun-Cadal noticed the lad's more resolute step. But he looked even more anxious than before. His face tense and wearing a frown, he quickened his pace and was walking beside the steward. A few more steps at the same speed and he would be the first to present himself before the Emperor. Frog would surely slow down at the last instant. The general smiled faintly. He was about to reply when a peculiar noise caused him to place his hand on the hilt of his sword. A blade hissed through the air to stop short against the boy's neck. The steward stepped to one side, alarmed.

'Peace, Daermon,' purred a strangely deep voice.

Dun-Cadal stiffened. The shine of his own sword had emerged between the scabbard and the guard. He hesitated over whether to yank it completely free. But he recognised the other man and knew he would be far too quick to respond. For it was the Hand of the

Emperor who had placed the cutting edge of his weapon beneath Frog's lifted chin.

'The lad is no enemy,' Dun-Cadal rumbled in protest.

'He comes from the Saltmarsh ...'

The timbre of the other man's voice was extremely unpleasant, a mixture of hoarseness and whistling, as if there were pebbles lodged in his throat obstructing his breathing.

'Ever prompt to defend me, Logrid,' acknowledged the voice behind the curtain as a servant poured more water into his bath.

Wisps of steam drifted along the stretched cloth.

'But I don't believe a mere child who has left his region in time of war would come all this way to kill his Emperor.'

The assassin tilted his head slightly to one side, like a wild beast studying the smallest details of its prey. He looked down at the boy's hand, which was ostensibly reaching for the hilt of his own sword. There seemed to be a tear brimming along the edge of Frog's right eyelid, ready to run down a face gone rigid with shock. Beneath the assassin's ample hood not a single feature was touched by the light. Nevertheless, he appeared to be closely examining the lad, who was glaring back at him.

'Logrid ...' growled Dun-Cadal. 'Leave him be.'

Logrid lowered his blade. As he advanced towards the general, he slipped his sword back into the scabbard which hung from his belt.

'So this is how we're welcomed back to court,' murmured Dun-Cadal as he stepped around the assassin.

'I'm only following your teaching ... Daermon,' Logrid replied in a low voice.

'The lad isn't threatening the Emperor, Logrid ...'

Logrid gave him a strange smile over his shoulder and, with a silent step, crossed the room to disappear behind a column. In his wake he left a boy who was paralysed by fear ... or by humiliation.

'Frog ...'

'Perhaps it would be better if you were to have a private audience with His Imperial Majesty,' the steward suggested in the general's ear.

Dun-Cadal nodded. Whatever had possessed Logrid to cause him to attack a child? The general knew the insurrection in the Saltmarsh was still far from being beaten, but to go from there to suspecting a mere boy of ... He sighed as the steward led Frog back to the door. The lad did not even glance at him, wearing a sullen expression on his face. Frog, who was so proud, had been frightened so badly in the presence of the most important person in the world. Worse still, he had been humiliated without being given a chance to display his own talents. It would teach him to be patient, the general decided; it would teach him to be humble. A day would come when, having mastered his anger, he would reveal himself to the entire world in all his splendour. Right now, the important thing was the war. The idea that the lad might influence its outcome had to be sown in the Emperor's mind. That hope had germinated out of chaos. When the double doors closed behind them, Dun-Cadal advanced towards the red curtain, certain that he had returned from the Salt-marsh with a truly precious stone. The shadow climbed from the tub accompanied by a certain amount of splashing and was immediately covered up by the slender silhouettes of the attendants. It looked like an angel folding its wings, assisted by chaste virgins. Or else a demon. The shape of a skull slowly rose up and the ladies stepped away. They appeared at last in flesh and blood, passing around the curtain, all of them young and beautiful and wearing long green gowns with gold embroidery. Four of them carried the still steaming bathtub. Out of the corners of their eyes they directed curious glances at the general before vanishing behind the columns. A door slammed shut and then there was only the whistling sound of breathing. The silhouette remained unmoving, still masked by the curtain.

'He saved my life,' Dun-Cadal said suddenly.

'I know that,' replied the Emperor. 'Forgive Logrid. The revolt has caused trouble even here in Emeris. Who are our friends? Who are our enemies? It's difficult to know for sure.' He paused, shifting slightly to one side. 'Logrid ... is only protecting me. Just as you did, a long time ago.'

He seemed to be looking for something at his feet, bent down and pulled up what appeared from the shadow it cast to be a stool.

'How good it was to learn that you were still alive, Dun-Cadal. How pleasant it is to have you here,' he confided as he sat down.

'My being alive is even more pleasant for me than for you, Your Imperial Majesty. I'm not certain, however, that Captain Azdeki is of the same opinion.'

The Emperor stifled a laugh.

'Yes, I've heard rumours. Don't worry about it. Despite his uncle's pleas, I've sent him to another front. I could not do more than that. He claims he believed that you were dead, and who can prove otherwise? We all believed it. Approach,' he ordered. 'Come close to me ...'

The general obeyed without saying a word, his sword slapping against his thigh. Outside, birds were singing.

'They're beautiful, aren't they? The songs of my Empire ...' the Emperor said dreamily. 'But what happens when some of them become discordant?' His voice was suddenly harsher. 'You visited Garmaret, didn't you?'

'I found Negus there after our escape from the Saltmarsh. He told me the news.'

'Ah, really? What news was that?'

'That the revolt has spread to other regions, Your Imperial Majesty.'

Behind the curtain, the shadow nodded its head ruefully.

'Like wildfire, I'm afraid.'

'Negus also told me that Uster's younger son is the suspected ringleader ...'

'Yes,' the Emperor admitted. 'Yes, that's what I think. Laerte of Uster, Oratio's second son ... His father was found guilty of treason and hung. He denigrated my power with his writings, the treacherous bastard! He denigrated the *Liaber Dest*, he denigrated the Order of Fangol ... Everything we believe in, he wanted to trample. I suppose his son is prepared to do anything to avenge him ... including inciting the people to rise up against me. Our people, to whom I've given my life, a people who are no more than ungrateful children! I am their father and they rebel against me without any thought. This Laerte, just like Oratio before him, must be judged! He has encouraged my people to tear themselves apart! And all of them are accomplices in shedding blood.'

'Your Imperial Majesty ...' murmured Dun-Cadal.

There was anger in the Emperor's voice, but also a degree of resignation. As if in the end all this was not completely unexpected.

'I can also shed blood if I have to. I can be ruthless, you know. I'm no longer the child you once protected, I've learned a lot since then. Oratio of Uster believed that the Empire could not endure, that change was needed, that I was unworthy! But it was set forth in the *Liaber Dest* itself that my family would accede to the Imperial throne! I am and I remain a Reyes, by the gods! Whatever my opponents say and however many they may be. Me, not worthy? And not worthy of what? Governing over a court filled with viperish tongues and flatterers seeking my favour in exchange for their lying compliments ...?'

The shadow of a sword rose into the air, perfect, slender and straight, its guard seeming to wrap itself around the balled fist. The curtain fluttered slightly.

'They are here, Dun-Cadal my friend,' the Emperor affirmed, brandishing Eraëd. 'They are here, the real rebels. The ones who caused all this. They slither like serpents around my feet. They flatter me, they seduce me, thinking I see nothing.'

Now disgust accompanied his words. He was more deeply wounded than he cared to admit, voicing a distress that only the general could perceive. He had known Asham Ivani Reyes for such a long time. The Emperor lowered the sword and its shadow disappeared into a scabbard which he held in a trembling hand.

'What was it like, the Saltmarsh?' he asked suddenly, as if the general had just returned from some leisure trip.

Disconcerted, Dun-Cadal took his time before answering:

'Wet ...'

'A whole year,' murmured the Emperor.

'I would have preferred a much shorter stay,' the general conceded before changing his tone. 'Don't be despondent, Your Imperial Majesty. This revolt doesn't amount to anything. If you fear losing then you might as well surrender to them right away.'

'I like that,' replied the Emperor. 'You're the only one to speak to me in this manner.'

There was a moment of silence before the Emperor's muffled voice made itself heard again.

'It is not here with me, however, that I have the greatest need of you, but at the front. You made a strong impression at the Saltmarsh. They required days to recover from your escape. To think that a single knight ...'

'And a child, Your Imperial Majesty.'

'Even worse,' laughed the Emperor. 'A mere child ...'

'He's gifted. He will make a great knight, I'm certain of it. I would have liked to present him to you at greater length. He was very nervous at the idea of meeting you.'

'I shall congratulate him when you return ...' sighed the Emperor. 'Both of you ...'

By this single sentence, Dun-Cadal understood that his apprentice had been recognised and placed under his sole protection. The child would accompany him if he, Dun-Cadal, decided so. Reyes slowly stood up again and the shadow of his head shrank, as if he had turned his eyes towards the balcony.

'I'm sorry, my friend, to be sending you back to war so soon.'

A rustling of wings could be heard in the room. Beyond the balcony, the tree tops stirred as a flock of sparrows took flight.

The Empire was shaking on its foundations, its regions set alight one after another. This was no simple revolt. Never before had Imperial power been threatened in this manner. For who could be singled out for judgement? It was the people who, little by little, rose up against their master. Children, the Emperor had said, angry children. As he walked the long hallways of the Imperial palace, Dun-Cadal tried to comprehend it. Most had food on their tables, taxes were not exorbitant, and the peasantry was not simply left at the mercy of an arrogant nobility: they owed their allegiance to the Empire and not to any tin-pot counts. The Emperor made sure that everyone received their due consideration and that justice was carried out. The gods had chosen his family and written an extraordinary destiny for them. To express any doubt about the legitimacy of their acts, the intelligence of their decisions, was to insult divine will.

But when he pushed open the wooden door he had dreamt of for so long now, he was no longer seeking answers to his questions. All he cared about was the simple scent of lavender.

'They told me you'd returned. But I didn't believe it,' declared a harsh voice.

He crossed the chamber with a firm step, encircling the woman by the window in his arms in order to kiss her. She immediately pushed him away, cursing. Although he tried to keep hold of her for an instant, the slap that reddened his cheek quickly dissuaded him.

'Emeris is no longer as welcoming as it used to be,' he grumbled, rubbing his face.

'You dog!' she exploded as she walked over to the door to close it with an angry slam. 'You didn't even think to send a letter to reassure me!'

'About what? From what I see, you've been busy enough without me.'

He was finally glancing around the chamber he had entered without ceremony. A broad canopied bed was surrounded by two finely sculpted night tables and the walls were covered with bright red tapestries with golden borders. When he had last left Emeris, Mildrel had merely been a courtesan like all the others, without a large income or fancy furnishings. In his absence, she had become the woman most sought after by noblemen and the most hated by her own kind. But as far as Dun-Cadal was concerned, she was the only woman who had ever existed.

She moved along the edge of the bed, her fingers trailing over the vivid green spread.

'I don't belong to you, Dun-Cadal. You've known how I am from the beginning...'

'You don't belong to me ... and yet you missed me,' the general said with a smile as he approached her.

'That's not the point,' she said in a grating tone.

His hands, normally so strong, brushed the woman's wrists before his fingers closed gently over the delicate skin. She did not move an inch. Her curly brown hair spilled over her bare shoulders, her full lips were shaded a light red. Her eyes, edged in black, stared at him without blinking.

'A year without any news, a whole year when everyone believed you to be dead ... you ...'

'You what?' he murmured, bending towards her slightly.

She could not finish her speech, having waited for him so long. Their lips met in a lingering kiss ... before their embrace made them forget everything and carried them far, far away from the rumblings of war and lurking death. There was no longer anything but their hearts against one another, beating hard and fast, at the same rhythm.

The sun was declining when Dun-Cadal went to the window. A naked leg emerged from under the sheets on the bed. Mildrel was observing him pensively. She took a deep breath, barely masking her disappointment.

'You're going to leave again right away, aren't you?'

Dun-Cadal didn't reply. His attention was focused on the section of the palace opposite his mistress's apartments. The golden roofs were tarnished by vert-de-gris and in the distance below, he could see the tall white houses of the surrounding city.

'What's he like …?' He turned his head towards her, a blank look on his face. 'The child from the Saltmarsh … Everyone gossips around here, you know,' she went on, her tone light. 'Your exploits have never ceased to amaze. Dun-Cadal, the general, has become a veritable myth. It wasn't enough for you to fight for the Empire, you had to go and leave your mark on men's minds—'

'It's not how it seems.'

'Was it written that you should bring the lad back with you?'

'Mildrel—'

'Written down in a book of which no one has ever read even a single page,' she commented sourly.

Dun-Cadal paused before replying. The *Liaber Dest* had always been the source of their biggest disagreement. She had never believed the Sacred Book existed and criticised his faith whenever she could. For every time she said she feared for him on the eve of combat, he justified the risks he took with simple fatalism. While she argued that placing such faith on a lost book was evidence of ignorance. Pragmatic by nature, she devoted herself to gleaning information from the rumours and murmurs at court rather than taking an interest in more arcane matters like the origins of the world. As far as the divine was concerned, she tasted its sweetness in the satin sheets on her bed. Ideas and dreams she left to those who were unable to love. This difference in perspective affected her relationship with the general, but their love ran too deep to wither because of an argument.

'It's how things are. The gods decide the course of our lives. The fact that the Sacred Book has been lost doesn't mean you can deny its existence. Whether you like it or not.'

'And what about him? Was it written that you would find him in a marsh?'

He raised an eyebrow. Mildrel sat up in her bed.

'I can't wait to meet him,' she said with a smile.

But there was sadness in her eyes. He knew what pained her, but could not speak of it. It did not interest him.

'He's just my pupil.'

'I didn't know you were so … kind. Gathering in and training a Saltmarsh orphan, taking care of him, looking out for him like a fa—'

'I must be going,' he broke in, in a studiedly neutral tone. 'I'll

102

remain in Emeris for a few more days before taking the road to the Vershan mountains. I shall see you again.'

He picked up his shirt from the edge of the bed and put it back on.

'Tell me, Dun-Cadal, what does he have that the others lacked?'

'He needs me . . .'

'I need you too! I don't want to be a courtesan my whole life . . .' Mildrel murmured.

'You don't belong to me.'

'I could.'

Holding his breastplate in his hands, he grew still for a moment before lifting his eyes to hers with a strange expression on his face. She immediately looked down, folding her legs under her like child caught doing something naughty. Without saying a word, he donned the pieces of his armour. Once he was presentable he headed for the door and, gripping the handle, he gave her one last glance.

'I'll see you again . . .'

He waited a brief instant, hoping that she would confirm their next meeting or beg him to stay a while longer, but she gave no response. It had always been like this between them and so it would surely remain. They could not live without one another but each shared moment had to come to an end. He was returning to combat and there was nothing she could do about it. She prayed for his safety. And, many times after he departed, she had placed her hands on her belly in the hope she would feel life slowly growing there; longing to keep a part of him with her always . . .

Dun-Cadal wandered for a time in the palace hallways, enjoying a moment of peace he had not experienced in more than two years. Until finally his steps led him to a large inner courtyard, surrounded by open corridors lined with columns. He lingered for a moment, remembering his arrival in this place as a very young man. Here he had attended his classes and learned the art of war before being judged unsuited for command. A smile curled his lips. How atypical his career had been and what a strange path he had been forced to take in order to achieve the highest military rank . . .

Some cadets were chatting near a fountain, dressed in red-and-white doublets. On their chests, drawn within a silver shield, they wore the image of a thin, proud rapier with a twisted guard. The legendary Eraëd, the Emperors' sword.

Dun-Cadal spotted a boy sitting on the lip of the fountain, frantically wiping at the blood running from his nose. One of his cheekbones was swollen and there was a cut on his lower lip. A fight must have broken out a short time before. The general went to join him with a slow step, knowing that those present were observing him with a certain deference. When the cadets recognised him, words dried up. Except for those of the general, which were barely audible.

'I see you've already been making friends ...' he murmured to the lad.

'It's nothing,' Frog grunted.

The steward had brought him here, and entrusted him to the palace master-at-arms to see that he was assigned a room. During their brief stay in Emeris, Frog would be just another knight's squire. And here, more than elsewhere, every newcomer had to earn respect from the very first day. Frog had just undergone the bitter experience.

'It's always hard to find one's place ...'

Dun-Cadal let his eyes drift over the groups of cadets. Their faces had gone pale. General Daermon had just appeared, in person, and a boy they had just shamelessly thrashed happened to be his protégé. Dun-Cadal did not need to say a word to make the culprits avert their eyes. He hesitated for a long instant. Should he punish them?

'It's always difficult to know what one is capable of, and as for revealing it to others ... Well then, violence is hardly a solution. Wine! Tavern keeper! More wine!'

Dun-Cadal contented himself with giving them a baleful stare.

'Come on, let's go,' he said with a sigh. 'We'll get that fixed up. And take your hand away from your nose, a few blows won't make it drop off.'

'You've had enough to drink, Dun-Cadal.'

Frog stood, sniffling, with his eyes lowered and his teeth gritted. He followed the knight with a quick step, passing between the cadets without giving them a single glance. A few feet away, a young Nâaga watched them enter the academy.

'An' my tankard! I hav'n't finissed my ... my tankard! Thief!'

'Dun-Cadal! Stop it!'

'My taaankard!'

'General!'

She'd raised her voice like she'd never done before. She was as surprised as the old man banging on the tavern door. But she had to admit that her sudden display of authority worked wonders. Dun-Cadal went from being a bellowing drunkard to a little boy caught in the act.

'He doesn't want to serve you. Night has fallen, you should go to bed.'

She helped him move away from the door. Inside the tavern, the customers were still carousing and, although the door muffled the noise, Dun-Cadal could hear the laughter along with the melodies of the fifes and penny whistles. With regret, he turned away and staggered off beside the young woman. The day had gone so quickly, as his story unfolded with the help of tankards filled to the brim. He had plunged into more than just his past . . .

'Come on, Dun-Cadal, I'll take you home.'

'Take me home,' he sneered, hiccupping. 'But I'm a hero! Who're you? A nanny . . . ha-ha! . . . a nanny . . .'

'And you stink . . .'

He leaned on her shoulder, his feet almost slipping out from under him with every step. In the muddy alley, barely lit by the dim oil lamps hanging from the balcony, anyone coming across this frail young woman supporting a man as massively built as Dun-Cadal would have been amused. Or intrigued . . .

Three men hidden in the shadow of an adjoining street spotted them. The target was too good to pass up and they came forward, sniggering.

'Hey!' jeered the thinnest of the trio, hefting a club studded with sharp points. 'Where do you think you're going, my beauty? Your grandpa there doesn't look too lively. How about giving us some money on this fine evening?'

Viola halted abruptly. Dun-Cadal, deprived of any strength, let his head fell upon her shoulder. A grimace passed across his face and his eyes rolled in his sockets as if he were seeking a point to focus on somewhere ahead.

'Wha's . . . all this . . . ?' he grumbled.

'Company …' Viola murmured, her voice suddenly tense.

In the darkness, the disparate silhouettes facing them did not bode well. One was almost a giant, the second, probably the leader, was as thin as a rail, and the third as round as a cannonball. All of them wore patched brown trousers and shirts of the same shade opened in a V at the neck. The thin one wore a sleeveless leather vest and an odd-looking hat which drooped around his head.

'Br-brigan's!' bawled the general, pushing the young woman aside with an elbow. 'Or swin'lers?'

He threw himself at the trio, stumbling several times.

'Come 'n' flight, yo' … yo' … yokels!'

'Flight?' snickered the round one. 'Yo-yo-yokels?'

'He's pissed,' the giant laughed hoarsely.

'General!' screamed Viola.

He wanted to strike the first brigand a furious blow with his fist but this simple gesture was enough to make him lose his balance. He'd seen his share of battles, he'd led men into combat, but this evening, Dun-Cadal Daermon was nothing but a falling-down drunk. Lying on the ground, looking surprised and ridiculous, the little amount of lucidity left to him wounded his self-esteem. Here he was … arse in the mud.

There were blows, sharp and quick. There were cries of surprise and the snapping of an arm when the Nâaga emerged out of nowhere to seize one of the bandits. Dun-Cadal tried to make out what was going on but he couldn't keep his head straight. All he perceived were blurred silhouettes and sounds like echoes rolling around inside his skull … and then finally there was silence, once the bandits had fled. He lowered his head, his belly knotted and his heart heavy. He should have made mincemeat of them. He should have used the *animus*; standing against them the way he had once defied the greatest warriors … A terribly cold hand gripped his wrist and helped him to his feet.

'Come on,' said a hoarse voice.

Was that a note of … compassion? It was a strong grip that had raised him from the ground. The grip of a tattooed colossus.

'Y-you …' stammered Dun-Cadal.

'Yes,' replied Rogant with a twisted smile on his lips. 'Delighted to see you, too, old ghost.'

'I'm no' … dea' … yet!

106

From behind the general's back came Viola's quiet voice.

'Thank you for intervening,' she said curtly.

Dun-Cadal attempted to turn his head to look at her, but sleep weighed heavily on his eyelids and every gesture was steadily becoming more strenuous. He thought, for the space of an instant, that Viola was looking at the rooftops as if trying to catch sight of something.

Then he passed out.

7

REGAIN YOUR DIGNITY

It's easy to fight with a sword.
But to vanquish one's demons
A blade is of no use.
If you are on your knees, pride gone,
Then stand up, even if you tremble,
And regain your dignity.
For it is the only weapon
Which protects you from the powerful.

'Aaaarrows!'

The desperate scream was immediately drowned out by a deafening whistling noise. A dark swarm plunged down upon the infantry, striking the breastplates and helmets of the lucky ones, piercing the leather surcoats of the less fortunate. The sharp stinging noise of metal on metal was followed by the heavier, punching sound of torn flesh and the deep wheezing of the soldiers who had dropped to the ground. The whole dire symphony finally faded into a stunned silence. The first lines did not disperse, however, the uninjured men rising up among their fallen comrades. The plain had to be held. They had been carrying out this task for more than a week now and many of them had seen previous fighting. The revolt had spread to numerous regions, but here at the foot of the Vershan mountains its forces were weakening. Soon, Imperial troops coming from the East, led by Captain Etienne Azdeki, would trap them in a vice and calm would be restored. They just had to keep their position a little longer.

'Hold the line! Hold fast!' ordered a deep voice at their backs.

Sitting on his horse, Dun-Cadal Daermon encouraged his men, the hooves of his steed pounding the ground as he rode back and forth. Some of the soldiers regained their posts, their faces contorted with fear. Others remained permanently still. On the far side of the plain, lying low near the woods at the foot of the mountains, enemy archers prepared a new volley.

'General! General Daermon!'

A young knight was galloping towards him, looking nervous. His armour had seen use in numerous battles and was covered with nicks and cracks. He was the well-bred son of a family entirely loyal to the cause of the Empire, one of those who followed in their fathers' footsteps without ever expressing a single doubt, justifying their complete submission by invoking tradition. In other circumstances, no doubt he would have been elegant and polite, displaying a degree of cultivation and even a touch of humour at banquets in Emeris. But since his graduation from the military academy he had been sent to the battlefield. The war had surely transformed him to the point that, in forthcoming festivities, he would limit himself to bringing a glass to his lips while nodding at the remarks of those who hadn't taken up a military career. For a young knight like this one, learning the art of war and the mastery of a force as delicate as the *animus*, Dun-Cadal felt only respect. From this battle, a young man like him should emerge a victor. One day perhaps, he might even save the life of his general ...

The knight pulled sharply on the reins and his horse came to a halt with a snort.

'General, the cavalry is prepared and ready. Captain Azdeki's troops have skirted around the Vershan and are awaiting your orders.'

Dun-Cadal nodded. The hour had come.

'Upon my signal,' he said gravely.

With a dig of his heels, he urged his steed into a steady trot behind the lines of infantry. It was time to launch the assault, they had already waited long enough. The Emperor had not sent him to hold on to a piece of ground, but to win back an entire county. He descended a small hill and rejoined the main force of his army. Hundreds of cavalrymen and knights, ready to defend their Empire ...

'It's time!' he yelled, drawing his sword.

At the edge of the plain, the infantry was enduring another shower of arrows when suddenly the ground began to tremble. There was a growing rumble as if something were approaching. The captains acted immediately, barking out orders. The soldiers formed wide

109

corridors lined with spearmen, regrouping themselves with perfect timing. And coming over the hill, the cavalry rushed into the lanes thus opened.

In the woods at the foot of the mountains, few had knowledge of the art of war. Some had served the Empire, others had distinguished themselves as mercenaries, but most of the rebel army was made up of peasants or modest artisans from nearby towns, plus some more well-to-do folk seduced by the idea of change. When they heard the strange rumbling, their hearts beat faster. Upon seeing the rising dust, some thought their chests would burst. Masked by the clouds thrown up in the cavalry's wake, the Imperial soldiers were advancing. Once the mounted knights had torn through the enemy lines the Imperial infantry would overwhelm their defences. Although some cowards fled, abandoning makeshift weapons and a few shreds of pride, most of the rebels resigned themselves to dying here in the shadow of the Vershan. For they were fighting for the ideal of a different world. Their hands gripped spears, swords, and maces as if they were the last things preventing their fall. And of their own accord, without anyone giving the order, they rushed forward to meet their adversaries in the most total confusion imaginable. Iron struck flesh, sharpened points punctured skin and the cavalry shattered their lines. Bodies flew through the air ... and the edge of the forest was engulfed in chaos. And then the forces to the rebels' rear joined the fighting. Coming down from the mountain, Captain Azdeki's troops attacked in their turn.

The rebels had nothing left to lose. They would not lower their weapons, not with so much depending on their resolve. A simple insurrection was on the verge of becoming a true revolution. Standing, they held their ground. On their knees, they fought. Lying down, they continued to strike. Nothing would make them give up, nothing short of death.

Dun-Cadal had reached the woods. Sword in hand, he forged on, hacking and slashing. Until a spear pierced his horse's neck. The beast whinnied and its legs gave away beneath its own weight, throwing the general to the ground. He regained his feet, nimbly, parrying a blow, then another, with the flat of his sword. And with his free hand, he shoved back his opponent without even touching him. The rebel was thrown into the air before crashing into a tree trunk with an awful thud.

Dun-Cadal caught a glimpse of Frog standing a few feet away. Visibly fascinated by his mentor's use of the *animus*, the lad had come to a sudden halt. The point of a spear brought him back to the brutal reality of combat, forcing him to take a quick sidestep. A man with greying temples stood with his arm at full stretch, surprised at missing his target. Frog lunged with his blade and planted it in the rebel's shoulder. The man screamed before collapsing, his face contorted with pain. Not so long ago, the lad would have been affected by the sight, but in the heat of action he had learned to forget all humanity. His gestures became mechanical, responding automatically to each attack, repeating parries and lunges over and over again. When two men charged him at once, he had no trouble dealing with the threat. Their swords clashed with his. He bent down before plunging his blade into the belly of one assailant and then, spinning round, dodged the attack by the second. With a kick to the ribs, he knocked him to the ground. The poor man saw the sword sweeping down towards him and the blade sank into his torso with an odd yielding sound.

'Frog! Stay close!'

Dun-Cadal too was battling without a break. Despite vigorously repelling a series of assaults, he kept watch over his apprentice out of the corner of his eye. Although he was worried on several occasions, he was reassured by the lad's ease in wielding his sword. Frog not only reproduced what he had been taught but, not content with achieving near perfection in each move, also improvised freely. His entire pent-up rage exploded on the battlefield and, although this could have served him poorly, in fact it lent his movements a precision worthy of the greatest swordsmen. A single stroke was enough to fell an opponent before dispatching the next with the same speed.

'I'm not going anywhere,' Frog grumbled as he shoved a man away with his elbow.

His attacker was a true soldier this time, probably a former mercenary from the North judging by his chain mail and pointed helmet. But the lad's skill would not be enough; others were already coming to the man's aid, running between the trees, heavily armed.

The general had to rid himself of two rebels, each visibly more used to working in the fields than fighting, given the way their arms trembled with each blow. He parried a spear thrust with a stroke of his sword before punching the first in the face. Stunned, the man fell to his knees, eyes half-closed. Then, with a flick of his wrist, Dun-Cadal turned his blade before lunging and stabbing the other rebel's hand. The peasant dropped his weapon with a scream of pain and ran.

For his part, Frog was holding off four mercenaries as best he could, and they were skilful and accurate fighters. Two of them were using studded maces, almost shattering his sword with each of their blows. Frog then attempted something unthinkable.

His mentor immediately understood when he saw the lad take a step back, his eyes closed. He must be trying to calm his beating heart, to breathe and feel the world ... To employ the *animus* himself. But up until now, Frog had only managed to shift a clay pot and even that effort had exhausted him to the point of fainting. How could he imagine himself capable of mastering such a force? He dodged a sword and halted, kneeling on the ground with one hand extended towards his four assailants.

'Frog! No, no, no!' roared Dun-Cadal, running towards the boy.

The general whirled his sword in the air and forced a passage through the enemy. The lad repressed a grimace, his chest quivering with spasms. Perhaps he could do it. Perhaps—

Frog never saw the blow coming. A mace struck his wrist. His sword flew through the air to plant itself in the ground a few yards away. The pain in his arm made him cry out before he leant away by reflex to avoid a blade. The cutting edge brushed past his nose with a hiss. He threw himself into a roll across the leafy carpet of the forest and got back to his knees.

'Frog!' yelled Dun-Cadal behind him.

The general would not arrive in time to save his pupil unless he used the *animus*. But was he even able to do so? His lungs were on fire and another effort so soon after the first would probably kill him. He would have to rely on a more mundane method of combat. Dun-Cadal seized a sword stuck point-down in the ground and, a blade in each hand, waded through the mercenaries. All around them the rebels were starting to disperse. Azdeki's troops were arriving.

'You dogs!' he howled as he ran, slashing the air with his weapons, cutting, slicing and shoving the unfortunate wretches who were in his path. 'Filthy scum!'

Just a few yards away, protected only by his light, dented armour, Frog did not move. The four soldiers facing him were ready to pounce. The lad leapt to one side, avoiding a first blow. But the other three men wielded their weapons so well he wouldn't have a second chance. A mace and two swords came plunging down at him.

The sound of hooves striking the beaten earth announced the arrival of Azdeki's cavalry. A blade slipped in front of Frog to halt the two swordsmen in mid-charge and jerked their weapons upwards with a powerful stroke. The man with the mace was thrown to the ground by an invisible force.

And as if to finish off the rider's work, Dun-Cadal came up from behind to plant his weapons in the swordsmen's backs, before despatching the third mercenary, who had been groggily regaining his feet, with a kick to the face. The soldier fell backwards, bleeding from the nose, his eyes rolled up in their sockets.

'A man without a weapon is nothing,' said a voice. 'He loses all, including his dignity.'

Sword against his thigh, hand firmly gripping its hilt, his proud, straight body comfortably installed in the saddle, those scornful eyes set above a hawklike nose. Dun-Cadal had no trouble recognising him. Basking in his own arrogance, Etienne Azdeki looked the boy up and down with a disdainful expression.

'Did your mentor never teach you that? Perhaps you chose the wrong master,' he spat, before spurring his horse and galloping away.

In passing, he almost knocked Dun-Cadal down.

'Captain!' the latter bellowed.

But Azdeki was already disappearing between the trees. All around them the rebels were fleeing. Behind them there only remained the soldiers of the Empire and, strewn across the dead leaves or lying battered against the exposed tree roots, hundreds of bodies. The tumult of battle subsided little by little as the odour of blood and sweat drifted through the forest undergrowth. Frog could now hear branches snapping beneath the general's feet.

'What did you think you were doing, you little bugger?' Dun-Cadal bawled.

'Who was that man?' the boy asked him with equal vehemence.

'What were you thinking, dropping your guard like that?'

'His name! What is his name?' Frog insisted. 'Tell me!'

His face twisted in anger and defiance, he advanced on Dun-Cadal. Only his teacher's firm hand on his shoulder stopped before he took a step too far.

'Calm down, you idiot! Calm down!'

'Who was he?' demanded Frog.

'Azdeki!' replied Dun-Cadal. 'That was Captain Etienne Azdeki and, although it pains me to admit it— Calm down, by all the gods!'

The lad tried to walk past, with Dun-Cadal almost gripping him by the neck to stop him.

'Frog! Frog, look at me!'

He was finally seeing his pupil's greatest fault. Frog wanted to have fought all these men on his own, without any help from anyone. And even more without someone saving his life. He had failed. He'd been humiliated.

'Look at me, lad,' repeated Dun-Cadal in a quieter voice. 'Calm down …'

He finally succeeded in capturing the boy's attention. Nearby, Imperial troops were helping the wounded, whose moans mingled with the sweet singing of the birds returning to their roosts.

'You'd like to take him down a peg or two, is that it?' said Dun-Cadal. 'Look at me, by the gods! Is that what you want? Me too! Believe me, I have a real itch to do something about him. But whatever you may think of Azdeki, he is a captain in the Imperial Army and comes from one of the greatest and oldest families at the Imperial court. That means you owe him the respect due his rank.'

'That dog …' growled Frog.

'You owe him respect!' insisted Dun-Cadal. 'And though it pains me to say so, he was right.'

'… piece of filth …' continued the boy, lowering his eyes.

'He was right, you pig-headed fool! What on earth were you trying to do, can you tell me? Use the *animus*?'

In a flash, the boy's gaze challenged the general's.

'Yes,' he snapped with a scowl.

'You're not ready.'

'I can do it!' Frog protested.

Dun-Cadal let go of him brusquely and then, after a pause, retreated a few steps, keeping his eyes on the lad.

'We'll see about that …' he murmured.

'No doubt about it.'

They glared at one another until Dun-Cadal turned on his heels and stalked off without saying another word.

The Empire had just retaken the valley of the Vershan and he was the strategist who made it happen. In the camp, there were cele-brations around the fires. Some soldiers had been dispatched to the closest town to restore order, but most were allowed a well-deserved rest. Dun-Cadal and Azdeki avoided one another. It was obvious that the captain held a grudge over being relieved of command in the Saltmarsh. His punishment would have been quite different if Dun-Cadal could prove he'd deliberately abandoned the general to the mercy of a rouarg. But no one could – or dared – assert as much to the Emperor. So there was a standoff between the two knights. Pursuing their quarrel would have been a hindrance to the prosecu-tion of the war. And Azdeki hadn't run away, this time.

The next day, in the dawn light, the men were slumbering in their tents, by the dead fires, or scattered here and there ... The peace was barely disturbed by the chirping of the birds. A morning fog had enveloped the silent camp. Lying on his side, near the horse corral, his arms tucked beneath his body, even Frog was fast asleep. A boot in his back woke him with a start. He turned his head violently, gri-macing. An imposing silhouette looked down him, but he couldn't make out the face. The dawn diffused a curiously wan light around the figure.

'On your feet.'

He seemed to need a few more seconds to recognise Dun-Cadal standing over him.

'What ...?' he grumbled, rubbing his eyes.

He was still sleepy.

'Get up,' Dun-Cadal ordered.

Seeing the stern expression on his mentor's face he must have re-alised that no amount of complaining would make him change his mind, because he said no more. Resigned to the loss of sleep, the boy rose from bed, his eyelids still heavy.

'What? What's going on ...?'

Dun-Cadal led the way. Shivering in the morning cold, Frog fol-lowed him reluctantly. They passed between the tents, wending their way among the sleeping soldiers. The smell of alcohol and grilled pig's meat lingered in the air and the boy had to hold his breath to quell the nausea it provoked in him. When they reached the edge of a small wood, the air was fresher and more pleasant.

'Master?'

Not a word. They entered the shadow of the trees, dead branches snapping beneath their feet. The birds were singing. After a time, Dun-Cadal finally halted and, keeping his back to his apprentice, appeared to be deep in thought.

'Master Dun-Cadal . . .'

'The *animus*,' the knight said, his voice muffled, 'what have I taught you about it?'

Frog hesitated. What was expected of him? Being woken up this way prevented him from replying intelligently and his voice betrayed his disgruntlement.

'Not much,' he complained.

'Not much?' repeated the general with a small chuckle. He turned round at last and for a moment his face seemed more relaxed. Then his features tightened into severity once again. 'I'm not asking your opinion on the matter,' he said, 'but what you actually know. So? What have I taught you?'

Frog could not bear the knight's gaze this morning. He struggled against his longing to close his eyes, lie down and rest a while, without fighting, without being afraid, without any of this. To simply close his eyes and not have to think any more.

'Everything breathes,' he replied finally.

'What's that?' asked the general, cupping a hand behind his ear.

'Everything is in movement, like breathing. That's what the *animus* is,' the boy explained, as if reciting a lesson.

He backed up a step, suddenly wary, when Dun-Cadal approached him with his sword drawn.

'So that's all you've retained . . . and yet you claim you're able to use the *animus* with the greatest of ease,' the knight sighed. 'Very well. Disarm me.'

'What?'

'Disarm me!'

He spread his arms as if inviting an attack. A strange smile played on his lips as he observed his apprentice's reaction. The lad was trembling. Was it down to the cold morning or the worrying prospect of confronting his mentor in a duel? It didn't really matter, because Dun-Cadal knew exactly what Frog was going to do. When he placed his hand on the hilt of his sword, the general's smile froze.

'Without your sword,' he instructed.

'You're crazy, I'm not going to—'

'Disarm me without using your sword. Since you know all about the *animus*, go ahead, surprise me.'

Although Dun-Cadal's face let nothing show, he was jubilant. Opposite him, Frog had no idea what to do. He hesitated, at a loss, a far cry from the arrogant boy who had defied him the previous evening.

'I'm waiting,' Dun-Cadal murmured.

Frog extended his arm towards him, hand open. The general bided his time. He saw the lad stiffen little by little, the muscles in his arm contracting until it was shaking like a piece of wood that had been struck hard ... but nothing happened.

'You don't know what the *animus* really is,' Dun-Cadal declared as he resheathed his sword with a snap.

Frog lowered his arm along with his eyes, looking hurt. All his anger had boiled up again, ready to explode. A rage that had no other cause than his patent failure. Dun-Cadal was right. He did not make the slightest movement when the general halted next to him, tilting his face towards Frog's with a hard expression.

'The *animus* is passed from knight to knight, it's not an innate gift. Whoever understands it is able to use it. So remember that. Feel your surroundings, Frog. You don't need to open your eyes to see them. You just need to know they exist all around you. Feel them live ...'

But the lad turned his head away as if refusing to listen. The boy's pride bordered on insolence.

'Close your eyes!' snarled the general.

He did not have to repeat himself. Insolent perhaps, but not stupid.

'Good ... Now,' he said in a voice that was suddenly quieter, 'try to listen ... the sound of the wind ... follow it between the trees ... fly with it ... listen to the birds ... not their song, no ...' He placed his hand on the boy's shoulder and leaned towards his ear. 'But the beating of their hearts ...'

Frog's face relaxed and his breathing became calmer, slower.

'The earth ... the entire world is like the air that comes and goes. The *animus* ... the breath and life of the world. Everyone can hear it ... But feel it? Control it? That's much harder ... You need to be alert, focused ... Feel the *animus*, be the *animus*.'

The lad's chest rose and fell more quickly now. When Dun-Cadal saw him frown, he knew that he had taken Frog where he wanted him to be. The rhythm of his words, the peaceful sound of his voice, were hypnotising his pupil.

'Feel the *animus*, be the *animus*,' he said slowly. 'Feel it, Frog! It's there, the magic. In every breath you exhale ... It's like music, Frog ... It's not enough to simply listen. Feel it ... legato ... staccato ... Now, picture the tree facing us in your mind ... Are you picturing it?'

There was no more anger, no more hurt, no more tension. Beside him, Frog was straightening up, full of confidence. Dun-Cadal paused ... before raising his voice.

'Feel the *animus*, Frog. And strike!'

With a brusque movement the boy extended his arm and with it came a noise like the howl of the wind in the middle of a storm. The dead leaves lifted in a whirl; a furrow dug itself in the ground at an amazing speed, running between Frog and the foot of a tree. The bark flew off near some protruding roots and then split open a few inches higher with a crackling sound like the rattling breath of a dying man.

At that same moment, Frog opened his eyes. The general was standing ready, his hands on the boy's shoulder. He had experienced this and knew the pain that followed the first real use of the *animus*. When he saw the lad's mouth open wide with his respiration cut off, he recalled the burning that had run through his chest and the way his muscles had felt as heavy as lead. Frog fell forward, his legs giving way beneath his own weight. His mentor caught him and helped him to kneel.

'Calm ... calm ... calm, lad,' he murmured, hugging him tightly.

'I— I promise ...'

And the boy coughed, so loud, so hard that it seemed as if he were literally coughing his lungs up, as tears came to his eyes.

'Frog ...'

'The *animus*, Frog ... it's something you learn ... do you understand now? You'll know how to use it one day. I promise you... but in return, promise me you won't try any more crazy stunts like yesterday's.'

'... *still sleeping, you can't wake him.*'

His body quivering with little jolts, still trying as best he could to clear his air passages, Frog nodded.

'*He's still sleeping!*'

'I— I ... promise,' he managed to say between two coughing fits.

'Wake him.'

'He's still sleeping.'

'Wake him up, I need to talk to him.'

The voices were muffled, yet he managed to clearly understand each of the words spoken.

'I must ask you to leave the premises,' one voice said.

'I have no intention of leaving without seeing him,' replied another just as firmly.

Finally, there was light. Little by little, his eyelids opened over his misty eyes. Above him the faded ceiling mouldings were bathed in a golden light. He wanted to turn his head, but there seemed to be an anvil lodged in his skull, the corners striking his temples with every sudden movement. Grimacing, he sat up in the bed. He was in Mildrel's home. Gradually, memories of the previous evening came to the surface. He held his head in his hands, cursing the fact that he was still alive. How he would have liked never to wake up, to be forgotten, not even a shadow, pure nothingness.

'You don't understand! It's important!'

The voice was young and determined.

'You aren't welcome here, sniffing around in other people's pasts.'

The two voices came from behind the closed door of his chamber, but he had no difficulty recognising Mildrel's. Through the curtains, rays of already bright sunlight penetrated as far as the foot of the wall facing him. In the neighbouring room, Mildrel and Viola were still arguing. The two women were polar opposites; a courtesan who had spent her life seducing men in order to climb her way into high society had little in common with a young supporter of the Republic.

'Leave him alone ...'

It was not an order, but rather a plea. As she sat down in an armchair covered in tarnished gilt, Mildrel sighed.

'You're after Eraëd, aren't you?'

'That's why I came and found him, yes,' Viola replied. 'Dun-Cadal fled Emeris with it. It's part of the history of our world, my lady.'

The historian stood near the doorway to the small salon, her hands joined before her. Although she'd raised her voice to make herself be heard, she was like a shy little girl when she mentioned the sword.

119

'It was forged by the kings of this world. Some say it's magical, capable of cleaving the hardest rocks, of piercing the hide of the greatest dragons ...'

She fell silent for a moment before tucking one of her red locks behind her ear. There was a dreamy light in her eyes as they peered through her round spectacles.

'But ... whatever you may think, it's something completely different that brought me here today, my lady.'

'He had nothing to with the councillor's assassination,' Mildrel assured her, seeking to forestall any accusation.

Viola nodded.

'I know that. I was with him when the councillor was killed. But he knows the assassin.'

If Mildrel was surprised by this piece of information, she let nothing show. She had learned to mask her emotions. A courtesan had to be a good actress in order to extract secrets and, even more, to pretend not to know them.

'I'm certain of it. He spoke of the ... Hand of the Emperor.'

Mildrel looked down. The sunlight coming through the window at her back lit up her bare shoulders. A few curly strands of hair fell gently upon her nape. When Viola had seen her the first time, it had been night. Her visit this morning gave her another opportunity to observe Dun-Cadal's former mistress. She was starting to understand some of the things she had been told about this woman. A flower that had barely begun to fade with time ... She had expected Mildrel to intervene in her business with Dun-Cadal. She had even come prepared for that.

'You think you can do as you please because we served the Emperor Reyes, don't you?' said Mildrel in a bitter tone. 'You, with your studies, your history and your little round spectacles. You come sniffing around people's pasts in your arrogant, impetuous youth, poking into our deepest wounds just to achieve your own ends ... Your Republic has given you the freedom to judge others. But only that freedom ...'

She brushed at her gown with a nervous gesture before getting up.

'I won't ask you again,' she declared. 'Leave my house. This is a place where a good many of Masalia's gentlemen gather. Several of them owe me favours and would not hesitate to deal with you ...

with the most complete respect for the very Republic you cherish so dearly.'

So it was barely veiled threats now. Viola felt her hands becoming damp at the idea that something ... painful might happen to her. She just needed to cajole Dun-Cadal along for long enough for him to lead her, of his own accord, to Eraëd.

'Madam ... it's a matter of life and death ...'

'For you, surely. I'd be surprised if *General* Dun-Cadal feels the same way.'

'I must speak with him.'

'All I need to do is send a message to the chief of Masalia's city guards,' Mildrel warned, joining her hands before her.

'You'll do nothing of the sort,' interjected a hoarse, almost broken voice.

The door to the bedchamber had opened without the two women hearing it. Dun-Cadal stood squinting on the threshold, one hand pressed against the door frame to keep his balance. He took an unsteady step forward with a grimace. This headache of his was obviously not going to give him any respite. He had been drinking for almost the entire previous day. He cleared his throat before speaking again.

'You'll do nothing of the sort,' he resumed, 'because you can't and you know it. The men who come to see your girls aren't upstanding bourgeois citizens of the Republic, but passing sailors ...'

'Shut up!' Mildrel snapped indignantly.

It didn't bother him that he was wrecking Mildrel's efforts to protect him. Both of them were living in the past and treated the future as their enemy.

'As hard as you're trying to frighten off this young lass, I'm not sure you'll succeed. She's very determined ... aren't you?'

He turned towards Viola. She gave him a brief nod.

'Yesterday you mentioned Negus,' said Viola without further ado. 'A friend.'

'Yes,' Dun-Cadal replied simply.

'A councillor,' she added.

The old man's gaze grew vague. His throat was so dry. Negus ... he had betrayed the very thing he had spent so many years defending, too ... His old friend Negus. His headache became so strong that he placed a damp palm upon his brow.

'He's arrived in Masalia.'

'What can I do about that?' he sighed.

'Warn your friend. I'll take you to him, he'll listen to you,' explained Viola.

Listen to him? Would they even still be friends after all this time? He exchanged a glance with the young woman. She was indeed determined. Her eyes held a spark similar to the one he'd perceived, so long ago, in a young boy.

'Will you be a phantom for the rest of your life?' murmured Viola. 'Or will you act like a real ... *general*?'

He seemed so weak standing there, with his bloodshot eyes and the greenish cast to his skin. She doubted it would be possible to revive a spark in him that seemed more dead than asleep. But she had to try.

'What right have you—?' the courtesan started to say angrily.

'Mildrel,' Dun-Cadal said, cutting her off.

He'd only whispered her name, accompanied by a simple look of sadness. All of this could not be due to chance: Viola's arrival, Eraëd, his memories becoming more vivid than ever ... the Hand of the Emperor. Something more powerful was at work ... was it the divine?

'Wait for me below,' he asked Viola.

When the sound of her footsteps on the stairs grew faint, the old warrior ventured further into the salon, still stumbling a little.

'You shouldn't have done that,' Mildrel hissed.

'Done what? Acknowledge that you were making stories up to scare her off?' he taunted, before leaning on a pedestal table as he rubbed his eyes with a trembling hand. 'You fled Emeris and the court just as we all did! You're surviving in a Republic that has forgotten all about us. None of the people who frequent this place have any power over this world. The only thing you think you still control is me. But you've mothered me long enough, my beauty. The young lass is right. She's bloody well right ...'

The courtesan looked at him sternly. He would have liked to see something other than reproach in her eyes.

'Mildrel—'

'And what about her?' she asked with a quiver in her voice. A smile stretched her red lips. 'What does she have that the others lacked?'

'She needs me?' he suggested.

He walked to the door with a firmer step and halted, touching the handle.

'He's not the Hand of the Emperor ...'

'But what if he is?' retorted Dun-Cadal, looking pensively at the lock.

'You want to avenge him, is that it? Dun-Cadal, you're no longer a—'

'A general?'

He spun round so abruptly that he had to clutch the handle to stop himself from falling. A mean scowl twisted his face.

'How do you see me, Mildrel? As a vestige? Leftover rubbish?'

'That's not what I meant—'

'How then?' he bellowed. 'A poor old boozer? That's what I am, Mildrel, a drunkard. I've lived outside the world for too long. What do I know about the Republic? About the people who survived after the Empire fell? If I can do something good before I die ... not for an Empire, not for a Republic, but just to save lives. Like a knight would. Like a general ...'

In Mildrel's face, haloed by Masalia's bright sunshine, he no longer saw any reproach, nor any anger or sadness. Merely affection.

'Tell me ... Mildrel. Tell me how you see me,' he insisted in a dying voice, before adding: 'It is him, it's Logrid, I'm certain of it. He wants to take revenge on all those who defeated the Empire, all the ones who switched sides. It can't be anything else.'

He opened the door.

'I'm sorry ...' he said.

'Why?'

'For you. You and me. How ironic ... I was always so good at sowing death ...'

He left the room and as he closed the door behind, he concluded hoarsely:

'... but I was never able to sow life.'

8

KAPERNEVIC

Let's see ... you called me Wader, didn't you?
Why don't I return the favour?
As you seem to like these wriggling beasties ...
You will be ... Frog.
I shall call you Frog ...

Each step cost him, each movement revived the pain in his head, like the din of some ferocious battle whose echo refused to die. He walked, doing the best he could to remain dignified, but his balance was so precarious that he had to keep to the walls and use them for intermittent support.

'Are you going to manage all right?' asked Viola.

In the street full of life and noise she was like a shining beacon, luminous, reassuring ... her sweet face framed by those two dangling locks of flamboyant red hair, brushing against her cheeks. And the scent of lavender which floated around her soothed him. Masalia's light-coloured walls were a torment to his eyes, reflecting the raw sunlight. He squinted, grumbling.

'I'll be fine ... I'll be fine ...'

'We've not far to go now,' she said to encourage him.

He leaned against a façade, livid, cursing his drinking habit. Why did he have to drink so much? The image of a tankard came into his mind, as if gulping its contents were the solution he needed to relieve his pain. He looked down. His right hand was shaking ...

'Make way! Make way!' a voice bawled.

People cleared a path as a squad of guards came into view. It was the fourth such squad they had encountered since leaving Mildrel's house. They always marched at the same pace, their feet striking the muddy ground, the tips of their spears sparkling above their helmets. They'd never been used. These soldiers had surely never been in combat but they marched, puffed up with pride... *Pathetic*, he thought.

'It's the assassination of the Marquis of Enain-Cassart,' Viola explained. 'Since yesterday afternoon, they've been searching the city for the assassin.'

'Ha ...' murmured Dun-Cadal. 'Good luck to them ...'

They passed before an old church with its doors opened wide. On the front porch stood four men in black monks' robes, their heads shaven. In the shade provided by the bell tower, they were reciting holy words in unison, holding a book open with their hands. Dun-Cadal recognised excerpts from the *Liaber Moralis*, one of the major texts of the Order of Fangol. He halted with a thoughtful air. How many times had he heard the monks' sermons? Could he still remember everything they decreed to be good or evil? They were chanting almost, with fervour, attracting a few groups of onlookers. There had once been a time when hundreds attended their services, but faith had vanished as other religions came to the fore. The Nâaga cult, venerating serpents, was tolerated again, as was that of the Sudies Islands, which named their gods. Worse still, there were rumours going around of a 'child of the waters', a messiah who would one day come to purify the earth. Dun-Cadal had grown up in the shadow of the *Liaber Dest*, in which the destiny of men was transcribed, thereby making it immutable. He had learned about good and evil through the *Liaber Moralis* and respect for the gods from the *Liaber Deis* ... Did the Republic still listen to the Order of Fangol in Emeris, or had it forgotten how hard the monks had struggled to create a just society?

'We need to hurry, Dun-Cadal,' said Viola as she stepped around him.

She resumed walking, the hood of her cape flapping on her shoulders. Everywhere, in the streets as in the squares, there was an astonishing mix of people the like of which would never have been permitted by the Empire. The poor crossed paths with the rich, Nâaga walked past without exciting comment, ladies dressed in beautiful, colourful gowns extended hands to well-trimmed young burghers. Even if they only exchanged few words, all of them had the possibility of speaking to one another, complimenting one another, or insulting one another. Order had been replaced with a nameless chaos, bathed in a constant jumble of foreign languages and odours, sometimes pleasant and sometimes not. It was thus upon this soft muck that the Republic proposed to set its foundations, a far cry from the strong, hard cement of the Empire. This world really was no longer his.

'So this is your ... Republic,' snarled Dun-Cadal, his lips twisted in disgust.

All this mixing, the scorn towards the Fangolin monks, the forgetfulness ... this was why he had closed his eyes against it for so long.

'Here we are,' said Viola, not deigning to respond to his comment.

They had reached a large square surrounded by imposing buildings. Upon the pediment of one, he saw the wolves' heads, displayed as if springing forward with open jaws. The building's façade displayed the ostentation typical of the reign of the Caglieri kings, who likened themselves to savage beasts hunting in packs. For three centuries, shortly before the advent of the Reyes, they had carried out a policy of conquest, invading kingdom after kingdom, all the way to the distant Sudies. They had established the roots of the Empire, until one of them finally declared himself Emperor. He was the only member of the Caglieri dynasty to bear the title. The last wolf had died alone.

A wide stairway led to a pair of doors guarded by four taciturn halberdiers. Without slowing, Dun-Cadal marched ahead of the young woman.

'Hey ... wait!' she said.

His step was quick and firm despite his fatigue. His headache was fading. He halted abruptly, looking over his shoulder.

'You wanted me to see Negus, didn't you?'

'They won't let you pass,' she said as she hurried to join him.

She was probably right. Negus had been his closest friend ... Was that still the case, now that he served those they had fought together? As soon as he arrived on the front porch, the halberds came down in front of his chest with a sharp click.

'We've come to see Councillor Negus,' Viola hastened to announce in a trembling voice. 'We request an audience with him.'

'No visits are permitted,' one of the guards said tersely.

Since the assassination, the orders were clear. No one was allowed to approach the Republic's councillors before the great festivities on Masque Night. Viola interposed herself between Dun-Cadal and the halberdiers, her hands raised in the air.

'I beg you to excuse my friend for the sudden manner of this arrival, but—'

'Tell Negus that an old friend wants to see him,' Dun-Cadal interjected. 'Tell him it's the man he believed dead in the Saltmarsh.'

And seeing the guards' reluctance, he added: 'He'll understand.'

Then, with a wave of his hand, he invited them to open the doors. After a brief moment of hesitation, one of the guards went into the building and came back out a good ten minutes later. He admitted them without saying a word, and led them to a large hall with wide windows made of red- and gold-tinted glass. The sunlight passing through them formed peculiar oblique beams that landed on the golden brown tiles. Two rows of columns formed an honour guard that led to the feet of twin staircases framing a wide oak door.

'Wait here,' ordered the guard, pointing to a series of benches beneath the windows. 'Councillor Negus will receive you in a few moments.'

Four soldiers descended the stairs with a measured step and took up position to either side of the door, their hands resting on the pommels of their swords. Were the pair of them really worth all these precautions? An old man with tired eyes and a young woman whose gaze shone innocently behind her fragile spectacles? Viola looked at one of the benches and slowly went over to take a seat. She was pretending to be calm, Dun-Cadal realised. She opened and closed her fists upon her thighs, as if trying to soothe her apprehension. He joined her, leaning back against a column with his arms crossed.

'How's your headache?' Viola enquired.

The stained glass gave the sunlight a golden gleam.

'It will pass,' he replied, raising his eyes to the big windows behind her.

'Did I ... say too much?' he wondered in a low voice, looking distracted.

He met her gaze, anxious to read the answer there before she uttered the first word.

'Not enough to suit me,' she answered with a faint smile on her lips. 'If you're afraid you told me where you left Eraëd, I can assure you that you failed to mention it. You spoke of Frog. Of the battle at the foot of the Vershan mountains.'

He nodded, pensive.

'You love him, don't you?'

He went still now, his eyes half-closed.

'Frog,' Viola specified. 'What became of him? There's nothing in the history books about him. And yet you seem to consider him a great knight.'

His face hardened.

'You don't need to be in history books to exist, girl,' he said angrily.

'That's not what I was trying to say,' she protested.

'Then what? You know nothing about him.'

He drew away from the column, looking ready to leap at her. On the bench, Viola shrank back against the wall in a panicked reflex. He leaned forward, his breath still smelling of alcohol.

'Nothing,' he repeated. 'You don't know anything about him. He was the best among us, the purest. The monks should have written of his great deeds. He would have been the greatest if ... He would have ...'

He suddenly faltered, his gaze turning misty and vague, before he slowly straightened up, clutching his belt.

'The Empire would still stand,' he said finally. 'All on his own, he could have defended it. In my time he was renowned, you know. But I suppose it's not in good taste to remember that under the Republic. He was renowned and respected. Have you ever heard of the Dragon of Kapernevic?

'The last red dragon?'

Dun-Cadal nodded, looking away.

'The greatest dragon in the North,' Viola added as if reciting a lesson. 'It terrorised the region for years until—'

'Until we arrived,' revealed Dun-Cadal. 'Most dragons are stupid beasts, often frightened by the approach of men. It's easy to fool them. Sometimes they even forget they can fly, which just goes to show. But the red ones, well they're ... big, rare ... and extremely violent. We were at Kapernevic. We were there. And Negus too. It was the last time I saw him.'

The creaking of a door could be heard. They turned the heads towards the far end of the hall and saw a small pudgy man dressed in an ample white toga with a green-and-gold cloth draped over his shoulder. He exchanged a few words with the guards and looked towards the visitors who had requested to see him.

'And ...?' asked Viola in a low voice.

'If there is no longer a red dragon at Kapernevic, it's thanks to Frog. And to him alone,' Dun-Cadal murmured without expanding further.

And with a brusque movement, he stepped around the column to advance towards the small man. Viola got up from the bench to follow him, her hands suddenly very damp.

'Negus!' boomed Dun-Cadal in an unfriendly tone.

'Councillor Negus,' corrected the small man as he walked forward to meet them.

'To me you will always be Anselme Nagolé Egos, also known as Negus ...'

The two men stood facing one another. There was at least two heads' difference in their heights but, although Dun-Cadal was glowering down at him, Negus did not appear intimidated. He challenged his former comrade with a certain arrogance in his bearing, one arm folded against his belly, his thumb slowly rubbing the inside of his palm.

'At Kapernevic. That was the last time I saw him.'

'It's been a long time,' remarked the councillor without betraying the slightest emotion. 'My old friend ...'

They remained thus, looking at one another, not saying anything further. And the worn features of their faces began to soften as heartfelt smiles crept upon their lips.

'At Kapernevic.'

'Too long,' murmured Negus, presenting an open hand.

Dun-Cadal looked down at the outstretched hand.

He proffered his own.

'Kapernevic ...'

... a hand with red fingers; thick blood ran in his veins to counter the region's biting cold.

He pushed back a branch to get a better look at the landscape below, a valley covered with pines and traversed by an icy river. Among the boughs of the trees he caught glimpses of the thatched roofs of the village of Kapernevic and its wooden watchtowers. When he released the branch, it snapped back like a whip, shedding the white coating that clung to its needles. The crunch of snow beneath his feet did not disturb the lad behind him.

'Have you finished?' groused Dun-Cadal.

Near the horses hitched to the trunk of a pine, Frog was slowly swaying back and forth, throwing his arms forward as he exhaled. A furrow immediately ran across the ground to end at the foot of a tree. At every halt, every time they pitched camp, every free moment, he practised, sparing no effort. Little by little, he was learning to use the *animus* without suffering for it. Although his lungs still stung after each attempt, the pain had become bearable.

They were both wearing ample black cloaks edged in fur and padded black boots to protect their feet from the northern cold.

Three years had passed since the Saltmarsh and the war continued, a string of victories and defeats that granted them little respite. On three occasions, they had returned to Emeris. Each time Frog had failed to meet the Emperor. However, although Frog had not witnessed the fact, Dun-Cadal had never ceased to sing his praises. As a result, Asham Ivani Reyes was following the progress of the general's apprentice with interest, even raising the prospect that Frog might be dubbed in his presence. For an orphan to become a knight was rare enough in itself, but for the Emperor to deign to honour him personally was unheard of. Only a few noblemen had enjoyed the privilege of having the Emperor attend their oath-taking, the last being Etienne Azdeki. The general had never said as much to Frog, no doubt for modesty's sake or to preserve his aura as mentor, but he was proud of the lad. Not a day went by without his performing his exercises, sometimes coming close to passing out. Nor did he speak of the pain. He continued to wait until his master was either asleep or absent to test his limits and each time, push them further. For modesty's sake, no doubt …

'Stop that,' ordered Dun-Cadal. 'A child like you will only do himself harm.'

'A child like me could knock you off your feet, Wader,' retorted Frog with a grin, rolling his shoulders to get the kinks out.

His face was more seasoned, his jaw squarer, his features sharper. Little by little, the man in him was becoming defined. A nascent goatee ringed his lips. Dun-Cadal noted it with amusement. Someday soon he would have to teach him to shave properly.

'Really? I wouldn't bet on it if I were you.'

'No, because if you were me, you would be years younger. And who was it who fought the rouargs in the Saltmarsh? Not you in any case. You were asleep underneath your horse.'

Dun-Cadal smiled as he nodded his head, putting on thick leather gloves. He enjoyed the gentle warmth wrapping his fingers and seized his horse's reins, putting one foot in the stirrup.

'Now you're bragging, Frog.'

'I'm just applying your lessons,' the lad protested as he imitated his mentor.

'I didn't teach you be a braggart.'

The pair mounted their steeds and set off at a trot down a small path, barely visible in the snow. Here and there the earth was churned up into muck, but otherwise a smooth white coat stretched off between the trees. Silence reigned, disturbed only slightly by the horses' hooves.

'That's because you don't take into account the lessons I absorb from observing you.'

'Flattery, is it now?' laughed Dun-Cadal. 'Are you afraid that I'll kick your arse once we reach Kapernevic, to be complimenting me so?'

'Why have they sent us here?' the boy complained suddenly, drawing up his fur-edged hood to protect himself from the cold. 'All the real action of the war is happening in the South.'

'You're not enjoying the countryside?'

'You're a general, Wader,' Frog said indignantly. 'And we've proved our valour many times, haven't we? So why have they sent us to seek out this ... this alchemist?'

'Perhaps the Emperor thought it was time to cool your ardour,' mocked Dun-Cadal.

Frog had grown up in many ways but he still tended to talk back to the general. Showing more restraint than before, to be sure, even giving matters some thought before responding. But his anger remained intact. 'Ardour' was a very feeble word for it, in fact. He was sixteen years old and sometimes behaved like a child, sometimes like a man. The day would soon come when maturity finally prevailed.

They crossed the snowy woods, descending to the valley, galloping through clearings covered by a heavy white blanket. They passed by several wagons carrying dull-eyed women and children who were fleeing the region. But where would they go? No lands were spared from the crackling flames; no valley, field, or road was safe from bloodshed any more. The war was everywhere.

They reached Kapernevic beneath a pale sky. Its wooden houses rose on the banks of the icy river, hemmed in by two conifer forests. The stone chimneys exhaled wisps of grey smoke that dispersed towards the four corners of the village, flying over the watchtowers before dying above the surrounding trees. The villagers who had decided to remain here, or who simply could not afford to abandon the little they possessed, were bundled up in thick patched clothing. They wandered about like phantoms with livid faces and dark rings under their eyes. On the porch of a dilapidated house a woman sat, holding in her arms a little girl who looked barely five years old. Among the filth that spattered the child's hair Frog could make out a few blond locks, like a vestige of happier times. Her eyes followed him without expression. She watched him blankly from the cradle of her mother's arms. Life seemed to have deserted them all.

It was beneath the impassive gaze of these poor people that the riders entered the village, advancing at a walk. Some soldiers escorted them to a watchtower on the far side of the settlement that looked out towards the tree-covered hills to the north. Not a word, not a murmur greeted their arrival. Until the chilling silence was broken by a laugh. Descending from the tower's ladder, a round man was almost choking with joy. Clad in heavy dented armour, an animal's hide thrown over his shoulders, he rubbed at his face with pudgy fingers, looking as though he could not believe his eyes.

'They told me someone would come for the inventor but I was a thousand leagues from thinking it would be you,' he confessed between two chuckles. 'You ...'

He pointed a finger at the general who was dismounting.

'You, here!' he exclaimed, spreading his arms wide. 'My old friend!'

'They should have sent you to the South instead! Has the cold in these parts given you an ever bigger appetite?' Dun-Cadal jested, before the two men fell into one another's arms. 'But I thought we were supposed to be escorting an alchemist?'

'Alchemist, inventor, he's a little of this and that, my friend.'

Frog got down from his horse, allowing one of the soldiers to lead the mounts to a drinking trough. Some villagers passing by the watchtower stopped to observe them with a haggard air. In contrast to all of them, soldiers included, the general and his pupil were wearing handsome kit that appeared to have never seen battle. Frog eyed the spectators with a wary gaze, a thumb in his belt and his fingers grazing the pommel of his sword. Wrenching himself from the embrace of his comrade in arms, Dun-Cadal glanced over at the lad. He was on his guard, as if this were enemy territory. What was making him so edgy? These poor ragged buggers? He read an expression it saddened him to see on his pupil's face ... contempt. Frog felt contempt for these people. His education was far from being complete ...

'Frog,' he hailed. 'Come here.'

'He's grown up,' Negus murmured.

'He hasn't become much wiser, though,' Dun-Cadal said before raising his voice once Frog had joined them. 'Do you remember Negus? From Garmaret?'

Without saying a word, the boy nodded before bowing slightly. Their first stop once they left the Saltmarsh behind had been the fort at Garmaret, then under the command of General Negus. Of course he remembered. Dun-Cadal had spotted him talking to a girl, a refugee from the Saltmarsh, and with his keen eye had understood that he was attracted to her. But now Frog remained unsmiling, displaying only the politeness owed to a general. Negus's face darkened.

'I've heard a lot about you,' he said. 'You've changed a great deal since we met at Garmaret.'

'As have you, since you lost that town,' Frog replied bluntly.

In the shadow of his hood, his grey eyes shone with a piercing light, looking straight at the dumbfounded little general. Time stretched between them, as though the boy's reply left them both stunned. Before Dun-Cadal could give voice to his indignation, Negus let out a breath of stupefaction. Then he tilted his head back to look at the sky and laughed loudly, striking his bulging belly.

'No doubt about it,' he chuckled. 'You are indeed his mentor!'

'He sometimes forgets who he's talking to,' Dun-Cadal fumed, giving the lad a black look.

But Frog did not seem to care.

Negus immediately calmed his comrade's wrath with a friendly pat on the shoulder.

'Bah ... he's right,' conceded Negus with a sweep of the hand. 'I lost Garmaret. But who could have held it, faced with the scale of the revolt?'

Dun-Cadal feared that a voice would pipe up to claim that he, Frog, would have done so, but the boy remained quiet. He had to be aware of his mentor's embarrassment. He nevertheless gave the general an amused glance full of mischief and provocation. Dun-Cadal stiffened, his fists balled, ready to deliver a reprimand. But deep down he'd grown fond of the lad's spiritedness. In other circumstances, facing people he disliked, he would have been entertained by such impudence.

'I didn't think the Emperor would send you here,' Negus remarked. 'Especially for mere escort duty. Is this inventor really so important?'

The scowl on his round face left little doubt as to his low opinion of the man.

'The inventor himself? I don't know. But the nobleman at court who requested his repatriation surely is, yes.'

'Bah,' Negus murmured. 'If the Emperor granted the request and assigned you to this mission, then he must have deemed it important too. And to tell you the truth, it suits me. A few more days and I would have skewered him.'

Dun-Cadal raised his eyebrows in puzzlement. Negus looked around the village, studying the houses.

'Aladzio! Aladzio!' he called out. 'Where is the blockhead? Aladzio!'

When a slender figure appeared around the bend in a street, a tricorne jammed on his head, Negus beckoned him to hurry.

'Aladzio! Get over here!'

'I'm coming, General, I'm coming,' the young man answered breathlessly. 'Just give me time to ... Oops!'

In his haste, he dropped four long parchment scrolls he'd been carrying under his arm. He bent down to pick them up, but in doing so he let slip some books he had been hugging to his chest with his other arm. On his knees in the snow, huffing, he tried to gather all of it up again. His breaths formed little clouds in the cold air, coming faster as his anxiety grew.

'Him? A genius?' sneered Negus. 'Three months he's been out here, studying I-don't-know-what kind of stone and the only thing he's achieved is to set fire to a barn.'

'An accident?' Dun-Cadal suggested.

'Three times in a row?'

Dun-Cadal held back a laugh, crossing his arms.

'I don't know which nobleman values this good-for-nothing so highly, but if he's planning to burn down his apartments he's found the right man for the job,' added the little general before shouting again: 'Aladzio! They're just bits of paper, let them rot in the snow!'

'Let them rot?' objected the alchemist, clumsily scooping up his scrolls. 'Works hand-copied by the scribes in their monasteries? You have no idea, General, of the sum of knowledge contained in these bits of paper, as you put it. The Order of Fangol would be appalled if I damaged these scrolls.'

And, shivering in his long grey cloak, he shuffled forward with tiny steps. When he arrived at the foot of the watchtower Frog barred his way, tapping the pommel of his sword. The alchemist looked to be about twenty-five years old, with a pale face and rings under his eyes. His high cheekbones were reddened by the cold and his hair tumbled out from beneath his jet-black tricorne to fall in curls to the nape of his neck. His cloak was spattered with odd stains, either the result of his experiments or simply dirt, it was difficult to say. Licking his thin chapped lips, he repressed a nervous giggle, stepped around Frog and presented himself to the two generals, looking highly embarrassed.

'A thousand pardons, I— I've found some ... some ... yes, some finds, I would say,' he stammered. 'Some stones in the mines near ... over there, the mines ...'

Crushing the parchments against his chest, he managed to free one of his arms to extend it towards the woods before the watchtower.

'The territory of Stromdag's men,' Negus explained, raising his eyes towards his friend. 'He's the one leading the revolt in Kaperdae, Krapen and the area surrounding us here in Kapernevic. The miners have joined him. He promised them their freedom.'

'The mines,' repeated Aladzio in a dreamy tone. 'There are plenty of finds there.'

His face lit up with a wide grin, almost like that of a half-wit.

'Just the idea, it's like ...' He hunted for the right words and then, leaning forward slightly, said in a confidential tone: 'It's like the kiss of a woman on your ... I mean ...'

Dun-Cadal looked away, both amused and shocked. Who had taken such an interest in this man that they must fetch him from this distant region of the Empire? Ignoring Aladzio, the general turned to his friend.

'Stromdag?' he asked. 'I can't stay long, but what's the situation here?'

'Oh, there's not much to be said,' Negus sighed.

Advancing towards the pillars of the watchtower, Dun-Cadal raised his voice.

'Frog, go with Aladzio to the inn and see about our chambers.'

'But ...' the boy whined.

Dun-Cadal barely turned his head. His tone was enough to quash any further insolence.

'Take care of Aladzio and don't argue. We'll be leaving at dawn tomorrow.'

He exchanged a smile with Negus upon hearing the lad mutter in discontent.

'Come here,' Frog said to the inventor in an icy tone.

And the pair of them went back up the village main street, heading in the direction of the inn. Aladzio almost trotted to keep up with the boy, taking care not to drop his precious scrolls.

A few soldiers passed by the watchtower, looking wan and tired. Their armour was tarnished and bore numerous nicks, while beneath it pieces of their chain mail hung down like tatters of old cloth.

'Stromdag,' sighed Dun-Cadal. 'Who's he?'

'He started off as a common thief,' Negus replied. 'A sort of bandit with a big heart, in the eyes of the peasants in these parts.'

He began to climb the ladder leading to the tower's summit, inviting his friend to follow him, and as he climbed he continued his account:

'A little over a year ago he became the leader of the revolt here in the North. The general in command at the time managed to push him back as far as Kaperdae, but it cost him his life.'

'And in this cold the rebels are still holding their positions?' enquired Dun-Cadal.

Negus reached the top of the tower and used the parapet to hoist himself into the lookout post. Some heavy logs tied to one another with braided ropes provided a thick platform protected by planks. Wooden poles rose from each of the four corners to support a sloping roof. Two guards paced back and forth keeping watch on the horizon, bows in their hands. A third guard was seated near an old sack and was whittling the tip of arrow with a big knife. Upon seeing Negus arrive he stood up as if caught doing something he shouldn't. Without saying a word Negus waved him away with a scowl. The man drew back and let them approach the parapet. Their hands resting on the edge, the two generals contemplated the forested expanse covered in a thin white blanket which stretched out below them. The horizon merged with the blindingly white sky.

'That's their territory,' Negus commented grimly. 'They know every nook and cranny in these woods, all the way to the mountains a little further north. They're at home out there.'

'Just like in the Saltmarsh,' acknowledged Dun-Cadal.

'In the Saltmarsh they sent the rouargs against us. Here they promise freedom to the miners ... and stir up the dragons ...'

These lands belonged to the Empire, but what general could claim to know them completely? Most of them had grown up in Emeris and when, like Dun-Cadal, they hailed from elsewhere, they had usually spent their youth cooped up in a castle. The war continued, quite simply, because the bonds joining them to the people had been broken. And the Emperor himself was unaware of the fact. For the first time, in all the fighting Dun-Cadal had known, he had the strange feeling that the Empire was really crumbling.

'Do you see that basin over there?' asked Negus, pointing his finger at a spot in the distance.

In spite of the trees covering it all the way to the foothills of the mountains, Dun-Cadal could make out the form of a valley.

'That's the only reason we haven't been defeated yet,' admitted Negus. 'The dragons are hemmed in by the forest. They don't try to fly over it to attack Kapernevic. You see? They simply charge into the trees, once Stromdag has drawn them out of their lair. It's the only reason we're still holding on here.'

'Animals,' groused Dun-Cadal. 'Just animals ...'

He knew that dragons were almost as dumb as sheep, but to that extent? The advantage they gave the rebels might turn out to be a weakness, after all.

'Animals, certainly, but ones that can tear our men to pieces, even when they remain on the ground,' Negus replied. 'Imagine what will happen the day one of them decides to fly over to this side of the valley ... So far, they've kept to the mountains.'

'There's nothing to worry about,' Dun-Cadal assured him. 'It's always the same with these dragons. You herd them into a corridor, under an open sky, and they'll follow it like stupid rats. Things never change, Negus.'

'Yes they do,' Negus said in a whisper, his eyes lowered. 'Some things do change.'

He drew in a deep breath before saying, as if it were a dead weight he wanted to be finally rid of:

'Nothing will ever be the same as before. This war has gone on for too long. You've just come from Emeris ... haven't you felt it?'

'Felt what ...?'

'The vipers' nest, my friend. The Emperor is receiving poor advice. Uster's son, Laerte, is still at large. He's embarked on a campaign near Eole, word has it. But although we know there's a revolt there, nobody can confirm that he's the one leading it. He seems to be everywhere at once, at the head of every rebellion that breaks out. They arrested rebels at Serray, you know. They were interrogated. They captured some others around Brenin. All of them said that Laerte was there, but none of them could say what he looks like. The man is so completely disembodied he's become merely a rumour. And do you know happens to rumours? They collect at the Imperial palace. Rebellion is brewing there too ... People fear most the things they can't see. Certain noblemen have already rallied to Laerte's cause. The ideas Oratio of Uster was peddling are becoming attractive. We made a martyr of him when we hung him. Laerte has realised this: he's waging a political war, through accusations and hearsay ... That's what's going on in Emeris. A war using no weapons but words.'

Standing with his forearms on the parapet, Dun-Cadal let his gaze drift over the strangely silent landscape. How peaceful Kaper-nevic seemed. The distant trees swayed gently, caressed by a slight breeze.

'Are there any suspects?' Dun-Cadal asked grimly.

The very idea that Emeris might be infested with traitors was un-bearable. The palace was his refuge, his lair ... his heart. He had protected the Emperor in inadmissible ways before later serving him as honourably as possible. And now the perfect world he had built for himself was tottering like some poorly made tower ... as rickety as the wooden watchtower on which he now stood.

'There are rumours about noblemen from families close to the Saltmarsh. The counties of Asher and Rubegond, the duchy of

Erinbourg, not to mention refugees from the Saltmarsh itself ... certain ones in particular.'

Fight. Strike. Attack. That was familiar ground for Dun-Cadal. But the struggle for influence in high places was totally foreign to him. He felt himself at a loss. On edge, he slowly straightened up.

'What are your plans for countering Stromdag?' he asked.

He might as well stick to discussing things he'd mastered.

'My friend ...'

Negus placed a hand on his forearm, looking sorrowful.

'The Emperor is wary of refugees from the Saltmarsh who are now in Emeris. Don't you understand?'

Dun-Cadal took a deep breath. Yes ... he understood. He had fully grasped the inference, but he refused to take it seriously. With a quick motion, he shook Negus's hand from his arm and left the parapet.

'Dun-Cadal,' called Negus.

'He has no need to be suspicious of Frog! No more of him than anyone else,' the general said coldly without turning round.

He prepared to descend the ladder, placing a foot on the first rung.

'Listen to me!' implored Negus as he joined him with an urgent step.

'He won't betray the Empire!' Dun-Cadal said angrily.

'Perhaps not, but be on your guard,' Negus advised. 'Some of those close to the Emperor think he is dangerous.'

Seeing his friend's stricken expression, Dun-Cadal responded with a savage smile. Frog was only a boy, yet the guileful advisers who were poisoning his Emperor with their vile words were afraid of him. There at least was one point all could agree upon.

'*They* have reason to be frightened of him.'

The idea pleased him. He knew nothing of politics and had no particular liking for the games of power. All that mattered to him was the respect earned by deeds, not empty words. Frog had risked his life so many times fighting the rebellion that to imagine, for a single instant, he could be accused of sedition was intolerable.

During the rest of that day, as he and Negus inspected the troops, Dun-Cadal kept thinking about what awaited them in Emeris. Although he was close to the Emperor, did he carry enough weight to defend his pupil if ...? No, it was inconceivable.

When he joined Frog again in the cosy warmth of the inn he was still not reassured. The lad held a small wooden horse in his hands. Dun-Cadal had seen him contemplating this particular object before, a child's toy he must have picked up on the road from the Saltmarsh. He brought it out on the eve of each battle they fought. The fact that he was holding it now did not augur well.

'The troops look tired, don't they?' Frog said as his mentor sat down at his table. A fire crackled with bright red flames in the inn's wide hearth. They danced above the logs, revelling in their wavelike movement, spreading a saving warmth throughout the room. All around them soldiers were making the best of their meagre hot meal. At the counter, some of them were getting drunk in silence, gazing blankly into space. A feeling of great lassitude reigned, as if the cold here at Kapernevic had frozen every desire.

'Weren't we the same at the foot of the Vershan mountains?' Dun-Cadal said lightly as he clasped his hands together on the table. 'Or at Bredelet after three weeks of fighting? You'd wear the same look if you'd been here as long as they have, believe me.'

'That's possible,' agreed Frog, looking down at his plate.

The remains of his meal rimmed the porcelain. With a nonchalant gesture he seized his steaming tankard and drank a mouthful. The scent of it reached the general's nostrils and he recognised the smell of hot berry juice with distaste. Too sweet for him. Out of the corner of his eye he caught sight of a serving wench with an impressive bosom filling a jug from the spout of a barrel. He beckoned to her and then brought his attention back to his pupil. He seemed troubled.

'Where's Aladzio?'

'He went back to the house he's been occupying to pack his bags. Is it true we're leaving tomorrow?'

'We have a mission. We're under orders to accompany this inventor back to Emeris. He's too much at risk here and there are important people worried about his safety.'

'I'd like to give him a thump,' Frog declared flatly.

Dun-Cadal bit back a chuckle.

'Don't laugh, Wader,' Frog said, looking aggrieved. 'All he does is blather ... words, words, words. He's more at risk spending ten minutes with me than he is staying here for the duration of the war.'

'Come now,' the general sighed. 'You'll get used to it. The trip won't last that long. And that's not what's bothering you. Out with it.'

Frog hesitated.

'Are we going to leave all these people here?' he asked.

'Negus is protecting them.'

'I heard talk of dragons ... of a red dragon, in particular. It seems it's the worst sort of beast in the entire world, attacking whole villages and not leaving any survivors.'

'So that's it,' smiled Dun-Cadal.

The lad wanted to slay dragons. He was longing to fight, to act, to do something concrete. Rather than serve as guard to a blithering inventor.

'Dragons are stupid beasts.'

'Not the red ones—'

'They're a little smarter, I'll grant you that ... bigger, crueller, and it takes a certain knack to kill one, but they're just beasts. Beasts that only attack men out of necessity.'

'The Nâaga don't say that. According to them, dragons are more than just beasts, they're the ancient ones.'

The fact that his apprentice was taking the Nâaga seriously did not please Dun-Cadal at all. Those savages worshipped anything covered with scales, arguing that they were the ancestors of men. To them, dragons were worthy of respect.

'Where did you hear that twaddle?'

Frog scowled.

'The Nâaga are brutes,' growled Dun-Cadal. 'They believe in the power of dragons, but they also believe they can acquire other men's strength by eating the prisoners of their tribal wars. They're ... beasts, just like the dragons, Frog. Remember that. And anyway, this dragon is not our business. It's only stirred up because it's caught between Stromdag and us. The day this war comes to an end it will go back to its lair, believe me. Has it attacked Kapernevic? No, never. People are talking about it because it's ... folklore. It's dangerous because there's a war going on. And we can't stay here, you know that.'

'Why not?' Frog exclaimed. 'You're a general. And I know how to fight. We've won battles together.'

'We've also lost some.'

'Not many! Between the two of us, we've changed the course of this war many times!'

'Is it because of these people that you want to stay and fight?'

'You don't understand anything,' muttered Frog, looking downcast.

The serving wench came to their table at last, depositing a tankard in front of Dun-Cadal which she immediately filled with a tilt of the jug. He gestured to her to leave everything. A single glass would not be enough. She immediately began to clear away the boy's place, bending slightly forward at his eye level. His gaze was inevitably attracted by her corset and then moved upward to her vertiginous cleavage before fixing on the smooth skin of her bosom. Dun-Cadal bowed his head, one hand over his mouth to hide his smile.

Frog was truly no longer a child. When the wench left the table, carrying away the boy's plate, Dun-Cadal broke the silence.

'On the side, just there,' he jested, pointing to a corner of his lips.

'What?'

'You're dribbling.'

The lad did not appreciate the joke, having naively almost wiped at his mouth. Looking piqued, he shook his head as he put the small wooden horse back into the pocket of his leather jacket.

'This girl . . . the one you see in Emeris,' said Dun-Cadal, gradually becoming serious again, 'you love her, don't you?'

Frog looked him in the eye for a moment and then drained his tankard in a single gulp.

'Come now, word gets around. Word always gets around in Emeris,' his mentor assured him in an amused tone. 'She's the same girl you found at Garmaret after our escape, isn't she? She's from the Saltmarsh too. Did you know her from before?'

'That's none of your business,' the boy replied brusquely, getting up from the table.

He crossed the inn and went out with a violent shove of the door. Dun-Cadal remained seated, pensive, his hands surrounding his tankard. He raised it to his lips and drank the entire contents. The wine ran down his throat, its pungency spreading a gentle warmth through his veins. He put the tankard back down, hesitated over whether to serve himself another drink before he went outside in his turn. He found Frog on the front porch leaning against the façade with his arms crossed and his hood pulled over his head.

Dun-Cadal paused before descending the steps and tramping across the snow with a crunching sound. The moon was full and lu-minous, sailing high in the sky. The entire village was tinted blue in the quiet night. On top of the closest watchtower, two guards looked out beneath the light of a wavering torch.

'I remember the first time I was in love,' he said as if speaking to himself. 'I was barely older than you are now. I remember the desire, the longing ...'

He turned round to look at Frog.

'How is it possible that a feeling can give you such an ache in the belly?' he asked lightly.

But the lad's expression remained stony. What was the general hoping for? That the boy's tongue would suddenly loosen and he would reveal all? That he'd reassure Dun-Cadal? Perhaps Negus was right after all, there were traitors scheming in Emeris ... and a young refugee girl from the Saltmarsh was using Frog, in his innocence. Supposing that an apprentice knight could still be innocent.

'Tomorrow ... we'll help Negus launch his assault against Strom-dag's rebels,' he decided.

Frog gradually separated himself from the wall, letting his arms fall, mute with astonishment. How could he possibly imagine the real reason for this change of heart? Dun-Cadal knew the lad was at far less risk out here, fighting visible enemies, than he would be in the vipers' nest in Emeris. As for Aladzio ... well he would survive a day or two more. A cry rose in the distance, a sort of harsh scream.

'Have you ever seen dragons before?' Dun-Cadal asked quietly, looking thoughtful.

And above the forests miles away four black shapes climbed into the sky in a great spiralling ascent. Their wings spread and their long necks became more distinct in the moonlight. The dragons were waking in the night.

At nightfall the following day they would go hunting for them, and for the men who sought to rouse them against the Empire.

SAVING A LIFE

Will you be a phantom for the rest of your life?
Or will you act like a real general?

Proud columns rose from the black-specked brown marble floor. Around the hall, the tall tinted windows conferred a golden brown hue to the sunlight. At its centre stood the small man with a face marked by age and a head bearing just a few grey locks of hair. Despite his plumpness, his white toga fell in loose folds about him, with a green cloth draped across his shoulder. He was a councillor of the Republic now ... Who would recall that he once led Imperial armies to victory, that he employed the *animus* better than anyone and that he had fought at Dun-Cadal Daermon's side for the last time at Kapernevic?

'I am Viola Aguirre, Councillor Negus,' the young woman introduced herself as she shook the small man's proffered hand. 'Historian at the Great College of Emeris.'

He watched her bow to him, charmed by her grace.

'We're grateful that you could accord us a little of your time, having just arrived here in Masalia. But it's a matter of the utmost importance, which—'

'He's here, Negus,' interrupted Dun-Cadal.

The councillor continued to smile, but his expression suddenly seemed wry.

'And here I was thinking you wanted to rehash old times ...' he murmured as if to himself.

Opposite him, Dun-Cadal appeared worse for wear, with stubble sprouting from his weathered face and his eyes bloodshot from alcohol, giving him a hangdog look. Anyone watching these two men

144

talk would never imagine they had been heroes.

'It concerns the assassination of Councillor Enain-Cassart,' Viola explained. 'We have every reason to believe—'

'Leave us,' ordered Dun-Cadal without taking his eyes from his old friend.

She hesitated, but finally nodded, turned around and went over to one of the benches under the windows.

Alone in the middle of the large hall, the two men stared at one another without any great show of affection. Yet there was a strange gleam in both men's eyes. What they had experienced together could not be forgotten. Which made what they perceived of one another's current state all the more unbearable.

'I thought you were dead,' confessed Negus.

'And I thought you were worthy,' replied Dun-Cadal in a mutter.

He swallowed his anger. Seeing his old comrade thus, wearing the colours of the Republic, revolted him. There must be an explanation for all this.

'Things change, my friend ...'

'This much?' Dun-Cadal asked gravely. 'To the point of forgetting what you fought for and siding with the enemy ...?'

'So you've come to judge me,' Negus said with a sad smile. 'A ghost from the past has come to judge me.'

'No ...' sighed Dun-Cadal

He shook his head and looked down, as if searching for something lying at his feet that would lend him courage.

'No,' he repeated.

Had he changed so much as well? He no longer recognised himself in this listless body that served him as a vessel, sailing from tankard to tankard, from a tavern in the slums to Mildrel's house.

'I was at the port yesterday when Enain-Cassart was killed ...'

Negus was no longer smiling. His normally affable face had become suddenly as hard as that of a statue.

'I saw the man who killed him,' Dun-Cadal continued.

'And who was it?' asked the councillor in a murmur.

At last he was showing signs of emotion, his eyebrows frowning.

'The Hand of the Emperor ...'

There was a brief silence while they eyed one another, unblinking. Dun-Cadal was the first to look away.

'The Hand of the Emperor,' repeated Negus, at last taking stock of the full gravity of the situation. 'And so ... here you are, to warn me?'

'To save your life,' declared Dun-Cadal.

But his face was livid, his eyes vague, his general appearance ... filthy. He was filthy and pitiful to behold. Negus looked him over from head to toe, barely disguising his sorrow.

'You're still living in the past, aren't you? Logrid is dead, Dun-Cadal. Enain-Cassart was killed by a madman, nothing more. The rest does not concern you.'

So that was it. This would go no further; but the old general could not accept being dismissed in this fashion, convinced that he could see what others were doing their best to ignore. Masque Night had been declared a national holiday. The evening festivities, when everyone shed their social rank and donned masks, celebrated the victory of the people over their oppressors. This year, by some quirk of fate, Masalia was playing host to the most important members of the High Council and the presence of an assassin raising the banner of a fallen Empire now was no mere coincidence. As Negus turned to walk back to the door at the rear of the hall, Dun-Cadal tried to reach out to his former comrade in arms.

'Negus, wait!'

He could not even catch hold of the other man's arm. Negus had gained weight over the years, but was nevertheless still nimble. He sidestepped his friend's clutching hand, looking both saddened and scornful. By the door, the guards stiffened in alarm.

'The affairs of this world are no longer your concern, Dun-Cadal! You cannot understand!' Negus exclaimed irritably.

'Understand what? That you've raised yourself from the ashes of what we once defended?' Dun-Cadal said in a trembling voice. 'You were a knight! A general! You took an oath!'

A combination of anger, hurt and disappointment choked him. Was this really his friend before him, wearing that awful toga which reeked of arrogance? Or was he just another opportunistic upstart ...?

'We had beliefs, Negus. The Empire ... the Order of Fangol ...'

'The Lost Book, is that it?' asked Negus, shaking his head. 'And what if we deserved something better than the destiny the gods wrote for us in the *Liaber Dest*? Is this degradation what they foresaw for you? You were great once, Dun-Cadal ... but you were never one for reflection.'

'I know how I lost my grandeur. Tell me what you did with yours!'

'That's what you can't understand,' replied Negus with equal rage. 'See me as a traitor if it pleases you, but as for the grandeur we achieved defending the Reyes dynasty? Tell me what it brought you. Take a good look at yourself and tell me how serving the Empire improved your lot.'

Negus turned away from his friend one last time and stalked off towards the door, but could not resist a parting shot:

'Both then and now, I've always served the people. You've never served anything but your dreams!'

In a daze, Dun-Cadal heard the door slam. He did not react as Viola came up behind him.

'Dun-Cadal?' she called softly. 'Is everything all right"

He gave her a brief glance, reluctantly meeting eyes filled with compassion. He had no need of it. He deserved better than that. Hadn't he once been something more than a drunk haunting the lowest dives in Masalia?

'No ...' he said, glaring balefully at the door on the far side of the hall.

But something was going on behind it. He could sense the air vibrating like a taut piece of string.

'You ...'

'We'll find some other way to convince him,' she said, trying to sound reassuring as a guard approached them.

'You stay ...'

She placed a delicate hand upon his shoulder.

'I've always been able to sense death,' he affirmed with a trembling voice and a tear in the corner of his eye.

Upon joining them, the guard prepared to usher them out of the building.

'Stay close to me, Frog ... Negus, are the traps ready?'

'It's here!' he snarled.

Suddenly, Dun-Cadal seized hold of the guard by the collar and with his other hand reached for the hilt of his sword. Before the man could make the slightest gesture, the general had shoved him to the ground and was unsheathing the blade from its scabbard. He rushed towards the door Negus had just vanished through.

'They'll be here soon ... I can feel it.'

He ran as fast as he could, his heart thumping fit to burst, his skull about to explode. His head was hammering so hard he thought he was boiling inside. His entire body seemed like a piece of old meat: rotten, useless, flaccid … burnt up.

'The dragons …'

'They're coming …'

But still he ran. He ran because the same odd sensation he'd felt at the port the previous day was now prickling at his temples again. He had dodged death so many times that he could sense its presence even before it struck. With a blow of his shoulder he smashed open the wooden door and halted abruptly.

'Are the traps ready, Negus?'

'This might be the last battle we fight side by side, my friend …'

'They're coming …'

Under the starry night sky, their mouths exhaled thick plumes of condensed breath. The cold seized hold of the men, wrapping them tightly and stripping away every degree of heat beneath their frost-covered armour. In the torchlight they held themselves ready, lying prone in the snow at the foot of the trees. Standing at their side, Dun-Cadal gripped the hilt of his sword, the creaking of his leather glove audible in the deep silence.

'I don't hear them,' murmured Frog, stretched out close by him.

'Trust him on this,' advised Negus, leaning against a tree a few paces away.

He gave the lad a wink before lifting the blade of his sword before his face. They had grouped themselves on a small mound in the heart of the woods bordering Kapernevic, hundreds of Imperial soldiers numb from the cold and nervously awaiting the assault. It had been more than an hour since the beaters had left their positions, sneaking through the trees with muffled feet to seek out the rebels' camp. Their mission was simple: simulate a surprise attack, pretend to retreat and draw the enemy army out, certain of its superiority, to the appointed spot. Dun-Cadal had come up with this plan at the last moment, based on Negus's advice and having considered all the alternatives. The dragons' stupidity was the keystone of his plan and the flaw in Stromdag's strategy. Now all that remained was to see the matter through to its conclusion. Curiously, it was due to Aladzio that the idea had occurred to him. It was time to see if it had been a wise choice.

'Hold your positions,' he ordered in a low voice as he knelt at the top of the mound.

In the darkness he could barely make out the movements of the pines. Was it the wind bending their branches? No. There were shadows running in their direction. Dun-Cadal's hunch was panning out. The clatter of their armour as they dashed forward became more distinct and, with it, a drumming sound just behind them. A first voice yelled:

'They're coming!'

A second:

'Get ready!'

Dun-Cadal and Negus exchanged a determined look. This moment would decide the outcome, and it was the only obvious weakness in their strategy. Everything depended on the inventiveness of a man who, so far, had only succeeded in burning down a barn. Frog had not been enthusiastic when the plan was explained to him either. And Negus had thought Dun-Cadal was joking.

'Spearmen!' bellowed Dun-Cadal.

It was no joke. The first line of soldiers readied their spears. Only a few yards ahead of them infantrymen armed with axes calmed their fears and pressed up against the pines. Cords had been wound around the trunks of the conifers. The drumming ... the clatter. The clatter, the drumming.

'They're here!' cried a man leaping out of the darkness.

Ten more beaters followed, gasping for breath. Numerous deafening roars resounded in the night. It was no longer a drumming but an infernal din, a mixture of shattering wood and shifting earth. When the maw of the first dragon became visible in the torchlight, there was not a moment's hesitation.

'Now!' shouted Dun-Cadal as he stood up.

The axes fell upon the ropes, sharp and brutal. It took no more than three blows to sever them, releasing the enormous net lying hidden at the foot of the pines. Studded with metal barbs, the trap sprang from the ground, throwing off the blanket of snow and pine needles that had been concealing it. The dragons had followed their unreasoning fury, rampaging through the forest, and the first of them was stopped dead in its tracks. Its brothers to the left and right suffered the same fate. Despite their instinctive attempts to deploy their twisted wings, beating them vigorously as they roared, their heads were trapped by the thick mesh of rope and metal.

The spearmen charged, screaming as their weapons punctured the leathery hide of the imprisoned creatures. Dun-Cadal completed the assault, planting his sword in the eye of the closest beast. Turning round, he spotted Frog standing motionless, his hand barely gripping his sword. He was gaping at the massive bodies mottled with grey swellings, their long maws bristling with fangs and glistening with drool, their thick nostrils expelling clouds of steam. Dun-Cadal had described them to the lad before the operation began but seeing the beasts before him, struggling to free themselves from the net hampering their movement, was another matter entirely.

'Frog!'

He did not answer. He did not move. He did not even hear the strident howls of the approaching enemy warriors.

'Frog! By the gods, get moving!'

They arrived like a tumultuous flood coming through the pines, of all ages and sizes, mercenaries, soldiers and peasants, skirting around the fallen dragons or climbing over their carcasses to jump into the melee. Their rage was the foam, their bravery the incessant waves. There was an indescribable pandemonium as blades clashed and arms, legs and heads were chopped off, the bodies slumping heavily to the ground, the death cries ripping through the night. The blows found their own rhythm, the roars of the trapped dragons echoing the screams of the wounded. Everywhere there was the same bestiality, the same violence, the same anger ...

Frog parried a stroke and dodged another before thrusting his own blade home. With his free hand, he punched a second assailant in the head.

'Frog! Over there!'

After delivering the coup de grâce to the silhouette facing him, the lad turned to Dun-Cadal, the point of his sword covered in black, sticky blood that ran down in a thin trickle. The general was battling a few feet away from him, for the moment simply warding off blows with the flat of his sword.

'The dragon!' he yelled.

The boy spun round. Ten yards further down the line, one of the beasts had succeeded in tearing apart the netting with great snaps of its jaws, crushing the unfortunate soldiers struggling to restrain it.

Without pause, Frog rushed towards it. The chaos of combat closed behind him.

'Daermon!' boomed Negus, close by him.

Negus' sword slashed into flesh, severed limbs, clashed against other blades with loud rings. At times he stopped to spread his arms, generating a powerful *animus* about him which projected his adversaries several yards backwards. In spite of his weight he demonstrated a certain suppleness, avoiding blows and bending low to plant his sword in an enemy cuirass. No faces stood out from the others, there were only moving shadows. The generals were used to this confusion, a tornado of strangers rushing at them with no names, no history, nothing worth remembering. Their opponents doubtless had a life, a family, their own dreams and fears, but to think of their humanity in the midst of battle, to consider them kindred beings, would be courting death. The gestures of the two commanders were mechanical, simple reflexes at times, the result of years of combat training. Dun-Cadal felled one of the attackers without noticing another behind him. A mercenary brandished his axe and swung it down on the general ...

'Godsfuck!' Dun-Cadal swore as the sound of the sword punching through the rebel's body caused him to spin round.

The man fell to his knees, his face frozen in a stupefied expression. Negus stood behind him, a savage grin twisting lips chapped by the bitter cold. Dun-Cadal let out a sigh of relief.

'I just saved your life, my friend,' Negus remarked proudly, immediately placing himself at his comrade's side.

The snow was nearly covered in blood, like an insult to its purity.

The pine trees bent beneath the struggles of the captive dragons. The black silhouettes of the combatants, dimly lit by the wavering torches, continued to engage in their lethal dance. Dun-Cadal desperately tried to locate the figure of his pupil among them. When he finally spotted him, Frog was clearing a swathe through the rebel ranks, spinning, rolling and leaping as he went. His blade sparkled with a reddish gleam each time he delivered a stroke and he was just a few yards from the big dragon, now busy tearing apart the net, which only restrained it above the shoulders.

'It's the red dragon,' Negus groaned. 'Dun-Cadal! The net won't hold it!'

It was bigger than the others, its muscles bulging beneath bright red scales, two spiral horns jutting out above the yellow eyes with their jet-black slits. Fumes of steam spurted from its nostrils, gracefully entwining in the air. It was an almost hypnotic sight to behold. Its roar halted the boy in his tracks and, with a final bite, the beast succeeded in tearing the net open completely and lifted its head in a circling motion. The mesh had been reinforced with metal barbs, it should have held! But red dragons were so rare and so aggressive that Dun-Cadal had never thought Stromdag capable of driving one towards the Imperial troops. Despite the risk of seeing the beast turn on his own army, the rebel chief had managed to make it his ally.

As it opened its maw wide to inhale, Dun-Cadal felt his friend's arm restrain him.

'Frog!' he yelled.

'Dun-Cadal, no!' Negus bellowed.

In a brusque movement, the red dragon stretched out its neck, its jaws still gaping, to reveal a slender forked tongue. Deep in its throat two pink rolls of flesh contracted and a torrent of fire gushed forth. The hungry flames consumed the men standing closest to it and spread hungrily to the pine trees. The blaze was so sudden that Frog found himself hurled backwards. Stunned, he watched as the beast beat its wings and rose into the air with a rumble.

'Frog! Run!' Dun-Cadal bawled, shoving Negus aside and ready to rush to the aid of his apprentice.

'Dun-Cadal! We need to sound the retreat!'

He spun round abruptly. The crackling flames, the weapons clanging against one another, all of it produced a deafening racket. Negus had to raise his voice to make himself heard over the din.

'We have to retreat!'

'We can't withdraw!'

A few yards away, Frog had regained his feet, still groggy, his gaze tracking the furious beast's immense shadow. It spewed out another tongue of fire before it slipped away over the pines. The screams of the soldiers, trapped in their white-hot armour, almost made him quiver in fear. The human torches flailed about as they were devoured by the flames, throwing themselves down on the snow in the hope of smothering them.

'Frog!' called Dun-Cadal.

Strident cries preceded the miners' arrival. They surged between the trees, armed solely with pickaxes, determined to gouge flesh and break bones with each mighty swing.

'Daermon!'

The two generals were quickly encircled and, back to back, they toiled to hold off the flood of their assailants. The pack closed in on them in waves. Thrust, parry, whirling blades, *animus* ... Miners flew through the air, crashing against the burning pines and then falling heavily upon rocks covered in melting snow ...

Negus ... my friend ...

All was lost. The liberation of the red dragon, which flew over the woods giving long, raucous, threatening cries, had broken their courage. The soldiers of the Empire began to flee.

The weapons continued to flash in the night, parrying, striking and slashing. And the miners were joined by more skilful mercenaries.

How long did the fight last? A few minutes? It seemed to last an eternity. If the two generals fell here, Stromdag would pounce on Kapernevic, stirring up the red dragon's wrath until it burnt everything in its path. No army of the Empire would be able to stop it.

We could have died out there, together ... Perhaps it would have been better if we had laid down our lives, side by side, when we weren't so different from one another.

Until the scream was heard. An inarticulate, powerful, bestial sound. It was a cry of distress that tore the night asunder and disrupted the enemy assault. In the distance, above the tree tops, the silhouette of the red dragon could be seen, beating its wings vigorously, bathed in the light of the full moon. Still high in the sky, it was being dragged down to the ground by some irresistible force. It struggled and shook its head frantically, roaring as it tumbled. Fear switched camps. Panic began to creep into the enemy ranks. The beast bucked and twisted in every direction but could not free itself of the invisible force. It was an awe-inspiring sight to behold. Dun-Cadal and Negus both recognised the nature of the power at work. But never had they witnessed such a demonstration of the *animus*. Could any other knights of the Empire boast of such mastery? It required an unshakeable resolve to risk putting the *animus* to such use. Any loss of control would leave the caster with deep injuries to their entire body, right down to the bone ... All around them, terror spread among the rebels. Already the enemy troops were scattering, dreading the fall of their key weapon.

The red dragon finally vanished from view among the pines. Its impact was marked by the sound of splintering trees followed by a deep thud, not unlike a brief but violent earthquake.

'By all the gods!' Negus whispered.

It was the turning point of the battle. Word of the red dragon's death spread like wildfire and Stromdag's men retreated. Soon there was no sound but the crackling of the flames feeding on the carcasses, the sighs of the survivors and the rattles of the dying. But even after scanning the forest Dun-Cadal could find no trace of his pupil. He checked every corpse lying on the ground, every battered and burnt face, lifting the human remains in a frenzied rage. But Frog was not among them.

'Dun-Cadal,' Negus called, behind him.

Not this body here, nor that one over there ... The only ones left were those of soldiers incinerated when the red dragon had torn itself free of the trap.

'Dun-Cadal!' Negus repeated.

He seized his friend by the shoulder and forced him to stand up.

'He's here,' he announced.

In the clear night, under the flickering light of the flames, Frog came limping forward, his hood covering his head, a trickle of blood at the corner of his mouth. And under his arm, he carried a horn ...

'You're not ready.'

'I can do it!'

... which he threw down at his mentor's feet before falling to his knees.

'I think ... I think we won,' he stammered.

Standing at Dun-Cadal's side, Negus was dumbfounded. The lad had just displayed a greater mastery of the *animus* than any before him.

'I shall be the greatest knight ...'

Dun-Cadal remained at the door's threshold, his fingers only slowly loosening their grip on the hilt of his sword.

You saved my life ... at Kapernevic ...

There, among some scattered scrolls and books, lay his former comrade, eyes still open but devoid of any living spark. His head rested on the edge of a stone fireplace.

I'm sorry I wasn't able to save yours ...

Leading from the hearth, a trail of soot circled around a spot near the dead body, then led off in a fading line which ended at the foot of an open window. Thin blue curtains rippled in a light breeze, allowing glimpses of the brown-tinted street outside.

'Halt! Halt, I say!' yelled the guard in the hall.

Dun-Cadal straightened up painfully under Viola's worried gaze. Halt? While the assassin was still in the vicinity? Folly! Dun-Cadal crossed the office with a rapid step and was straddling the window by the time the guard entered the room. He ignored the man's commands and dropped down into a paved alley that opened onto a busy avenue. His heart skipped a beat when he caught sight of the assassin's athletic figure, weaving through the crowd. His face masked by a thin hood, and he was wearing a dark green jacket that fell to the top of his thighs. He glanced over his shoulder and quickened his pace.

'The affairs of this world are no longer your concern ...'

Drunk with fury, Dun-Cadal charged up the alley and then plunged into the steady flow of people moving along the main avenue. He bumped into a man as he passed, almost striking him with his sword.

'Daermon!'

His heart pounding, he shook his head and spun around, searching for any sign of Logrid. But there were only people. Hundreds of people, some dressed in finery, some in rags, men, women, Nâaga, traders, notables ... odours, spices, perfume, roses, lilies of the valley ... sweat. Beneath the southern sun everything was mixed up, colours and perfumes, filth and stink. His head swam. And then he spotted him, running gracefully, moving without jostling a single passer-by. Dun-Cadal groaned and set off in pursuit, using his elbows without consideration. Cries arose at the sight of his unsheathed sword.

His legs were becoming heavy. His chest burned, his lungs wheezing with a rasping noise, his throat nothing but a scraped passage like a raw wound. And a few tears were streaming from his eyes. But he continued running, on and on, ploughing through a market stall with an almighty crash. He pursued the man down several streets, each time believing he was gaining ground. Or was the assassin deliberately leading him on?

Behind him came the drumming of guards' boots and with them citizens' cries of alarm.

He was growing breathless and his heart was beating irregularly, leaping in his chest as if it were trying to escape. His temples were hammering. He was about to fall.

No!

He continued on. He had to continue. He had fought whole armies and roamed the Empire to its furthest regions. A simple footrace would not defeat him. His pride became a lifebuoy from which he drew support and he redoubled his efforts as he entered an alley in the shadow of two tall buildings. At its end, a pile of crates rested against a wall twice a man's height. Trapped, the assassin stood motionless.

'You …' gasped Dun-Cadal, alarmingly short of air, taking great wheezing breaths. 'You!'

'Sometimes … I hate you.'

He brandished his sword before him with surprising difficulty. It seemed to have tripled its normal weight and required the help of his other arm to hold it straight.

'Turn around,' he ordered in a weak, hoarse voice. *'Turn around!'*

'It was necessary, Dun-Cadal … I am the Emperor, I have to take the most difficult decisions. It's my duty.'

Slowly … very slowly, the assassin obeyed. Not a single feature of his face could be seen in the shadow cast by his hood. The old man's head echoed with memories from the past, as sharp as the edge of a sword. His legs almost gave way as he advanced towards Logrid.

'Why … why did you kill Negus …?' he asked, still breathing heavily. 'Why did you come back from the dead? Bring out your sword! Out with it!'

'You're still too weak,' murmured the assassin without moving a muscle.

His voice was odd, sounding deep and forced.

'Weak,' groused Dun-Cadal.

He approached the other man with an unsteady step, shaking more from exhaustion than fear. Little by little his breathing eased, though his throat remained horribly dry.

'Don't underestimate me … Logrid,' he advised, a menacing smile

156

tugging at his lips. 'I am still General Dun-Cadal Daermon!'

His voice had gained a certain strength from the rage boiling within him. He slowly straightened his back, adopting a proud bearing. His gaze, without losing its glint of sadness, suddenly looked more resolute. At last he had a goal, a light that would guide him, a way to come full circle. Beneath the drunkard, the general was being reborn. His descent into hell had started after the assassin had murdered the councillor. It would end right here, in a simple alleyway in Masalia. With a suddenly supple wrist, he turned the sword before him.

'I am General Dun-Cadal Daermon,' he repeated in a low voice, as if trying to convince himself. 'I was one of the greatest in my day.'

In the shadow of his hood the assassin remained impassive, watching the general come towards him with a measured step.

'Even if time has done its work,' he continued in a voice that became progressively stonier, 'even if my heart, weary and broken, no longer beats steadily, I remain a general. Don't ever forget that.'

'*Sometimes . . .*'

'I'm glad that you remember that,' answered the assassin. 'But I will not fight you. Not until I have the rapier.'

The reply was so surprising that Dun-Cadal stopped short, though he did not lower his guard. Eraëd? Was he referring to Eraëd?

'Draw your sword!' the general roared, pointing his blade at the assassin with a challenging air. 'Draw so that we can end this now!'

The man backed up a step, his hand slowly inching up towards the hilt of his weapon.

'*. . . I hate you.*'

'I would trade hundreds of men like you for just one Frog,' the general ranted. 'You're worthless. You're nothing!'

'Found your pride, Dun-Cadal?' the man asked with what seemed a mocking smile as he tilted his head to one side.

He lowered his hand.

'At last, you are with us once again,' he concluded.

Dun-Cadal froze in surprise. The assassin had spun round with astonishing speed and was climbing the piled-up crates.

'C-come back!' stammered the general. 'Come back, you coward!'

The man leapt over the wall without looking back. Already the boots of the Republican Guards were clattering in the alleyway behind Dun-Cadal.

'By the gods, I'll kill you, Logrid! I swear it! I'll kill you! You'll pay!' he yelled.

'Halt there!' a voice commanded.

He did not move as the halberds were lowered in his direction. The guards surrounded him but he did not even spare them a glance. His eyes were still staring at the top of the wall where Logrid had vanished.

'You'll pay ...' he murmured into empty space.

'Lay down your sword, killer. Lay it down!'

He did not resist when they disarmed him. He did not say a word, nor did he object when they led him away to a prison cell.

'... *I hate you.*'

10

LOGRID

———

Don't ever forget, Dun-Cadal!
Don't ever forget where you came from
Or how you became a general.
It was not due, in any way,
To your sense of honour.

They had returned to Emeris covered in new glory. Kapernevic had been saved, its terrible red dragon slain and rumours flew about the identity of the hero who had accomplished this feat. Although few people knew the name of the exemplary knight whose skill had brought down a legendary monster, the cadets at the military academy suspected it was one of their own. One who, even when present among them, remained a shadow. The mysterious Frog, the only cadet who had actually seen a battlefield, and who had very nearly received honours from Emperor Asham Ivani Reyes for his deeds.

For each time the lad returned to classes, taking part in lessons on fencing, mastery of the *animus*, or strategy, he demonstrated the skills and progress acquired through his experience of war itself. Was it because of his obvious superiority that he preferred to keep his distance from the others? He did not seem to have a single friend. Truth be told, the young nobles who were in the same year at the academy regarded him with envy and jealousy, but also fear. Who could say what this Frog, who served with the legendary General Daermon, was capable of?

A dragon had fallen at Kapernevic. The fact that this brilliant man and his apprentice had taken part in the battle was hardly surprising. And the idea that Frog might have used the *animus* to bring the beast down, however unlikely given the difficulty of the feat, was nevertheless taken seriously. Wherever they went, word of their exploits, even in defeat, echoed around the hallways of the Imperial palace. All on their own, those two might just win this war ...

The cadet who was holding his sword with a firm grip in the academy's great courtyard could not rid his mind of this idea. Opposite him, Frog was staring at him with a keen gaze which never wavered but clung to its prey and took note of the slightest reaction. Forming a circle around the pair, their comrades watched them with apprehension. The courses in duelling allowed them to put into practice what they had learned in theory, and most of them took part with enthusiasm. Except when Frog was around.

'Engage!' ordered the instructor in the midst of the cadets.

The blades immediately crossed with a sharp clang. Leaning against a column with his arms crossed, Dun-Cadal watched his apprentice defeat his opponent with ease. After just a few attacks, he had the other boy on the ground, having disarmed him with a flick of the wrist before sweeping him off his feet with a movement of his leg. As if to sign his work, he let the point of his sword brush beneath his victim's right eye. Blood welled from the thin wound and the cadet didn't dare wipe it away with the back of his sleeve. There was no applause; not a sound except for the rustling of the wind in the trees bordering the inner courtyard. The cadet rose up on his elbows and gulped, his belly knotted. Frog stood over him in silence, his blade pointed at the other boy's throat. His gaze held no emotion, his posture alone demanding respect.

'Good. All of you saw the manner in which Frog won this duel,' the instructor said, advancing into the middle of the circle, hands on his hips. 'He'd already won, even before their blades met. Why is that, do you think?'

Because he will be the greatest of them all, Dun-Cadal thought with a faint smile before leaving, striding down the academy's long hallways until he reached the other courtyard where the fountain stood. He'd found Frog here, with his face bruised after a fight, the first time they had arrived in Emeris together. He looked at the fountain pensively, disturbed by a slight sense of remorse. Hadn't Frog slain a red dragon on his own? So why did he still feel a need to keep an eye on the lad whenever he had the chance? Perhaps to congratulate himself for having discovered him, alone out there in the Saltmarsh. The lad was a rough diamond, waiting only to be cut in order to become a gem. Or else ... was he still worried about his pupil's well-being?

'The gods watch over him, General, be certain of that. But they alone know what role they have assigned to him in this ordeal which is our life.'

He had been walking in the palace corridors for more than an hour, worrying over whether or not to go see Mildrel. He'd left that morning after another argument, and while he was ready to hold her tightly in his arms again, he feared that first she would force him to apologise. Which was something he refused to do. Whatever his feelings for her, she chose to remain a courtesan. So he continued walking ... until he finally pushed opened the heavy doors of the cathedral of the gods.

'I pray for him, every day ...' Dun-Cadal confided.

'As we pray for all the soldiers waging this war against the rebels,' said the bishop, sitting beside him with a smile.

On the pillars that ran along the choir of the cathedral were statues with fixed faces, representing men and women dressed in long togas with no details that might distinguish them from ordinary mortals. Here, the gods wore similar faces to those of men, their divine character indicated only by their inordinate size. Near the stone altar, illuminated by the light shining through an immense circular stained-glass window, empty wooden pews stood in perfect alignments. In the front row, Dun-Cadal had engaged in private prayer before the Bishop of Emeris, wearing a large white-and-gold toga and a red headdress that fell to his shoulders, came and sat down to his right. His grey face was covered with deep wrinkles and fine white hairs like silken threads dangled down the nape of his neck. Their tips brushed against his robe's vast rigid collar, which was dyed violet. With one brown-spotted hand, he patted the general's shoulder in a fatherly manner.

'And I pray in particular for you, my old friend.'

When he first arrived in Emeris as a youth, Dun-Cadal had sought refuge here on many occasions, in moments of doubt, weakness, or fear. It was thanks to his faith that he had followed his peculiar path to glory. And for good reason. The bishop was named Anvelin Evgueni Reyes and the current Emperor was his nephew. If the man hadn't seen some hidden promise in Dun-Cadal when he was a mere boy, he would never have been presented at court, would never have saved the life of the young Asham Ivani, and would never have followed his initial career as a bodyguard ... or become the first Hand.

'No one knows what the gods have foreseen,' the old man continued. 'There are difficult ordeals ahead, but to help you through them, I suspect they have granted you this boy's assistance.'

'He's worth more than that,' replied Dun-Cadal without animosity, as if he were simply stating the truth.

'Really?'

'I believe rather that the gods have sent him to me so he can win this war. And protect the Empire.'

The bishop nodded briefly, bringing a closed fist up to his mouth to combat a violent coughing fit. Then he feverishly hunted about his robe for a handkerchief which he used to wipe the edges of his lips.

'Then they picked the right man to teach him to become great,' he said.

He stood up, running a respectful eye over the enormous hall. The petrified gods stared at one another. Majestic, their stone effigies remained unmarred by any cracks. Each day, artisans came to make sure of it, repairing any signs of time's wear.

'The Empire is like these statues,' remarked the bishop, gathering his hands before him. 'As years pass, it grows fragile. It requires feats of arms and great battles for its splendour to shine. That's how Adismas Deo Caglieri became the first Emperor. He was a fervent believer. To the point of launching a quest for the *Liaber Dest*, persuaded that he would be the one to rediscover it.'

He paused with a thoughtful air, a faint smile on his thin lips.

'That's why his dynasty lost out in favour of ours, I dare say,' he said with a quiet chuckle before continuing: 'Deo Caglieri wrote numerous commentaries of the other two *Liaber*, for want of the Sacred Book itself. I should like, before leaving you to your prayers, to quote a passage from the *Liaber Deis*, along with the commentary he added.'

For the first time since sitting down on the pew, Dun-Cadal raised his eyes towards the bishop, unclasping his joined hands. And quite naturally, Anvelin lowered his eyes towards him, tilting his head slightly.

'The *Liaber Deis* says: "No one is as great as the gods. But the gods ensure that between men and themselves great destinies arise. Although the gods are nameless, heroes, in this world, shall be named." And Deo Caglieri adds here ...' The bishop leaned forward slightly in order to whisper: 'He adds, "It is strange to see how great names succeed one another ..."'

He straightened up slowly, turning his gaze away.

'If the gods put this child on your path, it was not just to save your life. He will be the echo of your greatness, for the good of the Empire. I shall pray for you and for this child. The Emperor will join his thoughts to mine, I'm certain of it. And no doubt the gods already know this and have foreseen all, so our prayers will be heard.'

He gave Dun-Cadal one last smile before he stood, turned on his heel, walked past the altar and disappeared through a small wooden door which he closed behind him. Alone once again, the general brought his fingers back together, closing his eyes with a long sigh. The bishop's words were certainly comforting to him. The gods had intended to link the destinies of mentor and pupil, so that the latter would become even greater than his master. Dun-Cadal was well aware of his notoriety and the victories that he had, alone, brought about for the Empire. The idea that one day Frog might do even better was reassuring. And trying to keep this thought in mind, he resumed reciting a prayer, almost in a whisper, repeating the same requests over and over again. That this war would end with glory, that Frog would survive it with honour, and that if his own life should end during the final battle, he would die with dignity. He clasped his hands together and squeezed his eyes shut as if his life depended on it. He prayed that the destiny traced for him at the beginning of time would be as great as he hoped. That was the true faith. To accept and to give thanks to the gods.

'Feeble words ...' hissed a voice behind him.

The general's lips froze as he slowly opened his eyes. *How on earth?*

'Vain, feeble words when, according to the bishop and all his sheep, what shall be is already decided. If the gods have written the history of men, then believe me, they have already closed the book and gone on to something else. So why praise them? What if it so happens that the destiny they foresaw does not suit you ...?'

How had he failed to sense the man sitting down in the row just behind him, spreading his arms across the back of the pew with a relaxed air, the tip of his scabbard scraping on the cathedral's flag-stones? Dun-Cadal slowly stood up. Then he turned his head, just enough to see the assassin's dark silhouette with a simple glance over his shoulder. The Hand of the Emperor looked as mysterious as always, the shadow of his raised hood completely masking his face. His green cape opened over a studded leather breastplate, a belt dec-orated with several daggers and the silvery pommel of his rapier. But in the black space occupied by his face, Dun-Cadal was certain that Logrid's gaze continued to size him up.

'I used to think highly of you,' the general suddenly said.

'I've never ceased thinking highly of you,' the other man retorted in a muffled voice. 'Only ... now I can see your faults.'

'My faith isn't one of them.'

'When it blinds you, it seems to me that it is, Dun-Cadal.'

The general passed an arm over the back of the pew, turning to the side, and balled his fist. He stared into the shadow where he sensed Logrid's eyes looking back at him. The assassin did not move a muscle.

'You were good, Logrid ... you were good once ...'

He shook his head in disappointment.

'Perhaps it's because I've been unable to expiate my sins, as you do, through faith ...' the assassin replied. 'Or as opposed to you, I have greater difficulty understanding why we are made. And what I'm expected to do.'

'Unlike you, I've never enjoyed inflicting death!' roared Dun-Cad-al as he stood up.

With a firm open hand he struck the back of the pew. The wood shook and the crack of his palm echoed loudly within the cathedral, followed by an oppressive silence. The other man did not seem dis-turbed, remaining immobile and serene.

'What about your ... little Frog?' Logrid hissed. 'Have you asked him what he thinks? It will be too late when you finally realise he's developed a taste for this power he's acquired.'

'You don't know—'

'Taking life while justifying the act,' Logrid continued.

'You don't know what you're talking about—'

'What new creature will you create, *General* Daermon ...?'

Dun-Cadal looked away, retaking his seat on the pew without re-alising he was avoiding a confrontation. He felt dismayed, recalling the hopes he had placed in Logrid before being appointed general and ceding his post as Hand to the younger man. He had been so skilful, so gifted in combat, so ... patient. When had he become perverted to the point of adopting this cruel manner?

'Are you going to make him into a new Hand of the Emperor, so that your creation will perpetuate itself?'

'That's enough, Logrid ...' Dun-Cadal sighed, bowing his head. 'It's jealousy making you talk like this.'

He paused, before adding:

'He'll be more than you ever dreamt of becoming.'

'He'll betray you.'

'Enough!' Dun-Cadal growled. 'He's worth much more than—'

'Than an assassin?' Logrid interrupted him brutally.

He seized the back of the pew before him with both hands and leapt over it with such nimbleness that he did not even make a sound. In one step, he was looming over the general, the fingers of his hand brushing the pommel of his sword.

'You were the first Hand, Dun-Cadal. You only trained me so your invention would not be forgotten. So that the Imperial family would remember your name! Out of sheer pride!'

'I chose you!' Dun-Cadal snapped in protest.

He stood up, shoving Logrid away. As the volume of their voices increased, so did that of the echoes within the cathedral, bouncing off the statues and the stained-glass windows in the choir. Cold metallic words that could still be heard reverberating with each new utterance.

'Oh yes, I was perfect for you. No attachments. A mother dead of syphilis, a father who never deigned to recognise me, but who, in his infinite kindness, paid for my studies at the academy. To be an assassin rather than a knight, you need to follow the path of anger ... don't you?'

'It's not a question of anger,' objected Dun-Cadal.

'Oh, but it is, don't deny it,' Logrid said. 'Anger against the rest of the world, this world which sees Reyes as a degenerate. Oh yes, it's far less glorious than the path you've since chosen for yourself, I agree, but it's more effective.'

'I believed in you. I thought—'

'And so, you don't believe any more,' Logrid cut him off sharply. 'All that matters to you are your gods, who never show themselves.'

Dun-Cadal's grip closed about the hilt of his sword. And then their two blades were drawn, meeting in mid-air before the altar.

'You blaspheme …' the general hissed.

'You're so quick to defend those who will do nothing for you. We've come back to the blindness induced by your faith.'

They remained still for a moment, each of them waiting for the other to launch the first attack, without sparing any thought as to the consequences of their duel. Something was pushing them to challenge one another in this manner, old resentments which had festered over the years, a mutual sense of disappointment, a feeling that they had both been mistaken. And above all else, the inevitable confrontation between master and pupil to test whether the balance of power between them had fundamentally altered. But never before had they crossed steel to decide the matter.

'You weren't wrong to believe in me. But you would be wrong to believe in that kid from the Saltmarsh.'

'And what do you know about that …?'

'Because if you're in here praying, it's not for the Empire. It's for him.'

Boiling with rage, Dun-Cadal lunged forward in a first attack, which Logrid deflected with ease. The second, in contrast, was more difficult for him to avoid. With a sudden lurch, he leaned backwards to see his opponent's blade pass over his face in a circular motion. He just had time to straighten up and parry a weak stroke to his side. And the duel finally took form, a *danse macabre* of blades vibrating in the air before they kissed with a clash. Their ringing blows reso-nated in the cathedral like terrifying death-knells. Beneath the fixed gaze of the statues, they fought one another with a dexterity few could boast of, each looking for a flaw in the other's defences, until finally they each became aware of a sudden change in their breath-ing. Time seemed to dilate, their movements becoming slower. Then each of them lifted their free hand.

The two *anima* collided in mid-air, propagating a shockwave which blurred their vision. They kept their feet despite the power of the impact, both of them backing away in a cloud of dust. They eyed one another for a few seconds, wheezing.

'You … you need to open your eyes, Dun-Cadal …' advised Logrid, still winded.

'About *what*?' the general thundered. 'About what, Logrid?

'About the bonds between the Count of Uster and the Reyes dynasty! About the duty he was entrusted with and the reasons behind this revolt.'

The two opponents observed one another, stone-faced. Both of them had seen their rancour explode into violence. Their words, poorly formulated or poorly received, had never been more than a spark, a pretext for this duel that both men had been expecting. Their paths had divided long ago.

They each took a step back as if trying to shake off their rage. The pride of the master pitted against the ambition of his former pupil ... They had never truly understood one another.

'There are supporters of the Count of Uster here in Emeris, Dun-Cadal,' the assassin continued. 'They took refuge from the fighting here and are scheming in the shadows! Against us! Open your eyes.'

'They're wide open,' retorted Dun-Cadal. 'And what I see before me does not please me at all ...'

'The Saltmarsh, Dun-Cadal. You brought the Saltmarsh here, close to the Emperor. Forget your new apprentice. He will never be strong enough to defend the Emperor against his true enemies.'

So that was it. In the heat of their duel, Logrid was finally revealing his jealousy.

'I chose you,' Dun-Cadal said sharply. 'I chose you among so many others to relieve me as the Hand of the Emperor. Frog will never take your place. Something else awaits him.'

It was enough of a peace offering, Dun-Cadal hoped, to put an end to Logrid's jealousy which he suspected had hatched even before their arrival in Emeris. A jealousy that had grown like a malignant weed with their recent success in the North and the slaying of the red dragon. But Logrid had the opposite reaction. He took a quick step forward, as if on the verge of exploding again, before changing his mind ... and slowly placing his sword back in its scabbard to show he no longer had any intention of fighting. Only his voice betrayed his anger. It rolled around his throat, as hard and heavy as a rock.

'You think I'm trying to separate you from your new pupil because I'm afraid he'll replace me?'

'He's gifted, I told you that. You took offence and I can understand that, but—'

'Dun-Cadal ...'

His voice had changed. There was now a certain sadness mixed with disillusionment.

'This is not a simple revolt that you can crush by force. Our whole world is changing. I'm doing my part, doing it better than anyone. I've taken many lives of the filthy bastards who are threatening us, but alone I will not succeed ... There are noblemen poised to change sides if the rebels reach the gates of Emeris. Some of them are already plotting the fall of our city.'

So many divergences had grown up between them. They no longer understood one another, if they ever had.

'I taught you to kill for the Emperor, to defend him, not to take pride in it,' Dun-Cadal said in firm condemnation. 'In my time, the Hand was feared *and* respected. Since you put on the uniform, everything —'

'— you built I've destroyed,' Logrid completed for him. 'As if I haven't heard that sermon before. I have ...'

He hesitated before lifting his gauntleted fist and pointing a finger at the general. He took a step towards the edge of the altar.

'... respect for you. You taught me everything. But you are such a ... peasant,' he spat. 'So crude and down-to-earth. Old-fashioned, that's what you are, Dun-Cadal. It's never occurred to you that I might be able to teach you a thing or two.'

'By the gods, Logrid,' Dun-Cadal fumed.

'Enough with your gods!' the assassin growled. 'Are they here, warning you about the dangers facing us? No. I am!'

He took a step back. The shadow of his hood disappeared in the warm midday light pouring through the big stained-glass window, revealing a mouth marked by a scar on its upper lip which was still visible beneath a nascent beard.

'There are voices murmuring against the Emperor. The evil that Oratio of Uster unleashed is here, right now. There are voices offering bad advice, masking the truth behind innocent words. The refugees from the Saltmarsh are conspiring against His Imperial Majesty and the nobles are preparing to abandon him if the revolt becomes a full-fledged revolution. They will preserve their places, believe me.'

'What foolishness ...' muttered Dun-Cadal, looking away. 'You hear things and then twist their meaning.'

'I am the eyes, the ears and the *Hand* of the Emperor, Dun-Cad-al. I am the guarantor of the Empire! I believe in him, not in any

divinity. I shall defend him, and his world, to the death. But you ...
you don't listen anymore, you don't see anymore ... and your hand
will tremble on the day when we need to fight.'

Dun-Cadal shook his head in disgust and decided he must leave
this place before his anger and his disappointment burst forth again.
They'd challenged one another and crossed swords already. This rebellion was sowing confusion, making former allies hate one another
to the point of murderous rage.

'The war is no longer being decided on the battlefield, Dun-Cadal. It's now a matter of words and promises. Of seduction, lies and
betrayals. Those who plot do so in the shadows. And who can ferret
them out better than me?'

Words, promises, betrayals ... What if the real duel between them
was made up of these things? Weary of speaking, Dun-Cadal tried to
deliver a final crushing blow.

'They will remember his name. Not yours ...' he said, his gaze lost
in the distance.

But he'd overlooked Logrid's own talents, talents he'd never been
able to perceive, including his capacity to use words to undermine
and wound more deeply than any sword.

'No one else has heard what I've told you,' the assassin admitted
coldly. 'No one else deserves my trust and my respect. No one else
could save the Empire like Dun-Cadal Daermon. This boy from the
Saltmarsh will be your burden to bear. When he falls, he will drag
you with him ...'

He retreated several steps before adding:

'... into the abyss.'

Dun-Cadal lowered his eyes. When he raised them again, the assassin had disappeared. He remained standing for a few minutes, one
hand placed on the back of the pew in front of him, not allowing
himself to lean against a pillar. He let his gaze drift over the flagstones leading up to the altar, lit by the sunshine tinged from the
stained glass. His mind was divided between anger and reflection.
He was a man of war, not of words. A general, not a courtier. An iron
fist poised to strike, not one of those who schemed in the Emper-
or's shadow to decide the world's fate. The only advice he willingly
gave His Majesty was the product of common sense, that of the land
where he had been born and raised. The son of a provincial nobleman
in the West, he had walked barefoot as a child. Logrid, on the other

hand, had grown up in Emeris among the elite before Dun-Cadal had seen his potential and made him his successor. A nobleman by the name of Duberon had seduced the daughter of a good family, but then had not dared recognise the child born of their dalliance and risk compromising his position at court with a scandal. He therefore bought the young unmarried mother's silence by agreeing to finance Logrid's education. Dun-Cadal had taken notice of the boy just as the Emperor offered to make him a general. Logrid seemed the ideal candidate to replace him. A perfect Hand of the Emperor, skilled in combat, agile and clever. The Hand of a sickly Emperor whose power was being contested by certain parties. An immortal Hand, nameless and faceless but not lacking in honour. Logrid had accepted. His mother's life had just been taken by disease, after she had sought to forget her former lover in the city's slums. A degradation the boy had witnessed without being able to do anything about it ... except endure it.

The gods work in mysterious ways.

The assassin's very first victim had been Duberon. The count was one of those who believed the Reyes dynasty was nearing the end of its reign ... With hindsight, Dun-Cadal could not deny Logrid's allegiance or doubt his initial intentions. Nevertheless, he remained convinced that jealousy had played a part in his decisions. That a plot existed now was no mere hypothesis. But to suspect Frog of being a participant seemed more like a settling of scores.

The general sighed.

He found no comfort, no answers from the statue of the god that rose behind him. No matter how hard he scrutinised the figure, its half-opened stone eyes stared ahead without taking any notice of the insignificant being at its feet.

'No one has the right to name them. They are everywhere and in everything.

'They are here, now. Before us, as they will be after us.'

Once, during his apprenticeship, Logrid had questioned him on the subject of the gods, and his mentor hadn't imagined for a single instant that his pupil's doubts would harden into certitude.

'But who are they? Are the things I believe I decide really written down? What right do they have to predestine us for anything at all? Are we just playthings to them?'

To all these questions, Dun-Cadal had only found one answer:

'They are the gods. They are not playing with us, but from our lives they make stories, tales, sagas. So that humanity can achieve its full potential. They know the beginning and the end of time. We thank them for having given us life and a destiny whose meaning belongs to them.'

And there, beneath the statue whose gaze he was vainly scrutinising, the idea of turning to any other answer seemed inconceivable to him.

THE FALL OF THE EMPIRE

How many years does it take to build an empire?
How many seconds to destroy one ... ?

He mopped his face with the back of his hand.

In the filthy cell, bathed in a warm orange light, sticky metal bars obstructed a small high opening in the wall, beyond which boots could be seen scuffing past. With each step, a little more dirt spilled down upon the prisoner's head. Lying on his hard wooden pallet, his fingers interlaced behind his neck, Dun-Cadal watched the light diminish along with the number of passers-by. For hours now, he had been waiting patiently for someone to come question him. Again and again, he went over the chain of events, trying to understand, to find a meaning in all this, a reason, something that would reassure him. He had left Negus while both generals still served the Empire and he had found him again working with those who had defeated their former cause. Whatever the reasons for such a change of heart, Dun-Cadal would surely never understand them. Even so, he would never have taken his friend's life; indeed, he'd tried to warn him. But what good would it do to deny it? Plainly, he was the ideal suspect. In this cramped space, he played with his memories like the pieces of a puzzle, trying to fit them together into a coherent picture. But nothing came to him. When the trap in the door slid aside, he ignored it. An eye appeared in the opening, accompanied by a sardonic laugh.

'Hey!' called a nasal voice. 'General! Howzit goin'?'

He couldn't see the man, but his tone was enough to picture him. He imagined him to be gaunt and dirty, bitter at a being a mere warden and, worst of all, stupid. Outside the prison walls, he was, no doubt, an object of contempt. In here, he had ample leisure to take his revenge by humiliating prisoners, from behind a heavy iron door, as they rotted in their cells.

'Ya were a grand'un, it seemz, zat it? A gen'ral 'mung gen'rals. Yer not so prad naw,' the voice chuckled. 'T'er wer' sum like ya who s'rend'erd. We'z niz t'em. But wunz like you wot din' s'rend'r, ya 'nowz wat we do t'em?'

Without taking his eyes off the daylight fading above his head, Dun-Cadal smiled thinly.

'You make councillors of them,' he murmured.

'We 'ang 'em,' the warder assured him as if he hadn't heard the reply. 'T'at, fer sure with yer ol' vet'ranz mug, iz wat t'ey'll do t'ya. Ya did t'ingz durin' t'war.'

His tone changed abruptly.

'Enjoy yerself,' he advised, full of scorn, 'cuz zoon, gen'ral 'r not, y'll jez be a poor booger at end offa rope.'

He shut the trap forcefully. The clack of the metal was masked by his sniggering and then the sound of his steps gradually receded. When they were no more than a distant echo, Dun-Cadal let out a sigh. Perhaps the warden was right. Perhaps he was going to face judgement. Mildrel had warned him: *You know what the Republic has done to generals who failed to rally to its side ...*

He had tried to save a councillor's life. Only Viola could testify in his favour. But where was she? What if she decided to abandon him? He tried not to dwell on it and closed his eyes. It was not the first time he had found himself locked up in a cell and, although on the previous occasion his life had not been in jeopardy, he did not recall the situation having been any more comfortable. Quite the opposite. It had been twelve years earlier ... far from Masalia ...

... he remembered having searched high and low for Frog in the military academy, without success.

'Aladzio!'

... in Emeris. The image of the shining city slowly took form in his memories and he left his putrid cell behind as he remembered walking towards the academy's great courtyard.

'Aladzio!!!' he hailed, approaching the inventor with a rapid step.

Wearing a blue cloak with gold piping, a tricorne perched on his head, Aladzio stood out among the grey tunics worn by the academy's cadets. But even more than his attire, it was his attitude that distinguished him. While the cadets at his side drew back with a show of deference, he did not even seem aware of the general's arrival. A few feet behind him, upon a wooden base, rested a long tube made of black lead. Whatever the new machine might be that the inventor was testing there in the middle of the school courtyard, Dun-Cadal was not interested. It was only when he was standing right before Aladzio that the latter finally noticed his presence, still preoccupied with resolving some tricky problem.

'Ah,' he murmured distractedly, 'General Daermon . . . to what do we owe . . . do we owe . . . ?

'. . . the pleasure of my visit, is that what you're asking, Aladzio?'

'Well yes, I mean, it's always pleasant to see you.'

Aladzio wasn't even looking at the general, still absorbed by the machine waiting behind him.

'Perhaps a little more sulphur . . . or saltpetre . . . unless we need a lighter ball,' he mused aloud.

'Aladzio . . .'

'The projectile must achieve a high velocity, while remaining on a precise axis, otherwise . . . Boom! It explodes,' he continued, miming a violent explosion with his two open hands.

'Aladzio.'

'Or else it's . . . But of course!' he exclaimed in delighted realisation. 'It's the humidity! The mixture is too damp! So the powder fails to react.'

'*Aladzio!*' rumbled Dun-Cadal in annoyance.

They had spent a long month on the road from Kapernevic to Emeris enduring Aladzio's unending flow of words. More than once Dun-Cadal had to prevent Frog from braining the man with his sword. But as they approached the Imperial capital, the two warriors started, if not to like him, at least to tolerate his chatter.

'I'm looking for Frog . . .'

'Ah, yes, yes,' jabbered Aladzio, rubbing his hands.

The inventor assured Dun-Cadal that he would find his pupil near the walkway, a sort of long stone bridge connecting the military academy to the armoury, and overlooking the palace's hanging gardens. The general left Aladzio to his device and crossed the courtyard. Since their return Aladzio and Frog had, against all expectations, become friends. Dun-Cadal was not overly upset by the fact that his pupil chose to hang about with the alchemist; after all, he was allowing the lad a well-deserved rest, far from the turmoil of the war. In fact, he was somewhat reassured that Frog was finally socialising with someone. He spent little time with the other cadets at the academy. His classmates had always viewed him with mistrust and jealousy, while he chose to keep his distance from them.

On previous visits, Dun-Cadal and Frog had never lingered so long in the Imperial city before being sent back to the front. But their last mission to Kapernevic had been such a success that the Emperor decided their present stay was the moment for Frog to swear his oath. Only the absence of His Imperial Majesty for reasons of health had cast a cloud on that day, but otherwise, what pride and satisfaction Dun-Cadal had felt when he tapped his sword upon his apprentice's shoulder.

'I hereby swear . . .

'. . . to defend the Empire . . .'

Even though the war went on and the rebellion gained a little more ground with the passing months, Emeris remained an island of tranquillity at the heart of the storm. The singing of birds had replaced the yells of soldiers. Sunshine bathed the white stones of the parapet with a soft light.

'. . . to never take the path of anger . . .'

He caught sight of Frog in his grey cape and, facing him, a young woman aged about twenty with a black braid falling upon her bare shoulder. Her dress was carmine red but plain, without embroidery or other signs of wealth. Perhaps she was the servant of some retired duchess in Emeris. But no, for as he approached he had no difficulty recognising her bright blue eyes and gleaming olive-coloured complexion. She had the same comely look she had at Garmaret . . . she might have grown up but he was certain there was no error on his part.

'Frog!' he bellowed.

'Knight . . .'

The young man turned round and his face hardened as the girl whispered something in his ear. She took her leave before Dun-Cadal joined the newly dubbed knight . . . almost his equal now. The two men watched as her slender figure reached the end of the bridge and descended the stairs leading to the palace's interior, before the general broke the silence in a scolding tone.

'I've been hunting for you for hours.'

'You used to be more effective than that,' replied Frog, his face remaining expressionless.

He continued looking towards the end of the walkway as if the young woman were still there. How he had changed in so little time, growing nearly as tall as his mentor. Although his features were more refined they were also harder, his cheekbones sharper and his brow creased by wrinkles whenever his wide eyebrows frowned. As for his grey eyes, they retained a juvenile gleam, although Dun-Cadal sometimes glimpsed a curious grimness there.

'Whenever you're not busy with Aladzio, then she occupies your time,' the knight grumbled. 'You know what I think about that.'

'I've been training with the other cadets, Wader,' Frog assured him in a phlegmatic tone.

'What if we're sent back to the front tomorrow? You shouldn't be training with the cadets. You're a knight now, you blockhead!'

'I'll be ready,' his pupil assured him, at last betraying a certain irritation.

His tone had become sharper and the delivery of his words brisker. Annoyed, he turned towards the gardens that descended in terraces, placing his hands on the walkway's railing.

'Anyway, you seem to be spending enough of your time with Mildrel,' he accused.

'It's not the same.'

'And the Emperor doesn't ask you to train all the time. Whereas I perform my exercises every morning. Even more often, since I was knighted. I have the right to see her.'

'It's not the same,' Dun-Cadal repeated quietly.

'And why is that?' Frog asked angrily, looking squarely into his mentor's face.

'Because Mildrel isn't a refugee!'

Frog turned away with a shake of his head.

'Not that again,' he muttered.

'I told you when we returned from Kapernevic. You should avoid going anywhere near her. Haven't you seen the way everyone is suspicious of everyone else? Negus warned me. And then I warned you.'

'I'm from the Saltmarsh too, have you forgotten that?' murmured Frog.

The lad understood nothing. He saw his mentor's recommendations as an injustice, although they weren't intended to oppress him.

'Frog ... it's only until this war ends. After that, you'll have all the time in the world to court her ...'

He was trying to be reassuring, but he did not sound convincing even to himself. For the war was not going well and it might well be years before it drew to a close.

'I don't want you to be suspected of anything.'

He hesitated before placing a hand on the lad's shoulder. With a brusque movement, Frog shook it off before drawing away.

'And even less now that you've been dubbed a knight.'

'Shouldn't that give me the right to see whoever I like?' the boy objected.

'Oh, don't go thinking you've been anointed, my boy. There's still some way to go before you become—'

'I don't understand,' Frog complained with a dark glare. 'I'm never good enough in your eyes, am I? Whatever I do, it's never enough. Have you ever complimented me, even once? Have you ever said to me: "Well done, *lad*"? Even after the oath-taking ... did you congratulate me? I would like to say you've been like a fa—'

He could not find the proper words, lowering his eyes. When he raised them again, his voice was as a steely as a sword.

'Sometimes ... I hate you.'

And fleeing any response Dun-Cadal might make, Frog walked away rapidly, his cape flapping in the wind. Alone in the middle of the walkway illuminated by a setting sun, the general heaved a disappointed sigh. He had the feeling they were no longer able to really talk to one another, that the words they spoke were never the *right* ones, or spoken at the *right* time. More than once, their discussion had ended with the lad leaving as if everything had been said and nothing needed to be explained, or calmed, softened ... At these moments, everything seemed to separate them. And each time it happened Dun-Cadal found himself thinking of Logrid, fearing Frog would turn out the same way.

Yet, their relationship was built largely on knowing glances and cutting words. In one respect at least, Frog was right. Dun-Cadal had never congratulated him for anything, why would he have done so? The lad was not particularly gifted, just bright and hard-working, driven by a force that no one was capable of understanding. Dun-Cadal had tried to uncover his story, learn what had happened to him before they met, which would surely explain his motivation. But over the years he had come to accept that nothing would be revealed, contenting himself with watching the boy grow up rather than hear him speak of the past. Only the future mattered. And it now seemed darker than before. The Emperor had summoned him, but he'd had no time to tell Frog what he foresaw happening. Something bad …

His intuition had never let him down. He felt death in the air.

'The rebels are approaching Emeris!' declared a voice like the crackling of flames, dry and unpleasant.

The doors swung open before the general and he crossed the room with an assured step, one hand on the pommel of his sword. Near some net curtains caressed by a light breeze, the Emperor's solid gold and silver throne, shone with a dark gleam. The seated Emperor was wearing a great black cape which fell to his feet. A gold mask hid his face and revealed nothing except his eyes.

'The West, the South and the Southeast all fell this morning.'

'It's here that everything will play out,' predicted an elderly man, leaning upon a cane of twisted oak wood.

'You should have acted sooner,' concluded the man with the unpleasant voice, his double chin swelling when he tilted his head.

His body almost concealed the Emperor from view, his obesity lost within a vast cloak with tints of blue. No one present could have denied his resemblance to Captain Azdeki, standing just a few feet away. But while Etienne had a slender, proud figure, his uncle looked more like a pile of flaccid flesh on top of which jiggled a sole lock of white hair. Baron Azinn Azdeki of the East Vershan baronies tended to frequent banquet halls, like the ones where the Duke de Page organised his feasts, rather than battlefields. No one reacted to the general's arrival, and only the Emperor seemed to pay him any attention, his gaze moving away from his advisers to stare at him. There were six advisers present. The Emperor's own uncle, Grand Bishop Reyes of the Order of Fangol, was at his side. The Marquis of Enain-Cassart, his white hair tied back and his firm hand gripping the pommel of his oaken cane, stood near the throne. To Baron Azdeki's right, his nephew narrowed his eyes pensively. To his left, the Duke of Rhunstag and the Count of Bernevin fidgeted, the first man robust in his fur cloak, the other dressed in a purple cloak cinched at the waist by a silvery belt. The two were used to acting together since their fiefdoms adjoined one another, like two inseparable neighbours who were not actually friends. It was almost as if they each found in the other what they lacked as individuals to play an important role, one possessing the fine intelligence of a politician, the other the typical characteristics of a warlord.

All these noblemen present had formed the Emperor's innermost circle during the last year. Little by little, as rumours grew that certain parties had allied themselves to Laerte of Uster and his rebels, the other members of the Imperial court had been ousted in favour of these six. Who were always ready to provide advice, generous with their compliments, and capable of expressing their viewpoint with surprising aplomb.

'We need to commission Uster's assassination,' said Bernevin. 'Without him, the revolt will be leaderless.'

'No, no,' retorted Enain-Cassart in a reedy voice. 'We don't even know where he is, or what he looks like. And it's not he who is conspiring against you here in the palace.'

'Your Imperial Majesty,' interjected Rhunstag, sticking out his chest to give himself substance. 'All the miners have joined the rebels' cause. And that's not counting the Nâaga who have been promised their freedom in the event of a rebel victory. Their troops have been reinforced considerably.'

'We must prepare the palace's defences right away,' nodded Azinn Azdeki. 'My nephew seems the best person to carry out this task which —'

Dun-Cadal gave a sigh, at last attracting a glance from the others.

'— this task which must be carried out with ruthless efficiency,' the baron concluded, his jaws clenching at the sight of Daermon.

Of all the generals in the Imperial Army, Dun-Cadal was certainly the highest in rank, but for many noblemen he remained an upstart of the worst sort. The Emperor had defended him from attacks within the Imperial court many times, arguing that he had won more battles than any other warrior. Like his grandfather before him, he had been wounded in the service of the Empire. He was at least as noble as any who merely boasted a title without ever having set foot upon a battlefield.

'We must not wait any longer, Your Imperial Majesty,' said Bernevin.

'It's time to face the facts,' added Rhunstag. 'The revolt is already running through the lower quarters of the city outside. We must make some examples.'

'The Empire has never been so fragile and only a decision on your part, wise and enlightened, can repel the enemy from Emeris,' assured Azinn Azdeki. 'Arrest those who are conspiring against you and hang them without further ado, as you did with that traitorous blacksmith!'

'Show the population that you are not afraid,' advised Rhunstag. 'Crush the revolt here in Emeris. And let us prepare our defences against Uster's armies. They will no longer have any support here.'

'I know you are reluctant to pass summary justice upon your subjects in this fashion,' Enain-Cassart said with a benevolent smile. 'But you did so in the case of Oratio of Uster. If his ideas have outlived him, then let us act now before they reduce your Empire to ashes. You must either punish those you suspect of plotting against you or else hope that the storm will somehow pass. I have no doubt you will choose the right course.'

Silence fell. The Emperor's eyes remained fixed upon Dun-Cadal, as if the general alone were worthy of his attention, the only person whose approval he sought. A flock of sparrows fluttered their wings, their black shadows taking flight behind the gauzy curtains.

'What do you think ... my friend ...?'

All the advisers waited for the general's response, hiding their enmity as best they could behind hollow smiles. Dun-Cadal paused, search for adequate words to express his opinion. There was no need to provoke the ire of the noblemen present by criticising their total lack of good judgement. And while he held them in part responsible for the current dire situation, he could not afford to raise their hackles by accusing them directly.

'I think they are right, Your Imperial Majesty,' he finally said. 'We must prepare for the coming attack against Emeris.'

'But beyond that?' enquired the Emperor in a terribly low voice.

'But hanging those you believe guilty of conspiracy is surely not the best means of aborting an uprising within this city itself.'

Azinn Azdeki stifled a harrumph of surprise, offended that anyone might contradict him. The advisers looked like barnyard roosters, swelling their necks and ready to beat their wings. Enain-Cassart managed to hide his discontent by simply lowering his eyes.

'On the contrary, it would stir one up,' asserted Dun-Cadal.

'Really?' sighed the Emperor.

'The revolt is already here!' Bernevin exclaimed angrily.

'Would you dare to deny, General Daermon, that certain noblemen have already lent their support to the rebels?' hissed Rhunstag. 'The Duke of Erinbourg fled Emeris two months ago. Everything leads us to believe that some of his men are still here, preparing the ground. Not for a mere revolt ... but for a revolution!'

And so they imagined that spectacle of alleged traitors dangling from the end of a rope would be enough to counter any leanings towards rebellion within the capital. They understood nothing about the common people, had no idea the courage the rebel commoners had displayed on the field of battle. All those mere *peasants* Dun-Cadal had been fighting since the beginning of the war ... none had laid down their weapons upon seeing their brothers fall at their side. Quite the opposite, in fact ... He noticed the glance the baron gave Enain-Cassart as the latter approached the Emperor.

'I suppose you have summoned me for a particular reason,' declared the general, preferring to cut short any debate. 'And evidently it's not for me to advise you on the proper course of action, as Bernevin does so ably.'

Ignoring the jibe, Bernevin looked away, raising his chin proudly. In other circumstances, Dun-Cadal would have liked to prove the man wrong, but not in the presence of Reyes. If the Emperor had called for the general, it was surely to entrust him with the defence of the palace. Otherwise, why hadn't he sent him to the front, along with Negus and the other military leaders?

Behind the golden mask, the Emperor's eyelids closed. He was duty-bound to make the right choice. Lives depended on it ... Or ... was there something else weighing on his mind? He lifted a hand to the bishop on his right. His uncle gripped it fondly, with a weak smile.

'I understand your point of view, my friend, truly I do,' the Emperor assured the general, nodding his head. 'So I ask you do the same with me, whatever it may cost you.'

'I beg your pardon?' the general blurted in surprise.

'It is written ... General,' the bishop added sadly. 'No one can evade divine decisions.'

The doors at the end of the room opened and a dozen soldiers entered very quietly. Dun-Cadal could barely hear them. But he perceived their presence, just as he noticed the unusual absence of one person in particular.

'You've said so yourself, my advisers are right,' continued the Emperor in a quavering voice. 'While the furious masses approach our gates on the orders of a madman, their poisonous ideas have already been filtering into the city ... for a long time now ...'

'Your Imperial Majesty ...' murmured Dun-Cadal.

He did not know what was being hatched. How could he have guessed it? All the same, his heart beat faster and he felt anxious. Logrid wasn't there. The Hand of the Emperor, the ruler's personal assassin, was not lurking in the shadows of the columns as he usually was, ready to defend his master. Only one thing could explain his absence ... he'd been sent away on a mission.

'Bernevin,' the Emperor called out. 'Make sure that the people understand that I will tolerate no disturbances and that anyone who calls into the question the greatness of my Empire or speaks in favour of this insurrection will suffer the consequences. And anyone with allegiances to Oratio of Uster shall be punished! Starting with all the refugees from the Saltmarsh region.'

'Very well, Your Imperial Majesty,' replied Bernevin, saluting him with a low bow.

'Your Imperial Majesty,' repeated Dun-Cadal.

'My friend, you have accomplished so much,' the Emperor sighed. 'So very much, and this is how I thank you. But your sentiments have blinded you.'

'What have you done?' asked the general in alarm.

Behind his back, the soldiers advanced.

'I welcomed them here ...'

The Emperor's voice trembled, from sadness as much as hatred, bearing a tone of wounded betrayal and the most complete contempt for those he sought to protect.

'... and this is how they thank me!'

'The girl,' intervened Etienne Azdeki brusquely. 'The one who hangs about with your Frog. Her name is Esyld Orbey.'

'The daughter of the Count of Uster's personal blacksmith,' his uncle added with smug satisfaction. 'Together, they were fomenting a plot. The two of them, along with others ...'

'What have you done?' roared Dun-Cadal, placing a hand on his sword.

But the soldiers had already started to encircle him, pointing their spears at him in a threatening manner.

'I am merely doing my duty!' the Emperor declared stoutly, straightening up in his throne.

A hand appeared beneath his cape, he grasped the armrest to keep his balance.

'And it is because you have accomplished so much that I am acting in this fashion,' he continued. 'Your pupil does not deserve to be dragged out in front of the public, like Orbey and his daughter.'

'By all the gods, what have you done?' repeated Dun-Cadal, on the edge of tears.

'Only what the gods expected of us!' affirmed the bishop. 'Nothing happens that is not in the *Liaber Dest*! Call upon your faith. Do not remain blind!'

So Logrid had been sent hunting. His vision blurry, Dun-Cadal searched desperately for a means of escape. He must leave here immediately, run and join Frog, stand against the assassin, fight, defend the lad, save his life, not let him down, not abandon him, fight, defend him ... not leave him ... alone ... without defence. It was as if Frog were still the child he'd found in the Saltmarsh, without experience, weak.

'Captain Azdeki, make sure General Daermon is treated with all due respect to his rank,' ordered the Emperor. 'And then, see to the defences of Emeris ...'

'You can't do this!' yelled Dun-Cadal, drawing his sword.

The soldiers stiffened, ready to intervene, but Azdeki raised his hand, signalling them to do nothing. Alone, surrounded, Dun-Cadal struck defiantly at their spear tips with the flat of his sword, hoping that one of them would break formation and give him a chance to flee. Where was Frog? In which hallway was Logrid waiting for him, hidden in darkness?

'He hasn't betrayed you! He fought for you! He killed the red dragon at Kapernevic! All on his own!'

'General Daermon—'

'Your Imperial Majesty, he's still just a child! He can be stupid at times, but he's the best we have! You have no right!'

'General Daermon!' the Emperor repeated, raising his voice.

Dun-Cadal began to turn around inside the circle, lunging on occasion with his sword, but each time the soldier he targeted retreated a step before retaking his position.

'He fought for you! He fought for *you*!' Dun-Cadal bellowed. 'He defended the Empire!'

Would Frog see the sword come plunging towards him? Would he have time to parry the stroke? Would he manage to defend himself? Alone ... bewildered ... unable to comprehend why those who had welcomed him were now treating him so despicably. He was still just a boy ...

In the shadows of the columns, Logrid's silhouette approached. How he would have liked to remove the hood concealing the man's face, to be able to see the spark of fear in his eye as Dun-Cadal charged towards him, howling in fury. But the soldiers took hold of the general despite his mighty struggles to escape their clutches. They immobilised the hand holding his weapon.

'*Logrid!*' spat Dun-Cadal, drunk with rage. 'Logrid! Scum, filth! *Logrid!*'

The assassin retreated a step, surprised by such fury.

'Logrid! I curse you!' the general yelled at the top of his lungs. 'By the gods I curse you! I curse you ...!'

Out of breath, his energy spent, he became suddenly weary, lost, devastated like never before. He who had always believed he would fall to an enemy's sword on the battlefield, was yielding to this stroke of fate. The assassin seemed to sway on his feet, head bowed, one shoulder leaning against a column.

'Is it done?' Azdeki enquired.

Logrid nodded his head briefly. And with a gesture of his hand, the captain ordered the soldiers to release their captive. Dun-Cadal fell to his knees, exhausted, his body shaking with sobs.

'You have no right ...'

'Lo and behold the great Dun-Cadal Daermon,' murmured Azdeki.

'Lo and behold the great Dun-Cadal Daermon ...'

'I am sorry, my friend,' confessed the Emperor in a shaky voice. 'I had no other choice. His treason will remain secret forever and only his honour on the fields of battle will be remembered. It was necessary, Dun-Cadal ... I am the Emperor. It is for me to take the most difficult decisions. It is my duty.'

'... the great Dun-Cadal Daermon ...'

'Arrest him ... but only for as long as it takes for him to come to his senses ...'

'Lo and behold ...'

The dank odour of the dungeon cell ... the clunk of the iron door, the helplessness that comes from confinement, as if he had been excluded from life itself. He had experienced all this once in Emeris. And now he was living through it again in Masalia.

'Lo and behold the great Dun-Cadal Daermon,' said a voice.

Asleep, he had not heard the man enter. The words roused him from his slumber with a certain gentleness before the clanking of the door closing again awakened him fully with a start. The dusk shed a weak light through the window and the silhouette before him remained in shadow for a long moment. Dun-Cadal sat on the pallet, massaging the back of his neck. He already knew who had come to see him. There was no doubt about it. He recognised the slender figure, dressed in a long white toga.

'More reunions ...' he muttered.

'As you say,' acknowledged his visitor in an ironic tone.

His hand on his neck, bent forward, Dun-Cadal paused, raising his eyes towards the shadow standing a few feet away from him. He looked just as arrogant as he had at the port. It was not Enain-Cassart who had most deserved to be assassinated ...

'Come in, Etienne, please, make yourself at home.'

Azdeki moved into the dim light, revealing his gaunt, smooth-shaven face, his aquiline nose above thin pinched lips, the grey hair combed back over his skull. With an arm folded across his stomach and a red cloth draped over his shoulder, he eyed the prisoner disdainfully.

'I was just reliving some old memories,' said Dun-Cadal bitterly. 'When you locked me up and they put you in charge of defending Emeris.'

'The past is the past,' replied Azdeki, keeping his calm.

The general longed to leap at his throat and strangle him until the man's haughty face finally showed some fear. It was inconceivable to him how Azdeki could have ended up in his present position. He, who had been the first Imperial leader to be confronted by the revolt and by those who would later found the Republic, was now one of their number. Yesterday's enemy was today's friend. But not for Dun-Cadal. For him, an enemy remained an enemy, and time would never change it.

'And only the future matters, is that it?' sneered Dun-Cadal. 'Should I congratulate you on having so brilliantly survived the fall of the Empire?'

Azdeki did not respond, but advanced towards the pallet, keeping his eye on the window feebly lit by Masalia's setting sun. Sitting on the edge of the board, Dun-Cadal observed him without saying a word, noting the mud staining the bottom of his toga.

'So you're not dead,' said Azdeki, still looking up at the opening.

'As you can see,' sighed Dun-Cadal. 'And you must surely be a better politician than you were a military strategist.'

Perhaps he'd rather leave this world than see so many old acquaintances, friends, or brothers-in-arms, flouting their oaths of loyalty to the Empire.

'I believed you had fallen at the time of the capture of Emeris and the death of Reyes.'

'The death of the *Emperor*,' corrected Dun-Cadal.

Azdeki nodded with a thin smile before sitting down next to the general.

'I didn't kill him, Azdeki,' he muttered, head bowed.

'I know,' admitted the councillor, joining his slim hands before him.

Hands far too well-groomed to hold a sword.

'I wanted to save Negus, I wanted to warn him of Logrid's return, that's why I was there,' Dun-Cadal continued, in a grave voice.

'The world has changed, Daermon ... Yesterday's saviours are no longer today's. But you're lucky. Given your identity, you would have made the ideal culprit. A young woman vouched for you.'

Viola ... Although he showed no sign of it, Dun-Cadal was relieved. The girl was definitely very likeable. His whole life seemed to have changed since she had come to see him, and now she had come to his rescue.

'You are extremely lucky. Without her ...'

He left his sentence unfinished, darting a discreet glance at the general as if imagining the worst kinds of torments.

'Because I never surrendered, is that it?' murmured Dun-Cadal.

'Hatred against the Empire still runs strong in some quarters,'

Azdeki conceded. 'But all of the renegade generals considered truly dangerous have been arrested.'

Dun-Cadal held back a burst of nervous laughter, passing a hand over his face. Of course he wasn't dangerous in the eyes of the Republic, despite having, in his days of splendour, so often changed the course of a battle. But now, without Frog, he was just a harmless shadow. His splendour had dissolved in wine.

'So you have nothing to fear on that score,' added Azdeki as he rose to his feet.

'Why, then?'

'Why come see you?' the councillor guessed. 'I'm marrying off my son on Masque Night. I am a councillor elected by the people and, I hope, loved by them. I've always associated with the powerful … and to think, once upon a time, I lived in the shadow of a general …'

Azdeki had his back turned now, with a proud bearing, savouring this instant by prolonging the silence. Dun-Cadal remained seated on his crude wooden pallet, his face haggard, the dirt on his skin hidden only by his beard. Now he understood why Azdeki had visited and he closed his eyes. It was painful for him to wait to hear this answer, knowing it would trample what remained of his honour. The councillor tilted his head to one side, without even turning round to address the prisoner. Why would he do so? To humiliate the general still further?

'I wanted to see what had become of the great hero, Dun-Cadal Daermon, with my own eyes.'

He walked slowly towards the door.

'Azdeki!'

The councillor halted, ready to pound with his fist on the metal to signal to the gaoler that the interview was over. But his hand remained suspended in the air.

'How many are there like you?' asked Dun-Cadal. 'Who else sold themselves to the Republic to hang on to a little power? Tell me.'

There was no hatred in his voice, just disappointment. He'd asked these questions in a long sigh. Facing the door, Azdeki did not make the slightest gesture. He took his time thinking before he replied in an icy tone.

'You never were very intelligent, Daermon. You never saw, never understood what was happening. The world could have crumbled beneath your feet and you would not have felt it.'

Negus had said the same sort of thing. Had he really been so blind? In the end, had he been no more than a simple warrior, a tool, an instrument ...?

'It was ... so predictable, readable ... as if it had already been written,' Azdeki said with a smile. 'It was how things were supposed to happen. The Empire was just like its Emperor ... sick.'

He turned towards Dun-Cadal, his fist still raised against the door.

'It's strange, I thought I was going to enjoy this more, seeing you in such a piteous state.'

Without even looking up, the general replied, joining his hands together before him as if in prayer.

'It is strange, Azdeki. But now I'm happy I couldn't stop Logrid.'

Then his gaze rose very slowly to challenge that of the councillor.

'Because none of your power games will protect you from his vengeance. And he will do what I'm incapable of doing.'

Azdeki's mouth twisted and then his jaws clenched. He hesitated before banging violently on the door with his fist. With an unpleasant clanking noise, the gaoler opened it up.

'The gods take pity on drunks, Daermon. You're free to go.'

For the space of an instant, Dun-Cadal thought he detected a gleam in the councillor's eye. It was enough to make him smile faintly.

For just an instant, he'd seen fear on that ever-so-proud face.

12

AT THE CROSSROADS

After his memories have awakened him,
I shall reveal myself.
Here, at the crossroads
Between what we were, what we are now
And what we will come to be.

'I know what you're thinking, my friend. I know you don't understand.'

The Emperor's voice was muffled by the heavy cell door. Plunged into pitch darkness with his head leaning against the cold metal, Dun-Cadal could hear his ruler's wheezing breath. The general was sitting on the damp earth, mute with rage. His fingers slowly dug furrows in the ground, as an outlet for his anger.

'But don't judge me too quickly,' the Emperor continued. 'This is what it's like, the burden of power, it's a curse. Sometimes, in order to preserve the integrity of my Empire I must wound someone close to me ... Don't judge me for it.'

He waited but Dun-Cadal did not speak.

'I had to protect you. I had to lock you up, and keep you here for as long as takes for you to regain your calm, your reason. Try to understand ...'

There was no answer to his plea. So the Emperor continued to speak.

'You knew, didn't you? That associates of Laerte of Uster had infiltrated the city, inciting even my most faithful advisers against me. You knew that. I welcomed the Saltmarsh refugees, thinking to show kindness, but they bit the hand I extended to them. What folly to believe that rotten fruit can become green again. The blacksmith's daughter was one of them; he is now dead. Perhaps she wanted to avenge him, what do I know? But I could not let her pervert someone as important as your apprentice. She incited him against you and you were blinded, Dun-Cadal. The knight Frog was—'

'Don't say his name!' snarled the general, close to tears.

His voice cracked like a clap of thunder, and after his words came a fraught silence … He tilted his head back, the cold of the metal studding the door immediately chilling his skull. His fingers continued to dig into the earth, and he slammed his head back against the door with three sharp blows, enduring the pain that ran into his temples. The hurt failed to ease the suffering that bore into his soul.

'Sooner or later he would have chosen his camp, Dun-Cadal,' the Emperor said in a sad voice. 'You know that, don't you? He loved her. He would have been forced to choose her side. A young man will do anything for love. Including losing his way … It had to be done.'

Something wasn't right about the way he was speaking. He enunciated the words in a curious fashion, as if he doubted them, or was restraining himself from saying the opposite. The only certainty, for Dun-Cadal, was that his Emperor wasn't telling the whole truth.

'I had no other choice,' he said, this time with astonishing assurance. 'The real culprit in all of this is Laerte of Uster, who has divided my people. And believe me, I will protect Emeris. I will push the revolt back into the deepest corner of the Empire. As for Laerte … Laerte … he shall have no rest, no refuge. Whether by day or by night, wherever he goes, he shall be no more than game fleeing from the hunt.'

He measured each sentence, each word, with such gravity that the air itself seemed to grow heavier. Asham Ivani Reyes had often confided in the general. He had known Dun-Cadal since his childhood. But this was no question of confidences; it was if he were seeking absolution.

'I lost my mother when I came into the world. I lost my father when I was ten years old. I had to learn to rule very quickly, my friend. I had a duty, that of leading my people. And you always knew how to protect me, from the moment of your arrival. You were always here to protect me, Dun-Cadal. You were so full of ambition; I respected you so much … right up to the day when I placed Eraëd upon your shoulder and made you a general. Was that not a mark of my affection?'

He paused to regain his breath. His voice was quavering and muffled. He sounded ill.

'The strong man from the West protecting a stricken Emperor, only half-standing ... a weak and foolish Emperor,' he murmured. 'You deserved to be knighted by me, personally, because Eraëd is the Empire, did you know that? Its power, its beauty ... its strength. Proud, straight ... perfectly balanced. Some say it has held magic ever since it was forged. It has always been worn at the belt of the fathers of this realm, throughout history. It has traversed time without being weakened by it. It has been more than all that, more than time, more than men, more than anything else of their creation. At the end of the world this blade, Eraëd, shall remain ... It is capable of breaking anything, they say. And while my people tear themselves apart, while this rebellion continues when it should have been broken, I have not even taken it out of its scabbard ...'

'You are weak,' said Dun-Cadal in a terribly neutral tone.

It was not even an attack. Just the truth proclaimed in a brutal fashion.

'I am weak,' the Emperor agreed with a laugh. 'I always have been.'

It was laughter drowning in sadness and, when it faded, there remained only sorrow in his voice.

'Is that not why my uncle and my father made you my Hand? You know how I am ... stricken. Weak. Repellent. I am a monster to so many, when in truth ...'

He paused, cleared his throat and then continued:

'In truth, I am a father to them. To the people, I mean. What will they do without me? They'll want to make decisions on their own. That's Oratio of Uster's famous *dream*, isn't it? But do they ever imagine what it would be like, being responsible for their own choices? They are merely ... children. I am responsible for them. For this Empire. It has been written so since time immemorial.'

'But you listened to them ... to *them*,' muttered Dun-Cadal. 'To Azdeki, Rhunstag, Bernevin ... They've made you their puppet. So don't speak to me about responsibility.'

He took the long silence that followed as a confession.

'It's not as simple as that,' the Emperor defended himself on the other side of the door. 'So many things happened here while you were away at the front, fighting for the Empire. I could tell you about them, yes ... but someone else would describe them to you in a very different manner.'

There was a metallic noise from behind the door. The clink of a coin against door.

'Like a coin with two sides,' murmured the Emperor. 'On one side, you have the image of my mother. And on the other ... the seal of the Empire. Two things that are as different in their forms as in their meanings, and yet ... it's still one and the same coin. And it's the same thing with events. Depending on who brings you the tale, the story may change altogether ...'

What was he trying to say? This man, who Dun-Cadal had defended since his earliest years, was now damned in his eyes. This same man had taken away the most precious thing he had ever acquired, more than his honour, more than his victories. He had ripped away a part of Dun-Cadal's self.

'I ordered Oratio of Uster's execution because he was dangerous. He was, Dun-Cadal ...'

The general heard the Emperor stand up.

'I know because they told me about it,' added Reyes.

Just as he heard the sound of his hand on the icy metal of the door.

'With your young friend, it was the same way ... That's how things happen, Dun-Cadal. It's all just murmurs in one's ear. And in truth, everything has already been decided in advance. This is how things must end ... without forgiveness on your part, I imagine.'

His steps faded away slowly, like a memory ... a very distant memory.

And the darkness of the cell dissipated beneath a soft light, tropical and warm. The sun was setting in the distance behind the tall houses with their flowery balconies. The Emperor was just a memory now and Dun-Cadal an old man with a weathered face covered by a salt-and-pepper beard.

'Don't bother thanking me!' exclaimed a sweet voice as he was walking down a deserted alleyway, preferring to avoid the tumult of the commercial avenue.

Glancing over his shoulder, he recognised the friendly face of the young historian from Emeris. She smiled at him. He had no desire for this and did not wait for her, rubbing the back of his neck as he went on. A stiff drink would do him the greatest good.

'Well, if you wanted to thank me, I'd take it as compliment,' continued Viola, almost running after him.

He carried on walking with a quick, determined stride. But she'd go on dogging his heels and he'd never be able to get rid of her, he knew that. Logrid's words were echoing in his head ...

'I will not fight with you. Not until I have the rapier.'

Eraëd. Viola wanted it. So did Logrid. He knew he could take the secret of its location to his grave, but his curiosity was piqued. Nothing happened by chance.

'They believed you'd killed Negus, I told them it was impossible,' Viola explained as she struggled to keep up with him. 'I had to intercede in your favour. But Councillor Azdeki was very clear that you are to remain in my custody from now on and I – damn it!'

Her voice had progressively risen in volume until it cracked like a whip, at the very moment when she came to a halt.

'You could at least listen to me for an instant, couldn't you?' she growled. 'Or is even that asking too much?'

She stood stiffly with her fists balled against her thighs, her eyebrows forming a deep frown above her round spectacles. Her green eyes pinned Dun-Cadal as he turned round. He felt lost in them, completely ensnared by her smooth, youthful face. Viola would never leave him in peace. But it was not simply self-interest that had prompted her to free him from gaol, no. He could see that in the depths of her pupils. He detected a touch of respect there. His own expression softened.

'Thank you,' he said.

'Well, that's something at least,' she sighed, relaxing her shoulders. 'You really don't make things easy, Dun-Cadal.'

At last, he gave her a faint smile.

'Why are you doing all this?' he asked.

'Doing what?'

'Making my life a misery,' he replied, keeping his smile.

She raised her eyebrows.

'For the rapier,' she admitted. 'I help you. You bring me the rapier.'

He nodded his head slowly.

'Very well.'

And he resumed walking.

'What? That's it?' said the young woman in surprise. 'But wait!'

She tried to catch up with him, but he was walking faster and faster, reaching the end of the alleyway.

'What about Councillor Azdeki, did you speak to him? What did he tell you? And Logrid? What happened?'

She was pressing him with questions, but he was far from inclined to answer them. They had joined a paved street where a few passers-by were strolling unhurriedly. There were no traders, no cries, no guards here. Just ordinary city life. Some of the citizens were going home, others were conversing on a bench near a fountain which spilled clear water into a basin covered with green algae.

'But ... where on earth are you going?'

He spied a statue at the end of the street. Standing in the middle of a small crossroads, no one seemed to take any notice of it, half-hidden by ivy, with a mossy coat joining the base to the damp paving stones of Masalia. It showed a man holding some sort of parchment scroll before him, about to announce an important piece of news.

'I'd like your tattooed *creature* to leave us in peace for a while,' he said suddenly.

When he turned to her, Viola grew pale.

'He's there to protect me ...' she assured him.

Behind her, the Nâaga's massive silhouette detached itself from the shadow of a balcony. Dun-Cadal gave him a black look before smirking at the young woman.

'You know what? I'm not so sure of that.'

Upset at being trapped in this fashion, Viola opened her mouth to protest, but Dun-Cadal had already started walking again, accelerating his pace.

'Is this how you thank me? You're being unpleasant again! What dreadful dive are you hurrying off to get drunk in, this time?'

'I'm not going to get drunk,' he replied curtly.

He slowed down once he reached the crossroads.

'Then what?' Viola asked impatiently.

Before him rose the statue, its base surrounded by an iron fence through which the stagnant water from the streets drained. The figure's nose had been broken, its features were dulled, and ivy climbed up as far as its shoulder, but he would have recognised it among a thousand others. He had not passed it again since he first arrived in

Masalia. He closed his eyes, drawing a deep breath to chase away his memories. But it only made matters worse. The images of the fall of Emeris came out of nowhere, blinding, reddened by the voracious flames that wavered frantically among the clouds of dirty smoke. He saw himself in the hallways of the palace, coughing his lungs up, lost ...

An explosion awoke him and he discovered, in a daze, that the door of his gaol cell was bent backwards and gaping open, beside a collapsed portion of the wall. The sound of detonations surrounded him, like peals of thunder shaking the building. They were mixed with the sound of distant fighting, the clash of swords, without his being able to determine their origin. He'd run through the hallways, his brow bloodied and his face covered in dust. Did he even know where he was going? Emeris was under attack and the rebels were taking the palace by storm. Azdeki had not held them back. Did he even know ...?

He halted before the double doors without understanding quite what had led him here. He pushed them open with all his might, unsure what grim spectacle he was about to discover within. Or what purpose was currently guiding him ...

And what bitterness struck him when he glimpsed the twisted silhouette draped in the black cape, the shining mask resting a few inches from the inert hand. The emperor was lying stretched out on the floor, silent, the flickering light of the flames outlining the contours of his body. Behind it, the net curtains rippled as they were consumed by the flames, moving to the echo of the raging battle. No birds sang in the tree tops that brushed up against the marble balcony.

Dun-Cadal knelt beside the body. He covered the face, now gone forever rigid, with the golden mask.

He almost left the room at that point, wallowing in his rancour. He had almost fled without even giving it a thought. But it could not be allowed to fall into the hands of the rebels, it represented so much. So he had taken it with him, crossing the remnants of an Empire in flames ... Eraëd left the Emperor's belt and had travelled with Dun-Cadal to this port city. It had passed through the former Kingdoms as they gradually settled back into a state of peace. Until it reached Masalia ...

'This statue ... it's one of those that were erected to mark the procla-
mation of the Republic,' Viola observed.

He reopened his eyes slowly. The monument was now haloed by
an orange light, gentle and warm. Much less harsh than crackling
flames.

'That's right,' he acknowledged, adding to himself: 'It's ironic
when you think about it.'

The young woman did not immediately respond to his remark,
watching him move around the base while darting brief glances at
the houses on the street corners. She frowned.

'What's ironic?' she asked finally.

He stopped short, his face seeming to harden at the sight of an
iron gate slightly hidden within a recess of the fence. More ivy fell
there, in a curtain.

'What I hid beneath it,' murmured Dun-Cadal as he approached,
looking preoccupied.

'You mean ...?' Viola gasped.

She looked back, desperately seeking some sign of the Nâaga.
Paying her no heed, Dun-Cadal was already busy opening the gate,
both hands gripping the bars to pull it towards him. He had to try
several times before he succeeded in loosening it with a strident grating noise. It had been ten years since he had last crossed over the
threshold.

'You hid it here?' Viola finally realised, looking thunderstruck.
'Right here in Masalia?'

It was quite obvious that she was not prepared for this. When
they'd first met, he'd mentioned the Eastern territories. The same
location he'd mentioned when, completely drunk, he had recounted
the fall of the Empire to others. And everyone had believed him ...
that he'd hidden Eraëd in the Eastern territories, not far from the
Vershan mountains. Dun-Cadal just restrained his mocking grin.

'I talk too much when I'm drunk, as you well know. Just think of
all those treasure hunters out there, roaming the Vershan region ...'
he remarked blithely, plucking a match from the pocket of his vest.

He passed through the gate, disappearing into the darkness of a
steep stairwell. An astonishing stink rose up into the square, pungent and salty. Viola grimaced in disgust before entering in her turn,
taking care to check that Rogant was just a few feet behind her.

Upon the stairs below, Dun-Cadal lit a torch and was using it to ignite others fixed to the wall.

The steps gleamed in the combined light of the sun passing through the fence and that of the flames. The staircase led downward in a spiral before reaching an underground tunnel through which fetid waters ran. In addition to the filthy wastes borne by the current there were also rats as big as cats.

'How exquisite . . .' Viola sighed.

Dun-Cadal was waiting at the edge of the channel, the torchlight flickering over the contours of his stern face. He completely ignored the rodents as long as his forearm that were slipping between his legs. Unlike Viola, who took carefully measured steps, instinctively lifting the hem of her dress with trembling hands.

'. . . exquisite and also swarming with vermin,' she added in a murmur.

She did not retreat, although she walked cautiously and with a sick look on her face, but she was determined not to lose sight of the general. Dun-Cadal was encouraged by this. Perhaps he was making the right choice after all, rather than giving in to sheer impulse. Whatever the reasons for Logrid coming to Masalia, and for the murders of the two councillors, everything seemed to point to Eraëd. If Logrid knew that Dun-Cadal had hidden it, perhaps he had also deduced that the sword was here, somewhere in the southern city. Better Viola than him. The old general was resolved to hand the rapier over to the young woman. In a certain sense, she had earned it.

He followed the channel to a wide chamber where its waters joined that of three more furrows emerging from other tunnels. Their currents met around a broad octagonal platform bathed by sunlight. Above them, the drainage gratings bordering the statue formed odd shutters smeared with black filth. Viola dropped her skirts, ill at ease. Carrying them had been slowing her down, and now she hurried to rejoin Dun-Cadal, stifling a cry when a rodent brushed past her calf. As she came up to the general, he gave her a brief glance which she answered with a sickly grimace. She should have cursed him for bringing her down here, into the city's excrement.

He had buried the ultimate symbol of the Empire in the putrid sewers . . . It was an astonishing act from someone who felt the Empire's passing so deeply and still believed it was the only acceptable regime. He crossed the chamber, walked over the platform and halted at the corner of a tunnel after counting the others by eye.

'So why did you say it was in the Eastern territories?' asked Viola as she watched him kneel and search around a crevice in the wall.

She gagged as she saw him push away the rats with the back of his hand. Then he stuck his entire arm into the hole.

'Why not?' muttered Dun-Cadal.

'I think I know the reason,' the young woman declared. 'If you're going to claim you hid a legendary item, it might as well be at the highest place in the world. Am I right?'

Years could have passed safely by until Eraëd and its location passed into myth and no one dared, or had an interest, in hunting for it. The Vershan mountains were reputed to be dangerous.

Dun-Cadal withdrew his arm from the cavity, holding a long object wrapped in thick brown cloth. And as he moved back to the centre of the platform, he started to remove the wrapping. Little by little he revealed a blade whose gleam had in no way been dulled by time, clear and smooth up to the twisted guard that spiralled around a finely sculpted hilt. Its perfection was so evident that no one could have regarded it as anything less than a divine creation.

'There it is,' Dun-Cadal sighed. 'Eraëd.'

He held it respectfully, lying across the flat of his palms, reluctant to grasp it by the hilt.

'Why?' Viola ventured to ask timidly, narrowing her eyes with an air of suspicion.

'It's what you wanted, isn't it?' Dun-Cadal replied brusquely. 'Eraëd. Here it is.'

He extended his arms to present her the rapier.

'Take it. It's the sword of the last Emperor, it must be worth something in your museum of the Republic. Take it.'

She hesitated, coming slowly around the platform, her gaze wavering between the sword and the expression on the general's face. It was the sole physical object which linked him to what he had once been. And he was prepared to relinquish it without any ceremony.

'Why?' Viola insisted on knowing.

'Because it deserves another setting than this one,' the general replied without conviction. 'And perhaps I think you are capable of protecting it.'

'Protecting it? From what?' she immediately asked.

'From whom, rather ...' he said.

She clasped her hands behind her back, without managing to conceal their shaking. Dun-Cadal looked down at the blade, knowing she'd understood him.

'Someone else asked you for the sword.'

'Logrid,' he admitted with a sigh. 'Logrid wants it too.'

She did her best to hide her relief. But it was obvious that the general was too absorbed in admiring the perfect blade to pay her close notice.

'You helped me,' Dun-Cadal said in a terribly low voice. 'You listened to me . . .'

His sad eyes turned towards her, plunging into her gaze as if he were trying to cling to something there. Until now, she had only relied on the scent of lavender to win the old man over. Her tenacity and her humour, along with her youth, had done the rest. Dun-Cadal liked her.

'You earned it . . .' he said. 'You wanted it, so take it.'

Once again he offered the sword to her, presenting it with a certain deference.

'It has never been of much use to me,' he explained. 'It belongs in a museum . . .'

'Why change your mind?' asked Viola, curious.

"Why?' he laughed nervously. 'It's only a rapier.'

'It's magical.'

He shook his head, smiling slyly.

'You don't understand—'

'It survived the great dynasties of this world!'

'It's not magical,' he murmured.

'It was forged in ancient times, and enchanted, it's capable of—'

'What do you know about it?' he said, losing his temper. 'You don't understand! It's just a sword. Do you think it saved Asham Ivani Reyes?'

His face twisted in anger. In the corner of his eyes, tears swelled. But standing before him, Viola was unperturbed. The Nâaga's massive silhouette was slowly coming into view behind the old general.

'Do you think it changed anything at all?' Dun-Cadal continued. 'The Empire fell . . . and I fell with it. So tell me, where did this alleged magic go? I never even saw the blade unsheathed. All those things that are said about it are twaddle. It served many Emperors, but it failed to protect them in the end.'

He saw himself again, bent over the still-warm corpse of the Emperor. An inert body lying at the heart of a palace in flames ...

'Perhaps that's not what its magic is meant to do.'

'It isn't magical!' he insisted. 'It's only a symbol! Don't you understand?'

His anger turned to bitterness and his voice faded into a sigh.

'Eraëd has never been more than a symbol,' he said.

But he still could not bring himself, even for an instant, to touch the hilt, preferring to hold it like a precious object on the palms of his hands.

'And who but Dun-Cadal Daermon could have attached so much importance to a symbol?'

Dun-Cadal froze, as if petrified. That voice. He knew it even though it had become deeper with age. It had the same diction, the same weight given to each word. Emerging from a tunnel, the man approached with a feline grace, his face masked by the shadow of his hood. The torches projected a halo around the outlines of his broad green cape and gilded the edges of his leather boots and gloves with a fine luminous tracing. His hand rested on the pommel of a sword hanging at his belt.

'But ... but ...' stammered Viola, turning pale.

'A symbol you took such care not to leave behind in Emeris. It's hardly surprising that a man who spent his entire life serving the Empire, who gave so much to it, would wish to take a piece of it with him ... before everything burned.'

Dun-Cadal remained completely still, his heart pounding fit to burst. His face had gone pale too. Out of the corner of his eye he saw the Nâaga detach himself from the darkness of another tunnel.

'This was not the plan,' Viola finally managed to say. 'This—'

'The plan ...' repeated Dun-Cadal in a murmur.

The man halted a few feet from the platform.

'I wanted to see it, Viola. And nothing could have stopped me,' he said in a flat voice.

The Nâaga was visibly unhappy about this surprise but merely crossed his arms, leaning against the curved wall of the chamber. With a kick of his boot, he sent a passing rat flying.

'I know who you are ...' Dun-Cadal started to say, his throat horribly dry.

The man acknowledged his words with a slow nod of the head.

Dun-Cadal could have sworn he was smiling. The general did not dare move a muscle, and with Eraëd still resting on his palms, he could not look away. He no longer had the strength to do so.

'I thought you were Logrid,' he confessed, a hint of sadness in his voice. 'But why ... why all this ...?'

'This isn't a good idea, you should leave now,' said Viola, taking the man in the green cape by the arm. 'We wanted the sword, and now we have it. This serves no purpose.'

But the man ignored her.

'There are so many things you did not wish to see,' he said accusingly to Dun-Cadal. 'You have no idea what I've lived through. None at all.'

'Stop this while there's still time,' the young woman pleaded, squeezing his arm.

This time, he pushed her gently away.

'If you knew how lost I became when I was with you, how I hated you, how I hated myself.'

'... *sometimes, I hate you ...*'

'Your old friends betrayed the Empire and now it's the Republic they are trying to subvert. Isn't it astounding that, in order to save it, we need the last Emperor's sword? The irony of fate ...'

There were so many questions burning the old general's lips, but which should he ask first, which would soothe the dull pain rising within him? As he stood there, wearing Logrid's cape, Dun-Cadal did not recognise him.

'And now ... now they want to destroy my father's dream,' the man said with the greatest calm. 'They shall not trample what remains of him. We need the sword—'

'Your father ...?'

A whole section of Dun-Cadal's life suddenly fell apart. He tried to reassemble the pieces, but nothing formed a coherent whole any more. The man nodded briefly before lowering his hood, finally revealing a face that Dun-Cadal had believed he would never see again.

'I lost myself, Wader. They even stole my name from me, for years. I chose my path. And I know it will not please you.'

'Laerte,' Viola said worriedly.

And Dun-Cadal felt his heart break.

'Uster ...' he let slip in stupefaction.

The man is so completely disembodied he's become merely a rumour.

201

*

'Like a coin with two sides . . . It's the same thing with events. Depending on who brings you the tale, the story may change altogether.'

Part II

I

DESTINY

Irony of fate
Or will of the gods?
To give a man the chance
To nurture his own enemy.

The first kiss, the first murmur of love, the first embrace ... A man's life is scattered with events that will be engraved upon him forever. The first weapon, the first blow struck, the first death delivered. Who can recall or be aware of the moment, among all these first times, when a life found its meaning? The moment when destiny seizes you and leads you down a single path. That moment arrived seventeen years earlier.

'That's not the right way of doing it, Laerte,' said a quiet voice.

The Saltmarsh was under the protection of the Count of Uster, a man respected for his good judgement, authority and clemency. He was a man of letters, able with a sword but so enamoured of the written word that he was known for leaving his blade sheathed where others would have used force to ensure obedience.

'Like this,' she explained, placing her hand on the quarrel to lock it in the crossbow's slot.

No one had any inkling that, two years later, war would set the entire region aflame. If Oratio was guilty of anything it was blasphemy, but even his most religious subjects had forgiven him that sin. It was true that, contrary to the edicts of the monks of Fangol, he wrote books of his own – and not merely registries but reflections on the future of this world – but he wrote with so much intelligence and thought that his words were being secretly discussed even in Emeris.

The young woman took the crossbow from Laerte's hands and demonstrated as she spoke.

'You hold it like this, then shoulder it, aim ...'

She paused, concentrating on the target.

'... and release,' she murmured.

She pressed the trigger and, with a sharp snap, the quarrel sped away to lodge itself in the trunk of a tree. Without saying another word she returned the weapon to the boy, a mocking smile curling her lips. She was beautiful, with long jet-black curls tumbling over her shoulders. Her green dress clung to the developing shape of her body, just emerging from childhood. She wasn't quite a woman yet, but she tried to look the part and as a result Laerte was utterly hapless in her presence. The works of Oratio of Uster were unfamiliar to him, as was the turmoil they were causing in high places. The man was his father, but his attention was drawn by something entirely different. Shyly, he studied each of her features, each curve of her body, with furtive little glances. And whenever she directed her blue, almond-shaped eyes towards him, he immediately looked away, blushing.

'It's simple,' she said in a suddenly high-pitched voice.

She was eyeing him with a sly grin. Laerte couldn't bear it when she behaved like this: haughty, almost disdainful. All because she was just turned fourteen and he was only twelve. He could still hear his father's master-at-arms shouting in his ear: *'You clumsy oaf! Even a girl can handle a sword better than you.'*

In her case, it was true. Her father was a blacksmith; she had grown up surrounded by weapons and had learned to wield them at a very early age. When they were little, she had always given him a hiding in their contests. Now, it was ... different. She no longer played, no longer amused herself with the same things he did. Other things interested her and sometimes he felt he was no longer included among them. Worse still, she had started speaking to him like an adult addressing a child. But then, if she irritated him so much, why couldn't he stop himself watching her every move?

'I know how to shoot,' Laerte whined, hefting the crossbow.

'Such a proud little boy,' she said with a smile before walking towards the tree.

She pulled out the quarrel and, when Laerte joined her, they stood there together, not saying a word. Below them stretched the

Saltmarsh's placid wetlands. A few salt harvesters were going about their tasks, on their guard because the swamps a little further away were teeming with rouargs at this time of year. It was the start of summer, when the females emerged from their lairs with their offspring to hunt. It was not unusual for some poor wretch to end up in their maw.

'It's beautiful,' she said.

But rather than the heat haze drifting above the marshes, it was she who drew the boy's gaze. When, out of the corner of her eye, she noticed Laerte's attention he immediately looked at the landscape in his turn. In the background, two wading birds were standing on one leg, the other folded beneath their bellies. At this distance, their long slender beaks looked like sharp sword blades.

'Yes, well … it's the Saltmarsh,' he sighed.

She smiled faintly before starting to laugh.

'"It's the Saltmarsh," that's all you can find to say about it?'

'Well, what of it?' asked Laerte, offended.

'Your tutor hasn't taught you any words to say something more about a landscape than,' she leaned towards him, '"it's the Saltmarsh"?' she concluded in a soft voice.

He smelled her perfume, saw her lips inches from his own, her smooth olive skin. A longing seized his belly, stronger than ever, and he had to force himself not to kiss her.

'What are we going to do with you? You're not very gifted with weapons—'

'The master-at-arms says I'm making progress!' Laerte lied.

'And you're not as inclined to letters as your father … What is it you actually like to do?'

She did not wait for an answer, descending the hill towards the horses hitched to a tree at the edge of the forest. Behind the tree tops, in the distance, stood the wooden ramparts of Aëd's Watch and a tall stone keep at their centre.

'I like riding,' said Laerte as he trailed behind her.

'And that's all?'

No, of course not. He was lying, anyway. The only thing he was sure he liked was being with her. As for the rest … he felt very little enjoyment, if truth be told. His path was already traced out for him. His older brother was destined to military service, while he would one day take his father's place. That's how things were. The eldest son offered to the service of the Empire, while the second ensured the succession. But even if his destiny had not been so clear-cut, he had no ideas of his own about his future.

He was no longer a boy but not yet a man, and it was difficult to know what interested him. Sometimes, he liked to play with his little wooden soldiers. On other days he put them away, telling himself that he was too old for such games and wanting to ride off wherever he pleased. Only, although he felt himself growing up, everyone else, like his friend, continued to treat him like a *little boy*. Besides, wasn't she right to think so? He still kept his favourite toy at the bottom of his pocket; a tiny wooden horse his father had carved for him.

'Iago knows how to wield a sword. He likes to ride, he's a good archer and he knows his poetry,' she confided to him.

He had the strangest sensation that his legs were giving way beneath him. But he remained standing, his hands feeling terribly damp when she passed him the reins to his horse.

'He's a better rider than you and he would have found marvellous words to describe the landscape,' she added as she unhitched her mount from the tree.

Laerte tugged at the horse behind him, swaying as he walked, his head bowed. When she spoke of Iago like this her eyes shone with a glow that he did not like at all. Too lively by half. Iago was the son of the captain of the guard, and he had leanings to follow in his father's footsteps. And he was sixteen years old! And he was fair-haired. And tall. And whatever else he might be, Laerte would have seen it as a fault. Iago was the very image of a handsome young man that no one and nothing could resist. Laerte and the girl walked to the edge of the woods at their horses' sides.

'Oh, a frog!' she exclaimed as they approached the little path that wound through the trees.

She threw him her horse's reins and ran after the alarmed amphibian. Although her snatching gesture was swift, there was no roughness when she imprisoned the poor animal in the hollow of her hands.

She let the green head with black stripes peep out and placed a kiss upon it. When nothing happened, she opened her hands and the frog hopped away before disappearing in the grasses in the direction of the marshes.

'That's … nasty,' said Laerte, revolted. 'Do you really have to do that every time you see one … ?'

'Yes, because each time, it's possible that the frog will be my prince charming,' she defended herself with a shrug of her shoulders.

She came back to him and placed a finger upon his nose, narrowing her eyes.

'Who knows which frog a prince charming may be hiding behind?'

'Well, not that one. And who's to say you won't catch warts doing that?'

She led her horse to the dirt path which plunged into the forest, wending its way between flowering copses until it was no more than a faint trace between the tree trunks.

'Frogs don't give warts!' she said indignantly. 'My grandmother taught me they have all kinds of virtues, whatever people may say!'

'I know, I know …' Laerte agreed in an indifferent tone.

'The urine from rush frogs is a very good medicine! And they're not just poor little creatures, you know. Some of them could teach a thing or two to the finest strategists.'

She mounted her horse and her skirts rode up, revealing her legs to the thigh. Laerte swallowed, gripping the reins as tightly as he could. He wanted to kiss those legs, let the palm of his hand slide along them, smell their scent. It was a new and sudden feeling, so he lowered his eyes. Not to drive away these ideas which, in the end, were enjoyable, but in order not to encourage them further. He too mounted his horse and with a dig of his heels urged it to a walk.

'Did you know that the Erain frog feeds on wasps and hornets?' the girl continued saying. 'It has a peculiar technique for hunting them. Its skin takes on the colours of its prey as it approaches a hive, and they almost accept it as one of them. And then, at the very moment when they lower their guard …'

She tilted her head to the side, directing a sly glance in his direction.

'The Erain frog waits until it is as close as it can be to its enemies before striking. So you see, little count, how much one can learn from a simple frog.'

'Don't call me "little count",' he said sullenly.

'Sounds like someone's feelings are hurt … As much as they will be if you arrive last at the Watch's gates?'

She tapped twice with her heels and her horse broke into a gallop down the path. Startled, Laerte's horse reared, almost throwing him off. He wavered between anger and amusement as he watched her escape into the distance. Her curls seemed to float above the olive skin of her shoulders.

She was named Esyld Orbey, daughter of the blacksmith at Aëd's Watch. And Laerte of Uster, son of the count of the Saltmarsh region, had loved her day after day without daring to admit it to anyone. He launched into a gallop in his turn.

His path was already laid out ahead of him, just like the track he followed through the forest towards the town. One day he would be himself count of the Saltmarsh, and he had no idea if he could govern with the same easy assurance as his father, and without being able to rely on help from his brother, who would surely become a general, ensuring peace within the Empire. He would have a wife, and children. And then what? He was content with what he already had, without dreaming of more: doing what was asked of him, without giving more; learning to love in secret, without saying more. But there was one other thing he wanted. To be like Iago. Not Iago the handsome, the fair-haired and the talented. But to have a little of his charisma, a little of his skill ... and a little of Esyld's attention.

He caught up with her in the thickets. She had stopped, her face grim, and was staring beyond the trees at an odd black smoke rising from Aëd's Watch. When he finally drew up beside her, soothing his suddenly nervous mount, Esyld gave him a commanding look.

'Stay right here.'

'What? Why? What's going on?'

And then he saw the smoke. The keep was burning. His heart skipped a beat and his face turned pale. He did not dare move forward although Esyld spurred her horse and galloped towards the town's wooden ramparts. What would she find there? Laerte could have followed her, riding into the town to see for himself what was happening. But he, the Count of Uster's younger son, a mediocre swordsman, an average student, endowed with an ordinary physique, lacked even the ounce of courage needed to ride escort for his beloved.

The hooves of her mount hammered the dirt road leading to the gates of Aëd's Watch, before she disappeared in the distance behind a cloud of dust.

For more than an hour he waited at the edge of the forest, hesitating. What should he do? Join her? Stay here? What was going on? He dismounted and tethered his horse to a branch, then paced like an animal in a cage, his gaze fixed upon the town's walls. He leaned against a tree trunk, breathing heavily, as he heard the sounds of combat in the distance. There was a dry crackling noise behind him. He was just turning round when a slim gloved hand fell upon his shoulder. A second hand placed itself over his wide-open mouth to stifle his cry.

'Shh!' ordered a voice. 'Laerte, it's me.'

And beneath the blue cloak, he recognised Esyld. Why had she changed? Before he could ask she pulled a second cloak, this one black, out of a bag and held it out to him.

'Put this on, quickly. We need to get away from here. They've sent patrols out looking for you.'

'Who did?' he asked in a trembling voice. 'Esyld, what's happening?'

He put the garment on over his shirt. Esyld placed her hands on his shoulders and looked deeply into his eyes.

'The Empire. Your father has been arrested. So has your entire family.' She said it without betraying any hint of emotion.

'But ... why?'

'My father is with Captain Meurnau. They're in the northern part of town. Come on, we need to hurry. Let's go!'

The features of her face were so hard and tense that he barely recognised her. She took him by the hand and led him back into the forest. Meurnau, the captain of the guard ...

'A girl leaving town attracts less attention than a boy,' she said, sounding terribly nervous. 'Someone told them you'd gone into the marshes so they're combing the area all around the Watch, looking everywhere for you ...'

They reached the edge of the forest again where they found a small cart with a covered rear section waiting for them.

'But there's one place they won't imagine you would go. Hide in there, we might run into some soldiers ...'

The smile she gave him was so tense that he was not at all reassured. She helped him wriggle under the canvas. The sky was starting to become overcast and a rain shower was threatening in the distance. Between two soft bags stinking of manure, Laerte curled up like a newborn babe. His blood was pounding at his temples and his hands shook. He closed them into fists. His father had been arrested by the Empire without Laerte even knowing why. And if they were looking for him, they must want to subject him to the same fate. What crime had the House of Uster committed? It was not solely Oratio's writings that justified such an act. So why?

He heard the snap of the reins followed by the sound of hooves striking the ground. The cart began to move off.

'Whatever you do, don't move,' Esyld ordered.

During the few minutes that the trip took to the town gates, he only heard the sound of his own breathing, coming in heavy gasps. A mantle of anxiety enveloped him, while his skin was damp and his throat dry. When he detected the muffled calls of the soldiers hailing Esyld he held his breath. There was a tense exchange. The soldiers' voices were clipped, their tone conveying both authority and contempt. A single word taken the wrong way and it would be over for them both. Under the canvas he gathered his knees in tightly and closed his eyes. If a soldier attacked Esyld, would he have time to crawl out and come to her rescue? Would he even try? Would he shield her with his own body, allow a blade to pierce him? He held back a moan and tears trickled down his face. There were several small taps above him. A soldier must be running his hand over the cloth. The sound became more pronounced and the tapping increased ... No, it wasn't a soldier at all, but raindrops. The raincloud had reached Aëd's Watch.

Finally, the cart moved forward again. When it halted and someone lifted the canvas cover, Laerte's eyes were reddened from crying. Although the first face he saw in the dim light of a damp barn was that of bearded man and not Esyld's, he felt no less ashamed. Out of the corner of his eye he glimpsed the girl, soaked by the rain, watching him with a sad expression. He immediately wiped his eyes with the back of his eyes, gritting his teeth in anger. She must not see him like this. Not cowardly, lost, or unable to contain his feelings.

'Sir, you are safe. Come,' said the man, urging him forward with a hand on his shoulder. 'I thought they'd caught you in the woods. Time is running short.'

It was Esyld's father and, evidently, they were in the barn adjoining his workshop. He still wore his dusty apron over a black shirt, which strained to contain his broad shoulders. Behind a closed door, wood crackled in the forge's hearth, its orange light pulsing between the panel boards.

'Esyld, saddle the horses, we need to leave within the hour!' he informed her, as he led the boy towards a ladder giving access to a passageway.

They climbed without waiting for her, following the passageway to a small door upon which Master Orbey gave three rapid knocks followed by two slow. Over the railing Laerte glanced down at Esyld. She was busy preparing the horses, looking scared. In her haste she dropped the saddle she was carrying and swore at herself with a sob in her voice. She had seemed so resolute when she had come back to find him in the woods. How he would have preferred to stay with her and take her in his arms. At least he was sure of managing that.

The door creaked as it opened. Behind it two guards with hands on the pommels of their swords eyed the two new arrivals suspiciously. Recognising Orbey, they drew apart to let them enter. The room was cramped, with a few crates full of blacksmith's tools and a wide anvil retired from service placed in one corner. A man with a thin face marked with scars was seated at a table close to the single window overlooking one of Aëd's Watch's streets. Master Orbey's forge had been built in the highest part of the town. From here they had a view all the way to the big square at the foot of the church. Upon the table rested a county guard captain's helmet, recognisable from the dragon's head with the open maw above the nose guard. The man placed an iron gauntleted hand upon it.

'Captain Meurnau?' Laerte exclaimed in surprise, his throat still dry.

If he was here hiding in Master Orbey's workshop it meant the situation was even worse than he had imagined. Meurnau stood up and with a brisk nod of his head indicated a small stool by the crates.

'Sit down,' he told the boy in a firm tone.

Then, turning his back on Laerte, he invited Orbey to join him by the window.

'There are a great many of Azdeki's soldiers searching the area surrounding the town,' the blacksmith informed him in a murmur.

Passing a hand through his ash-blond hair, Meurnau inhaled deeply as he listened to the other man. It was as if they both trying to exclude Laerte from their conversation. He would surely not have

213

heard anything if he had sat down as the captain had instructed.

'They will come back when they find nothing and then we will be unable to leave by the north. We have to leave Aëd's Watch now, Orbey.'

'I know,' the blacksmith nodded. 'My daughter is already saddling the horses. But after that?'

'After that, we'll decide. The southwestern baronies have always respected the count and some there were open about sharing his vision of the world. We need to find a safe haven where we can organise the uprising.'

'The uprising? Meurnau, surely you're not contemplating that?!' Orbey exclaimed indignantly.

'Captain ...' said Laerte.

But the two men by the window were not listening to him. Orbey was seeking to draw the captain's elusive gaze. In the distance, in the square in front of a church, Laerte watched a gallows being erected.

'It's not what the count wants!'

'It's exactly what he wants, blacksmith,' retorted Meurnau. 'The Empire is dying, it's time for a change of governance.'

'Not by force!'

'Captain!' Laerte repeated, stepping forward a pace.

He balled his fists and felt the blood boiling in his veins. And in his head, one question was supplanting all the others ... but no one was paying him any attention.

'Since the Empire is depriving the Saltmarsh of its master without the consent of its people, then the Saltmarsh will declare its independence!' roared Meurnau. 'We've bent the knee long enough to the whims of a tyrant. To call Uster an outlaw and treat him with such contempt after all he has done for those barnyard roosters, it's disgraceful. Disgraceful!'

'*Captain Meurnau!*' Laerte yelled.

The two men spun round, seeing the boy's determined expression with astonishment. Meurnau had trained him in duelling several times, without hiding his doubts as to the boy's aptitude as a swordsman. Of Uster's three children, Laerte knew he was the quietest, the least forthcoming, the most timid on all occasions. For him to raise his voice like this, without arrogance, but with an authority similar to that of the count, surprised even himself. But he was so filled with anger that he could not remain silent.

'Where is my father?' Laerte demanded. 'My mother?'

'Laerte, we are trying to deal with the situation as best we can,' explained Meurnau. 'I must request that you remain in your—'

'Tell me what is happening here!' the boy exploded, locking eyes with the captain. 'Where is my family being held? Why has nothing been done to prevent this? Tell me!'

The captain blinked. It was the first time that Laerte had given him an order, from all of his twelve years of age. But in view of the respect Meurnau owed him, he was ready to defy the man in order to obtain answers. The blacksmith intervened instead, approaching the boy.

'Sir, there is a great deal of commotion within the town,' he started by saying. 'Captain Azdeki has come to arrest your father the count and your brother, accusing them of high treason against the Empire. Your mother and your sister have also been taken, we're unable to—'

'Your father is no traitor, Laerte,' the captain muttered angrily. 'This is all political manoeuvring by the Azdeki family and others,' he added in disgust.

'But why are they inventing such lies?' asked Laerte, in a dazed tone. 'Why would they do that?'

'I fear the Order of Fangol wants to reassert its status,' replied Meurnau. 'And the Emperor, in his weakness, has not opposed this.'

'Your family . . . possesses many things that make men jealous, sir,' Orbey added with an uncomfortable air.

Although Laerte had heard him, it was not what he wished to know, not the most important thing. Fear bore a hole in his stomach.

'Where is he now? Where is my father?'

His voice was trembling now. He imagined the worst.

'Master Orbey! Where is my father?'

The blacksmith took one step to the side, revealing the window behind him, and stood with his head bowed.

'They have already judged him, sir . . .'

In the distance, behind the wooden roofs of the houses below, the gallows could be seen. Someone was about to be hung. Laerte looked back and forth between the window and the men beside him. He didn't understand. He did not want to understand. In the end the why, how, when mattered little to him. The only thing he took angry note of was the guard captain's failure to take action. Obeying the inner rage that invaded him, he lost all self-restraint.

'And you're going to let him die?'

'Laerte …' Meurnau sighed.

'Go and rescue him! Stop this from happening!'

'Laerte, calm down!'

'You coward!' the boy screamed. 'Go and fight! You are under our orders! Obey me! My father is your count! Save him!'

'By all the gods, sir!' intervened Orbey. 'Get hold of yourself!'

Would they listen, take up arms and rescue his father? And liberate his mother, his brother and his sister? No. Neither Meurnau nor Master Orbey, nor the two soldiers present, seemed prepared to act. Overcome with anger, Laerte rushed to the door, taking all of them by surprise. He bolted down the passageway, reached the ladder and let himself slide down, his legs hugging the uprights. Behind him the captain's stern voice rang out.

'Laerte! Come back!'

He gave no thought to the risks he was taking. His reason had been obliterated by fear. This same fear was turning into a fierce determination. He had to see, with his own eyes, what was taking place on the forecourt of the church. The idea that he was powerless to prevent it did not even occur to him.

'Laerte?' said Esyld in astonishment as she saw him pushing open the barn doors.

'Sir!' Orbey was calling from the passageway.

Meurnau was already descending the ladder. Without even giving the girl a glance. Laerte mounted the horse she had just finished saddling. As the captain rushed forward to stop him, he spurred his mount and galloped away through the deserted streets of Aëd's Watch. The absence of the town's inhabitants did not worry him, for in the distance the sound of the crowd guided him. Their clamour was joined by the sound of the rain, like the roll of drums. When he was only two streets away from the square, spying the halberds held by soldiers in black uniforms at the corner of a house, he slowed down and covered his head with the patched hood of his cloak. He dismounted, releasing the horse without even attempting to tether it, and continued forward. He almost retreated, heart pounding, when a squad of soldiers passed in front of him, their boots stamping across the ground swept by the rain shower. He finally thought of the danger he was courting, of the folly he was committing with this sudden outburst of passion. The Empire was hunting for him. His father was going to be executed. Instead of fleeing, he had thrown himself in the wolf's jaws. What could he possibly do against an entire army ...?

Yet something forced him on. A strange fire burned inside him that he could not name or even describe. Perhaps hope still ran in his veins, to make his heart beat so fast. He had the sense that his clothes had suddenly become too small for him. He walked to the forecourt. A crowd pressed round the wide gallows that had been hastily erected. There was no joy, no enthusiasm, only cries of dismay, and some of outrage. And for good reason. His father stood straight and proud, gazing into the distance, on the platform, ready to be executed. At his side, his eyes lowered despite his attempt to remain dignified, his elder brother was murmuring a prayer. A rope was knotted around his neck and his hands were tied behind his back. Laerte almost fell to the ground.

He inhaled deeply.

'Silence! Silence!'

At the front of the platform, a man with a gaunt face and a hawk-like nose tried to calm the crowd's ire with quieting gestures. He wore silvery armour and a wide red cape attached at his shoulders and falling to his heels. An eagle was painted upon his breastplate, crushing a snake in its talons.

Led by a man in light armour, undoubtedly a young knight, spear-men positioned themselves in front of the gallows to hold back the crowd. Laerte made his way through the spectators without anyone noticing him. Just as he paid no attention to them. He hunched slightly, lowering his head towards his chest. The rain made his cloak even heavier. He was allowed to pass and no one recognised him, all those present stunned by the spectacle of their beloved count standing at the end of a rope. When Laerte drew close to the line of soldiers at the foot of the gallows, he read upon their faces a determination that sent a chill down his spine.

'Silence!' repeated the man on the platform.

There was a semblance of quiet during which he looked out over the crowd with a piercing gaze.

'I, Captain Etienne Azdeki, am here in the name of His Majesty the Emperor Asham Ivani Reyes, to judge the traitors you see before you ...'

He pointed an accusing finger at the two prisoners standing a few feet from him and then looked back at the crowd with a grim expression.

'The man who has governed you all these years has fomented a plot against your Emperor, spread false words and sowed dissent and doubt in your hearts and minds! His Imperial Majesty himself has observed his high treason. The Order of Fangol has also laid charges—'

Protests rose from the crowd. Huddled together near the gallows, a group of monks in black habits tried to maintain brave faces.

'—charges against him,' Azdeki continued. 'Count Oratio of Uster has committed numerous offences and, despite many warnings from our Bishop of Emeris, has expressed no remorse! In light of the many accusations against him and despite the Emperor's sorrow, it is with sad resignation that I must now pronounce their sentence!'

Resignation? Azdeki showed no sign of it. Laerte gave him a baleful look, taking care to memorise the tiniest feature of his face. This man had brought calamity into the boy's life and now he knew his name: Etienne Azdeki. Nevertheless, Laerte still did not believe for a single second that his father and his brother would lose their lives. In the next few instants, surely someone was going to rescue them.

'My hand . . .' said a quiet voice beside him.

Laerte became aware of people shifting about behind him and, turning his head, he met Esyld's stricken gaze. He immediately lowered his eyes.

'Hold my hand. Take it,' she insisted in a murmur. 'Hold it tight.'

The young woman's fingers slipped between his. He gripped her hand as if it were the most precious thing in the world. Her skin was smooth, her warmth comforting. Her presence alone slowed the beating of his heart. He fought a mad urge to seize her in his arms for fear that she might escape.

'Lord Oratio Montague, Count of Uster, has been found guilty of high treason against the Empire and His Imperial Majesty Asham Ivani Reyes, and of offending the gods and their representatives, the monks of the Fangolin Order. For this, and as prescribed by law, he and all his descendants shall suffer the penalty of death.'

An angry growl ran through the crowd. The guards brandished their spears to pre-empt any attempts to interfere. The monks stepped back, lowering their hoods over their shaven heads, and started to chant. Azdeki turned towards the count and met his black eyes without any trace of hesitation. Sure of his power, he stepped towards the condemned man.

'Death ... by hanging,' he added, staring deep into the count's eyes.

There was dried blood on the prisoner's white shirt and in his full beard, and bruises beneath his tired eyes. His split lips twisted into a snarl.

'Smile, Count,' whispered Azdeki, feigning a downcast expression for the benefit of the spectators. 'You've bitten the hand that feeds you ... and now here you are ... at the end ...'

Azdeki brought his mouth close to Uster's ear and murmured:

'... of a rope ...'

How filthy and worn-out the count looked in his rumpled clothing, despite the dignified bearing he struggled to maintain before his people. At his side, his elder son choked back a sob. The count had defended his family, he had opposed their arrest, fought the Imperial soldiers in the hallways of the keep. But his valour had not been enough. Now here he was, on the gallows, in the company of his first son, and dreading the fate awaiting his wife and daughter. There were only two things that let him stand tall and proud at death's door: the need to die a martyr, so that his life's work would not be swept away by his last breath, and the comfort of knowing that one member of his family was still at large. Laerte. His little Laerte had wandered off again, into the marshes with the blacksmith's daughter. There was at least one Uster that Azdeki could not torture and then execute in public.

'Squeeze my hand,' Esyld's said in the boy's ear.

'Hangman!' Azdeki called out loud and clear.

And at that moment, among the crowd, the count was horrified to see the sad, grave face of his younger son.

'Do your duty!'

'Squeeze it as hard as you like ...'

For the first time in his life, Laerte saw fear in his father's eyes.

The hangman lowered a lever abruptly. There was a drumming sound ...

And the sharp crack as the boards gave way beneath the condemned men's feet.

Two thumps ...

And then only the sound of the wind blowing the rain over a

crowd struck dumb with horror while two bodies dangled at the ends of their ropes. Laerte closed his eyes, his chest squeezed by an unbearable pain to the point of drawing tears from his eyes. His hand still gripped Esyld's and he bent his knees, feeling a cry growing in his throat. She put her arm about him and took him through the onlookers as they slowly began to stir from their state of shock.

'People of the Saltmarsh!' hailed Azdeki. 'You have been freed from the rule of a usurper! You have returned to the light of the Holy Empire!'

Laerte was not seeing the light. He could barely make out the figures of those in front of him, among the raindrops, among the tears. They passed a squad of soldiers marching slowly towards one of the streets leaving the square and Esyld dragged him beneath a coach gate. When they came to halt, and after making sure no one could see them, she lowered her hood and took the boy's face in her hands.

'We have to leave, we must leave now ... Be courageous, proud little lord, be the bravest of us all ...'

She brushed the boy's cheeks, her sad gaze connecting with his.

'My father ...' he managed through the sobs, 'my brother ...'

Terror seized him then as his mouth twisted in pain. His throat was squeezed so tightly, his heart scraped so raw, he could not say another word. His mother and his little sister were still being held prisoner, alone and helpless. Unless Meurnau had freed them? Yes. He must surely have.

'You will weep for them later,' Esyld said gently. 'But please, do not run off again. Your life is precious to us.'

She let her fingers climb along his face and she pressed her brow against his, closing her eyes.

'Your life is precious to me,' she added in a murmur.

Through the haze, everything became clearer for Laerte. He concentrated on this one single priority: follow Esyld wherever she went, wherever she wished. All the questions he was asking himself, all the torments afflicting him, were covered by a warm veil. He allowed himself to be taken back to the barn, looking haggard and bereft. Meurnau did not say a word to him. Orbey treated him with kid gloves. They hid him in the back of the covered cart again. Then they left the town in the greatest of secrecy while men belonging to the county guard, still loyal to their dead master, distracted the Imperial soldiers by taking them on in a series of skirmishes.

Night fell quickly upon the Saltmarsh. Aëd's Watch was lit up by a thousand torches upon the wooden ramparts. And throughout the region, Azdeki sent his men to ensure his domination.

In a hamlet by the marshes, a few miles from the town, Laerte saw the flickering flames in the dusk, like the fragile light from a past life. He could no longer cry. Behind him, Meurnau was arranging watch duties with the handful of men who had joined them. There were barely a dozen wooden houses in this salt harvesters' village, but Azdeki would leave no stone unturned to find the count's missing offspring. The entire region would be put to the sword in order to eliminate the House of Uster.

'Where is my mother?' asked Laerte without detaching his eyes from the town in the distance.

There was no reply.

'And my little sister?'

'I'm sorry ...'

He had sought them out with his eyes during the chaos of their flight, as he was carried away roughly by Meurnau's guards. Since their departure from Aëd's Watch, this was the first time he had spoken. Esyld emerged from the shadow of the house they had chosen to spend the night. She placed herself to his right and their fingers brushed.

'They killed them too?' he asked with icy calm.

She burst into sobs.

'I'm sorry, Laerte ... so sorry,' she repeated, burying her face in her hands.

In a single day, Laerte of Uster had lost everything. His entire family, his town, his future ... He was no more than an empty husk, ready to be broken.

She tried to take his hand but he moved away from her. For the first time he snubbed her, without his usual fear of alienating her affections. He fished about in the pocket of his trousers and brought out the small wooden horse. How many times had he played with it? How many battles had he led against imaginary hordes? His fingers closed about the polished curves of the tiny sculpture and he squeezed it so tightly he thought his palm would bear the mark forever. Then, with a swift gesture, he threw the toy as far as he could away from him. The wooden horse disappeared into the night. There was no more Esyld, no more Aëd's Watch, no more Meurnau, no more Orbey. It was only him and his rage. And he realised what he desired above all else.

One day, he would be the greatest knight in this world ... and, all on his own, he would bring the Empire crashing down.

2

HUNTED

He shall have no rest, no refuge.
Whether by day or by night,
Wherever he goes he shall be
No more than game
Fleeing from the hunt.

They fled. Constantly. Endlessly. They roamed the Saltmarsh region in silence, penetrating the marshes, making their way through the tall grasses and the mud. From village to village, from makeshift camps in isolated spots to the thick of the swamps, their only goal was to protect Laerte and to keep him as far as possible from the growing shadow of Etienne Azdeki. The boy felt it at his back, menacing and vicious. Sometimes he looked back, fearing he would see the Imperial captain's proud figure challenging him with his gaze. But there was never anything but whichever bumpy road they were following.

Their party numbered twenty in all, for the most part soldiers of the county guard who had left their armour behind them, playing the role of simple peasants. Often they placed the boy in the back of a cart, Esyld at his side, and all of them wearing rags; they travelled like poor wretches leaving the war-torn region. Azdeki's troops continued to comb the area, searching the columns of refugees. The few times they were stopped they came close to being unmasked. Each time Esyld drew close to Laerte, taking his hand in hers and whispering soothing words in the hollow of his ear.

And always the soldiers ordered them to be on the way, looking frustrated. Who could claim to recognise Laerte of Uster? Who even knew what he looked like? And what inhabitant of the Saltmarsh, who crossed his path, would been vile enough to hand over an innocent child to be put to death? Oratio of Uster had been loved by his people. His death was a cause for grief and surrendering his last living child to the Emperor's wrath would have been an insult to his memory. The registers were burned. Mentions of Laerte, erased ... The few people who knew the boy's age and appearance kept quiet.

This silent form of support protected them during their flight, a silence accepted by all as the only possible defence against the folly of a captain of the Empire. No tongues wagged and Azdeki was forced to acknowledge that he'd made his first mistake. In his haste, he had let a single child, a mere boy, slip away from him. The rumour of his survival was enough to foment rebellion. Little by little, people took up arms, farms rebelled and hamlets were transformed into fortified camps. Revolt was stirring. And Captain Meurnau was prepared to do everything in his power to make it become a loud roar.

'Drink,' he said to Laerte, one day when they were halted by the side of a road.

Sitting in the rear of the cart, a wide, thick cloth covering him from head to toe, the boy extended a pale hand and took the flask proffered by the captain. They had been travelling for months now with no real destination, if there had ever been one. And during that time Laerte had only uttered a few words. He often remained mute, as if absent, and his gaze grew darker with each passing day.

The boy took a gulp and returned the flask, wiping his mouth with the back of his hand. Meurnau did the same as he took a seat to the boy's right, on the edge of the cart. He sighed as he contemplated the marshes bordering the road. In the distance, thick black smoke rose into a charcoal-grey sky.

'They've burned the village of Aguel,' he murmured.

At the approach of winter, the villages nearest the Watch had risen up following the example set by more distant towns. Once the stupefaction caused by the summary judgement of their beloved count has passed, anger had taken hold.

Even dead, Oratio of Uster remained a thorn in the Emperor's side ... Worse still, his memory stirred the crowds to the point of rebellion. Aguel was not the first village to be razed in this fashion by Azdeki's troops, and it would surely not be the last.

'Do you know why they're doing that?' asked Meurnau.

Laerte had been asking himself the same question. Just as he tried to understand why his entire family had been judged unworthy by the Empire it served. He had always imagined Emeris as a city of wise men, where everything was decided, watched over by a benevolent Emperor. And, like an omniscient god, he took care of the world … He had so often been proud of the fact that his father was the Emperor's representative here in the Saltmarsh.

'They thought we were idiots,' the captain answered himself.

He passed a hand over his sunken-cheeked face before smoothing his fine jet-black moustache with his fingertips.

'They thought that once your father was dead, we would all bend our knee. But Oratio of Uster is stronger than the Emperor, here. It was he who governed. It was he who was loved.'

Laerte remained beneath his cover, his gaze blank, giving no response. He heard, he understood, but in the end it made little difference to know why, how, or even who … Only two things mattered to him: why he had been spared and why he had been unable to save his family …

'That's why he was killed,' admitted Meurnau. 'That's why he was judged. Because he was loved. But the Emperor decided—'

'He wasn't a traitor,' Laerte said bluntly.

Surprised to hear the boy's voice, Meurnau remained silent for a moment, observing him out of the corner of his eye. But the child had once again become as still as a statue.

'No, not really,' agreed Meurnau, getting down from the cart, his gaze turning towards his men seated not far from them, engaged in a discussion.

Close by the ragged-looking soldiers, Orbey and his daughter were busy hiding swords in big canvas bags.

'But your father's dreams ran contrary to the Emperor's rule,' continued the captain. 'He wanted the world to be free from the decisions of a single man … He thought that people were capable of choosing for themselves. It's too complicated for you to understand now, but always remember one thing, Laerte: if your father is dead, above all he died for his people. He would never betray them.'

The boy lowered his eyes when Meurnau turned to face him. No, he didn't understand. Nor did he feel any urge to try. The present moment did not count. Nor did any thought of tomorrow enter his mind. There was nothing but emptiness.

'In a few days we will be stopping at Braquenne,' the captain announced coldly. 'There we'll teach you how to fight. And we will prepare the revolution. Do you hear me, Laerte?'

Yes, he heard the captain, but there were tiny pebbles upon the road and Laerte preferred to look at them rather than this austere captain always spouting words devoid of any significance. The pebbles were so small, so brown, lying upon a grey earth that had started to crackle from the frost.

'Laerte,' insisted Meurnau.

But the boy no longer paid him any mind. Weary of it, Meurnau swept the air with his hand before moving away.

And they continued on the road for days on end. One morning, a new column of black smoke rose into the sky. Another burnt village. Laerte was surprised not to feel anything as he pictured the villagers being consumed by the flames. They reached Braquenne at last, a small village composed of fifty broad single-storey houses built of stone, in the middle of the marshes. They had been travelling for months... and yet Braquenne was no more than two days from Aëd's Watch. What a complicated path they must have taken to throw off the Imperial troops, But at last they had a place where they could stay, somewhere they could hide. Oddly enough, the safest place for them right now was as close as possible to their enemy. Azdeki had sent his troops out over greater and greater distances, convinced they were fleeing towards the other counties.

While Meurnau endeavoured to plan the rebellion, Laerte fell into the care of a bald colossus named Madog. Sturdy and proud, he had been Meurnau's second-in-command within the Count of Uster's guard. The scar running from his right eye to his upper lip instilled both fear and a certain respect, and Madog was charged with training Laerte for combat. During the year that followed, he tried to teach the boy to wield a sword properly. Without success.

Although Laerte's general attitude changed for the better, he remained sullen during classes. Between the wide houses he railed, sword in hand, after falling on his arse. But he was still far more interested in the moments he passed with the blacksmith's daughter, avoiding the tedious attentions of his master-at-arms.

Madog took him aside. The first time, he refrained from scolding the boy for leaving the village and risking his life. It wasn't Azdeki's men who worried him, truth be told; there had been no patrols within two days of their hideaway. But the rouargs were populous in the area. The second time Laerte ran away, Madog seemed to realise that nothing would stop him short of attaching the boy to a stake, and that he would have to make the best of a bad situation. He therefore gave the boy an unusual present.

'This is a whistle.'

'A whistle?' asked Laerte in surprised.

Seated on a bench along the wall of one of the stone houses, he examined the strange piece of hollowed wood.

'A rouarg whistle,' Madog explained. 'When you're out roaming the countryside, I can't protect you. If the Imperial soldiers spot you, I hope you can run fast. But as far as the rouargs go, you won't be able to shake them off.'

He pointed to the whistle.

'This whistle imitates the growl of a male rouarg. It's the females who hunt, rarely the males. So when a male approaches, the females flee out of fear of . . .'

A carnivorous smile lit up the man's marked face.

'. . . of receiving one hell of a thrashing. If rouargs are chasing you, use it.'

Very fortunately, Laerte had no occasion to do so in the following months and, while Madog spent hours searching for him in the village to keep up pretences, the boy escaped out into the marshes in more pleasant company. With Esyld, he could forget who and where he was, and no longer thought about or dreaded what might become of him. The girl devoted her attention to studying frogs. One spring day, she spotted an Erain frog. Dull green in colour with golden stripes, it was nonchalantly hopping through the tall grasses. They followed it, and the risk of running into Imperial soldiers only added spice to their expedition. The fear spurred them on rather than slowing their progress. Hearts beating, they watched the frog rush towards an upturned cart. It surely belonged to fugitives, like themselves, who had had an accident and been forced to abandon their load here in the middle of the marshes.

'Shh,' Esyld ordered. 'We mustn't frighten it. Look.'

She lifted the hem of her dress, revealing her smooth knees, and halted a few yards away from the creature. Slowly, she knelt down upon the damp earth and, placing a gentle hand on Laerte's shoulder, invited him to do likewise.

'It's hunting,' she remarked. 'There's a hornets' nest over there, do you see it? And do you see how it's changing colour? And underneath its eyes, look closely and you can see the skin there fluttering like insect wings. It's pretending to be a whole group of hornets. They can't see the difference … they think it's part of the hive.'

In the bottle green of the tall grasses, sitting on a wet rock, the frog turned a darker shade, while its golden stripes lightened to a bright yellow. The slow swelling of its throat produced an oddly hypnotic effect. Esyld and Laerte remained completely still, watching the amphibian. There was nothing to disturb its apparent repose. In a corner of the cart, a barely completed hornets' nest quivered. All around the oval shape covered in a brown resin, the big insects went about their business without being alarmed by the frog's presence.

'My grandmother told me it can wait like this for days,' whispered Esyld, an admiring smile on her lips. 'Some hornets will come out to look at it, but it won't move. Then, when it feels the time is right, it will attack and they'll have no idea what's happening. Do you see how beautiful it is?'

But Laerte was no longer looking at the frog. He was watching the long curling hair slipping over the delicate nape of her neck, her shoulders lightly covered by a dusty dress, and her slender, fragile fingers joined in a worshipful pose. His heart was beating so hard, and without any pain. Quite the contrary.

'What?' she asked, noticing him staring at her with a rapt face.

'It's not beautiful,' he replied timidly. 'But you are …'

He turned his eyes away. And Esyld placed her hand on his without either of them uttering another word.

When evening arrived he could still feel that sweet warmth upon his skin. He hoped life would go on like this, that the commotion caused by the loss of his family would die away. He continued to train with Madog, for days on end.

'Lift your sword,' yelled the colossus. 'Keep your grip! Arggh! Meurnau told me you were clumsy, but I never thought you were such a butterfingers.'

Weeks on end.

'Watch your footing,' scolded Madog. 'Be careful, blast you!'

And summer followed spring.

'Come on, Laerte!' encouraged Esyld, seated on a barrel near one of the houses. 'Come on! Defend yourself!'

'You can parry better than that! Parry!' ordered Madog.

Although he gradually improved he was far from standing any

chance in actual combat. He was too stiff and while he memorised certain sequences, he reproduced them without any great conviction – to the despair of his instructor. Perhaps he didn't take after his father at all ...

After the summer came autumn and another winter. During all this time, Meurnau rallied many villages to his cause and, little by little, the resistance organised itself. Ordinary peasants agreed to take up arms, driven by an anger that had been pent up for far too long. The death of their count had still not been accepted and the very idea that his son Laerte could be leading the rebellion at the captain's side emboldened them. And then there were the terrible rumours concerning the deaths of Laerte's mother and sister, and the torture inflicted upon these two innocent victims; barbaric crimes perpetrated for no reason but bestial cruelty ... The Empire no longer had any justification for its existence when those who served it succumbed to their basest instincts. The captain envisaged retaking Aëd's Watch shortly. He had his army now.

One evening, in the biggest of the houses at Braquenne, heated by a wide, austere fireplace, Laerte observed his second meeting between Meurnau and his men. Not that he had been invited to it. He was nothing more than a symbol for the rest of the Saltmarsh. His own identity had been blurred into an altogether larger, handsomer and older figure. But at this moment, he hadn't yet realised he had vanished in favour of a ghost. There he was, enjoying some hot soup while Esyld darned his jacket by the hearth.

'The attack will take place in the spring,' explained Meurnau standing behind a table, his hands resting upon a map of the Saltmarsh.

His lieutenants, including Madog, gathered around him and listened attentively. Some had come especially from the neighbouring villages where they were training the inhabitants to fight. The number of skirmishes had multiplied for several months now, and it was murmured that Azdeki was beginning to doubt that the region could be pacified.

'We will surround Aëd's Watch without alerting them to the fact, approaching here ... and here.'

He pointed at two places on the map.

'They don't imagine for a single instant that the entire population will take up arms,' he assured them with a satisfied air. 'But already, in the neighbouring counties, some are calling the validity of the Emperor's actions into question. And once the people start to doubt …'

'Here you go, proud little man, this will keep you warm.'

'Thank you,' he answered shyly.

The flames crackled, devouring the log with passion; their light shone in her eyes. He could not tear his own eyes away, hoping to read something more than mere … affection there. Perhaps he should confess what he truly felt, or simply kiss her. Yes, he should ask her to accompany him to the house next door where he slept and there, on the porch, he should place a kiss upon her sweet lips. She would not push him away. She had taken care of him, out of more than compassion. She loved him. It could only be that. He would ask her. He had to.

He was going to do it.

'Esyld …' he murmured.

'Esyld, go fetch some wood,' ordered a voice behind him.

And Master Orbey's firm hand fell upon the boy's shoulder at the very moment when he was preparing to get up. Because Esyld had nodded to him before leaving her wooden stool. She moved towards the front door while her father took her place with an embarrassed air. She disappeared into the cold night and the door slammed behind her.

'Sir,' said Master Orbey, rubbing his hands near the fire, 'I saw you the other day, training with Madog.'

He brushed his beard with the back of his hand, looking thoughtful before taking the plunge:

'You aren't very attentive, sir. I'm worried.'

Laerte gave him a brief glance before turning towards the door. He was only waiting for one thing: Esyld's return. Unless he found a way to escape her father's sermon and join her in the settling night.

'I know you have been through a terrible ordeal, but … every wound closes.'

The blacksmith hesitated. Laerte looked sharply towards him, his eyes blazing. Neither of them dared to say a word. Until at last, Laerte broke the heavy silence.

'I will not forget my family,' he muttered defiantly.

'I'm not asking you to,' Orbey seemed to excuse himself, raising his hands before him. 'Not for anything in the world. What I'm trying to say is that this wound eating away at you, you need to put it behind you. You must learn how to fight. For the memory of your father.'

'You know nothing of him,' the boy snapped, on the edge of tears.

By what right did this mere blacksmith evoke Oratio of Uster? Although he had been in his father's service, he had no family bond with him. Any more than with his son.

'I'm not asking you to forget him,' Orbey insisted with greater conviction. 'You can never do that. All wounds heal, although the scars remind us of them. And if the pain is less keen, it still cuts deep.'

He slowly stood up.

'This loss, nothing will ever fill it. But ... I dread that we will lose you if you don't listen to Madog more closely.'

The boy did not have time to respond. The door opened with a sudden bang and two men, holding a third by the shoulders, entered the house shouting.

'Come on, you cur! Tell them what you did!'

'What is it?' rumbled Meurnau.

'It's old Bastian from the Creeks house,' explained one of the two men.

The third man did not attempt to hide his fear, his white hair tousled over a weathered face. Gaunt-looking, lost inside a thick cloak that fell to his worn-out, muddy boots, he cast wild eyes at the pair holding him in their grip.

'Mercy ... mercy,' he begged in a high-pitched voice.

'He was in Aëd's Watch two days ago and not just to stock up on provisions. He's a coward! A traitor!' raged the other man.

Meurnau went to Bastian and gripped him by the throat.

'What?'

'I-I ... I beg you,' stammered Bastian.

'What have you done?'

'He's sold us out,' snarled one of the soldiers.

'No, I-I just said ...'

'You said what?' rasped Meurnau.

A distant voice interrupted the interrogation.

'To arms! To *arms*! The Empire is coming!'

'I didn't want to,' sobbed Bastian. 'But they gave me money for my family. I told them you were in Braquenne, that you were protecting

231

Laerte of Uster. He gave me money so that my family could eat. The winter is hard, sir, and—'

'Who did you tell?'

'Captain Etienne Azdeki,' the old man confessed.

'We can't do anything against a knight with the *animus*,' lamented Madog.

'Laerte!' Meurnau called.

Outside, the voices of the soldiers could be heard beneath the flickering torches. Azdeki was coming. Of the tumult that followed, Laerte only had a confused memory. The lieutenants drew their swords, people ran to and fro, and there was an increasing din. Until finally Meurnau's hands lifted the stunned boy and carried him to the other end of the room, near a small door.

'Laerte, you have to go,' he said.

When the boy did not move, he raised his voice.

'Do you hear me, Laerte? It's Azdeki! I don't know if we can escape him. You must flee. At least we can lead him away from you. Flee, Laerte! Go!'

But Laerte still didn't move. The lieutenants left by the front door, and he heard their war cries. He heard the dry ring of swords striking one another, screams, and a rising roar ... Yet everything seemed so slow in the boy's eyes, so surprisingly blurry, and ...

The hand that slapped his cheek brought him out of his torpor, his heart leaping in his chest. The Empire. The Empire was here. Fear held him in its grip and would not let go.

'Flee, Laerte! Go on!' shouted Meurnau as he opened the door.

Without further hesitation, the boy plunged into the night, barely hearing the door slam behind him over the pounding of his heart. He fell to his knees on the frozen earth and the din of the battle became more distinct. He feverishly regained his feet. To his right, the gigantic shadows of the combatants were projected against a wall. Deformed, yet splendid and frightening, they sometimes merged together, haloed in the reddish light of the torches.

'Laerte?' called a small voice.

She appeared out of the night, her breath whistling and her cheeks crimson from running. There was fear in her eyes. In the distance, the clamour of the battle continued to resound.

'Run,' she said brusquely. 'Go away.'

He stood there at a loss, without knowing what to do or where to go, whether to fight or take flight, to die somewhere far from her or perhaps here in her arms or ...

'Go away, Laerte! *Go!*'

Her voice cracked like a whip, stinging him. She was not asking him to go, she was ordering it. Her fine features were twisted by a savageness that was quite unlike her.

'*Go away!*' she insisted.

He darted off into the night, making his way between the tall marsh grasses that lashed his face. He ran as fast as could, until the fighting was no more than a distant echo and only the icy starlight lit his path. His legs became heavy, his breathing painful, his throat dry and prickly, but he didn't stop. Esyld's voice repeated in his head, so harsh and brutal: '*Go away, go, go away!*'

His boots sank into stagnant water but still he went on. He almost became mired in a patch of thick sludge. He went on. He fell, scraping his knee against a jutting rock, and almost smothered himself in the mud as he wept. He got up and went on.

His chest was on fire and he felt dizzy. His breath rasped in his throat and his heart felt ready to explode; and tears ran down his mud-stained cheeks in a steady flow. There was only blackness before him, a series of barely distinguishable shadows, and the sound of hoots and snapping wood carried on the slow breeze. He was all alone out here, in the dark ...

He fell forward. And this time he did not get up. There was nothing but pitch blackness and a long soothing silence. Then a murmur, like a distant chirping.

Laerte blinked. Something viscous, with a bitter taste, was obstructing his mouth. He coughed once, closing his eyes.

The wind caressed his cheek, lifting his filthy hair. He coughed again, harder this time, and gradually recovered his wits. He was lying on his belly among the tall grasses, sunk in the mud with part of his face immersed. He rose with a start before immediately folding in two, coughing up the soggy earth that was choking him. When he finally felt better, he stood up. He had no idea how long he'd been running. Swamps surrounded him for as far as the eye could see. Except for ... protruding from the tall grasses, turned upon its side atop a small dry mound, he recognised the cart with the hornets' nest. He decided to make his way towards it, taking stumbling steps. He was exhausted, his mind empty and he collapsed on the dry ground a few yards from the cart and passed out again.

When he regained consciousness, a host of question assailed him. What would become of him now he was alone? What could he do? Where could he go? How would he survive? Had Meurnau fought off the attack? Esyld ... she'd survived, he felt certain of it. She could not die. He would go find her and ... no. He knew nothing for sure, except that Empire had killed his family and was hunting him like a cur. He was reduced to the state of a beast at bay.

Amidst his worries, he gave a cry of joy upon seeing the broken hornet's nest lying on the ground. This simply discovery offered such relief that he almost sobbed. The Erain frog had stuffed itself full of insects, leaving only the dried-out empty husk of their shelter. The cart was suddenly as welcoming as any of the houses at Braquenne and the boy began to search the crates, looking for the means to arrange a comfortable hideaway. He spread old fabrics on the ground, devoured peaches from jars as if he hadn't eaten for days, and finally fell asleep when the sun was at its zenith.

Over the following days, this consolation faded away to be replaced by a terrible sense of despair. Not a soul passed through the neighbouring marshes; Laerte was well and truly alone. Meurnau had probably died during the attack by the Imperial soldiers. The days became weeks and the spring arrived in a timely manner to warm the Saltmarsh's breeze. Tormented by hunger pangs, Laerte had been forced to learn how to hunt hive frogs, remembering Esyld's claims that their tender meat was similar to chicken.

He tried to make fire without success, managing to cut his hand several times in the process. He had to content himself with eating the frogs raw, almost vomiting with each mouthful. The flesh was slimy, the blood sticky, the nerves hard to chew. But it was the only food available to him. Everything he had learned from Esyld, which had seemed so useless at the time, he now used to survive. Because the marshes were a veritable breeding ground for frogs with multiple virtues. The mucus from one allowed him to prepare an ointment, while another turned out to be a nourishing dish.

Several times he pondered leaving his hideout and trying to reach Aëd's Watch. But was he even certain of finding the right path through the swamps and, if he did, what would he find in the town? Meurnau and his men, if they had survived, would surely have combed the countryside looking for him. But what if they believed he was dead?

The days passed and his despair grew so oppressive that he became incapable of doing anything at all. He remained prostrate, famished and weary ... and then came a morning when he finally came close to death and found he lacked the courage to face it. He finally stood up, and decided not to let himself die in this place.

The weeks became months, the mildness of spring became the heat of summer. Until that day when, moving through the tall grasses far from his lair, hunting hive frogs, he heard a voice roar:

'*Azdeki!* Godsfuck! Tomlinn!'

Through the grasses, he could make out a man on horseback sweeping the air with his sword. And circling him were three growling rouargs.

'Tomlinn! Azdeki!'

When one of the beasts leapt upon the knight, toppling both rider and steed, Laerte fought the urge to run away as fast as he could. But it was not morbid curiosity that led him to watch the massacre, no, it was a sense of vengeance. The Imperial troops had killed his family ... and now it was if his own region was avenging the Count of Uster and his people. He stood up to get a better view of the man being devoured but then immediately crouched down again, nervous. In the distance he'd seen at least sixty other soldiers carrying heavy pieces of wood, parts of what looked like a dismantled bridge. When he dared to lift his head again, he watched them march away without any hint of concern for their comrade.

'Azdeki! Tomlinn!' screamed the knight, just a few yards away from him.

The rouarg's snarling covered his voice; the knight would soon be torn to shreds. Laerte decided to leave the scene, preferring not to hear his death screams. Especially since he risked the same fate himself if one of the rouargs noticed his presence. He turned around, still crouching, when his hand brushed against the bulge in his pocket. The whistle. The rouarg whistle. A feeling of guilt came over him, more cutting than a sword, heavier than lead, unbearably painful. To watch a man die, whoever he might be, was one thing. But to fail to intervene when one had the means to save that man's life was another. The satisfaction he derived from seeing vengeance done collapsed beneath the weight of a shame as unexpected as it was sudden. Would he really allow the man to die like this?

He heard a strange sound behind him.

Throwing a frightened glance over his shoulder, he witnessed the unthinkable. The rouarg was thrown into the air by an invisible force and, along with it, the mauled carcass of a horse. A terrible scream rang out, harrowing, so awful that Laerte sank into the mud and covered his ears. Was it possible to suffer so much? The cry had nothing human about it and, when it died, it was like an icy silence had fallen on the marshes. Laerte plunged his hand into his pocket and seized the whistle. He held it so tightly it felt as though the piece of wood had pierced his palm and when the wind carried the thuds of an approaching rouarg, he brought it to his lips. He tried to blow, hard and fast, in bursts. No sound came out. His throat was too constricted and he gasped for breath. The thudding drew closer and the grasses bent beneath the wind. He inhaled, swelling his lungs, and blew, stronger still, forcing as much air as possible into the tiny piece of hollow wood. He needed to blow harder. There was a growling noise, so close that he thought he could feel the beast's fetid breath on him. He filled his lungs and blew again and was rewarded with a dull snarl. Then a second. And a third which he continued until his face turned bright scarlet.

Believing they heard the roar of a male, the female rouargs immediately fled and Laerte found the courage to stand up, still short of breath. The Imperial troops had vanished over the horizon. The tall grasses waved slowly beneath a sparkling white sky. Little by little, nature emerged from its torpor and the croaking of frogs became audible again. Not far from them, a harnessed horse came towards him at a walk, looking lost. Its reins hung from its neck, and a badly clawed red saddle sat on its back.

'Why ...?'

He examined the knight's body and almost fainted when he saw the crushed leg, the blood mixing into the marsh mud in odd spirals.

'Why didn't you tell me?'

It was perhaps simple compassion that made him try to save the knight when he was at death's door. His respiration was weak. His skin was pale.

'I thought you were dead ... I thought you were ...'

It was perhaps mercy that made him bring the man to his hideaway ... and then watched him gradually decline without feeling anything, neither pity nor hate. When he saw the empty scabbard at the man's belt, he went back out into the heart of the marsh to look for the sword. He spent more than an hour searching the thick mud in the rain. A foul odour assailed his nostrils but it was nothing compared to the fear churning inside his belly. Several times he halted, listening for any sound other than the drops striking the soft earth. But no rouarg interrupted him before his hand, at last, touched the pommel of a buried sword. He started back towards his makeshift camp, his heart still pounding, but his fear faded as each step took him closer to home.

Lying near the cart, the wounded knight was babbling deliriously, his face soaked with sweat, writhing in pain.

'Why, Frog...?'

'Why what, Wader?'

That first night he spent kneeling beside the dying man, firmly gripping the sword's hilt in his damp hands. The rain fell heavily. And the drops, which filtered between the cart's boards, mixed with his tears. Sobbing, he lifted the blade over the body as it twitched in pain. He could lower it, split the armour, pierce it and put an end to all this. They had killed his father.

'Why didn't you let me die there, in the Saltmarsh?'

The second night, when he had already begun to clean and bandage the man's wounds, he wondered again if he should finish the knight off. The sword was heavy ... he only needed to add a little force to the blow for its weight to do the rest and penetrate the man's torso.

He wept ... he couldn't do it. He longed to do it, to avenge those he had lost, to answer the deeds that had stripped his mother and little sister of all dignity. They had been broken, he could do the same ... Or so he believed ... But he was not capable of it, not yet.

'You were merely a child...'

He let himself fall to the side with a moan, crying hot tears, cursing himself for being so weak. Between sobs, he opened his eyes.

'You could have let me die...'

A few yards in front of him, an Erain frog looked at him without moving, the pale glow of a wan moon reflected in its black eyes.

An Erain frog...

'You were just a child...'

237

'You could have let me die ... You were just a child ...'

'My childhood ended the day I hesitated for the first time, ,' Laerte replied.

He could barely remember the warm humid air of the Saltmarsh now. Here in Masalia, the nights were dry and stifling. Times had changed ...

'And the day I saved you, believe me ... I hesitated,' he added in a frighteningly calm voice.

Leaning against the wall of a kitchen, arms crossed, his piercing grey eyes lingered on the old general sitting at the table. Before them, placed on the brown cloth that had hidden it for so many years, Eraëd glittered in the light of an oil lamp. By the door, Rogant stood watch like a guard. On the other side of the room, her red hair ruffled by the light breeze coming through the half-opened window, Viola leaned against the ledge with both hands. They had brought the general to this house not far from the port. It had been their hideout since their arrival in Masalia, while Viola tried to win the old man over.

'Laerte ...' sighed Dun-Cadal as he passed a trembling hand over his face.

What he wouldn't give for a jug of wine right now ... Laerte gave him a brief nod of the head.

'Dun-Cadal,' he said as if they were meeting for the first time.

It hurt him to see the general who had once taken him under his wing in such a filthy state, with his features so deeply drawn and a defeated expression on his face. It was like discovering an entirely different man from the one he had known. How could he have fallen so low? He tried to guess what the general was thinking, what questions were passing through his mind now that he knew Laerte's true identity. He had prepared so long for this meeting that no query could have surprised him.

'Frog ...' the general said, looking blankly into space.

It was as if he were recalling a dead person. In a sense Frog truly was dead, if he had ever existed at all. The general's gaze fell upon the rapier's perfect form and stayed there.

'You're here for this ... for this sword ... but why ...? Why these deaths?' he mumbled.

Laerte advanced to the table and grasped the sword's hilt with a firm hand, to heft its weight.

'For many reasons, Dun-Cadal,' he replied. 'Vengeance, duty ... obligation ... but mostly will.'

He stared at the general, waiting for a reaction. But none came. Out of the corner of his eye, he glimpsed the sceptical expression on Viola's face. But he knew the old man better than anyone; he knew how to rouse the general sleeping inside.

'You're angry with me, aren't you? For never telling you anything, for hiding who I was ... I know that.'

Dun-Cadal continued to look into space without saying a word ... but little by little his jaw tensed.

'It wasn't part of our plan that I would see you. Rogant is somewhat put out about it, in fact,' said Laerte, sounding a little amused.

In the corner, the Nâaga shook his head in exasperation.

'But I always do as I please, you know me.'

The general's eyes met Laerte's with an aggressive challenging glint.

'Really?' he asked.

And for the first time during this face-to-face encounter, Laerte looked away. He lowered his head, letting silence settle. But his former mentor did not break it as he had expected. So with slow, deliberate steps, he started to walk around the table, and continued speaking.

'When I heard that a former Imperial soldier was recounting his adventures in return for a few tankards, I never thought it was you. And then came that moment when, for whatever reason, you started talking about the sword. Oh, I'm certain there are many people looking for it in the Vershan, Wader. But not me ... Once I realised it was you, I knew you would never have hidden it so far away. Even as pathetic as you are now, even filthy and as stinking as shit, you'd never abandon this last piece of the Empire. The Hand of Reyes, the great general, the relic of the Empire watching over ... a symbol, was that it?'

Dun-Cadal endured his speech without stirring. And when Laerte reached his side and slowly bent towards his ear, he did not move in the slightest. An angry tear, however, emerged at the corner of his eye.

'You've been reliving your past, haven't you? Did you recall your former glory? Here. Take it.'

239

With a flick of his hand, he rolled the sword towards the impassive general.

'I can sense you boiling inside.'

'Laerte,' intervened Viola. 'That's enough!'

She could not stop herself from blushing when he gave her a black glare. Trying to mask her apprehension, she had left the edge of the window and stood with her hands joined before her.

'He doesn't deserve this,' she said in a low voice.

She thought Laerte was going to react violently, perhaps even slap her, but nothing happened. Beneath Rogant's expressionless gaze, he left the room with the same slow step.

He could barely take stock of the emotions assailing him. It had been so many years since he had last seen Dun-Cadal. So many years to understand what had forged his own destiny . . .

Viola seized him by the wrist in front of the closed kitchen door.

'Wait,' she demanded. 'What are you trying to do? Tell me.'

Although there was a note of reproach in her voice, she tried to remain friendly enough not to aggravate the situation. He was forced to admit she was gifted when it came to calming things down. But she was young, too young to comprehend what he felt in the old general's presence.

'He shouldn't be here,' Viola continued, darting brief glances at the kitchen. 'We have what we wanted. What are we going to do with him now? If we let him leave he might reveal everything. Even if he's a drunk he could attract attention and that's something we don't need.'

'Rogant will keep an eye on him here,' Laerte replied curtly.

'But when de Page finds out that—'

'He won't say anything. I know what I'm doing,' he assured her. 'Trust me.'

With a brusque movement, he raised his hood.

'And you're right, he doesn't deserve this . . . he deserves much worse.'

Before she had time to reply, he turned on his heel and left the house.

3

GARMARET

It's your own innocence you'll kill over there, lad.
And believe me, I'm the first to regret that.

He had let himself fall to one side, lying hidden as best he could in the thick grass.

'Is this how you were taught to stand guard?' a man roared nearby.

'What? I was just havin' a piss,' a second man answered nonchalantly.

The night was clear, and just one step in his direction might allow the two soldiers to see his outline in the grass. He was barely fourteen years old. And he was fleeing the Saltmarsh.

'Don't ever leave your post without warning the others!'

'We only arrived yesterday,' the soldier defended himself. 'Us lot, we don't know what's up yet, do we? They just told us, line up the catapults.'

'Where do you come from?'

'From Avrai Wood, Cap'n. There're fifteen of us.'

His wooden weapon. It was only a few inches from his outstretched arm. Lying flat on his belly in the damp earth, as if crushed by fear, he did not have the courage to make even the slightest movement towards it. His heart pounded violently, echoing in his temples, while his chest felt constricted and his breathing too heavy.

'You should always be—'

A few yards away, a captain with shiny boots took one step forward.

'What on earth have you done?'

'We lined up the catapults, didn't we?'

A single step, allowing the man to make out a dark shape in the grass. When he heard the hiss of a sword being drawn, Laerte had no choice but to attack. Agile, he seized the wooden sword as he rolled over and stood with astonishing ease. He had trained hard these past months.

But tonight it was no exercise where mistakes were allowed. His life depended on the choices he made.

'You?' the man gasped. 'How?'

The scarred face, dimly lit by the camp's tall torches, was frozen in stupefaction. The officer was bald, broad-shouldered and had a split lip.

'When you're out roaming the countryside, I can't protect you. If the Imperial soldiers spot you, I hope you can run fast.'

Laerte also hesitated for an instant. In his trouser pocket, the rouarg whistle felt heavy.

'I can't protect you.'

Opposite him, Madog still seemed stunned, his sword almost loose in his hand.

'What are you—?'

'. . . protect you . . .'

He woke with a start at sunrise, soaked in sweat and gasping for breath. Every night since they had left the Saltmarsh, he relived that moment, that terrible decision. Each time he slept he was burdened with the same nightmare, where he irrevocably chose to commit murder. Because he had not plunged his wooden sword into the man's throat to defend his own life. The moment haunted him to the point where he despaired of ever seeing the guilt fade. He tried to forget, to persuade himself that he had acted for the best, that he had no other possible choice.

'Who is Madog?' asked a voice at his back.

They had ridden for two days straight, only pausing to allow their mounts to rest. They had galloped as far as the great forest of Garm, a border of pine trees between the saltwater marshes and the arable plains of the county of Garm-Sala.

Behind him, Dun-Cadal was harnessing the horses while giving him brief glances.

'No one,' Laerte replied, drawing in his legs.

'No one?' the general said with a surprised laugh. 'And yet you call out to him every night. So this Madog must be someone . . .'

Laerte ignored him, determined to reveal nothing more.

Dun-Cadal was only a tool, a pawn who would take him to the Emperor. He had no cause to know Laerte's secrets. And if the general learned his true identity, then without a doubt, it would cost Laerte his life. He did not understand much about the Saltmarsh rebellion; his only goal was the death of the Emperor. Nothing else warranted his attention. Truth be told, he was barely aware of the rest of the world.

For months he had thought, reflected and imagined the deed right down to the last detail. Looking after the knight so that he would become his teacher was only the first step. He had been drawn into the game little by little, certain that one day he would be as respected as his father ... and above all, feared by his enemies. He had trained until the point of exhaustion, overcoming pain, repeating the movements endlessly as soon as his mentor fell asleep.

'Come on, get up, lad,' Dun-Cadal sighed. 'We're in the county of Garm-Sala, Garmaret is only two weeks from here. Soon we'll be enjoying a warm bath.'

By the time they reached Emeris, he would be the greatest knight in the world, capable of challenging the Emperor himself. Like the Erain frog, he would take on the colours of his prey ... all the better to fall upon him. He got up, still feeling tired.

'Get a move on!' Dun-Cadal urged him.

The general mounted his horse unsteadily, grimacing. Was his leg still bothering him? Laerte caught himself feeling sorry for the man's suffering. He had feared the general's injury would be a handicap during their flight, but to his great surprise, Dun-Cadal had shown an impressive mastery in actual combat. He'd helped Laerte escape before facing the rebels alone. Laerte had to respect him for that, at least.

Two weeks, he'd said. Two weeks riding through the forest until they reached the green plains where the fortified town of Garmaret awaited them. Two weeks during which he dreamt of Madog, and was subjected to the same questions each morning from his mentor. During their journey, the general taught him some rudiments of hunting, and he was glad to eat something other than hive frogs.

Even so, Laerte experienced some difficult moments. The man was boorish, cocky and inquisitive. He was always trying to learn more about Laerte, asking him questions out of the blue to which the boy struggled to find answers. To his relief, whenever he deflected his mentor's curiosity with evasive responses, Dun-Cadal changed the subject.

At every halt, his apprenticeship continued. In the dim light, he fought invisible enemies until his muscles felt like burning coals and he fell to his knees, drained. He wearily returned to their camp and lay down to sleep for barely three hours before he awoke with a start at dawn.

Jouncing along on his mount, he almost fell asleep more than once. And then finally they reached the edge of the forest and he saw the Garm-Sala plains. Beneath the gentle spring sunshine, hundreds of fields spread before him, ranging from the dark green of mowed grass to the golden hues of grain. Here and there dirt tracks meandered between them, travelled by a few rickety ox-carts. Small dark silhouettes walked at their side, quiet and peaceful. Some odd white shapes floated in the air, tiny and beautiful, borne aloft by a slight breeze.

'Those are dandelion seed heads. The wind blows them,' Dun-Cadal explained, before saying, with a sigh of pleasure, 'Garmaret ...'

His arms resting on the pommel of his saddle, he indicated the town and its crude ramparts with a nod of his head. From here, the place looked like a simple stone square with a watchtower at each corner.

'We'll be there by the end of the day if we maintain a steady pace.'

Laerte contemplated the landscape with a stoical expression. He allowed none of his astonishment to show, too used to masking his emotions.

'Well ... you look delighted ...' Dun-Cadal remarked as he patted his mount's neck. 'A little well-deserved rest doesn't appeal to you?'

'It does ...'

His laconic reply seemed to irritate the general, so he thought it best to explain himself.

'It's the first time.'

'That you'll have had a bath?' mocked Dun-Cadal.

'No ...' He shook his head. 'I've never seen anything but the Saltmarsh,' he clarified.

Fear gripped him along with a thrill of excitement which he carefully concealed. Was the Empire so immense that it would take him years to reach Emeris? Instinctively, he looked over his shoulder, back towards the Saltmarsh.

'Hey, boy!' called Dun-Cadal. 'Look at me.'

When he met the general's eyes, he was so upset that he felt tears rising within him. He saw kindness in the man's eyes. Why was he starting to dread the moment Dun-Cadal discovered he'd been nurturing his own enemy?

'You are at home here, lad.'

And with a dig of his heels, he spurred his mount into a gallop. Being at home here ... was not at all reassuring.

They rode along the tracks at a goodly speed, passing wagons and peasants without any of them showing signs of surprise. He had expected to be stopped, for one of them to block the road and shout that he was from the Saltmarsh, or worse. Everyone in these parts was bound to serve the Emperor and his court; they must all have cheered when they heard about Oratio's death and the initial occupation of the region. Why then did they show so little interest in two horsemen galloping towards the fortified town? When they reached the gates of Garmaret, as the sun was setting, Laerte understood the reason for their indifference.

Beneath the hard gaze of Imperial soldiers, dozens of wagons were queued up before the gates, packed with ragged, weeping women and children. Men in their hundreds slowly advanced at their side. They were all fleeing the Saltmarsh to seek refuge here at Garmaret. The rustling of war had reached as far as this town. And far from enjoying a calm respite, families found themselves being rudely searched, and sometimes separated from each other, before passing beneath two raised portcullises and being escorted through the town.

The general and Laerte made their way through the crowd, crossing the town's heavy gates and walking their horses through the narrow alleys that climbed to the Army's camp. It surrounded a small stone tower standing a few yards from a wide gate blocked by a portcullis. On the far side was the beginning of a great road which was watched by soldiers wearing dark armour.

As he rode, not once did Laerte lower his eyes towards his people who had come here seeking peace. He dared not meet their gaze for an instant, for fear of being recognised ... or of seeing the depth of their suffering. Anxiety weighed heavily upon him when a squad of soldiers passed behind them. He was just dismounting from his horse at the foot of the tower and the thought that he was now in the jaws of the wolf squeezed his heart. Everywhere he looked there were soldiers and refugees. Here at the entrance to a tall, wide tent, a woman was soothing her baby by rocking him slowly. Over there, soldiers were arguing with a defeated-looking man, his features drawn with weariness. He barely heard his mentor's voice, speaking with a young lieutenant wearing shiny armour.

'Who commands this camp?'

'General Negus, sir.'

The young officer was clean, carefully groomed, and clearly intimidated. The general had spent months in the marshes, was filthy and stinking, wearing dented armour, and his unkempt hair crowned a face marked by exhaustion.

'Call him, quickly.'

He immediately snapped his fingers to recall the lieutenant before he hurried off.

'Tell him Dun-Cadal Daermon is here.'

At this the lieutenant lost his composure completely. Beneath the marsh muck that spattered the other's armour, he could make out Imperial colours. And any military man could spot the rank engraved on his shoulders. But General Daermon had been given up for dead almost a year ago. The lieutenant nodded and climbed the stone staircase leading to the top of the tower without demanding further explanation.

And Laerte suddenly noticed that people's gazes were not directed at him. Dun-Cadal was drawing all the attention. Soldiers were whispering amongst themselves, guards stopped in their tracks upon seeing him, and others, on patrol, gave the general a wide berth without taking their eyes from him.

He attached the reins of his horse to a large wooden beam that jutted from the stone and Laerte followed suit, before joining him as he came around his mount.

'Behave yourself, Frog, don't make a bad impression,' Dun-Cadal said in a firm tone.

'Yes, Wader—'

'And stop calling me that!' his mentor snapped. 'I am General Dun-Cadal Daermon here, so use my rank, blast you!'

He yanked nervously at the bottom of his breastplate to adjust it. Although everyone was observing him with a certain reverence, the only thing that worried him was that Laerte should make a good impression. He'd saved the man's life, helped him cross enemy lines and this was how Dun-Cadal treated him. Like a child who might embarrass him at any moment.

'By the gods! *By the gods!*' someone cried.

And turning round, Laerte saw a small round man, stuffed inside a golden suit of armour, coming towards them with outstretched arms.

There was a radiant smile upon his face, and a gleam of joy in his eyes.

'Is it you? Is it really you?'

'Who else could it be?' replied Dun-Cadal in an amused tone, as he placed a hand on his apprentice's shoulder.

Slowly but surely he drew the boy out of the way as the little general approached. The two men fell into one another's arms, accompanying their embrace with hearty backslaps. Wearing a surly expression, Laerte watched them laughing out of the corner of his eye, lost in their joy at being reunited.

'They told me you'd fallen! I did not believe it. A rouarg? Kick your arse? The arse of Dun-Cadal Daermon?' the small man guffawed.

'You were misinformed,' Dun-Cadal said as he stepped back, 'but I confess it was a close call.'

'Tomlinn?'

Laerte's mentor shook his head sadly.

'And I would have ended up like him if this lad hadn't saved my hide. Frog!'

With a wave of his arm, he beckoned Laerte to come forward and gripped his shoulder again.

'This is General Negus, one of my closest brothers-in-arms. Negus, allow me to introduce Sir Frog.'

'Frog? Sir Frog?' Negus asked with a laugh.

'That's what I decided to call him,' explained the general.

He talked about Laerte with a hint of disdain in his voice, as if he were some kind of pet animal.

'What a proud look he has,' remarked Negus.

'He's an orphan of the Saltmarsh, my friend, and he has a temper. But never mind. We have a lot to say to one another ... before I grant myself the pleasure of finally taking a bath.'

'Now that, I can understand,' smiled the small man, looking back and forth between the general and the boy. 'I could smell your stink for ten leagues.'

He led them into the heart of the tower, climbing the external staircase to pass through a small door, where they found themselves in a maze of hallways lit by weak torches. The entire edifice was made of large brown stones and there was a fine coating of dust on the floor. It had been built before the Empire had even arisen, when Garmaret was still a mere kingdom. Despite some recent renovations, it had a primitive appearance similar to all the fortifications dotting these lands. There was no delicacy in its architecture, no attempt to embellish the stone, just one shade away from dirt.

They entered a large room and Negus recounted to them the events that had led to the Imperial retreat towards Garmaret. They had sought to retake Aëd's Watch but had been driven back by a much tougher army than they had anticipated. And for a good reason; one of the neighbouring counties had decided to throw in its lot with the rebels, proclaimed its independence and pledged complete allegiance to the new leader of the revolt. For a long time they had believed this was Meurnau, the former captain of Oratio of Uster's guard. But in fact, persistent rumours mentioned the younger son of the deceased count: Laerte.

When he heard his real name the boy had the impression that Negus winked at him. His hands became clammy, his breathing laboured. He grew visibly pale and thought he was about to keel over when Dun-Cadal seized his wrist.

'Frog, are you listening?' he repeated.

He realized this was not the first time he'd been asked.

'The boy is exhausted, Dun-Cadal. I'll ask for someone to see to his needs,' declared Negus, coming from behind the big table around which they had been conversing for more than an hour.

Laerte had only been vaguely following the discussion, distracted by his fear of being unmasked from one moment to the next. The simple mention of his name had finally scrambled his wits.

'If you're not feeling well, then say so,' Dun-Cadal said in reproach as he helped the boy to the door.

A soldier was charged with taking him to a little room. Two serving women prepared a hot bath for him, into which he plunged, trembling. When he was alone, he almost burst into tears. The fear tormenting him was so strong he felt crushed. His arms dangling over the edges of the wooden basin, he stared blankly at the curls of steam intertwining over the hot water. Above the veil they formed, a skylight admitted the glow of dusk and the martial sounds within the fort: hooves on the paved path, footsteps, and the clatter of armour … loud voices shouting commands. And the weeping of his people, lost here in Garmaret, so far from home. Little by little, he regained his strength and, stepping out of the bath, found a pile of clothing awaiting him on the small bed. He dressed, relishing the soft contact of clean cloth upon his skin. He had some difficulty pulling on the new, polished boots due to the condition of his feet, after wearing the bits and pieces of his old pair for so long. When he was finally clean and dressed from head to toe he lay down on the bed, absorbed by his thoughts. He had no idea what might become of him. Would he be able to see things through to the end without being discovered? Despite his doubts, giving up was out of the question.

He recalled the first time he returned to Aëd's Watch after spending months out in the marshes. He had left the general dying by the cart, seeing his horse as the best means of reaching the town without expending too much effort. He became lost several times, but finally found the right path. He'd been greatly surprised to learn that Meurnau had not only escaped the attack by the Imperial troops, but had retaken the Watch.

Yes, he remembered his joy, his restored hope as he ventured into the peaceful streets … At least, until he reached the main square and realised that his entire life had been stolen from him. Laerte of Uster was alive and roaming the Saltmarsh, it was said. Laerte of Uster was leading the rebellion and had just won another battle, people murmured. Laerte of Uster was twenty years old? He seemed much younger …

They spoke of him everywhere … as if he were someone else. Here and there they told tales of the latest exploits of a man who was not him. And worse still, people believed it all without expressing the slightest doubt. While everyone guarded the image of his beloved father in their memory, who really remembered him? He was barely fourteen years old; no one would have believed him if he told them who he was. And he feared Meurnau's reaction if he ever learned of the real Laerte's survival. He feared the guard captain had taken advantage of the situation to seize power in the Saltmarsh, and would kill him at the first opportunity rather than repudiate the rumours of Laerte's martial feats.

Laerte recalled all this and fell asleep with a heavy heart.

They spent four days at Garmaret, enjoying a restorative rest, and each day more refugees arrived. Dozens of columns of them, which eventually marched along the great road, once the portcullis was raised, in the direction of Emeris. Garmaret was only a stage in their journey. The Emperor had signed a decree promising every inhabitant of the Saltmarsh that they would find asylum in the capital. Laerte often stayed in his room, alone, excluded by a master too busy gathering information about the course of the war and haranguing the troops on duty near the gates. The boy was snubbed several times when he followed Dun-Cadal as he carried out these impromptu inspections. Very quickly he was forced to recognise that the general did not wish to have him underfoot, except during the few hours they set aside for training at the end of the day.

On the morning of the fourth day, when the portcullis was raised to allow a new procession of exiles to depart, Laerte decided to leave the tower wearing a blue cloak that a servant woman had kindly lent him. His face thus masked by the shadow of the cloak's hood, he descended to the middle of the external staircase and, hand gripping the railing, he observed the wagons inching forward in a cloud of dust beneath the spikes of the portcullis. Soldiers were shouting to either side of the column, ordering the poor wretches to move more quickly.

Laerte continued to walk stealthily, keeping his eyes down, and skirted around the Army camp in the direction of the great road. He tried to make out a familiar face among the crowd, an acquaintance, anyone whose mere presence would have comforted him.

Between two large tents, in the middle of some barrels, he sharpened his gaze, examining each refugee passing only a few yards away from him. He watched them march by, heads bowed and listless. They had been dispossessed of everything, their dignity along with their goods.

'Always remember one thing, Laerte: if your father is dead, above all he died for his people. He would never betray them.'

But in the end, what did it matter to the people that his father had died for them? Now they found themselves on the roads, with the only possessions they had worth defending: their lives. Wearied by this spectacle he decided to return to his room, feeling more despondent than ever. He wended his way through the camp and though he still kept his head down, it was no longer because he feared being recognised but because he was taking stock of the cost of the conflict. What had he really seen up to now ...? He halted suddenly, and then lifted his head. A few feet away from him, a girl was crouched between two tents, removing a trembling hand from an open bag lying at her feet.

'No, I-I ...' she stammered. 'It's not what you think. I found this bag, I didn't ...'

Her dress was dusty and her hair was tied hastily at the back of her neck. Despite her disastrous appearance, Laerte gaped at her.

'Laerte ...' she murmured. 'Laerte? Is it really you?'

Collecting his wits, Laerte glanced around to ensure that no one was watching them and almost threw himself upon her. But instead of kissing her, he pressed the palm of his hand over her mouth to stifle her words.

'Frog,' he said quickly. 'I'm called Frog, don't call me Laerte any more. Here, everyone knows me as Frog. Do you understand? Nobody must know.'

She tried to say something behind his hand, but no intelligible sound emerged. Her wide-open blue eyes became damp with tears, not of sadness, but of joy.

'Do you understand, Esyld? If you reveal who I am, if you're heard saying my name, I'm dead. Do you understand?'

He paused. The girl's eyes were smiling now. She nodded her head in agreement. Slowly he drew away his hand, feeling her fine lips leave his palm with a gentle kiss. They looked at one another without saying a word, lulled by the jolting of the passing wagons.

'Is it really you?' she murmured.

Her fingers brushed his. They had never been so close to one another before, and he wondered if he should kiss her at long last, taste her lips and abandon himself completely. But anxiety won out over longing.

'We thought you were dead ... we spent days searching for you, and—'

'What are you doing here?' he asked bluntly.

He did not believe a word of it. Meurnau knew the marshes, he should have found him. Had he not turned the name Laerte of Uster into a banner that all had rallied to? No, his fears were true, Captain Meurnau had taken advantage of Laerte's disappearance to make him a stronger, grander and more unifying figure than the boy could ever have been in real life.

'I fled the Saltmarsh,' she replied, surprised by his tone.

'Why? Aëd's Watch was liberated, wasn't it?'

Although he was happy to have found her again, he could not bear the idea of her being here. If something happened to her ...

'My father surrendered,' she confessed. 'But it's not what you think. He is going to infiltrate the palace. Meurnau has a plan and he has many allies ...'

She could not continue. Laerte had turned away from her, moving along one of the tents to draw closer to the road. The column stretched into the distance, a succession of dilapidated carts with wobbling wheels drawn by exhausted horses. Their bits were covered in thick slaver.

'I'll be safe there,' she said in a reassuring tone.

She approached him, placing a delicate hand on his shoulder.

'I'm on my way to Emeris too,' he said in a distracted tone.

'What? Your place is at Aëd's Watch, Laer—'

He bent his head towards her.

'Frog ...' she immediately corrected herself.

'My place is nowhere except before the Emperor,' he railed. 'Meurnau is waging his war perfectly well without me.'

'Frog,' she sighed. 'That's not what is being asked of you, you're only fourteen years old.'

He spun towards her with a scowl on his face. Of course he was just a child in her eyes. Of course ...

'He killed my father.'

'I know,' she acknowledged, caressing his cheek to calm him.

'So I will kill him.'

Her hand halted while her eyes froze, briefly lit by a gleam of horror.

'Yes, I'm going to kill the Emperor,' he confirmed. 'I am now Frog, for them. I helped a knight who was lost in the Saltmarsh. I'm his apprentice now. I will become the greatest knight of all and I will avenge my family. Meurnau never even searched for me.'

'What? But how can you—' sputtered Esyld.

'I know it,' he asserted in an imperious tone. 'I heard it myself ... all those tales about a Laerte leading the rebellion. He no longer has me under his thumb so he's using my name to give himself credibility.

So he can wage war as he feels fit. As for me, I shall not rest until I've killed Reyes.'

'You can't seriously be thinking—'

He locked eyes with her, seeking to convince her of his firm resolve. 'I've decided, Esyld,' he warned her. 'I've done things, I've ...'

Madog!

'I can't back down now ...'

He remained dignified, keeping calm as he had never believed himself capable of doing before.

'If this is what the gods intend,' said Esyld with downcast eyes.

'The gods have nothing to do with it,' he said. 'I choose my life.'

Finally he realised that he was master of his own destiny. In the Saltmarsh, ever since he was born, and even after the start of the rebellion, he had done as he was told without ever influencing the course of events.

'I decide my future, Esyld.'

Looking wan, she forced herself to smile. She could see how determined he was and realised there was no point in arguing with him.

'My proud little lord,' she humoured him, plunging a hand into her bodice, whose edges were black with dirt. 'But if you pass yourself off as someone else, don't you risk becoming him?'

She pulled out a small wooden figurine he had no difficulty recognising. It represented a crudely carved horse. She hesitated for an instant before offering it to him.

'Hey, you! Over there!' called out a hoarse voice.

On the far side of the road, a soldier supervising the column was headed towards them. Without waiting, Esyld took Laerte's hand and deposited the little sculpture before folding his fingers over it.

'Return to the column!' the soldier ordered before seizing hold of her.

'Let go of her!' Laerte snarled.

But a loud voice immediately immobilised him.

'Frog!'

Behind him, leaning on the railing of the tower stairs, Dun-Cadal was glaring down at him. Before he could find an explanation for his conduct, he felt Esyld's hand squeeze his.

'Don't forget, Frog,' she said, as the soldier was leading her back to the road. 'Don't forget who you are. Ever.'

With a brusque gesture, she escaped from the soldier's grip.

253

Everything happened so quickly that Laerte had no time to react. The young woman's lips joined with his in a soft caress, her slender and gentle fingers placed on his cheeks. The kiss was moist, surprisingly moist. But so pleasant, intoxicating ... She was pressed against him, as if she had always been there, as if whatever she did, or wherever she was, her true place was here next to him ...

'Cooome here, you!' growled the guard as he tore her away from the boy.

Laerte stood there in a daze, still tasting the sweetness of the kiss upon his lips.

'That's so you won't forget me,' she murmured.

And as the soldier dragged her back into the crowd, her murmur became a cry, a truth screamed in the face of the world, tearing his heart in two.

'I love you. I'll always love you. Forever. Don't forget me. Don't forget us, Frog! Don't forget who you are ... Don't ever forget! I love you!'

When he finally decided to run after her, the soldier had already lifted her onto the back of a wagon. The column passed beneath the portcullis, a cloud of dust rising behind the jolting wheels.

'Frog! Come back here!'

Dun-Cadal had already descended the stairs to catch up with him in a few brisk strides. In his hand, Laerte squeezed the small wooden horse tight. The column came to an end and the soldiers were preparing to lower the portcullis. It fell behind the last swaying wagon to depart on the great road ...

4

THE FACE OF HIS ENEMY

'They are merely ... children.
I am responsible for them. For this Empire.
It has been written so since time immemorial.'
'They've made you their puppet.'

He lay there, listless and disoriented, in a drab house in the heart of
Masalia. Rogant had accompanied him to the upper floor without
saying a word, before showing him into the chamber. Lying down on
the moth-eaten blanket covering the bed he recalled the course of his
life in the hope of finding some meaning there. The latest events had
strengthened his conviction that he had failed at everything, while
the other generals who served alongside him now held power. He
had been incapable of saving the Empire and he had been unable to
secure a dignified position after its fall. Any ideal he still preserved
had become a burden to him.

When the chamber door opened he did not move but continued
to stare at the ceiling, his mind elsewhere. A scent of lavender wafted
into the room and only then did he turn his head to the side. For a
moment he hoped to see Mildrel standing at the threshold. Strangely, he wasn't disappointed when he recognised Viola's slender figure.

'I know it's rather bare, but at least it's better than a gaol cell,' she
said without daring to enter.

When he did not react, she came forward. She was wearing her
plain green dress with a cape attached to her shoulders, as if out of
modesty. Her hands clasped behind her back, she seemed anxious.
Once she had advanced as far as the bed, she bent over slightly to
enter his field of vision and tilted her head to the side.

'Tired?'

He grumbled and resumed his contemplation of the ceiling.

'Oh, I know what you're thinking. I feel the same way.'

He stiffened and almost sat up when she continued.

'I feel betrayed too.'

He heard her draw up a chair and sit down.

'To begin with, when you spoke to me about Frog, I was a thousand leagues from ever suspecting that it was him,' she explained. 'Any more than he warned me that the man I was supposed to find was the most famous general of the Empire.'

Intrigued, he rose up on his elbows, but did not glance at her. His mind still seemed to be somewhere else.

'What did he tell you?' he asked in a dull voice.

The young woman's lips sketched a smile. He was hoping for answers and even if she were unable to provide all of them, perhaps she would help clear his thoughts a little. Like him, she seemed to be somewhat taken aback by events.

'I was supposed to find a soldier, a man called Dun who was telling all and sundry how he had fled Emeris taking the sword with him. I was supposed to coax you into leading us to Eraëd ...'

At last he deigned to look at her.

'You see,' she confided as she leaned towards him, 'I didn't lie to you. But, let's say, I didn't tell you everything. And in that—'

She raised her eyes with a pensive air.

'—in that, I take after him, I suppose ...'

Before Dun-Cadal had time to lie back down, she resumed speaking.

'It's strange, isn't it?'

When she saw him slide his legs over the edge of the bed to sit up, she knew she'd captured his attention. Over the past few days, she'd developed a certain fondness for the old warrior. She'd understood what had shattered him. She imagined how he must have been in his days of glory: boorish, arrogant and authoritarian. Now he was a broken sword. He had wanted to offer the world to a boy from the Saltmarsh, whose loss had crushed him while the Empire to which he would have given his life collapsed around him.

'What's strange?' he mumbled.

'To be so angry with him while still loving him,' she said, lowering her eyes.

The general stared at her, noting her sudden embarrassment as she realised the full import of her admission.

'You and he . . . ?'

'Oh, no, no,' she hastened to reply. 'In truth, I do not know him well . . . And I'm not sure he's aware I even exist . . .'

Her cheeks were flushing. No, of course they weren't together, but how could she now deny she harboured feelings for Fro— Laerte . . . ? The boy was whoever he wanted to be, that didn't concern Dun-Cadal any longer. The old man simply wished to leave this chamber, forget what he had seen, and drink to his heart's content.

So why didn't he just get up, go through the door, descend the stairs, knock out the Nâaga in the salon below, and melt away among Masalia's night revellers? Why stay here? He had lost Frog. He'd discovered Laerte of Uster instead. He did not have the slightest idea of what had taken place in the meantime, which no doubt would have made sense of all this. In the chaos of his thoughts, Viola was the only fixed, reassuring landmark.

'Why are you here?' he asked, feeling distressed. 'Are you even really a historian?'

'Yes . . .'

She nodded slowly.

'That much, yes, I really am a historian at the Great College . . . but tuition is expensive, you know, and girls such as myself, whose parents are simple, ordinary folk, must have recourse to sponsors. Mine is a councillor by the name of de Page. A good man, honest . . . but to whom I am somewhat indebted.'

'de Page? Then he has managed to do well for himself too,' the general grumbled softly.

One more to add to the list. Another of those who had enjoyed the Emperor's favour, had sought out his company, and had finally discarded him as if he were of no account. Duke O had been known for his astonishing feasts, his casual attitude, and the unpleasant rumours about him. He'd been a pervert who, even when the nobility still existed, Dun-Cadal had despised. A worm in the fruit, whose appetite the Emperor had been unable to restrain . . .

'If you are as indebted to him as much as that . . .'

'He's the one who sent me here,' concluded Viola, nodding again

A craven man . . . yes, a craven man who was always fawning. It was beyond belief. Was it through fawning that he'd saved his life and become a councillor? And the others, had they trampled their own dignity in order to remain in power? Was there even an ounce of honour left in this world? His head swam.

'But why here?' he asked angrily, his belly knotted. 'For Eraëd? Why kill those councillors? What are you seeking?'

His throat felt terribly parched. And he struggled to ask one last question, perhaps the most important one in his eyes.

'Why did he never say anything to me?'

Tears accumulated at the corner of his eyes, ready to submerge him. His jaws clenched as he desperately sought to hold them back, but some spilled down, and with them his disgust at no longer being as solid as a rock. When he felt the young woman's soft hands upon his, he had the sensation of falling, endlessly, with no hope of containing anything at all.

'I don't know ...' she answered quietly. 'Perhaps he came to you in order to give you an answer ...'

He did not believe her for an instant. Years of his life had been built upon a lie. This boy, he had loved him ... But why else would he emerge from the shadows when their plan didn't call for it? He tilted his head and contemplated Viola's hands as she gently caressed his withered skin with the tips of her thumbs, as if it were old leather.

'Azdeki gave the order to have his father hung. Is that why he's here?' He suddenly asked, regaining control of his emotions.

He glared at Viola, who still seemed moved by the tears he had just shed. She held his gaze without saying a word.

'Azdeki, Negus, all those who served the Empire, those who condemned Oratio of Uster to death ... That's the link, isn't it?' continued Dun-Cadal. 'There's a reason Fro—'

His throat suddenly tight, he inhaled deeply

'—that he disguised himself as Logrid. But ...'

He stared at Viola to keep the thread of his thoughts, hoping that his muddle of questions would not overcome him again. Every event, every sentence, every detail that he had ever registered deep in his memory, he now tried to regroup into a coherent whole. The presence of Rogant in front of the harbour, the same Rogant who had prevented him from turning into an alley, the fight provoked by a Nâaga to draw the attention of the guards just before Enain-Cassart was assassinated ... the lavender Viola wore which reminded him of his lover.

'No. It's not a question of revenge,' he mused. 'You were seeking the sword ... So it's not *only* Azdeki.'

She turned her eyes away, pensive. Then, she spoke.

'It's not a question of vengeance, Captain,' said a weak voice. 'It's a question of faith. Your faith ...'

'I am a councillor,' Azdeki replied sharply.

He took a step towards the cell's bars and stared down at the prisoner with a haughty gaze, one hand gripping his sword. He had removed his councillor's toga in favour of more military attire, with tall black boots and a light leather surcoat. In the shadowy cell, the old man covered in a plain filthy robe remained seated, his bare feet in the damp earth. Once upon a time his hair had been long, silky, white and pure. Now what little he had left was stuck together beneath a layer of muck.

'Don't forget what I've done,' Azdeki continued with a menacing air. 'Don't ever forget it.'

'How could I?' the old man laughed sadly. 'You've destroyed my dynasty by abusing our trust. Boast as much as you like of your success, you will never be anything but a mere ... captain to me.'

'Councillor!' shouted Azdeki, seizing the bars with both hands.

He scowled in anger, hesitating over whether to enter the cell, his face livid. Shaking his head, he let go and ran a hand through his grey hair, taking a deep breath.

'I know you're involved in this somehow. I don't know how you managed it, but you are responsible for all this,' he accused, slightly out of breath. 'Why else would the assassin look like Logrid? Tell me, Anvelin ...'

'... Evgueni Reyes ...' sighed Dun-Cadal, incredulous.

'He's holding him prisoner in the Palatio's gaols,' nodded Viola.

Dun-Cadal passed a hand over his face, looking blankly into space. The bishop of Emeris, uncle of the last Emperor. A man who had helped him, long ago, and then betrayed him. Like all the others. He wavered between anger and satisfaction, imagining the old man in a miserable cell, suffering a thousand agonies. He was so struck by this picture that he forgot to question Viola further.

'Dun-Cadal?'

Hand over his mouth, wearing a tormented expression, he turned his eyes to her. She remained surprisingly serene. Once again he found himself soothed and her gentle gaze did not leave his.

'Why?' he murmured at last.

'To make an example?' she suggested with a sad smile upon her lips.

He stood up with feverish energy, pressing his dry hands against the cell's dank wall, and moved with an unsteady step to the barrier separating him from Azdeki. Placing his hands upon on the sticky bars he glanced at the captain with his bright blue eyes and, despite his exhaustion, summoned a scowl to his face.

'You're frightened, Azdeki. He's here. The phantom of the Empire you betrayed. Of the faith you left behind you. It was written, Azdeki. You can't escape your destiny.'

'I'm not afraid of phantoms,' the councillor replied calmly, approaching his face to the bars. 'Any more than I'm afraid of your words. You have never respected the Sacred Book ... you betrayed the Fangolin Order in the interests of your family. All that was written, Anvelin, was the pitiful fall of your nephew and the advent of my Republic. And soon you'll be able to see proof of it for yourself.'

'What did he know? Viola!' Dun-Cadal asked impatiently.

He stood up suddenly, unsettled now he was discovering all the things he had been unable to see before. Back when he thought himself glorious, powerful and proud, at the service of an eternal Empire.

'What did the bishop know?'

He looked down at her from his full height. Viola remained seated without flinching, staring at the empty bed before her, her hands joined upon her knees.

'He knew what Oratio of Uster had in the Saltmarsh,' she confessed quietly. 'The reason why the Azdeki family turned against him, before they turned on the Emperor. He knew what the Uster family had been protecting for centuries; what Oratio wanted to reveal to the entire world ...'

Then she gently lifted her head towards him, before her eyes followed the movement and met the general's incredulous gaze.

'The Book.'

'What book?' asked Dun-Cadal, almost choking.

'The ... Book,' repeated Viola, nodding her head.

'You won't convince anyone, Azdeki!' cried Anvelin with all his might. 'No one may read it! No one!'

The councillor's silhouette receded down the arched corridor, trailing a gigantic shadow cast by the torchlight. The sound of his steps climbing the stone stairs faded, leaving only the sputtering of the flames.

'... no one,' the old priest concluded in a muffled sob.

Weary, Anvelin let himself slip down the bars, falling to his knees. He did not hear the new footsteps coming towards him. Only the shadow that shrouded him made him to look up and a rare smile illuminated his face, hollowed as much by starvation as by wrinkles.

'Are you there?' he rejoiced in a rasping voice. 'You're always there, yes ... always. Like a memory ... you never leave me.'

The shadow was silent. It examined him from behind a golden mask, split by a crack, showing no expression.

'It was written, wasn't it?' Anvelin said shakily, torn between joy and exhaustion. 'The gods had always foreseen it. If my lineage fell, you would return to avenge us, yes, oh yes. We weren't wrong to believe ourselves fit to rule, no, oh no. We weren't wrong. I pray every day to thank the gods, you know. Every day.'

His face suddenly twisted in remorse.

'I did not doubt, no! I never doubted the *Liaber Dest*, but it had been thus for centuries. To the Usters the Book, to us the Sword. That's how it always was.'

And his smile returned.

'... are you there?' he repeated as if the shadow had just appeared. 'You're always there, yes ... always. Like a memory ...'

The shadow's green cape flapped as it moved towards the stairs.

'... you don't leave me ... ever ...' sobbed Anvelin.

Dun-Cadal was sitting against the wall, his gaze lost in the grain of the wooden floorboards, without having any clear idea of where he was, how he arrived here, or why. He no longer thought, no longer reacted. His entire being was drowned in a flood of contradictory feelings overlying a terrible sadness. There it was, the dull pain, the wound that never ceased to bleed and was tearing his heart in two.

Beyond the manipulations, beyond the betrayals, there lay only one thing. But what a thing, to be the very root of his downfall.

'The *Liaber Dest* ...' he muttered.

He barely heard the chair creak when Viola got up to come over to him. Her lavender scent drew him out of his confusion and he met her gaze.

'After his son's wedding, during Masque Night, Etienne Azdeki will present the Sacred Book to the councillors he has invited,' she announced gravely, measuring each of her words. 'Can you imagine what a man could do, holding the destiny of the world in his hands? The aura of power he will gain in the eyes of the people?'

'He'll be a god among the gods ...' Dun-Cadal suddenly murmured.

'And thanks to Anvelin Evgueni Reyes, he has won over the Fango-lin Order,' Viola continued. 'The fate of the Republic will be decided on Masque Night. Our policies and our beliefs alike. That's why we are here, Dun-Cadal.'

'And the sword?' he asked.

He felt stunned, trying to find his place in this story. Knowing why his presence was required was unlikely to reassure him, but at least it would have shed some light on the abyss into which he seemed to be falling, with no end in sight.

'You already know more than enough,' Viola apologised with a wan smile. 'Laerte would not approve my telling you all this.'

She immediately drew away, heading towards the door but her scent lingered around Dun-Cadal. The old man did not move an inch when Viola asked, embarrassed:

'Do you know why you are here?'

She had halted in the doorway, hand on the latch, hesitating. The light from the oil lamp hanging on the wall blended with her freck-les, like two fires merging on white silk. Her green eyes glowed with tenderness.

Dun-Cadal shook his head, fearing she had an answer.

'I don't know much about him,' she said, 'but from what I do know, and from what you've told me of your own tale, I think ...'

She let her gaze drift about the room as she searched for the right words.

'I think he needs you, Dun-Cadal.'

Laerte walked with sure but quiet steps, ducking behind the columns bordering the corridors whenever a patrol squad came by. Alert, he continued onward, blending into the shadows without losing sight of Councillor Azdeki's stately figure. He followed him through the palace's maze, passing the great interior balcony that overlooked the ballroom before coming to the great stairway whose steps broadened as they descended.

Laerte stopped at the edge of the first step and watched Azdeki go down, his pace quickening and looking irritated. The councillor hurried across the coloured marble floor, passing before the great statues of the gods without sparing them a glance. The ballroom was immense, circular in form, with a vaulted ceiling painted with numerous tableaux recounting the history of the Caglieri dynasty, from the founding of their first city to the great battles against the Majorane kingdoms, the gods blessing their destiny until the advent of the first Emperor and his quest for the *Liaber Dest*, and lastly the portrait of a half-naked woman stabbing the heart of a strange-looking man with a shining spear. Adismas Deo Caglieri was represented in the centre, his eyes looking down upon the marbled floor studded with black stars, wearing a broad red cloak and a sumptuous beard giving him the air of a sage. His left arm was folded against his torso and his hand held a book. At the end of his raised right arm, Eraëd was haloed by a divine light.

'In my left hand, the Book, in my right, the Sword ...'

Azdeki disappeared through the large open doors at the far side of the room. This was not the place, and still less the moment, to act. Laerte knew it, but nevertheless the desire was overpowering. He could have charged after him, run him through with his sword and ended matters there, without delay, without risk.

'... and at my feet, the World.'

No. Azdeki was not the only one responsible. And if the others, like Bernevin or Rhunstag, had not fled Masalia after the assassination of two of their number, it was thanks to their leader's strength.

Etienne Azdeki would never give up. Not this close to his goal. He was far too ambitious, and if he had shown patience up until now, he could wait no longer. The day of his son's wedding would also be that of his consecration.

Laerte took a deep breath and went back the way he came, deciding to skirt around Azdeki. He recalled the plans of the Palatio to guide himself, seeking the surest path to intercept the councillor's route. Doubt nagged at him, sinuous and insidious. He knew he

263

was capable of facing this ordeal, he'd fought *his* dragon already. But when he confronted Azdeki, would he be able to contain the anger that had been devouring him for so many years?

For reassurance, he repeated the final stage of their plan to himself, the instant when, finally, he would have Azdeki to himself without risk of compromising anything else.

He took the building's smallest hallways, preferring to move through the cramped spaces the guards neglected when making their rounds. In two days' time, the Palatio would no longer be accessible in this manner. The tiniest nooks and crannies would be searched before Masque Night, and throughout the evening the palace would be impenetrable. Although he felt capable of taking on an army to achieve his goal, Laerte knew there was only one way to gain entry. As paradoxical as it might be.

So he ran, hoping he would arrive in time to catch Azdeki. He spotted an alcove where he could tuck himself away, relying on the shadows to mask his presence. Then he waited patiently, leaning against the wall, close to where a small hallway exited into a vast room lined with full length windows. Footsteps could be heard, coming closer and closer at a steady pace.

'*Es it allae ...*'

He had long pondered what he would say first, how he would accost Azdeki. He would have liked to scream his anger at the man, reveal who he was, make him relive their last encounter, but it would be a prideful act and put their mission at risk.

Azdeki had come to a halt, looking neither surprised nor afraid, his sharp face as still as the mask worn by the man a few feet in front of him. Standing with his arms crossed in the shadow of the recess in the hallway, Laerte took a step forward.

'... *Es it alle en ... Es it allarae*,' he continued reciting in a grave voice. 'Isn't that Masalia's motto: what you were; what you are; what you will be?'

Upon the walls draped in red, darkness struggled against the light shed by the oil lamps. It was here, not far from the grand private salons looking out over the outdoor gardens, that Laerte would begin the final act.

'Who are you?' Azdeki asked in a stern tone.

He had seized the sword in his belt, lifting the edge of his cape with his elbow. Laerte wondered if he could resist a duel with the man. Would he be able to retreat as planned, or, consumed by his lust for combat, would he give in to the temptation of finishing off his enemy? He could stand up to him. This time, yes.

'What you were? A more courageous man, a more intelligent man than you seemed to be, in order to manipulate those around you more easily. Isn't that so? Did you really think you could emerge intact from the role you cast for yourself?'

'That mask,' Azdeki scowled before raising his voice. 'Do you think you frighten me with this display?'

'The mocking, the contempt shown to you by the other generals,' Laerte continued as if he hadn't spoken. 'That's what you were. A whipping-boy, in the end.'

'Take off that mask,' Azdeki ordered.

'As you removed yours before Reyes?'

'Take it off!' he cried angrily.

He drew his sword with a swift jerk and Laerte retreated a step, now standing at the end of the hallway.

'What you are: a man at bay, as close to defeat as you are to success. An entire lifetime rides on the outcome of a single moment ...'

Azdeki brandished his sword, taking one step forward. He did not tremble. No. He would never fear this assassin, but he would dread the masked man's appearance at the very moment of his victory. He would double the number of guards and, thinking he was protecting himself, he would only weaken his defences.

'And what you will be, Azdeki? You'll be a dead man.'

Laerte continued to retreat, entering a wide vestibule lined with large windows. Behind the glass he could make out the shadowy forms of a garden, its gravel paths lined with tall torches burning beneath a clear night sky.

'I know you,' Azdeki warned him. 'Whoever you are, I know you. And if you haven't managed to stop me so far, you won't do it today. Nor tomorrow.'

'I'll take that wager.'

'Enain-Cassart, Negus ... they were better men than you.'

'Not better enough to defend their lives,' Laerte replied calmly.

'At least they defended what they believed in. And did it without hiding their faces behind another man's mask—.'

'Until Masque Night, Azdeki,' Laerte promised gripping the hilt of his sword. 'On Masque Night, the two of us will finally remove our masks.'

With a brusque movement, he turned towards the windows and took a flying leap.

'Guards!' Azdeki called, barely making himself heard over the sound of shattering glass.

Laerte had passed right through the window. His arms folded in front of his mask, ready to break his fall with a roll on the cool grass.

'Guards, to me!'

The reflection of the torches ran along the blade of Laerte's sword and the clatter of running men in armour rang out. Lifting his head, he saw the guards halt at the shards of broken glass beneath Azdeki's furious gaze. He had plenty of time to lift his weapon and prepare his first parry.

The spears he broke with two precise strokes, before seizing a soldier by the collar of his breastplate and bending him in two with a blow from his knee. The whistle of a blade at his back made him duck. He spun around and pierced his attacker's armour at waist level. The man fell back a step, his face distorted by pain and horror, his hand covering the open wound. There had been five guards trying to stop him and he had disposed of two. But soon there would be more. In the distant darkness of the gardens, shadows took form, and with them came the sound of clanking armour.

He had to flee now or lose all chance of executing their plan.

He used the *animus* and the three swordsmen still challenging him flew through the air like wisps of straw, to fall heavily at the foot of the building. At the window, Azdeki stiffened.

The message was clear: the man in the mask was more than a mere assassin.

The two men eyed one another for an instant. When Laerte returned his sword to his scabbard, Azdeki almost came after him through the window but changed his mind, shaking his head. The new soldiers approaching shouted at him.

'Halt!'

'You there!'

The first to arrive brandished his spear, certain of hitting his target, but Laerte retreated promptly. With a firm hand he seized the wooden haft, pulled it towards him, and knocked the guard out with an elbow to the face. Laerte looked at Azdeki the whole time.

He tilted his head slightly and then charged at the other guards. He forced a passage with his bare hands, deflecting their spears, lashing out with his fists and his feet, before leaping over the melee and racing away through the gardens.

He easily outdistanced them, weaving his way through a labyrinth of hedges until at last he saw the wall surrounding the garden and reached the top in a single bound. From there he overlooked the city, seeing a sheer drop of some thirty feet to the ground below. On the far side of the street a series of houses stood like a castle's crenellations. As he was about to take a leap to reach the first roof, he changed his mind. Hooves clattered on the cobblestones below and a procession of coaches appeared.

The parade passed just beneath him while the soldiers' voices were drawing nearer. He hesitated.

The coaches were painted in dark colours and bore coats-of-arms on their roofs which he had difficulty identifying. But he guessed they were guests arriving for the wedding and saw an opportunity to take his little demonstration one step further.

He took a deep breath and jumped into thin air.

When he crashed heavily upon the wooden roof, the coachman barely had time to turn his head before Laerte disabled him with a kick to the jaw. The horses whinnied, cries of surprise rang out, and the procession came to a shuddering halt. From the sound of their voices, he knew there were women inside the coach. He rolled across the carriage roof and landed on the cobblestones, feeling a twinge of pain in his chest. He was losing control of the *animus*. He would have to pull himself together before he was overwhelmed and his body broke down. He calmed himself, breathing heavily.

His senses remained more acute than usual, so he still had some time remaining before the effects of the *animus* dissipated completely. To his right and left he was aware of coachmen dropping to the street and armed men leaving their vehicles. He only had to turn, step into a side-street, and vanish.

But when he stood up his self-assurance was reduced to naught; his heart skipped a beat and his legs almost gave way beneath his weight.

A woman was looking at him with a stunned expression from the coach window, one hand holding the curtain open. Her surprise in no way detracted from her beauty. Age had barely touched the perfection of her olive skin and the curly hair flowing over her bare shoulders still had the characteristic black lustre of the West.

It was only a brief moment, but to him it seemed to last an eternity.

'There he is!'

'Don't let him get away!'

'It's the assassin!'

The voices were only murmurs, while the *animus* made the beating of this woman's heart loud in his ears. She was stone-still. And then he realised that she recognised the Emperor's mask on his face, that she was not seeing the man inside but instead a broken memory, like the crack running across the gilt mask. Her lips made a slight movement without any sound emerging. Nothing, he heard nothing but her heart. When a man took hold of his right hand, he offered no resistance. A second gripped his left.

Esyld ... He wanted to rush to the door, wrench it open, snatch her from the coach and bear her far away. It could all come to an end this very night.

'I have him!'

'Don't move!'

She withdrew her hand. The curtain immediately fell back into place, masking her face, and for a moment he thought he'd been dreaming. But her heart was still beating, so hard, so quickly, so frightened. He barely heard the sound of weapons being unsheathed. He was surrounded by a fog, unable to see clearly, as vague silhouettes came to the assistance of the two men who were forcing him to his knees.

He felt himself weaken, his legs bending.

'Proud little lord ...'

'Advance! Advance!' ordered a voice.

Hooves clattered on the cobblestones, and the wheels started to turn with a squeal. The heartbeat moved away. The blood on Laerte's lips had a salty taste that brought him out of his dazed state. He could see them clearly now, the coaches resuming their journey, the two men holding his arms loosely, while a third stretched a hand towards his belt to disarm him.

'Flee ... flee, Laerte!'

He rolled his shoulders forward, knocking the men restraining him off-balance, and then with a single movement he pushed his arms in front of him to strike at the third. The hands restraining him relaxed, and he freed himself from them completely. The procession of coaches was moving off into the distance, more soldiers were coming, and Laerte was out of time. He had to rid himself of these three men and leave the scene.

He punched the first with his right fist, followed by his left, delivered a spinning kick to the jaw of the second and then, kneeling, he seized the last by the belt and the collar before lifting him into the air. He tossed him over his head as if he weighed no more than a feather. He stood up, his heart heavy and his chest aflame and dashed into the adjoining street, ignoring the curses of the soldiers at his heels.

He ran desperately, turning at each street corner, his vision blurred, seeking a way out of his predicament. The soldiers' voices echoed in the deserted streets and with them the hooves of galloping horses. He was the prey, a fox being hunted by hounds on foot and riders on horseback, and if he did not find a means of escape quickly then the trap would close around him. Distant and faint, he spotted some flickering lights over the rooftops. As he drew closer, the sound of singing and the clinking of tankards came to his ears.

He turned into an alley on his right, almost crashing into a pile of crates. He slowed down as he came out into a wide street illuminated by lanterns hanging from strings. The crowd was dense; men and women were singing, drinking, coming and going from taverns whose doors stood wide open. He removed his mask, tucking it into his belt, and caught his breath. Here he stood a chance. He melted into the crowd.

When he left the neighbourhood he could only hear laughter and cheering behind him. He found an alley and climbed up the side of a building. And when he reached the rooftop he enjoyed a hard-earned rest.

Esyld ...

He repeated her name silently, as if to assure himself that he had not been dreaming. But no doubt was strong enough to disturb his sudden intoxication. Whatever the reasons for her presence in Masalia, and Aladzio's silence on the subject, he would reflect on them later. Another irony of fate. His life seemed defined by ironies of fate. Unlike his mentor he had never believed man's destiny was set out in a book, any more than he had accepted the idea that the gods had written it. But he had to acknowledge that chance worked in curious ways.

Looking out over Masalia, he spent several long hours watching the masts of the ships rock gently in the distant harbour.

5

REMEMBER WHO YOU ARE

Whatever the reason for your acts,
Whether you can justify them or not,
There will never be any excuse
For taking someone's life.

The Emperor.

Since the Saltmarsh, Laerte had never stopped thinking about it, imagining the day when, ready at last, he would plunge a sword into Reyes' heart. He would take his life, showing no mercy, he would avenge the Usters without shedding the smallest tear. He had already judged the man guilty; all that remained was to carry out the sentence.

From the Saltmarsh to Garmaret, from Garmaret to Sainte Amanne, Serray and Sopira Galzi, he had listened to Dun-Cadal's advice, trained hard, and never faltered despite the pain. His will alone allowed him to overcome all obstacles. They had passed through so many towns; from villages gradually darkened by the shadow of war to Emeris itself, flamboyant and majestic. Perfect and Imperial.

He would soon be fifteen years old and he reckoned he was capable of knocking down every wall separating him from his goal. What a surprise it was when he first saw the capital and its tall white towers, with the waterfall tumbling down at their feet, and how anxious he became when he tried to imagine the cursed Emperor. What did he look like? He must be a giant, a monster of muscle and strength, an implacable warrior.

During their journey he had seen the rebellion spreading and, more than once, he had been obliged to take lives. Each time he shed blood, each time he saw the dying gasp their last breath, the image of

271

Madog rose in his mind. All this violence, this rage, this turmoil. He was growing up amidst a war whose causes and meaning he barely understood.

Each life destroyed was one more reason the Emperor should pay for his crimes. It was his fault that Laerte was forced to act in this manner. Asham Ivani Reyes was the sole person responsible for this implacable anger. So Laerte rid himself of any doubts, not without some difficulty, for a dark idea persisted within him, as hot as a coal about to burst into flame. His guilt rose to the surface and nagged at him until he managed to push it into the deepest corner of his being, along with Madog's shadow. Through his experience of combat he gained in confidence and mastery without Dun-Cadal ever seeming to take notice. Not once did he compliment Laerte on his efforts or end a training session with an encouraging word. The general limited himself to repeating the same advice, sometimes mocking Laerte, *teasing* him, as he put it.

Laerte did not like it. Laerte put up with it. Dun-Cadal was an enemy; one of those who had attacked the Saltmarsh; one of those who had taken Aëd's Watch; one of those who had murdered his family. At least, that's what he kept telling himself . . .

For upon arriving at the gates of Emeris he found, against all expectation, that he'd grown used to the general and even come to enjoy certain moments in his company. Dun-Cadal's frankness pleased Laerte but did not excuse everything. He was boorish, hard and uncultivated. He thought he knew everything under the sun, that he'd experienced so much he had nothing left to prove and saw no reason to bow down to anyone except the Emperor. Only his opinion mattered, only his vision of the world was correct, only his words commanded silence. The Empire he served was righteous and just, worth sacrificing his life for. It mattered little to him that men had been hung in its name, and women raped and gutted . . . Or else he did not know of the torments inflicted upon the Uster family.

Naïs . . . my sister was called Naïs.

'Are you mute, then, having said nothing until now?' asked the man. 'I've heard of you, you know. You're Frog, am I right?'

A man wearing a white toga with a red cloth draped over his shoulder was leading them through the hallways of the Imperial palace at Emeris. Dun-Cadal had introduced him as the Emperor's steward.

'Yes.'

'Frog . . .' said Dun-Cadal reproachfully.

From the corner of his eye, he saw his mentor's stern gaze and corrected himself with ill grace:

'Yes, my lord.'

'Your devotion to the Empire has caught our attention . . . as well as our respect, young man,' added the man.

'Thank you, my lord.'

At the end of the hallway lined with mirrors were two great doors. And hidden behind them was the lastborn of the Reyes dynasty. Laerte felt his body stiffen, ready to pounce. There was no room for error. Once he passed the threshold he would have to seize his opportunity without hesitation. The steward pushed the doors open.

He would not get another chance . . .

They creaked, revealing a large room with a black-streaked marble floor.

Never get another chance . . .

Dozens of smooth, shining columns led up to a thin red curtain stretched near a large balcony that was brushed by tree tops. Was that the Emperor? The shadow behind the blood-coloured curtain? Was he that black figure over which the female silhouettes were pouring steaming water? Was that really Asham Ivani Reyes? Laerte grew tense. A hand pressed him in the back.

'Advance,' ordered Dun-Cadal. 'And don't speak until he addresses you.'

There would be no need for words. Only his deed, quick and precise, would count. Behind the curtain, the shadow bent over. The steward beckoned them to follow him.

'Your Imperial Majesty,' he announced loudly. 'General Daermon, returned from the Saltmarsh and his young protégé.'

'Have you brought back a son?' a voice jeered. 'Is that what took you so long?'

They advanced towards the silhouette, propped up in his bath. Only a shadow, but what a shadow! Imposing, strong . . . hateful. Laerte quickened his pace, coming up alongside the steward. His heart was beating so fast, his brow was beaded with sweat, his hands becoming damp as he approached his goal. His fingers brushed the pommel of his sword.

Quickly and well. That was how he must strike. Quickly and well, straight to the heart, his blade piercing the curtain, its colour

273

blending with the red of Imperial blood. Then it would all be at an end, the war along with his sorrow. His father, his mother, his brother … his little sister. His sweet little sister would be avenged. Tears rose to his eyes. His hand slipped to his sword's hilt. Only a few more yards and he would be in range, only a few …

A blade whistled through the air to stop short at his throat. Laerte came to a sudden halt, holding his breath. At the end of the weapon, a hand gloved in leather gripped the hilt tightly. The man wore a dark green jacket and a cape tossed over his shoulders, whose hood covered his head. His face was nothing but a patch of darkness from which a deep quiet voice emanated.

'Peace, Daermon.'

Laerte tried to detect some trace of humanity in the voice. His attacker only had to make a single move, just one, and it really would all be over. The boy resigned himself to releasing his sword out of fear of immediate decapitation. For the first time – having seen battle, experienced fear, fled from Imperial and rebel troops alike in the Saltmarsh – for the first time, he realized he was facing death. He was forced to admit that, on seeing it so close, he was not ready to confront it. A tear appeared at the corner of his eye.

Was he going to die here without honouring his family's memory? Without putting an end to this war? Without becoming the greatest knight of all time?

'He's not an enemy,' his mentor rumbled in protest.

Laerte did not know who this man was, but judging by the tone of Dun-Cadal's voice, even the general seemed to fear him.

'He comes from the Saltmarsh …' the voice replied.

'Ever prompt to defend me, Logrid,' commented the Emperor, in a stronger and more commanding tone.

A servant poured water into his bath as he passed his hands over his face. Wisps of steam drifted along the stretched cloth.

'But I don't believe a mere child who has left his region in time of war would come all this way to kill the Emperor.'

Laerte felt the tear brimming at the edge of his eyelid. He had failed so miserably … his one and only chance, he had let it slip by.

Trembling and close to actually sobbing, he glared at the hooded man.

'Logrid …' growled Dun-Cadal. 'Leave him be.'

The so-called Logrid lowered his arm. But Laerte could still feel the coldness where the blade had lain against his neck. From the corner of his eye the boy saw the assassin step around the general, replacing his sword in its scabbard.

'So this is how we're welcomed back to court,' murmured Dun-Cadal

'I'm only following your teaching, Daermon,' the other man replied in a low voice.

'The lad isn't threatening the Emperor, Logrid ...'

Laerte balled his fists. *That's a lie*, he thought. *A lie!* He would do more than simply threaten the Empire, he could break it, destroy it, annihilate it. One day he would do it. He wasn't a *lad*! He wasn't a *child*! He had not made this long journey for nothing. But although he was boiling inside, his entire body remained paralysed by fear.

'Frog ...' said Dun-Cadal.

Logrid had disappeared. All that remained in front of him was the red curtain behind which the shadow of the Emperor sat hunched over in his bath. He heard the steward murmuring in his mentor's ear.

'Perhaps it would be better if you were to have a private audience with His Imperial Majesty,' the steward proposed.

So he left the room without even glancing at Dun-Cadal.

Upon reaching the door he almost turned round and ran back towards the Emperor. Would this Logrid block his path again? Reason, or fear, prevented him from acting.

He followed the steward through the palace corridors, full of anger and regret, but refusing to admit defeat and flee far away, in the vain hope of leaving all his pain behind in Emeris.

When he discovered the military academy and the steward presented him to the instructors, he remained silent. He was taken to his chamber where he was asked to remove his sword. Then, dressed in the grey tunic worn by the cadets, he let himself be guided by one of them to a courtyard in the middle of which stood a fountain. In the shadow of the open gallery's arches, his gaze met those of his new comrades. They observed him as though he were a curious beast, some of them exchanging a few words. From their smiles, Laerte knew they were mocking him. But he did not react, still too stunned to defend his pride. He had sought to throw himself into the jaws of the wolf, thinking to strike a fatal blow, but now found himself lost, ready to be swallowed.

What would become of him?

'Come on, tattoo man! Come on, defend yourself!'

'Gods, does he stink!'

Laerte watched the Nâaga carrying two heavy crates, his head bowed. He kept his balance despite being shoved. He was massively built despite his youthful appearance. His heavily muscled arms emerged from his brown jacket full of holes, a physical trait that owed as much to his cultural heritage as to being a slave condemned to hard labour. His body was continually sculpted by exercises that were both cruel and painful. Withstanding blows to the torso while keeping one's feet was just one example among many, as Dun-Cadal had described them to Laerte in a tone of disgust. From infancy, the Nâaga learned to endure.

Stoically, he tried to reach the mouth to a chain-bridge without dropping his burden, while the cadets taunted and harassed him.

'Skin like that is repulsive!'

'You should go wash yourself!'

'The Nâaga are animals.'

'Hit him!'

They felt only scorn and disgust. One of them struck the slave in the face with his fist and the Nâaga made no attempt to avoid the blow. He did not utter a sound, continuing as best he could. No one intervened, viewing this sort of behaviour as natural, and Laerte was surprised to find himself thinking of his mentor. Dun-Cadal would never allow an inferior to be humiliated like this.

Laerte believed that he had failed this day, that he had not learned enough from his mentor to confront the Emperor. But perhaps it wasn't a failure after all, only a trial run; a first attempt which had allowed him to penetrate the monster's lair. Perhaps there was only another step to climb before he achieved his goal.

And the lessons he'd acquired during his journey from the Salt-marsh to Emeris had not been lost.

'What a brainless creature,' jeered a cadet, pointing at the Nâaga. 'Nothing between the ears!'

'Go on, punch him again!' urged a second.

As the third cadet prepared to strike another blow, a firm hand gripped his wrist. Before he had time to turn round, a foot kicked the back of his knee and forced him to the ground. Then a fist landed on his jaw beneath the stunned gaze of his comrades. They were quick to gather their wits, however, pouncing on Laerte and, very quickly, others joined them. He dodged as best he could, striking back at any who came within his reach, but he soon found himself surrounded. Finally forced to the ground, he rolled himself into a ball as fists and kicks rained down on him.

Laerte endured the pain … and he endured the humiliation. The Nâaga was able to escape. Right there and, as a dozen cadets pummelled away at him, he forged an unswerving friendship.

The days that followed, and then the months and years, only reinforced this bond. Laerte did not fit in at the academy. He was not like the other cadets and many of them disguised their jealousy as scorn. They envied him, they hated him … but they also feared him. He was the only cadet who had actually seen combat. And done so in the company of one of the Empire's greatest knights, no less.

When he was sixteen, Dun-Cadal and Laerte returned from the Vershan, on the heels of a hard-fought victory at the foot of the mountain range. This was the third time he'd returned to Emeris and he'd had no further opportunity to confront the Emperor. The war had dulled his ardour for vengeance. Although he had not forgotten his mission, other desires had taken precedence.

Esyld had found refuge in the great city, taken on as a servant by some of the nobles who lived in the Imperial palace. He was eager to see her again, but on the way to the servants' quarters he halted in a large inner courtyard in the centre of which a familiar structure had been erected.

The voices thundered like drum rolls. Cadets from the academy, completely devoted to defending the Emperor and blinded by their education, were massed around the scaffold. Among them, soldiers, male and female courtiers and their servants witnessed the scene with less enthusiasm. There a sharp thump, followed by a terrible snapping of bones. Three men, their bodies slashed, hung from the ropes and swung slowly in the air, their faces frozen in a sudden grimace. Laerte could not bear to look at their blank gazes and lowered his eyes.

'They came from the Saltmarsh,' said a hoarse voice behind him.

'There's no need for proof when people fear a plot. Rumours alone were enough to convict them.'

Laerte glanced briefly over his shoulder. The familiar face helped to alleviate the disgust he felt seeing such a spectacle and a flat smile tugged at his lips. It had been months since he had last seen the man and finding him here, visibly in fine form, was comforting. Rogant had changed. Like Laerte he had grown and was now a good foot taller than his friend.

'It seems I never return at the right moment,' Laerte said.

'It seems they never hang the right people, Frog. You're the one who should be swinging at the end of a rope,' Rogant said, joking.

'And who would defend you then?'

The Nâaga didn't appear to appreciate that gibe, revealing his shining white teeth in an aggressive smile.

'That only happened once,' he grumbled, crossing his arms.

His bulging torso was concealed by a leather surcoat. Strange-looking tattoos slithered down his face to his shoulders, following the contours of his neck. He wore loose linen trousers over polished leather boots and a dagger hung from his belt. Yes, things had certainly changed during Laerte's absence.

'You're armed now,' Laerte observed, passing before his friend to descend a small stairway leading inside the palace.

Rogant followed him through the narrow hallways.

'I thought slaves were denied the right to defend themselves?'

'I now serve Duke de Page as his bodyguard,' Rogant said. 'Let's just say he detected the makings of a warrior in me.'

'He must have a sense of humour.'

'Coming from an apprentice knight who goes by the name of Frog, that lacks any real sting.'

The day was drawing to a close when they entered the servants' quarters. Here, in the middle of a narrow hallway, Laerte halted. Shadow and light battled one another in even-handed combat, the torchlight flickering across his features. Giving a brief glance to the right and left the two friends assured themselves that no one had followed them. Then they fell into one another's arms, laughing.

'It's so good to see you've returned alive!' Rogant confessed, giving the boy a slap on the back.

'I have some things left to do before I give up the ghost.'

'The Vershan?'

'Wearying,' replied Laerte, drawing back from the Nâaga. 'And you? How are you?'

'I'm still not free ... but being in de Page's service almost amounts to the same thing. It's best if that remains between us. Times are complicated. Anyone who says a word against the Emperor is suspect.'

'And what if your master knew about our meetings?'

From Rogant's amused expression Laerte guessed that the Duke de Page's name had been added to the ever-growing list of nobles who had secretly joined the opposition and were offering the rebels logistical support. But Laerte ... how was he helping his cause? It was difficult to reconcile fighting the rebels, to maintain appearances, with his sympathies for the rebellion itself. Yet he carried on without questioning his own choices. All that mattered to him was the day when he would be ready to stand against the Emperor.

Rogant knew this. Although Laerte had never revealed his true identity to the Nâaga, they agreed on numerous points. Hadn't the Emperor authorized the enslavement of Rogant's people? Without telling him the reasons for it, Laerte had shared the secret of his vendetta against Reyes. And Rogant was determined to help him.

'You're much more at risk than he is, Frog. You come from the Saltmarsh ... and from the day you arrived here, you defended a slave. Believe me, de Page could be useful to you one day. In any case, I'm watching out for you.'

'I'm the one who protects you,' Laerte smiled.

'Little knight,' retorted Rogant, thrusting his chest out.

He tilted his head towards Laerte with a mocking air. No one dared to bother him now that he'd reached his adult size.

'It's only a warning,' Rogant admitted in a more serious tone. 'I wouldn't want anything to happen to you.'

Laerte nodded.

'Go quickly and see her ...' his friend murmured. 'She's been waiting for your return for two days now.'

Although Rogant had seen them meet in secret several times, Laerte was certain that the Nâaga did not know much about her. The boy had never spoken to him about his life before arriving in Emeris. And still less about Esyld. But Rogante must have guessed that she counted more for Laerte than anything in this world. He therefore had no qualms about cutting short their conversation. His friend knew him well. Laerte was indeed anxious to see her again after his prolonged absence.

His heart racing, he followed the hallways that still separated him from his beloved.

How overjoyed he had been when, two years previously, he had glimpsed her familiar silhouette in one of the palace gardens. She had just joined her father in Emeris and was working as a servant at the Imperial court.

She was his vessel in a raging sea, the only person capable of keeping him afloat. He had told her everything ... even what he intended to do, when he was ready.

When he opened the door to the little room, ducking his head slightly to pass through the arched door frame, he didn't even bother to check if anyone had followed him. He had waited too long.

She was there, her hands joined before her, her hair delicately arranged with blue ribbons. The pale light of day, which entered in a single beam through a skylight, wreathed her face in a diaphanous veil. In the corner was a plain bed with a rickety table beside it. Esyld was the light guiding his path. He did not say a word, quietly closing the door behind him. And when she turned towards him, her lips formed a relieved smile.

'At last,' she said simply.

'The journey was longer than planned ...'

He approached her hesitantly. His hands were damp. She had grown even more beautiful since the last time they met. Her features were more refined. She was a woman now. He did not dare to touch her. It was she who pressed herself against him, resting her head against his shoulder. The scent of her curled hair intoxicated him.

'My proud little lord,' she said. 'You took so long returning since the news of your victory at the foot of the Vershan reached us.'

'I came as quickly as I could ... It's only been two hours since we arrived. As soon as Dun-Cadal took his leave, I came to see you.'

'Won't he come looking for you?' Esyld worried.

'He's in Mildrel's arms right now,' smiled Laerte.

'And you're in mine ...'

His smile faded as his gaze plunged into hers. Very slowly, he bent his head and their lips brushed in a restrained kiss.

'You must not stay long,' she warned him in a murmur. 'You should report to the academy before someone notices your absence.'

She slowly drew away from him, avoiding his eyes. Surprised, Laerte remained silent for an instant. Was she not happy to see him again, to be waxing hot and cold in this fashion?

'They're hanging people now ...'

'I'm Dun-Cadal's apprentice. The old blowhard will protect me, don't worry,' he tried to reassure her.

'Don't you understand?' she asked angrily.

She turned her back on him, her fists balled at her hips, and she sighed bitterly.

'My father and I agreed not to tell Meurnau anything about you. To pretend you did not survive ... but you should have returned to the Saltmarsh. It's far too dangerous here.'

They had discussed this more than once but Laerte had always been adamant. He recalled his last visits to Aëd's Watch. All those people talking about him as if he were an entirely different person. Ever since then, his confidence in Meurnau had died.

'Meurnau has made me a symbol, I'm no use to him *alive*. He's leading his rebellion,' Laerte said. 'So on the contrary, I'm much safer here. Whatever else might be said about him, Dun-Cadal looks after me well. I've learned a lot with him.'

'Just a year ago, you hated him,' noted Esyld with a small laugh.

She was mocking him. But could he deny that he'd had a change of heart concerning his mentor? Sometimes he defended him now.

'That's still the case. I'm only using him to become strong enough to kill the Emperor,' he justified himself.

'Kill the Emperor ...' she sighed. 'Well then, do it, if you've learned so much from your beloved general.'

She glared at him as if he'd committed the most heinous of crimes. For her to be so angry with him, without his knowing the reason why, left him completely dumbfounded.

'Esyld—'

'Go on! Go and do whatever seems right to you!'

'I'm not ready,' he admitted. 'But soon I promise you I will be and that will put an end to this unjust war and my family will be avenged and—'

'So, you still haven't grown up,' she interrupted.

She turned away from him and went to the window, lifting her dress daintily with both hands in a dignified manner.

'What's got into you?' asked Laerte, taken aback.

He had never seen in her in such a state before, so aggressive towards him.

'What's got into me?' she said in an unbearably sharp and determined tone. 'What's *got into me* is that my father is risking his life here to ensure that Oratio of Uster's ideas survive. Rallying the nobles to the cause of the rebellion so that Emeris falls. Every day brings him closer to swinging from the gallows. Who knows when he will be caught, Laerte? But you don't think of any of that. All that matters to you is revenge.'

Her eyes were full of tears.

'We're taking enormous risks here! Each day, refugees from the Saltmarsh are being questioned. Each day, those nobles who have stayed away from the court are being summoned by the Emperor. Some of them have disappeared and it's whispered that the Hand of the Emperor is responsible. That the Hand, his assassin, is immortal. That he has always served the Reyes dynasty and that he will continue to serve its Emperors by killing all those who plot against them. Tell me, Laerte. Tell me how my father will die. On the gallows? Or murdered like a dog, while you are out there fighting *against* the rebellion? The rebellion that praises the name of Laerte of Uster to the heavens! Sometimes I wonder whose side you're on ...'

'It's not easy for me, Esyld, I ...' he tried to defend himself.

Images of the battles he'd fought passed through his mind. At what moment had he realised *who* he was actually fighting? Was there a single instant, since Madog, when he'd admitted to himself that he was killing those who were fighting for his father's dream ... the dream that one day the people would take control of their own destiny?

'No, of course it isn't easy,' she continued. 'The day you attempt to kill the Emperor, as you've been dreaming about for so long, his *Hand* will fall upon you ...'

This Hand who had already stopped him once ... Out of pride, he'd never dared to tell Esyld of his failure. He wanted to preserve her good opinion of him, not have her see his weakness.

'Perhaps at that moment you will remember who you truly are. Because for the time being, it is not Laerte I see before me but Frog.'

That was enough to break down his usual timidity. Without hesitating, he pressed her against him and pushed her hand into his pocket.

'I am one and the other, Esyld. It doesn't change anything. I have never forgotten where I come from or who I am.'

He pulled her hand out again; between her slender fingers she held a small wooden horse. The mere sight of it made tears to trickle from the corners of her eyes.

'I have never forgotten it.'

She slowly put it back into his pocket as he brought his face close to hers. She stiffened.

'I have never forgotten you ...' he murmured.

The kiss they exchanged was so intense he thought the world had disappeared around them. Only his body registered fully in his awareness, pressed against her, perfumed by her sweet scent. Little by little Esyld relaxed in his arms and it was she who seized the initiative from that point. Laerte had never dared to take things further despite his longing to. He had dreamt of it so often that every time he held her in his arms, his anxiety overwhelmed him to the point that he could only give her a kiss.

He discovered her that day, beautiful and naked. Together they lay entwined on her small servant's bed in the dim light of the room, with no other sound than that of their breathing. And their hearts, the one next to the other, beating in the same rhythm. Tasting her skin, caressing the curves of her body with the pads of his fingers, he abandoned himself to her completely. The more tightly she held him, the more he curled up against her. He would have liked this moment to last an eternity.

When he returned to the academy he felt changed inside. Who he was, Frog or Laerte, no longer mattered now that he had become a man. He saw Esyld several more times, but they never had the chance to relive the embrace they shared that day. The tension within the palace had increased a notch and, as the days went by, the impression that they were being spied upon grew stronger. The Emperor was suspicious of everyone, and of the refugees in particular.

Laerte took part in several classes at the academy without inci-dent. The other cadets avoided him ... Some of them even started to regard him as if he were Dun-Cadal Daermon himself. Laerte had never felt so confident of himself. He was sure of who he was, what he doing, and why he was doing it.

Yet Esyld was right. In reality he was losing sight of his goal, fighting battles instead, constantly postponing the confrontation with the Emperor, sometimes even forgetting the origin of the rebellion. The excitement of combat took precedence. His rage blinded him to the point of having no motivation except that of satisfying it. It had become an unquenchable thirst he carefully preserved, an unbreakable addiction.

Frog was losing himself in anger and violence.

It would continue until he confronted himself and the dragon full of rancour that roared within his heart. This inner dragon, which every man must one day fight, he would finally meet far away from Emeris, in the northern reaches of the Empire.

At Kapernevic, where he met an ingenious inventor by the name of Aladzio for the first time.

6

MASTERING THE DRAGON

Feel the *animus*, be the *animus*.
Feel it, Frog! Breathe as one life with it.
It's there, the magic.
In every breath you exhale

'Get up.'

He gave the bed a violent kick before turning round and going out the door. The old man grumbled where he lay. Laerte waited a few minutes to make sure he was up and then descended the stairs of the small house. In the salon, sitting comfortably in the hollow of a large armchair, Viola lifted an eye above her book. Surprised, she set it down on her knees when she saw Laerte walk past with a determined step. A few seconds later, Dun-Cadal appeared, still looking sleepy.

'Good morning,' she greeted him uncertainly.

The general ignored her and crossed the room, his eyes swollen. When he saw Laerte in the doorway leading outside, he sighed and shook his head.

'Oh, this is going to be a good morning,' Viola thought aloud as Dun-Cadal went out in his turn.

Neither man had uttered a single word, but they left a palpable tension floating in their wake. Viola stood up slowly and glimpsed Laerte slipping past one of the windows. She approached cautiously.

The two men were walking in a little gravel-surfaced courtyard overlooking the houses that descended in terraces towards the heart of the city. From here, they could contemplate all of Masalia, its high towers and buildings decked with flowers, the three cathedrals and the glittering dome of the Palatio. In the distance, ship masts swayed with the movements of the tide. The bright reflection of the newly risen sun danced upon the sea. Dun-Cadal advanced to the low wall enclosing the courtyard, looking down at the succession of red-tiled roofs. In his younger years he could have jumped from one to the next like the steps of a stairway. Was he still capable of racing down them? Simply leave all this behind and resume his life in the taverns? But he no longer wanted to flee. A few feet away from him, Laerte was hefting a sword.

'What do you want?' muttered Dun-Cadal.

In place of a reply, he watched the blade fly through the air to plant itself at his feet. Laerte swept aside his cape with a movement of his arm to reveal the pommel of his sword. Since his mentor did not dare to wield Eraëd, perhaps he would consent to use another weapon.

'Pick it up,' Laerte ordered.

'So ... you want to finish me off here and now,' concluded Dun-Cadal. 'The final reckoning ...'

'When you saw me at the port, assassinating Enain-Cassart, what did you try to do?' Laerte asked him, an odd smile at the corner of his lips. 'After Negus's murder, when you chased me? Weren't you planning to challenge me then? I'm giving you the chance now. Go on!'

'At the time I thought I was chasing Logrid,' Dun-Cadal replied drily.

'Another one of your students, wasn't he? Are you disappointed with the results of your teachings now?' the young man asked ironically as he spread his arms. 'Here I stand before you after all these years. I lied to you all this time. Don't you feel any anger about that? You know it. You feel it. When the Empire collapsed, it was because of me ... The shadow of Laerte of Uster ...'

Dun-Cadal tilted his head, his eyes on the pommel of the sword before him.

'The man I knew would have fought ... and then burnt this house to the ground before leaving,' Laerte continued. 'He would have stood up for himself. But you let yourself be pushed around ... It's not just your body which has grown old, it's also your soul.'

Laerte saw the old man quiver. All the features of his face hardened and his gaze shifted away from the weapon planted at his feet. Dun-Cadal was containing his anger. Out of the corner of his eye, he could make out Viola's face behind the window. Although she did not like the situation at all, at the same time she did not seem ready to intervene.

'I thought you were saving me for the end ...' Dun-Cadal smiled sadly. 'But that would have been too great an honour.'

'Honour is something you never had,' Laerte said in a grating tone. 'Oh yes, you were an exceptional general. An uncouth man who, in the age of the nobility, managed to get himself invited to the banquets of the high and mighty.'

'That's enough,' murmured the old man.

'Did you ever realise to what extent *he* took you for an idiot? A mere weapon in his hand? A great warrior, to be sure, but one with the brains of a sparrow.'

'Stop it.'

'The man of the West at the Emperor's feet. Yet you swore to defend him,' Laerte continued speaking calmly.

'Stop it!'

'You lost everything, Daermon. The world you devoted your life to has gone, along with what small glory you once possessed. No one respects you now. Not even yourself, which tells how far you've fallen. If Frog had ever existed, *your* Frog, believe me, he would never have wanted you as a father.'

With a swift movement, the old man reached for the sword. The hilt lodged itself snugly in his hand. While Viola looked on in alarm, Laerte lunged forward and delivered the first attack. Dun-Cadal just had time to lift his blade and parry the stroke. He tried to push his attacker back with his knee. Laerte evaded the blow, spinning, and struck the general's groin with a closed fist. The two swords clashed again and the blades slid against one another with a grating noise.

Behind the window Viola turned pale. But she had barely taken a step towards the door when Rogant's hand fell on her shoulder.

'Wait,' he advised her.

Reluctantly, she returned to the window and resolved to remain a mere spectator of a combat whose outcome she dreaded.

'Is that it?' taunted Laerte. 'You're even deader than I thought.'

'You won't kill me that easily,' retorted Dun-Cadal.

'Really? Have you found some of your passion, Wader?' the younger man asked mockingly. 'Is there still a soldier living inside you?'

'I was ... a ... general!'

'One who had the wool pulled over his eyes by a mere lad,' Laerte smiled, aware that his jibes were having the desired effect.

A violent blast of air dug a furrow across the courtyard, heading straight towards him. Laerte leapt backwards to avoid the wave of wind and gravel and fell heavily to the ground, one hand touching the earth. He had barely looked up when he saw Dun-Cadal swooping down on him. He evaded the attack with a sideways roll before using the *animus* in his turn. Gravel pelted the general's face, almost making him fall.

'You loved him, didn't you? Your Frog ... Although he felt nothing but contempt for you, and laughed at your weakness when you were asleep.'

Furious, Dun-Cadal aimed the point of his sword at the young man, small drops of blood running down his face.

'Shut up! You are nothing but a lie! Deceiver!'

He lunged forward but Laerte sidestepped away. He struck at the general's blade with his sword before tripping him up.

'Azdeki played you for a fool. I played you for a fool. Don't you deserve to end your life in this city, dying in a gutter?' Laerte asked as he walked around the old man sprawled on the ground. 'But you don't deserve to have me kill you right here and now, that would be too much of an honour.'

'So what do you expect from me?' roared Dun-Cadal as he struggled to his feet. 'You won't break me! You cannot take away what I've lived!'

'You're already broken.'

Indeed, Dun-Cadal was shaking, and not solely from rage. His thirst had taken control of his nerves, turning them white-hot. His need for alcohol was burning up his heart. Laerte recognised the despair in the old general's eyes when he attempted to strike another blow.

Laerte evaded it easily, again, watching as his opponent doubled over with sweat pouring off his brow and his breath wheezing.

'Try again,' Laerte urged him, turning his sword with a flick of the wrist.

Dun-Cadal charged at him, unleashing a flurry of blows, but Laerte's blade turned away each strike with precision.

'I gave you everything!' the old man bellowed. 'Everything! And you betrayed me! You should have killed me! That's what you should have done! So kill me, come on! *Kill me!*'

Suddenly, Laerte leaned over and struck Dun-Cadal right in the sternum with his elbow before sweeping him off his feet with an out-stretched leg. The old man fell flat on his back, stunned. Laerte stood over him, watching his head wobble, his face drenched in sweat.

'I will not kill you,' the former apprentice declared in a grim voice.

When he was still a child he had dreamt of this, the moment when he would surpass his mentor. But today, although he had Dun-Cadal at his mercy, he no longer felt anything but pity. The man was right. He had given Laerte *everything* ... including his dignity.

'You could do it,' sobbed Dun-Cadal. 'You killed a dragon ... Me, I'm just a cockroach ...'

'Sometimes appearances are deceptive ...'

He held out his hand. Dun-Cadal looked up at it, hesitating over whether to take it.

'What if you only saw what you wanted to see?' suggested Laerte, an odd smile playing at the corners of his mouth before it promptly vanished. 'And what if Frog ... what if he truly respected the man who saved him from the Saltmarsh?'

Dun-Cadal remained on the ground for a few more seconds, with tears in his eyes, before he caught hold of the young man's hand. Laerte helped him regain his feet. Instead of swords, now they matched gazes.

'You'd rather I finish you off,' Laerte acknowledged.

Dun-Cadal turned away with a stricken air. After a brief glance around him, he massaged the back of his neck.

'I'm thirsty ... Is there even a single jug of wine here?'

'You don't need wine.'

'Ha!' laughed the general, rolling his eyes. 'At least let me die as I see fit! You hate me! You've always hated me!'

'No. You will always be the general who taught me how to fight.' His tone was direct and cold.

'That general is dead ... he died with Frog!' cried the old man, his mouth twisted in rage. 'I taught Frog everything I know. He had honour, he had intelligence, he ... he had passion. He would never have assassinated men as you have here in Masalia. Do you want to kill me like Enain-Cassart? Like Negus? Then go ahead! Carry out your revenge to the bitter end! That's why you've revealed yourself to me, isn't it?'

Laerte took a step towards him and then halted.

'But what if things aren't what they seem?'

'It's crazy ...'

'The dragon at Kapernevic ... The red dragon ...'

'Wader, you can't rely on that ... that ... He's a fool!'

'I didn't kill it.'

'Aladzio is just a little different from the rest of us, Frog. But his plan seems judicious to me.'

Dun-Cadal turned around slowly. Laerte had already disappeared and the sound of his footsteps soon faded to no more than a distant echo inside the house.

'A judicious plan?'

'Judicious ...'

'Judicious?' Frog repeated as he quickened his pace to keep up with his mentor. 'Relying on that cretin is anything but judicious. Negus told you: he burned the barn down several times with his experiments.'

Dun-Cadal gave a satisfied smile before halting at the edge of the forest. Behind them, the tracks of their steps in the snow formed an odd dotted path leading back to the blurry outlines of Kapernevic. The chimneys of the stone houses released a heavy grey smoke that wove its way up into an immaculate white sky. The afternoon was coming to an end and, since dawn, Negus's soldiers had been pressed into service building the dragon traps designed by Aladzio the previous night. The fact that the inventor played a major part in the plan had greatly displeased the boy, he found it unbearable. Aladzio had one enormous fault: he talked constantly, about everything and anything, became ecstatic over the slightest thing, and was enthused by every passing idea.

When Dun-Cadal proposed that he help them defeat Stromdag's troops, his loquacity had vanished. Nervous at first, he set to work and devised a system of nets capable of trapping the dragons.

'Stay here, I'm going to check on things with Negus,' ordered Dun-Cadal, before he continued to make his way between the pines.

Negus was pacing up and down a long mound behind which his spearmen were preparing. Dun-Cadal went to meet him under the baleful eye of his young apprentice. A few feet away, Aladzio was supervising a team of four soldiers kneeling around a net.

'Judicious ...' muttered Laerte, before letting out a long sigh. 'We're digging our graves here ...'

The two generals conferred in the distance without paying any heed to him. When Laerte saw Aladzio heading towards him, he regretted not being nearer to them; at least they would have drawn the inventor's attention. But before he could take more than a single step in the snow, hoping to escape the man, Aladzio's voice forced him to halt.

'Frog!' Aladzio called. 'What a pleasure!'

Watched by the soldiers, Laerte had to give up any attempt to dodge the inventor. He waited until Aladzio reached him, his cheeks reddened by the cold and his tricorne jammed tightly on top of his head.

'We didn't have a chance to talk yesterday, I'm sorry about that. I left you alone at the tavern but—'

'Don't trouble yourself over that,' interrupted Laerte

'—I had baggage to prepare,' continued Aladzio as if he had not heard. 'And yes, I thought I was leaving today, but, well ... no. Instead, we're doing this.'

He placed his hands on his hips, gazing out at the forest with a bemused expression.

'That's how things are,' he sighed. 'That's life. Sometimes one thinks a thing ... and sometimes it turns out not to be the case. One thinks one is leaving for a destination and in the end fate has a quite astonishing surprise in store for us ...'

Laerte gave a brief nod of the head and started to sidle away slowly from the man.

'Tell me,' Aladzio asked, to Laerte's dismay. 'During the battle, I don't have to stay here, do I? I mean, would it be possible for me to return to Kapernevic? I'm not certain I'd be of much use here, and ...'

His voice had suddenly become nervous. He clasped his hands together anxiously, exhaling a milky-white cloud with each breath.

'That all depends,' replied Laerte with a nasty smile.

He slowly turned towards the inventor, the snow scrunching beneath his feet, and gave the man a mocking glance.

'If your traps are any good, Stromdag's men won't get past our lines. So what risks would you be taking then, if you watched the battle from the edge of the forest?'

'N-none,' stammered Aladzio, before smiling doubtfully. 'None, of course. It's just that, obviously, as in any science, there's a degree of uncertainty. I am a scientist. And this is ... experimental.'

'Are you claiming there's some *uncertainty* involved in your dragon nets? That you're experimenting?'

With each step Laerte took towards Aladzio, the inventor retreated. The apprentice knight kept hounding him with a stern glare.

'No, I'm not one to claim anything,' Aladzio defended himself without abandoning his smile. 'I performed a rough mass-weight-speed calculation based on what we know of the grey dragons inhabiting the Kapernevic mountains ... But if there's a red dragon ...'

'Scientist!' snorted Laerte. 'We'd be better off with a magician.'

Aladzio shook his head.

'Oh, no, no. Believe me, I know a little magic and it's not very effective.'

He lowered his eyes once Laerte was right in front of him.

'Well, when I'm the one trying to perform tricks, anyway ... I carried out my calculations correctly, I assure you ... I-I am gifted that way.'

The inventor looked so embarrassed that the boy didn't think he needed to add anything further. He took a step to the side, letting his gaze drift over the nets that the soldiers were stretching between the trees. In just a few hours a small party of Imperial troops would simulate an assault on Stromdag and draw the rebel forces to this very spot. Them and the dragons they'd driven from their lairs. It was the same tactic that they'd used with the rouargs in the Saltmarsh, adapted to the circumstances here. Laerte heard the crunch of snow beneath Aladzio's boots. Although the inventor was trembling from both the cold and fear he remained standing at the boy's side.

'Duke de Page did not tell me about this,' he sighed.

'de Page?'

'My patron,' explained Aladzio, placing himself on Laerte's right. 'Well ... for the moment. Indeed, that's why you're here ... at least, I suppose that's why. There are others besides him who seek to obtain my services. But he sent me out here to study. Not to wage war.'

His voice suddenly grew faint as his gaze wandered to the edge of the snow-covered forest.

'With all due respect, apprentice knight, frankly I don't understand much about this ... war.'

When Laerte glanced over at him, Aladzio did not blink. Although a certain fear could be detected in his eyes he continued to speak.

'It's true. I have nothing, personally speaking, against these people. They are simply fighting for ... well, they just want to be listened to, don't they? They want to have a say in their own destiny, at least I-I—'

'You could be killed for saying what you just said to me,' Laerte said gravely.

Aladzio looked away, a thin smile on his lips.

'For giving my opinion?' he objected in an uneasy tone. 'I'm just trying to understand ... Well, what I mean to say is that ...'

Laerte shook his head disgustedly. The inventor had started another monologue, one he preferred to ignore. Close by, the soldiers were finishing rigging the nets. Would they really be enough to stop the dragons? The boy could not understand how a man like Dun-Cadal could have built his plan around such an uncertain linchpin. There was both anxiety and excitement mixed with his doubts. Each battle offered him an occasion to forget himself, to see himself as someone big and strong when he vanquished his enemies, whoever they might be. Each confrontation let him reassure himself, to be certain he was becoming what he needed to be in order to avenge his loved ones. It mattered little to him that he was fighting people who proclaimed they were defending the ideals of a Republic. His father's dream mattered little – he'd been killed and his dream had been shamelessly appropriated by Meurnau and his supporters ...

None of this mattered much to him. Here at Kapernevic, in the blinding whiteness of the snow, there was more than the desires of Oratio of Uster at stake. There were his own. Stromdag and his men counted for little compared to the dragons.

As far as he knew, these furious beasts were as stupid as the rouargs. But among them was a breed superior in every way: bigger, stronger and more intelligent. The legendary red dragon. Dun-Cadal had minimised their dangerousness but nevertheless warned Laerte about them. His ambiguity itself was an indication of just how dangerous they were.

The red dragon represented the greatest challenge Laerte could hope for in this world and he was praying for a chance to meet one.

At nightfall, the soldiers took up their positions at the edge of the forest, hidden by the mound of snow. Pressed up against the trees, men with axes were preparing to cut the ropes holding the nets against the ground. The stars started to twinkle in the sky like distant fires in the icy darkness. Dun-Cadal ordered torches to be lit all around the traps and remained standing on top of the mound, only a few yards away from the pine trees. The tension increased among the Imperial troops. Next to the boy, a soldier was trembling, and not just because of the cold.

The squad chosen to act as bait had been gone for more than an hour when Negus took up his position against a tree trunk, his sword drawn. There were a few fits of coughing and the sound of the wind lifting the branches.

'Uhh ... excuse me ... please?' called a voice as someone tapped Laerte's shoulder.

The young man glanced back and was not surprised to see Aladzio's hunched silhouette. In the settling night his face was as pale as the moon. He was nervously crumpling his hat in his hands.

'Is it really necessary for me to remain here, my lord? I won't be of any great use to you. I suppose I—'

'Be quiet!' Laerte commanded.

He gestured at the inventor to step back.

'Well, I guess I should take that to mean: "By all means, go warm yourself in Kapernevic",' Aladzio said in jest. '"You've devised your trap well, you deserve to enjoy a spring chicken by the fire."'

Laerte could not help smiling. The inventor annoyed him so much he chose to be amused by him. The man left, accompanied by the crunching of his footsteps upon the mantle of snow. Then Laerte heard a few murmurs. Not loud enough, however, to cover the beating of his heart echoing in his temples. Instinctively, he brought his hand up to the hilt of his sword. The cold was numbing his entire body and he was impatient to get moving in order to feel alive, impatient to leave his position here, crouched down behind the mound.

Dun-Cadal's gloved hand slipped within the guard of his sword ... Had the general sensed something?

'They're coming,' he announced.

'I don't hear them,' Laerte murmured.

'Trust him on this,' advised Negus, standing against the tree a few feet away.

He punctuated his remark with a wink and then brought the blade of his sword up before his face. Laerte was not calmed by this at all. According to Dun-Cadal, Stromdag would send the dragons first. While the beasts busied themselves hunting those unfortunate enough to be standing in their path the rebel leader would try to overrun Kapernevic, given their advantage in numbers. They would arrive here certain they were superior in strength, while the torch-light would enrage the dragons. At that point the Imperial soldiers would spring forth from behind the mound. That surprise would create doubt and disorganisation in the rebels' ranks. As for the drag-ons? That was where Aladzio's contribution would tilt the balance in the Imperials' favour. The dragons' charge would crash into the nets ... so long as they were strong enough to contain the beasts ...

'Hold your positions,' ordered Dun-Cadal, kneeling on top of the mound.

Laerte observed the strange movement of his mentor. The general placed a hand upon the snowy blanket as he stared into the distance. Behind the wall of torches there was only darkness.

Little by little, a curious noise could be heard. Growing stronger and stronger, it was like the clash of metal on metal. *The clatter of armour*, thought Laerte as he slowly drew his sword. The drumming sound that followed reinforced his impression. The beaters sent out by the general were coming back, and behind them came Stromdag's army.

'They're coming!' a voice yelled.

A second added just as loudly: 'Get ready!'

Laerte stood up but the sound of his mentor's calm voice made him kneel again. It was not yet time to throw himself into battle. Not now ... but soon.

'Spearmen!' shouted Dun-Cadal.

The soldiers obeyed, readying their spears. A few yards ahead of them, their comrades were preparing to sever the ropes restraining the nets with their axes. The branches of the pine trees lifted slowly, announcing the approaching storm. Clumps of snow fell from the tree tops with soft thumps. Not nearly as brutal as the clatter of armour or the heavy breathing of soldiers running through the forest.

Clattering ... drumming ... and then a roar.

'They're here!'

A man came hurtling out the darkness, soon followed by ten more. Behind them the pine trees bowed and rustled.

Laerte finally stood up, his heart pounding, feeling as breathless as the soldiers who ended their mad dash by leaping over the mound. And looming between the trees, an enormous maw with gleaming fangs opened wide, ready to swallow the first victim that came within its reach. Two huge rolls of flesh vibrated at the rear of its throat and it gave a terrible bellow.

To the right and to the left, its brothers answered with their own spiteful cries, one of them raising hackles of torn flesh. From the cream-coloured spots on their scales to the striping of their leathery wings the differences between them were obvious. But all of them were driven by the same rage and their powerful jaws gaped ready to snatch men up in their charge.

'Now!' commanded Dun-Cadal as he stood up.

Laerte was speechless, looking in horror at the furious beasts stampeding out from between the trees. The axes plunged down several times upon the ropes before the nets suddenly sprang up, wrapping the dragons' voracious maws in their mesh. One by one, the dragons were trapped.

Dragons of the same colour as the darkness that enfolded them.

There was just enough light from the torches to make out the smallest details of their wings as they deployed between the pine trees. The spearmen charged, screaming at the top of their lungs. They rushed at the enraged monsters, planting their weapons in the beasts' necks. Watched by his astonished apprentice, Dun-Cadal leapt upon the snout of the first dragon and, with a quick, precise stroke, pierced its wide-open eye before falling heavily into the snow. But when the general turned round, Laerte was no longer looking at him. He was only interested in the enormous dragons, with their long snouts caught in the nets, a thick slaver glistening on their fangs. Clouds of white smoke swirled upwards from their wide nostrils and their bodies were covered with swellings that mottled their damp scales, except upon the thin wings that beat violently at the air in the hope of escaping the snares. But the nets held firm ...

'Frog!'

The frenzied beasts writhed, clawing the ground with their powerful legs.

'Frog! By the gods, get out of the way!

The sound of Dun-Cadal's voice surprised him. The tide of howling warriors who surged through the pine trees was even more surprising. Mercenaries, soldiers and peasants. All of them driven by the same anger, brandishing swords, flails, hatchets, or common pickaxes, gleaming in the torchlight. They skirted around the floundering dragons or climbed over the still-warm carcasses of the dead beasts, ready to sacrifice their own lives for the cause. They would never give up.

Going over the mound of snow, the Imperial troops' charge was equally unwavering. The impact between the two armies was violent, producing a din like thunder. Screams mixed with the clash of weapons, the death rattles of the dying with the roaring of the trapped dragons. At the very heart of the chaos Laerte parried, dodged and leapt, striking again and again, always with precision. His breathing accelerated and his heart raced. Everything became fast, violent ... and sublime. There, in the middle of the battle, he became someone strong, powerful, invulnerable.

He caught a blow from his right on his blade and then took a quick step back to avoid a second. With his free hand he struck at the mercenary's head before whirling his blade to keep his adversaries at a distance.

'Frog! There!'

A single warrior had decided to continue the fight, standing proudly before him, sabres in either hand. When he charged, Laerte merely had to kneel, raising his sword so that his opponent impaled himself without a sound. The apprentice knight extracted his blade from the man's flesh with a swift yank and turned back to Dun-Cadal. The general was gamely fighting on, surrounded by several rebels, parrying blows firmly and waiting for an opening that would let him to deliver a killing stroke.

'The dragon!' he yelled.

He indicated a distant heaving form with a brief nod of his head. It was much larger than the others and was struggling mightily within the netting. Its entire head, surrounded by hackles with blood-red glints, was caught in the mesh and it was trying to bite through the ropes with its fangs. It hammered the ground with its powerful legs, heedless of the unfortunate soldiers trying to restrain it. Their spears broke against its skin, the blast from its roars shaking the closest pines.

... as the net gave way.

Laerte rushed towards the scene, elbowing other men aside to force his way through the thick of the fighting. Several times he almost fell in the snow, parrying blows with a flick of his sword and jumping over bodies that were still warm. When he found himself blocked by a line of peasants he did not stop moving for even a second. Gripping his sword tightly he swept his blade through the air, spinning, rolling, striking. His blows were quick, accurate and deadly while the cries of the dragon grew louder.

Laerte was edging ever closer to it and could make out its perfect muscles bulging beneath bright red scales. Two horns grew above its yellow almond-shaped eyes with their pitch-black slits. Its powerful jaws snapped at the net and it roared again. Laerte halted suddenly, his breath taken away.

Coils of smoke rose gracefully from the creature's nostrils. It looked so big, so monstrously terrifying, lit by the flickering flames of the torches. Laerte remained completely still, his arms suddenly limp. He was hypnotised by the regular movement of its neck as it sought to extricate itself from the trap. Only when the dragon managed to rip the net apart from top to bottom did he retreat a step, feeling as much excited as afraid. Soldiers rushed at the monster, brandishing their spears. Free at last, the dragon's neck curved around before it lowered its snout towards the ground. Then it opened its jaws wide, something deep in its throat contracted and its forked tongue undulated as it inhaled deeply.

How did one defeat such a creature? Plunge a sword through an eye into its brain? Strike between its horns, between its eyes? Or behind those wide red hackles? Laerte searched desperately for a weak point in its armour, a plan of attack that would increase the odds in his favour. It was here, tonight, that he would prove his worth, facing this final challenge before becoming the knight capable of bringing down the Empire.

'Frog!' yelled a distant voice, just when he started to move again.

The red dragon stretched out its neck suddenly, its gaping maw releasing a torrent of fire. The snow melted into a thick steam as pine trees and soldiers were set alight. The fiery blast was so powerful that it threw the boy backwards like a rag doll. Lying full-length and stunned in the cold snow he caught sight of a gigantic shadow taking flight. A rumbling rolled over the burning conifers, almost drowning out Dun-Cadal's voice.

'Frog! It's too late! Run!' bawled the general.

A mind-numbing clamour announced the arrival of a new wave of enemy warriors. They were buoyed by a feeling of invincibility now the great dragon was free. Gliding over the forest, wings stretched wide, it poured fire down upon the Imperial soldiers. If it continued like this the battle would be lost. That couldn't be allowed to happen. Laerte tracked its progress and set off without anyone trying to stop him.

Dashing through the trees, the pine branches lashing his face, he left the clamour of war behind without losing sight of the dragon above him. The enraged beast circled high in the sky. In just a few more moments it would dive back down to the forest to unleash another flood of fire. Laerte was determined to prevent it, but he had no idea how. Running as fast as he could he tripped on a root and tumbled down a slope in a ball. The snow braked his fall, but did not cushion a painful landing on a bed of flat stones. The battle was no more than an echo now, the war cries like a distant memory haunting the woods. He stood up, his breath wheezing, his heart thumping hard and his temples aching. He was in a dried-up stream bed which weaved its way towards a wide grotto dimly visible in the moonlight. Rivulets of snow among the pebbles ran up to some oval objects as tall as a man, rising in the entrance to the cavern. A hoarse scream drew his attention and, looking up, Laerte almost lost his footing. The red dragon was circling overhead, craning its neck and trying not to lose sight of him. It had changed its flight path, foregoing the chaotic battle to devote its attention to the boy. Why would it do that? The oval objects . . . could they be a clutch of dragon eggs?

When the creature folded its wings back to dive on him, Laerte had no choice but to run.

His lungs on fire, he saw the shadow envelop him. At the moment the dragon's putrid breath reached him he threw himself down on the ground, his hands protecting his head. He heard the snapping of teeth and felt the powerful breeze that accompanied the monster's swoop. He thought he was going to die when a spurt of flame gushed down in front of him and almost sobbed when the thrashing tail lifted his cape.

Then it passed . . . the dragon had passed right over him. He would not get a second chance. He picked himself up off the ground, seeing the monster rising towards the moon with strong beats of its membranous wings. Then it tilted to one side, banking over the forest. The boy brought his hand up to the hilt of his sword.

'Damn ...'

The scabbard was empty. He had been running with the weapon in his hand and must have dropped it when he fell. Searching desperately for the gleam of his blade, he retraced his path. But in the dim light he saw only the dark blue snow and the black pebbles.

His heart was beating so fast and so hard he feared that it would give out; his chest was so tightly squeezed that he could not draw enough breath.

In the distance the red dragon was completing its turn and he had no weapon to face it.

No.

He still had the *animus*, wild and untamed and liable to obliterate him if he was unable to control it. But the *animus* made anything possible. It was the life force of the world.

'The whole world is like the air, it comes and goes. The animus ... *Feel the* animus, *be the* animus.'

He made sure of his stance, planting his feet firmly upon the pebbles with his knees bent. He drew in a deep breath, eyes closed, and concentrated. The urgency of his situation left no room for doubts. He must do this. He could do this. He was the greatest knight of all. He had promised. It wasn't a lie: he was capable of this.

From his head to his feet he could feel his entire body awaken, from his most recent raw wounds to the aches caused by his fall, from his burning lungs to his fluttering heart. He almost lost his grip for an instant; a tear ran from the corner of his eye.

The pain receded as the sight of the pebbles encircled by snow returned to him. He saw their strength, their hardness, reaching all the way to their unalterable heart. The roots of the pine trees, their branches bending beneath the snow, the thick bark protecting their trunks and the breeze caressing their boughs. And then he was submerged by a powerful current: an indescribable force that ran through his entire body before surrounding him. He felt the life animating the beast's bulging flesh, running beneath the scales to the veins in its leathery wings. He did not see the dragon; he became the dragon, sensing each heartbeat, each movement, each breath. The beast was about to pounce on him ... But no, it was neither stupid nor mindlessly aggressive. It was afraid.

The dragon folded back its wings.

He had it.

Now.

Laerte opened his eyes, stretching out as if to grasp an invisible rope. He balled his fists and, with a sharp movement, pulled them towards himself despite the pain. The beast screamed, unexpectedly held captive. It opened its wings wide, jerking its head about as if something were strangling it.

Laerte could not contain his own scream of pain. The sensation was unbearable, burning and spreading. His life seemed to be draining out of him as he tried to bring the dragon down. His feet slipped upon the pebbles. The beast was struggling frantically. He inhaled again, his throat terribly dry. But he wasn't just battling his own suffering . . .

He could also feel the dragon's torment.

A trickle of blood escaped from his right nostril and the world seemed to be spinning around him. The glow of the moon became as blinding as that of a sun.

He released his grip, drained. He could not contain the power, it was impossible. His heart was beating so fast he could barely breathe.

No . . .

Give up?

Not here. Not now.

He backed up slowly, redoubling his efforts, drawing his closed fists towards him and gritting his teeth. He bent his knees, screaming with effort.

His heart stopped for an instant. Everything went black.

Then there was silence. It lasted a few seconds . . . a minute perhaps.

At the instant the dried-up stream bed reappeared around him, he brought both fists down with a sharp jerk before he could think about it. The dragon was reeled in, plunging towards the ground with a final roar. It crashed in a cloud of snow and shattered rock. Laerte fell to the ground as well, exhausted. His whole body felt as if it had been trampled beneath the hooves of a maddened horse. Eyes half-closed, lying on the cold pebbles, he watched the injured dragon. Its yellow eyes had lost their spark, the heavy lids slowly covering the irises. Its nostrils released coils of grey smoke in brief spurts. It seemed so weary. The boy slowly sat up.

'That was it . . . wasn't it?' he murmured. 'You're protecting your nest . . .'

At the entrance to the grotto, he saw the eggs as clearly as in

301

daylight. They were the reason for the beast's fear. They were the reason it had left the battle when he'd tumbled down the slope – the same fear that Stromdag had used to send it against the Imperial forces, when they invaded its territory. Laerte approached the dragon, limping, and the monster did not stir. It accepted its defeat.

'You were protecting your family ...'

Laerte placed his gloved hand gently against the fuming nostrils and slid it slowly up towards one of the yellow eyes with its black slit. The dragon seemed to be watching him sadly. How could he kill it? What right did he have to end its life?

Out of the corner of his eye, he spotted a pile of bones ... and buried among them, a milky-white horn as big as the ones that jutted out from the monster's skull.

Slowly, the defeated dragon closed its eyes.

When it opened them again, Laerte was gone.

7

ESYLD

***

Who makes my heart beat?
Who wounds it or embraces it,
Holding it in the palm of their hand?

His father safely dead, he had indulged in orgies, some seeing this
as the expression of his grief, others his joy at finally being free of
paternal scorn. The small world of the Imperial court gathered in his
vast apartments to forget the rebellion with the help of great gulps
of wine and uninhibited sex with anyone, anywhere. Noble titles
mattered little when you were drunk.

By day, Duke de Page was considered the most amoral man there
was. By night, he was worth flattering in order to gain access to his
residence. His promiscuity was the object of public disapproval, although many secretly hoped he would offer them an invitation and
an open door to debauchery. He was host to the capital's most unbridled festivities: the reveller, the court entertainer.

He mingled at private parties like this one, lithe, wearing a black
leather jacket with puffed shoulders over a shirt of purest white. A
lace-trimmed mask disguised his face, but anyone observing him
would have seen his curious brown eyes roving from one couple to
the next. The guests' laughter mixed with cries of joy and the thump
of tankards was accompanied by the splash of wine being poured.

In an adjoining room, Laerte could hear their unbridled carousing.
The memory of Kapernevic still fresh in his mind, he felt nothing but
disgust towards the nobleman. The fact that he'd been summoned
here tonight, in secret, by de Page was incomprehensible to him, but
Rogant had insisted he attend. Leaning against the frame of a small
doorway, his arms crossed over his leather surcoat, the Nâaga stared

at him without blinking. A dagger in its scabbard hung down over one thigh. Visibly he took his guard duties so seriously that he gave Laerte no sign of friendliness. Or was there something else making him adopt such a stern manner?

Weary of the noise coming from next door, Laerte sat down on the small salon's red divan. Since his return from the North he'd barely had time to regain his quarters and sleep for a few hours before Rogant had come to fetch him.

'The dragons are our ancestors,' the Nâaga said suddenly, his voice hoarse.

Laerte nodded without giving him a glance. So that was it. Of course he knew about Nâaga culture and its beliefs, and of course he was aware of the significance of his deed in the eyes of his friend.

'You think I killed it,' he said.

'That's what the rumours claim. Few can believe they are true, whatever your mentor says. But if there is anyone capable of slaying a red dragon, I think it could be you,' Rogant admitted with a note of reproach to his tone.

Although the Nâaga had not meant it as such, Laerte was flattered by the compliment and smiled faintly. He leaned back in the divan spreading his arms to either side.

'There have been no more attacks on Kapernevic since we left there.'

'A dragon won't attack unless it is in danger. It defends itself,' Rogant remarked. 'Stromdag made use of that.'

'I know,' agreed Laerte.

'It wasn't necessary to kill it.'

'I know that, too.'

He tilted his head to the side and gave Rogant a wink.

'Don't worry about your big reptile. You can venerate it for a few more years.'

The Nâaga remained silent and still. If he felt any satisfaction at those words he was not one to display the fact.

On the other side of the wall there was a burst of laughter, so loud the door seemed to shift on its hinges. Music could be heard and, along with it, applause which covered the sounds of gasping. If de Page was hoping to win him over by offering him nights of ecstasy he was sadly mistaken.

Laerte had never met the man and was relying on what his mentor had told him. And those things Dun-Cadal had to say about the new duke were hardly favourable.

'What did you do?' asked Rogant, his face betraying no hint of his curiosity.

A voice coming from behind two rich red curtains reached them, coming closer and closer

'I'll be back! Don't you worry! I'll be back soon, my kittens!'

The words seem slurred, spoken carelessly by lips heavy from drink. Laerte glanced briefly at the curtains and, when no one appeared, he replied:

'I didn't kill it. I didn't have the strength to do it ...' he confessed. 'But I mastered it, Rogant. I managed to master it. And now that Stromdag is no longer using its territory its nest is safe, isn't it?'

Rogant raised an eyebrow. Then he nodded, a small smile tugging at the corners of his lips.

'Mastering a dragon means you're an adult,' asserted the same voice, still blurred by alcohol.

Laerte gave a start. Passing between the velvet curtains behind him, a young man came stumbling into the room. With a clumsy gesture he removed the mask covering his face. Wearing thigh boots over his riding breeches he stood out from most of the nobles living in Emeris, who were more often vulgar than elegant. This man, however, could have worn rags with delicacy. His only ostentatious touch was a golden seal ring on his third finger. His cropped hair shone with perfumed oil. Laerte stood at once but didn't offer him a bow. The nobleman did not seem offended, going over to a pedestal table which held a bottle of liqueur and two crystal goblets. His steps had become steadier.

'In the literature of the Caglieri era,' he said, slurring a little less and placing his mask beside the goblets, 'certain philosophers compared the dragon to our inner rage, the one that awakens when the world takes on a real significance.'

He no longer seemed drunk at all when he filled the two goblets and offered one to Laerte. He continued speaking, gradually regaining perfect diction:

'As children, we see nothing, either submitting or living protected from everything until the world and its injustices reveal themselves. That is the moment when the dragon takes hold of us. But then there comes a time when we must confront it, or it will enslave us. Rather than being prisoners of our anger, we must—'

Laerte hesitated before taking the proffered goblet. De Page lifted his as if in a toast.

'—master the *dragon*,' he murmured before taking a sip.

Standing in his corner, Rogant observed the scene in silence. He did not react when Laerte gave him a questioning look.

'But, please, sit down,' invited the duke with a sweep of his arm.

His guest did not blink, did not move, merely tracked de Page with a grim look in his eyes. The nobleman installed himself comfortably in an armchair by a stone fireplace and, crossing his legs, set his glass down on the armrest.

'Take a seat, Frog,' he insisted.

But Laerte had turned away. The game unfolding before his eyes did not please him at all and, although his interest was piqued, he was reasonably sure he would end up the dupe. The duke had gone from playing the drunk to being perfectly poised, like an actor shedding his role after taking a curtain call.

'What's the meaning of this?' he asked Rogant, raising his chin towards him.

'Calm down, Frog ...' his friend simply replied.

'I've taken off my mask,' intervened de Page, pointing to the one he'd dropped on the pedestal table. 'I hoped to win your trust. Our interview requires frankness. And it's an entirely informal interview, so I beg you ...' He stretched out a hand towards the red divan. 'Take a seat ... and let us exchange a few thoughts.'

Rogant's expression remained severe, and the duke's affable.

'What about?'

'About ourselves,' de Page replied at once, looking Laerte in the eye.

Laerte sat down slowly, masking his curiosity behind an unfriendly expression.

'As far as I know, with all due respect, my lord, we have nothing in common.'

The duke nodded his head, looking down at his full glass. A woman's cry of joy rang out loudly, before fading beneath a round of applause.

'Perhaps,' conceded de Page. 'Or perhaps we are both lost in a world that does not want us. Perhaps we have each chosen a disguise in order to fit in.'

Laerte's fingers instinctively stiffened on his thighs. The idea that he could be unmasked had never crossed his mind, so obsessed was he with his ultimate goal. He sought to contain his fear and, hoping to hide his distress, he bent his head forward. If de Page noticed he made no comment.

'I can imagine how difficult it must be, not to feel guilty when fighting those who were one's own people,' the duke continued, turning the base of his goblet between his thumb and forefinger.

'Is my loyalty to the Empire in doubt?' enquired Laerte tonelessly.

'No more than my own.'

They eyed one another without saying anything more. Next door, violins had started playing a ritornello, punctuated by much laughter and handclapping. De Page raised his eyes to the closed door.

'No more than theirs is. The people out there fucking, drinking and wearing their finest clothes as they await the fall. But they prefer to remain masked out of fear that someone will recognise them ... and expose their vices. Why should it matter to them? Everyone knows my vices: I'm the infamous pervert. Always have been and always will be. My father certainly told me that often enough. And yours? Did you know him, in the Saltmarsh?'

'My sincere condolences,' Laerte evaded the question curtly.

De Page pretended to take a sip and replaced the goblet on the armrest of his chair.

'What politeness. If you had known my father you wouldn't speak of sincerity. He was a pig. An intelligent pig, full of malice and political cunning, but a pig all the same. Anyway ...' He shook his head with a faint smile. 'We're not here to speak of the dead, but about the future,' he said in a brighter tone. 'I heard that General Dun-Cadal has insisted on you taking your oath soon.'

Laerte did not blink but his throat had suddenly gone dry. He did not take his eyes off de Page, looking for any hint of duplicity.

'I hear a lot of things. Information flows as easily as the wine at my parties,' he explained to head off any question. 'Congratulations, you will soon be a knight. And since rumour also says the rebels are approaching the Imperial city itself, you'll be on the front line. Your origins will no longer be a cause for suspicion.'

'Suspicion?' Laerte hissed.

'The noose is tightening around the conspirators. Particularly those who come from your region, whom His Imperial Majesty deigned to welcome in our beautiful city.'

'I serve Asham Ivani Reyes,' Laerte defended himself coldly.

His hands were damp, his body rigid, but his heart was racing madly.

'I'm fighting the rebellion,' he added.

'Your count was loved, as I understand it.'

Laerte measured the weight of his reply before his voice cracked like a whip.

'He was a traitor.'

The echo of the trapdoor opening beneath his father's feet shot through his mind. He kept his head held high, staring at de Page intently. No matter what it cost him, he would not betray himself.

'I serve the Empire and I will defend it to the death.'

He saw them again in his mind's eye, his father and his brother, dangling at the end of a rope. He felt the all-consuming fear he'd endured during his flight into the marshes, with Azdeki's shadow poised to pounce on him.

The duke raised his eyebrows.

'Is that you speaking, or General Dun-Cadal Daermon? I sense no passion in your voice.'

With a nod of his head he indicated the door.

'Rhunstag. Not even the great and mighty Rhunstag makes that kind of propaganda speech,' he said calmly. 'Only your mentor is so wilfully blind and, on his own, he will not save Reyes.'

Laerte remained silent. Out of the corner of his eye he looked for any clue on Rogant's face, a smile or a glance that would indicate what was expected of him here. But he saw nothing but motionless tattoos, closed lips and black eyes which watched his slightest gesture.

'Everyone is waiting for the outcome of this revolt. Particularly those enjoying a spanking this evening ... who will be wearing stern, dignified expressions tomorrow,' de Page continued. 'They have this tremendous capacity to adapt, it's really astonishing. Funny, even. But one mustn't let them see that, they would think it was mockery.'

Was he trying to make Laerte reveal his identity? Or was the duke alluding, in his own way, to where his own loyalties lay ... Laerte tried to withstand his gaze, but a growing turmoil assailed him. What should he do? How should he reply? And what was Rogant expecting of him? Wasn't he Laerte's friend?

'Which is the case, quite obviously,' admitted de Page, suddenly thoughtful. 'Anyway ...'

He pretended to drink again and then licked his lips.

'It matters very little how much effort you put into defending what you believe in, Frog. You're just a small stone on a riverbed, and as far as I know one stone will never make the river change its course. Isn't that the case?'

Laerte glanced briefly at Rogant. Wasn't he going to intervene? Just one sign from him, one look other than the one he'd worn on his face since the beginning of the interview, one word, would make Laerte feel a little less like cornered prey.

'I hope you'll make the right choice when the rebellion reaches Emeris,' de Page said, sounding sincere. 'For you are – or you will be, I should say – a great *knight*. Rogant has spoken extremely highly of you. And the events at Kapernevic have only reinforced my opinion. That is precisely what I wished to discuss with you.'

The goblet ... the goblet on the armrest was now empty. Its contents had somehow disappeared in the short instant when he had glanced over at Rogant. Where did it go? Had de Page finished it in one gulp? No ... no, of course not. Since the beginning, he'd only pretended to drink and been quite obvious about it.

His drunkenness was a manner of disguise, it was all merely illusion. As in the neighbouring room, de Page had resorted to trickery. Laerte may not have drunk a single drop, but that was the not the case with the duke's guests next door. Tongues loosened and de Page listened.

Laerte glanced again towards the Nâaga, and this time Rogant nodded with the shadow of a smile.

'Kapernevic ...?' murmured Laerte, suddenly interested.

'Aladzio ... he worked for my father. Did you know that?'

Laerte didn't have a moment to reply.

'Yes, of course you knew,' acknowledged de Page with a nod. 'My father ceded his contract to another family and, for the transfer to be concluded, it was important that he return here alive. I am indebted to you for protecting him ... he is of great value to me.'

There was no trace of irony or even scorn in his tone.

'Great value ...' he said again in a low voice. 'Although I say, wherever I go, day or night, that the man is an idiot. It's now public knowledge that I'm very glad to be rid of him.'

'Is that right?' Laerte asked tersely.

'And what do you think about that?' de Page smiled quickly.

In the big room next door the festivities seemed to be gathering speed, the music and the cries, the laughter and applause. Like heartbeats, repeating without any pause.

'What I think is of no importance.'

'On the contrary,' retorted de Page as he leaned forward.

He placed his elbows on his knees, joining his hands together. His smile had disappeared.

'If they come to my parties,' he said, darting a glance at the door, 'it's because they're sure no one will see anything of them but their mask. Indeed, it's probably the only thing, right now, they're still wearing. There is nothing more important than this ... Frog. Aladzio is, and to me shall remain, an idiot. Who but a half-wit would leave work like this behind?'

He looked over at Rogant and, without saying a word, the Nâaga disappeared behind the red curtains. He came back with a large rolled-up bundle of plans in his hand.

'I don't believe these plans could be of any use to anyone,' de Page said as Rogant placed the roll upon the divan. 'They're just hideous drawings.'

Laerte started to unroll the parchments with his fingertips, revealing an assortment of sketches. They represented an odd elongated structure, accompanied by some hastily scribbled notes.

'And then there was this ... powder substance he was always blathering on about before my father sent him to Kapernevic,' recalled de Page, his mouth twisting into a scornful scowl. 'He was certain he had discovered a powder capable of propelling projectiles through this ... this thing.'

He indicated the plans with a jerk of his chin.

'To me, these are nothing but stupid drawings,' continued the duke, rolling his eyes. 'But he claimed it was a weapon capable of putting an end to this war, and—'

He halted for an instant, pensive, and then frowning, he placed his index finger on his lips.

'Anyways, you can understand how ridiculous all this seemed to me. *Cannons* that would make our catapults obsolete? It's ... absurd.

Because leaving plans for an invention like this behind, risking them falling into the wrong hands, is the ultimate proof of his stupidity …'

The duke stood up and slowly walked over to Rogant with a stately demeanour. The Nâaga did not move an inch when he approached.

'Take these scrawlings back to Aladzio and let me hear no more about them.'

'Wait …' Laerte called.

With a brusque movement the duke turned back to him.

'Why …?' asked the apprentice knight, looking down at the perfect sketches of the *cannon*. 'Why insist that these documents are of no value to you?'

'That isn't the question you want to ask, Frog.'

Laerte saw him pat the Nâaga's shoulder with a firm hand before picking up his mask and walking slowly towards the curtains at the rear. In the neighbouring room the party had reached its climax, but the noise was nothing compared to the tumult of the young man's thoughts. He knew Rogant well enough to be open with him, at least to a degree. And the reverse was also true. Rogant had high hopes and had never hidden the fact that he saw the fall of the Empire as the only way his people could reclaim their freedom.

Although Laerte had complete confidence in his friend, he needed to believe he had correctly understood the underlying implications of this conversation. And as if to prove it to him, de Page added without turning round:

'The real question is: have you seen the man behind the mask … or simply the mask? Make the choice that seems wisest to you. About me, and about these plans and their use.'

He put his mask back on, conscientiously, before drawing apart the curtains. Laerte stood up, wondering whether he should question the man further, tempted by the idea that he'd found a powerful ally here. Cannons? More powerful and more destructive than catapults? Aladzio's work could end up in the hands of the rebels and give them a way to enter Emeris.

'There was one other thing …' the duke said in a grim voice. 'It seems you are acquainted with some of the Saltmarsh refugees. Unfortunately, one of them was found guilty of treason and hung this morning. But you serve the Empire, so you probably didn't know the man. He was the blacksmith at Aëd's Watch. The traitor should have spared a thought for the daughter he has left an orphan. I hope she will find a comforting shoulder ...'

He passed through the curtains.

Laerte thought his legs were going to collapse beneath him. He had not been able see Esyld again since his return the previous evening, and this was how he learned of her father's death, from the mouth of a perfect stranger. He did not recall ever coming across Master Orbey in the palace hallways during his previous short stays here. The last time they spoke they'd been in the Saltmarsh, just before Laerte had been forced to flee. Just before he'd met Dun-Cadal Daermon. Just before he had changed lives.

Esyld had often spoken of him, however, explaining the dangerous role he was playing here. All these years Laerte had spent wandering around battlefields, the blacksmith had been here working behind the scenes, organising the resistance among the Saltmarsh refugees. Until the nobles who were hostile to the Emperor had approached him. He had done everything he could to be sure of their good faith, while staying in the shadows. And among these noblemen, so prompt to join the rebellion, was the duke ...

'This war is coming to an end, Frog,' said Rogant, staring at him intently. 'Trust me on this. There's what de Page says, what is necessary for others to hear, and what he is. The inventor you saved ... he's going to train soldiers in the academy to use the cannon, if he manages to build one that works ... Speak to him. That's my advice as a friend.'

There was a long silence. Rogant finally bowed his head slightly before turning round.

'I'm sorry for her,' he said before leaving the small room in his turn. 'She will need you now.'

Alone for a moment, Laerte struggled to hold back his tears. His eyes damp, he stared at the plans spread out across the red divan. It only took him a moment to gather them up.

He travelled through the palace hallways as discreetly as possible, keeping to the walls, skirting behind the marble pillars, avoiding indiscreet gazes. He hurried to the servants' quarters and finally reached the familiar small door.

When he entered Esyld's chamber he found her huddled up at the foot of the bed, her curls falling over her face along with the tears.

She let out a little sob when she saw Laerte kneeling in front of her and she fell into his arms, clinging to him.

They remained like that for a long while, saying nothing, without even looking at one another. When she finally caught her breath she told him of her father's arrest and how close she had come to being hung, too. She owed her survival to a nobleman whose name she did not mention, who claimed to have taken her into his service and protested at the prospect of losing her to the executioner. Laerte did not press her for more details. He had a good idea of the man's identity. He was certain he had just met him.

When she had told him, in detail, how her father had lost his life, her voice quivering in pain, he hesitated for several minutes before speaking.

'He will not have died in vain, Esyld,' he murmured finally, his mind made up.

He unrolled the plans at their feet and crouched on the other side. 'What are these?'

'Something that will bring the Empire to its knees,' he promised her in a low voice. 'We need to get these plans to Meurnau as quickly as possible.'

Thanks to Orbey's network, Esyld knew of Saltmarsh refugees who had become couriers for some of capital's merchants. And that was how the parchments left Emeris; passed from hand to hand, until they finally reached the closest rebel camp.

Strangely, and without his fully understanding why, Esyld barely spoke to him over the following month. She avoided him as much as possible. He accepted, not without some difficulty, that she might blame him. Orbey was dead; while he had been fighting against their own rebellion for years. Worse still, he refused to take on his true identity and had always rejected the idea of joining Meurnau and his troops. He was hurt that she did not approve his choices. And his own guilt did not help matters.

During his last month at Emeris, his time had thus been divided between classes at the academy, enduring Dun-Cadal's authoritarian tirades, and conversations with Rogant and Aladzio, who he was getting to know better. And even coming to like. But this period of waiting did not last long. The rumblings of the rebellion had finally reached the Imperial city's gates. As de Page had warned him, the war was drawing to a close. He was finally ready to confront the Emperor and his Hand without trembling. Hadn't he mastered a great red dragon? Asham Ivani Reyes was just a man and the task would be less arduous. He was sure of it.

'Tomorrow ...' said Esyld.

The sunlight made the white stone walkway glow. A braid slid over her bare shoulder, delicately caressed by a beam of sunlight. Her hands joined before her carmine red dress, she conserved her full beauty despite her drawn face. Frog desperately sought to catch her gaze, but his efforts were fruitless. Distracted, she looked at the palace gardens which descended like the steps of a flowering staircase.

'I thought they were merely rumours,' he confessed quietly. 'Emeris seems so calm ...'

'Meurnau and his troops are well and truly near the city,' she assured him sharply.

'Esyld ...'

'They've built your friend's cannons and they'll be able to enter the city without any problems. But the Emperor remains and I know this is your moment to act. A nobleman who supports the cause will see me safely out the city. I trust him, but you, I ...'

'Esyld, look at me ...'

She glanced briefly at him and then looked away.

'I need more time, Laerte,' she explained coldly. 'I need time to forgive you, despite loving you.'

'I did not want this—'

'You know why I blame you,' she interrupted.

Yes, of course ... What part had he played in this rebellion? He'd fought against it instead of leading it.

'I am an Erain frog,' he protested in a murmur. 'I will strike when the moment is right. And tomorrow will be the right moment, Esyld. I shall not falter, I promise.'

'I believe you,' she said without much conviction. 'But what about Dun-Cadal?'

She finally met his gaze and her expression gradually softened. He was ready to embrace her, to kiss her until his heart burst. He desired her so much he was ready to give up his life for her.

'What about him?'

'When the moment comes, will you kill him?'

Kill his mentor? His enemy ... Dun-Cadal Daermon would rather

314

die than let the Empire collapse; that was certain. The very idea that he might stand between Laerte and the Emperor chilled the young man's blood. Would Frog take precedence over Laerte? Although he had tried many times to deny it, he felt affection for the man. Would he be able to put that aside in order to take his vengeance?

'I'll do whatever's necessary,' he muttered, his gaze drifting over the white flagstones. 'I'm ready. Trust me. I will succeed. I'll bring down the Empire all on my own ... and I'll do it for you.'

'Laerte—'

'Frog!' a voice bellowed.

He spun round, annoyed to see his mentor's massive silhouette bearing down on them. Esyld's soft hand, placed upon his shoulder, had the effect of a caress. When she rose on tiptoe to whisper a few words in his ear he longed to flee with her, far from here, from this war, from this violence ... and forget everything.

'Never forget this... I will always love you ... Be careful, tomorrow.'

He watched her move off down the walkway in the golden sunlight. Shadows slid over the perfect curves of her body until she reached the door to the tower. When she disappeared inside the palace he felt Dun-Cadal's oppressive presence at his back.

'I've been hunting you for hours,' he said in a harsh voice.

'You used to be more effective than that,' Laerte replied, masking his nervousness as best he could.

He was staring at the end of the walkway, as if Esyld were still there.

'Whenever you're not busy with Aladzio, then she occupies your time,' Dun-Cadal sighed. 'You know what I think about that.'

'I've been training with the other cadets, Wader,' Laerte assured him.

'And what if we're sent back to the front tomorrow? You shouldn't be training with the cadets. You're a knight now, you blockhead!'

'I'll be ready,' Laerte said irritably.

He finally turned around to face the general. Dun-Cadal's weathered face did not inspire sympathy. His clear eyes shone with a cold, severe fire. Laerte advanced to the walkway's parapet, hoping to cut his mentor's criticism short. It was not the first time Dun-Cadal had warned him against Esyld, claiming she was a distraction from his studies, causing him to lose focus ... That she was a bad influence on his apprentice, was that his fear? This man wasn't his father, he had no right to tell him who he could see or what he could do!

'You seem to be spending enough of your time with Mildrel,' he accused.

'It's not the same.'

'And the Emperor doesn't ask you to train all the time. Whereas I perform my exercises every morning. Even more often, since I was knighted. I have the right to see her.'

'It's not the same,' Dun-Cadal repeated quietly.

It was unbearable when the general used this gentler, benevolent tone. Every time a discussion started to become heated he adopted this attitude. But instead of soothing Laerte it only enraged him more. Why should that be the case? Perhaps he thought it was how a father would behave . . .

'And why is that?' he asked angrily, looking his mentor in the eye.

'Because Mildrel isn't a refugee!' Dun-Cadal snapped, raising his voice.

'Not that again,' Laerte muttered, shaking his head in disgust.

But the general was right. The entire court was buzzing with rumours. People were plotting against the Empire and the Saltmarsh refugees were the first to be suspected. The fact that the daughter of the hanged blacksmith from Aëd's Watch was still alive was a miracle. She had benefited from a nobleman's protection, but that wasn't enough to stop people from talking.

Dun-Cadal was truly worried for him. A keen pain pierced Laerte's heart. He was literally being torn in two by his feelings. For the first time he felt he was betraying someone he loved . . .

'When the moment comes, will you kill him?'

'I told you when we returned from Kapernevic. You should avoid going anywhere near her. Haven't you seen the way everyone is suspicious of everyone else? Negus warned me. And then I warned you.'

'I'm from the Saltmarsh too, have you forgotten that?' Laerte murmured.

'Frog . . . it's only until this war ends. After that, you'll have all the time in the world to court her . . .'

How he wanted to answer back, to tell the general that it would all end tomorrow, that Dun-Cadal would finally discover who he really was, what he'd accomplished, and what a powerful knight he'd become.

316

'I don't want you to be suspected of anything.'

He sensed Dun-Cadal's hesitation when the general sought to place a hand on his shoulder. He immediately shook it off and took a step back.

'Will you kill him?'

'And even less now that you've been dubbed a knight.'

He had taken the oath, yes. He'd been knighted by the great General Daermon himself. His mentor . . .

'Will you kill him?'

Laerte clung to the idea that the man had only been using him. They had been using each other as mere tools. Feeling affection for him was a weakness, when he should be concentrating on everything he hated instead. He repeated it to himself: Dun-Cadal had never behaved that well towards him. Always delivering sermons, telling him to work harder, ordering him to be silent in the presence of the great and mighty. He had never once acknowledged that he was a gifted pupil.

'Shouldn't that give me the right to see whoever I like?' he objected.

'Oh, don't go thinking you've been anointed, my boy. There's still some way to go before you become—'

'I don't understand,' he interrupted with a dark glare. 'I'm never good enough in your eyes, am I? Whatever I do, it's never enough. Have you ever complimented me, even once? Have you ever said to me: "Well done, *lad*"? Even after the oath-taking . . . did you ever congratulate me? I would like to say that you've been like a fa—'

The words caught in his throat. It was filled by so much anger that simply he did not know how to express it. Worse still, a new feeling of sadness squeezed his chest and made it difficult to breathe as tears rose to his eyes. He tried to get a grip on himself and conceal how moved he was. Dun-Cadal must not suspect anything at all.

He lowered his eyes for an instant and then forced himself to meet the general's gaze once again with a resolute air.

This man had taught him so many things, he could not deny it. But from the beginning he had known that Dun-Cadal Daermon had always been on the same side as the men who had killed his father.

'When the moment comes. Will you kill him?'

'Sometimes . . . I hate you,' he finally said.

'Does madam have everything she requires?'

The last words he'd exchanged with Dun-Cadal had been words of anger.

'When the moment comes . . .

The words Esyld had whispered in his ear had only ever been words of love.

'Madam?'

'I'm fine, Marissa, you may leave.'

Her voice, although a little deeper, had kept all of its sweetness. Standing on the cornice, pressed against the wall next to a window which looked in at the sumptuous apartments within the Palatio, Laerte remembered watching her leave the walkway, that last day before—

A door closed behind the servant and then all he could hear was the rustle of Esyld's dress as she approached her four-poster bed. He'd waited for night to fall before climbing the palace walls, crawling up drainpipes in complete silence until he finally reached the balconies. From there he'd crept over the roofs surrounding the tall cupola until he located the window belonging to the woman he'd recognised the previous evening in the big square.

He had not told anyone he was making this visit. He was certain Rogant, or Viola, would have done everything in their power to stop him . . . How could they possibly understand: all this time he'd clung to the hope of seeing her again. His memories of Esyld had prevented him from sinking into despair.

For years now he'd tried to find out what had become of her. He hadn't believed for a second that she had died during the final assault on Emeris. This evening he set aside his mission in Masalia. He needed to see her again, to hold her in his arms, to kiss her. And never leave her again.

The chamber was luxurious, furnished with wide armchairs upon which dozens of dresses had been laid out, but Laerte took no notice of them. His gaze was irresistibly drawn by Esyld herself, sitting on the edge of bed, rearranging her hair before a cheval glass. She was wearing a long violet gown with two slender straps across her shoulders. Golden threads were entwined in her curls. He didn't stop for a moment to ask himself questions or wonder how she had come to live in such elegant surroundings.

Obsessed, he threw caution to the winds. He threw one leg over the edge of the window and waited for an instant, gaze lingering on her bare back, her gown open in a V to reveal the curve of her waist. He entered the room.

And his reflection appeared in the cheval glass.

'Don't be afraid.'

She gave a start, almost letting out a cry, one hand in front of her mouth. He slowly lowered his hood to his shoulders, revealing his face.

'Laerte ...' she whispered.

She looked at his reflection, her face pale, without uttering a word, without making a gesture.

'I've dreamt of this moment for so long,' he confessed, trembling.

'You're alive,' she said, as if she'd never suspected it.

He wanted to draw closer and take her in his arms, but she leapt up and spun round to face him, her hands sliding over her belly in a nervous gesture.

'You're here ... alive,' she repeated. 'How ... how did you find me? How did you—'

'You're just as I remember you,' he cut her short.

She retreated, almost knocking over the mirror. The surprise must have staggered her. Trying not to upset her further he forced himself to stay where he was, staring at her with longing. So much time gone by, without her.

'Laerte ... what are you doing here?' she asked with a sob.

'No, don't cry,' he begged. 'You see? I'm here, quite alive. I know a lot has happened since the fall of the Empire, I know that—'

He searched for the right words, aware that this was hardly the moment to improvise but, after all these years, he was afraid of spoiling their reunion. He had pictured this moment in his mind so often.

'I tried,' he apologised. 'I tried to find you, but it was already too late. Something happened to me that meant ... I couldn't, it was too late. Believe me. But not one day, not a single day, has gone by when I didn't think of you.'

As he spoke, she seemed to pull herself together, drawing in deep breaths. No, she hadn't changed, she was exactly as he had always dreamt her – except that she seemed anxious rather than joyful at seeing him again.

He walked slowly towards her and she didn't step back this time. When they were finally face-to-face, he shyly raised a gloved hand to her cheek. His fingers brushed her skin, lifting a curled lock of hair. His eyes held hers and he sensed the rapid beating of her heart. The scent of her skin intoxicated him as did the carmine lustre of lips, the same shade as the dress she'd worn on the walkway that day before the fall—

Worn at their last meeting.

'What are you doing here?' she murmured, seeming at a loss.

'This is where I should have been a long time ago ...'

She tilted her head to the side, as if expecting a kiss. Laerte leaned towards her lips.

'No!' she said, and pushed him away with both hands.

'The assassinated councillors,' she said, starting to tremble. 'Was that you?'

He did not know what to say. Should he confess everything? Trust her with it all, when they had only just found one another again?

'Many things have happened, Esyld,' he admitted.

'So, it was you,' she sighed.

'It's not what you think,' he defended himself. 'After the Empire fell I finally learned why my father was killed—'

'It was seventeen years ago, Laerte!!'

She had raised her voice and he heard the anger in it. No, this really wasn't how he'd imagined their reunion.

'Events occurred thus because the gods wanted them to, don't you understand? You come back to me now, believing that—'

'Esyld! I know who planned my family's destruction and now those same people are threatening the Republic!'

'Are you doing this for the Republic or to satisfy your lust for revenge?' she demanded in a very low voice.

She glanced towards her chamber door with tears in her eyes.

'I thought you would be happier to learn I was alive,' said Laerte, attempting a smile.

'You said it yourself: much has happened,' she confessed. 'When I left Emeris, the day of the final assault, a noble family took me under its wing. The same family that saved me during my father's trial ...'

She raised her eyes towards the ceiling, letting out a sigh. She wanted to tell him something, but was evidently unable to summon the courage to do so.

'I love you as I did the first day I met you,' he said.

He could sense her slipping away from him and dreaded what she was about to say. He finally examined the chamber more carefully, seeing the tapestries on the walls, the chairs with their embroidered armrests, the drapes hanging near the door. The luxury here . . . Esyld was no longer a servant.

'All this time,' he murmured gravely, 'I survived by thinking of you—'

'While I had to forget you, Frog.'

Hearing her use his former name, he felt he really had lost her. But that was impossible: she'd said she would always love him. She had promised. She came back towards him, taking his hands in hers, her head bowed.

'I prayed for you, you know . . . I hoped that after the Republic was established someone would speak of you, that entire cities would praise your name and . . . and that you'd finally be recognised as a hero.'

'I couldn't, simply because—'

'Good people saved my life, Laerte,' she continued. 'People who welcomed me into their family . . . and who have been elected to rule the Republic.'

'All that's over now, we're together at last,' he said, leaning forward to touch her brow with his. 'I just need to accomplish one very important mission. Can you promise me that you will wait, until the day after Masque Night?'

'Laerte, look at me . . .'

He obeyed, looking deeply into her eyes.

'Times have changed. Nothing is the same as it was.'

'Just until after Masque Night,' he begged her in a murmur.

'Laerte—'

'And then we can leave together, it will be all be over . . . finally.'

'Laerte . . .'

She was trembling. He wanted to take her in his arms but she drew away from him, her eyes misty with tears.

'I'm getting married . . .'

He thought he was suffocating. His heart seemed to have stopped beating. He could not force a single word from his dry throat. Of course. The wedding, before Masque Night . . .

'His name is Balian. He's Councillor Etienne Azdeki's son.'

In the hollow of his belly burned a terrible, devouring, pitiless fire. His soul seemed to have been torn from him, while his heart lay in shreds. He was reliving the same pain that had ravaged him when his family died, but this time it rang through him like a death knell. The one person who had kept him standing had just put a dagger through his heart ...

'He's the one who took me in,' Esyld explained, on the verge of tears. 'I had no choice. And as time passed I learned ... I understood what they had done and why. They've been so good to me, Laerte ... I had to forget you. I needed to. I could die of sorrow; or I could live again!'

'You love me ...'

'I love Balian,' she replied.

I love you. I'll always love you. Forever.

'You told me—'

'That was a long time ago!' she protested. 'It was true at the time. But things change. People change. This world is no longer at war, Laerte!'

'*I am at war!*' he shouted, waving a closed fist in the air. And she shuddered, her face drained of colour. 'The Azdekis are dangerous!''

'You don't know Balian. That's not true,' she replied.

'His father killed my family! He put the Empire to fire and the sword. It's *their* fault your father is dead!'

'No!' she cried angrily. 'It's yours! You weren't even *there*! How dare you?'

Her mouth twisted into a grimace. Tears ran down to the corners of her trembling lips. She looked away.

'You don't know everything, Laerte,' she muttered. 'You don't even know what really happened.'

His entire body was boiling, his heart beating fit to burst. He could not accept this.

'Am I so cursed that the woman I love will marry the son of my enemy?' he moaned, before seizing her in his arms. 'Tell me you don't love me, Esyld. If it's really true, tell me. I dare you to say it!'

'We're not responsible,' she tried to explain. 'It's the gods who decide ... we simply live out their murmurs.'

'Never! Never! Do you hear me?'

He released her and turned in a circle, his hand on the pommel of his sword. Gasping for breath, he had the sensation he was falling, endlessly, with no solid hold he could grasp ...

'I refuse to be misfortune's plaything – I refuse to be anyone's murmur ... Never!'

He suddenly came towards her again, but before he reached her she turned her back on him, holding back a sob. Her shoulders shook, as much from sadness as from fear.

'Laerte, go. You can't stay here. I'm begging you. Go away.'

'For you—'

'Leave, Laerte'

'For you, I will be more than a murmur. I will be a cry.'

'Guards!' she called.

There was silence. She glanced over her shoulder.

'I dare you to tell me you no longer love me,' Laerte challenged her.

And her response crushed his heart.

'I don't love you any more.'

A clatter of boots could be heard on the marble floor out in the corridor.

'Run, Laerte ... I won't tell them who you are but you must never come back. Don't ever try to see me again. Things have changed ... everything except you and your vengeance. And that's meaningless now.'

She stood with her back turned, her head bowed, in tears.

'Go ... proud little lord.'

'Esyld ...' he sobbed.

The footsteps came closer.

'*Guards!*' she screamed.

Only when the door flew open, revealing a squad of worried soldiers, did Esyld turn. On the edge of a table, by the window, she spied a strange shape, half-lit by the moonlight.

It was a little wooden horse.

8

PAIN

―――――

He loved her.
He would have been forced to choose her side.
A young man will do anything for love,
Including losing his way ...

He had never, ever imagined their love could disappear. It had always seemed so eternal, so unalterable, that he couldn't understand how Esyld could have forgotten it. His heart was in tatters as he leapt from rooftop to rooftop, avoiding the squads sent in his pursuit. He wasn't fleeing them but his own sorrow. He ran as fast as he could, moving further and further away from the Palatio, from Esyld, and from their shared memories. But he was still there in her chamber, feeling his heart break, when he reached the house.

Thin white clouds slipped slowly across a backdrop of stars. Reaching the courtyard he lit two torches and drew his sword from its scabbard. Then, in the flickering light, he practised lunges and parries. He was nothing but pain. The sound of gravel crunching beneath his feet grew faint while his rage gave rise to a heart-rending howl.

'I love Balian ...'

His sword stabbed the air, slaying invisible enemies, and his lungs burned when he used the *animus* to lift the torches, setting them spinning around him. He imagined the wood splitting, the fire being extinguished, and he closed his fist.

'I love Balian ...'

And everything broke.

He fought a thousand men, a thousand armies, with the perfect moves he had learned years before. *Azdeki*, he thought. *Azdeki*. That family had stolen everything from him. He was cursed.

'Perhaps I'm mistaken,' said a small voice. 'But … is something bothering you?'

He stopped, one knee on the ground, frozen in a lunge which skewered an invisible foe. Standing in the doorway with her arms crossed, Viola's slender silhouette was haloed by the light from the oil lamps in the salon. He glimpsed a smile playing at the corner of her mouth.

'Or are you just working off some excess energy?' she guessed again. 'I know men like to fight, but I thought it took two to make things interesting.'

Hidden in shadow, her smile vanished when Laerte stood up, more intimidating than ever.

'I'm here if … well … if you want to talk about anything,' she offered weakly. With a flick of his wrist, he turned his sword. The blade slashed the air. 'You were gone all day … and you returned just as night fell … And …'

He looked at her, his eyes shining in the dim light. He said nothing, and did not smile, maintaining a stony expression. She linked her fingers together nervously before her.

'You so rarely speak …' she sighed.

'Go inside, Viola,' he said, his voice hoarse and carrying no hint of friendliness. 'It's late.'

'I may be young but that doesn't mean you can treat me like a child,' she complained, rolling her eyes.

'Go inside,' he repeated more forcefully.

'Such a nasty temper,' she immediately fumed, her fists balling at her sides.

But she reluctantly obeyed, stalking back into the salon. Stretched out on the divan with a pitcher of wine in his hand, Rogant barely raised an eye when she passed him, grumbling to herself.

'I just wanted to help,' she groused.

And meeting Dun-Cadal on the stairs, she snapped:

'You know, the two of you share the same vile character!'

The old general frowned, halting in the middle of the staircase to let her pass, without her giving him another glance. Seeing the girl in this state, her face flushed with anger and framed by locks of her red hair, was the last thing he'd expected.

The sound of footsteps on the gravel in the courtyard had roused him from his torpor and, curious, he had decided to come downstairs and see what was going on. When he entered the salon, however, it wasn't Rogant who drew his eye but the jug of wine in his hand. After two days without drinking a drop the temptation was too strong; he rushed over to the drowsing Nâaga and seized the pitcher before the other man could react.

'Hey! You miserable old ghost!' growled the colossus as he leapt up from the divan, still glassy-eyed.

Dun-Cadal paid him no attention, too busy pouring as much wine as he could down his parched gullet. Almost choking, he wiped his mouth with the back of one hand while halting the irritated barbarian with the other.

'You,' he said in a strangled voice. 'I'm starting to like you a little more.'

With his fist raised, ready to smash the old man's jaw, Rogant froze. Dun-Cadal was nodding, looking so contented and smiling that the Nâaga could not contain his laughter. He snorted and finally let it burst forth.

'It's true,' Dun-Cadal insisted. 'You don't seem like such a bad sort after all …'

'Go on, then,' Rogant said, between chuckles. 'Keep it.'

With a firm hand, he patted the old man's shoulder before bringing his smiling face close to his.

'You were once a great warrior, old ghost,' he muttered with a touch of derision. 'But wine puts you to sleep. So go ahead: get drunk. I'm not sure how much Laerte will like it though, and then … Well, then I'll be eager to see how you'll settle your little dispute. Believe me.'

Through the open door to the courtyard, Dun-Cadal could make out Laerte's shadow. That explained the sound he'd heard in his sleep: the whistling of the blade through the air, like an echo from the past. No, not an echo … a deformed reflection. This boy wasn't the Frog he had known. Stopping on the doorstep he took another gulp, savouring the fruity taste of the wine as it ran down his throat. Glancing over his shoulder he saw Rogant sit down on a corner of the divan with his arms crossed and a sly grin upon his face. No doubt he was hoping that Laerte would start another fight. He would be disappointed: Dun-Cadal didn't plan to defend himself. He felt so tired.

'I don't know what you have in mind,' he said finally, as Laerte slashed at the air with his blade. 'But it seems to me it's off to a bad start.'

Laerte halted, slightly out of breath. The moonlight lent a pale gleam to the outline of his silhouette. He turned towards the general, his head lowered.

'Anger,' sighed Dun-Cadal as he sat down on the low step in front of the door. 'You always had so much in you and now I understand why ...'

If he was expecting a reply, he drowned his disappointment with another mouthful of wine. Laerte remained silent and still, eyeing his former mentor grimly.

'So much hatred towards me ...' the old general continued. 'Is it an irony of fate, or the will of the gods, to give a man the chance to nurture his own enemy? It's so ... so humiliating that I had no—'

'You were right,' Laerte said suddenly.

He sheathed his sword with a sharp move. On the front porch, Dun-Cadal raised an eyebrow.

'Right about Esyld. Her father organised the rebellion in Emeris while I—'

His throat constricted, Laerte felt tears about to flow along with the rage boiling within him. Fists balled he took a step towards Daermon, but the former general didn't flinch.

'While I fought at your side, betraying her. The only thing that mattered to me was Reyes ... and the prospect of slamming my sword through his heart.'

His voice rose and the tears brimmed in his eyes.

'I was so blind, and I didn't know it. So ignorant, young, stupid ... Reyes was never to blame. Nor were you, you were never anything but a ...'

Seeing Dun-Cadal's lined face and weary gaze he could not continue. The old general was so ravaged, his skin weathered by the southern sun as well as by years of drinking. He drank again before tossing the pitcher away. It broke on the gravel.

'I loved her ... I've always loved her,' Laerte admitted as he turned his back to the old man, seeking comfort in the lights of Masalia below.

No. Not seeking comfort but to hide the tears he could no longer contain. He'd been trying to convert his pain into slashed air and broken torches, but the mere sight of his former master looking so bruised and pale had drained his aggression. Now he was afraid he'd overplayed his hand and, for the first time, he saw a real possibility that he might fail.

'She's here, Wader. She's getting married to …'

He clenched his fists.

'To Azdeki's *son*,' he managed to say, strangling a sob. 'So … where does the real irony lie?'

His tears dried in the heat of his renewed rage. He inhaled before turning on Dun-Cadal, looking into his dull eyes.

'Tell me,' he ordered in a firm voice.

'Logrid! You scum. You piece of filth! Logrid!'

Laerte scowled. For a brief instant he felt a jolt of pain in his shoulder which quickly faded. A memory … someone had cursed him.

'You are nothing to me,' Dun-Cadal said tonelessly. 'I loved a boy called Frog. And you killed him. I could curse you for that.'

They glared at one another. Looking at them together, it was difficult to see they'd ever they felt anything but pure hatred for one another. With the help of a hand pressed against the door frame, Dun-Cadal rose to his feet, an expression of disgust twisting his features.

'You've already done that,' Laerte assured him without blinking.

'Logrid!'

Dun-Cadal's face darkened. He remembered; he understood. The Empire's final moments … it all made sense now.

But could he imagine how much Laerte had suffered that day? Did he have the slightest idea what the boy had endured during the following days? The hatred in the old man's eyes slowly faded and Laerte thought he detected a hint of a more familiar expression. The look he had whenever he was worried for Frog.

'Yes,' said Laerte. 'You cursed me on the eve of Reyes' death …'

He had just left Dun-Cadal. On the morrow the Imperial city would come under attack. The rebels had a major advantage: Aladzio had feigned a lack of success with the cannon that could offer the Empire a decisive victory, while the rebels had made good use of the inventor's own plans. Their big new guns were gathering in the vicinity of Emeris and would soon roar unchecked.

328

Laerte regained his quarters, already imagining the fury of the final battle while he raced through the palace to reach the panic-stricken Emperor. The young man would remove his mask, look him in the eye, and watch the fear creep into the sickly ruler's face as he realised who Laerte was.

And after that?

He felt a strange distress come over him as he imagined plunging his sword into the tyrant's heart. What would happen after that?

He arrived at the door to his chamber. There were no cadets loitering in the hallways, they had all hurried off to the academy refectory. Now that he was knighted, and already experienced on the fields of battle at General Daermon's side, Laerte himself was excused from following their ordinary schedule.

He'd just touched the door handle and was turning it when a violent blow from behind sent him stumbling into the room. He hit the edge of his bed, reeling from the impact. The door shut silently behind him. Instinctively, he reached for the pommel of his sword but he was too slow to grasp it. A powerful hand gripped his forearm and, with a perfectly executed manoeuvre, twisted it with ease. Laerte yelled with pain as his arm was wrenched up to touch his shoulder blade. He ignored it as he straightened and leaned against his assailant, pushing hard to force him to step back. He kept pushing and the dull thud of their bodies against the closed door barely covered his cry of pain.

Stunned, the man loosened his grip for an instant, enough for Laerte to break free, his shoulder on fire. He spun round and was not very surprised to see Logrid, his gaunt face just visible within the shadow of his hooded green cape.

If the Emperor's personal assassin had been sent to kill him, did it mean Laerte's true identity had been revealed? He had no time to worry about it. Logrid drew two daggers from his belt in total silence. Laerte barely evaded the first blow by leaning backwards, the blade leaving a furrow of blood on his cheek. The following strikes were quick, precise, and would have been fatal if Laerte hadn't been nimble enough to dodge them. He seized the hilt of his sword to draw it at the very moment when the assassin charged at him and the blade blocked the daggers with a sharp clang. A sudden movement of his arm forced Logrid to drop both weapons and Laerte kneed the man sharply in the belly. The assassin doubled over with a gasp, one arm folded tight against him.

'Splendid,' he managed to mutter between his teeth.

It was now or never for Laerte; to strike hard and fell his enemy. His heart was pounding, his cheek stung and his shoulder was on fire. When he lifted his arm to deliver the mighty blow he was convinced the duel was over.

Still bent over, Logrid drove his free hand towards him and, with incredible force, he projected the boy against the wall opposite. Laerte struck the edge of the chamber's small window before falling heavily onto the book-covered table beside his bed. It cracked and collapsed beneath his weight.

'If you only knew how long I've been waiting for a match with you,' Logrid murmured.

With a lithe movement, the assassin drew his own sword and advanced on Laerte. A stabbing pain ran through the boy's temples. Lying in the shattered remains of his table he rose up on his elbows, full of rage and brashness. His best chance was to use the *animus*, to use it and hold nothing back. He breathed in deeply, feeling the blood beading at the edge of his nostrils. Suddenly, time seemed to pass more slowly, the world became clearer to him, as if each wall, each object, each sound, even the beating of Logrid's heart, registered in his mind. Ignoring the pain squeezing his lungs, he pounced like a wolf upon his prey.

The duel resumed with a fearsome clash of blades. Thrusts, parries … the two men moved gracefully in the cramped space. Splinters of wood flew through the air and the walls crumbled as their bodies slammed into them, but they continued to strike, dodge and counter each other without either gaining the upper hand. They were like two reflections trying to foil one another.

A particularly powerful blow forced Laerte to draw back. He immediately held his sword out horizontally, hoping to block another thrust, but Logrid surprised him: dropping down, he stretched out his leg to sweep the boy off his feet with a swift kick. Laerte fell to the floor, hitting his head sharply on the edge of his bed. The ceiling became hazy and bells chimed in his ears … the *animus* began to slip from his control, his heart stumbling with the force of it, and blood continued to run from his nose. His eyelids seemed turned to lead.

He had barely regained his wits when Logrid's shadow fell over him. The assassin's knees pressed down on the boy's arms, pinning him to the floor while a gloved hand covered his mouth. As the sword blade sliced through his shoulder, his cry was stifled by the leather, and could only be heard inside his head. The tearing pain ran through his body, forcing him to arch his back. Distress shone in his eyes when he glimpsed Logrid's sardonic smile above him.

He could not die. Not here, not now, not like this. The assassin continued to muffle his scream with a firm hand, whispering something incomprehensible in his hissing voice ... It was unbearable and yet hypnotic. If only he would stop speaking! Along with the pain! If only this would all end ...

No, Laerte could not let himself to succumb. He needed to breathe deeply, fill his lungs, and resist this blade tormenting his body. He had to fight; that's what he had learned to do these past years, fight to avenge his family. The ghostly image of his father hanging from the gallows haunted him. The silhouette of his brother dangling from the end of a rope ... the murder of his raped mother, of his little sister ...

He could not contain his tears. Rage was keeping him afloat. Neither despair, nor his sense of loss, and still less this damn pain was going to stop him. He would not give up! Force of will alone reasserted his control over the *animus*—

—a chair slammed into Logrid's head, shattering into pieces. Barely dazed by the blow, the assassin turned and Aladzio stepped back, furious, holding two broken chair legs in his hands. One arm freed from beneath Logrid's knee, Laerte seized this opportunity, lifting a widespread hand. And the *animus* did its work.

Logrid was lifted into the air. But he did not fall back down. He remained suspended there, spinning slowly, one hand upon his chest, his fingers bent as if trying to remove something piercing his chest. Laerte felt his pain. He lived it, endured it, desired it. He felt the assassin's heart throbbing; like an orange being squeezed in his hand, a wretched thing to be crushed between his fingers. And as he squeezed it, he saw the life slowly draining from the suspended body.

When he felt no more than an icy sensation and saw Logrid's head hanging limply, Laerte lowered his arm. And fainted.

*

A distant voice pulled him from the darkness, when his only desire was to immerse himself in it completely. The words became sharper and more urgent. The creaking of the floor sounded like an entire forest being chopped down.

'Frog? Frog?'

'Laerte ...' he murmured hoarsely.

Just saying the name felt like needles clawing his throat.

'No, don't move,' the voice told him.

By the time his mind took in the instruction it was already too late. He had attempted to sit up, and the wound to his shoulder had made it clear it was a bad idea.

'I removed the sword and I tried to make a quick bandage.'

'Your two students, Dun-Cadal ... how ironic.'

Kneeling beside him, Aladzio was looking at him with great sorrowful eyes. Laerte glanced at his shoulder. It was wrapped in a piece of blood-stained cloth.

'Your two students fighting one another ... Who would you have wagered upon, hmm, Dun-Cadal?'

'You passed out for a few minutes. I-I did what I could,' the inventor stammered.

'Thank you ...'

Next to him, Logrid had fallen to the floor, lying motionless on his green cape, one leg bent beneath him, his twisted hand still clutching at his chest. The cape ... Aladzio helped Laerte to stand up.

'That's the Hand of the Emperor, isn't it?'

'He was,' corrected Laerte with a sigh. 'I'm glad you were here.'

'de Page,' said Aladzio with an embarrassed expression. 'He asked me to keep an eye on you ... You need to flee, Frog. If the Emperor sent his assassin after you, you're no longer safe here. They must have discovered something—'

'No,' he snapped, making his way to Logrid's body with determination.

It was now or never, flee or fight, succeed or give up altogether. Like the Erain frog creeping as close as possible to its prey, he would take on the appearance of his enemies one last time.

'And that's how ...'

Despite his wounded shoulder, despite his fatigue and Aladzio's advice against it ...

'*... that's how ...*'

... he donned the leather jacket, the boots and the gloves. And he disguised himself in the Hand of the Emperor's green cape, drawing the hood over his head, its shadow hiding his face.

Hadn't he always planned to become the Emperor's assassin?

'And that's how you had the idea ...' repeated Dun-Cadal.

Seated on the doorstep, he contemplated the shards of the pitcher scattered across the gravel. The young man had reined in his emotions, savouring the quiet of the city below, illuminated by a thousand fires. At night, Masalia's torches rivalled the stars above.

'*Logrid!*'

'So it was you I saw ...' recalled the general in a low voice.

'*Logrid! You scum. You piece of filth!* Logrid! '

'You thought you were cursing Logrid ... but you cursed me.'

Laerte saw the general again in his memories, being escorted to the double doors by the soldiers, hurling a thousand insults at him. He had looked away, unable to bear the sight of his mentor's tears, and his face twisted by hatred.

'I was ... hurt, Wader,' he explained gravely. 'I felt as if I was falling, rolling downhill ...'

He took a deep breath. The scene had been so painful, so traumatic, that he could not simply think of it. He was forced to relive every instant.

'I was fourteen when I saved you. I was barely seventeen, that day. And the Emperor was only a few feet from me. Just a few ... feet.'

He stood silently for a moment and then resumed his account, weighing each of his words carefully.

'They hung my father and my brother in the Saltmarsh.'

'I know ... it was the law,' the general groaned.

'And was it the law to rape my mother?'

He shot a dark look at the old knight. Dun-Cadal masked his surprise beneath an impassive face. But Laerte knew his mentor was only now realising the extent of the terrible punishment that had befallen the Uster family. And that it had nothing to do with ideals, with a desire for change, or with building a republic. Nothing at all ...

'My little sister,' Laerte said, voice trembling. 'She was only four years old.'

She'd endured horrors the high and mighty justified, cynically, by explaining to those who chose to listen that no war was ever clean, that violence engendered violence, and that cruelty, if not excusable, was simply inevitable. Laerte stepped closer to Dun-Cadal, his throat choked and his eyes shining with pent-up tears.

Bam!

'They left her nailed her to a door like some kind of animal.'

Bam! Bam!

Laerte turned away, regaining his calm and wiping the corners of his eyes with the back of his hand.

'I waited. I waited until the next day.'

'Frog,' murmured the general, 'I didn't know, I—'

'I waited until the next day, for the rebels' attack to begin,' Laerte continued as if he hadn't heard.

'Logrid! Stay by my side! I must leave the city right away.'

He leaned towards Dun-Cadal.

'Logrid?'

'That evening, I learned just how closely the Reyes family and my own were linked ...'

9

THE END OF A WORLD

One day you'll understand.
Be certain of that.
I shall be the greatest knight
This world has ever known.

'Logrid?'

The voice was quavering and high-pitched ... surprisingly high-pitched for someone who reigned over the world. In front of him, Laerte merely beheld a frail figure wearing a long black robe with a golden mask upon his face. Standing in the middle of an empty throne room, lit by the explosions that were causing dust and debris to rain down on the balcony, the Emperor Asham Ivani Reyes had lost his splendour. One of his arms was bent in front of his torso, while his back was twisted and one shoulder was noticeably higher than the other. As the cannons thundered outside, he was revealed to be nothing more than an ugly monster, overcome with fear.

The previous evening, Laerte had resisted the urge to take him by the throat and run a sword through his body. Still feverish from his fight with Logrid, he didn't feel strong enough to defeat the Emperor's remaining guards.

So he had waited. He had rested.

When the first cannon salvoes shook the city and the generals left the palace to defend Emeris's fortifications, he had seized his chance. Although the wound in his shoulder was seeping blood beneath its bandage and a dull ache persisted, he was determined not to back down this time.

'Logrid? What are you doing?'

Reyes had come rushing into the throne room in a state of panic.

He had been even more frightened to see Laerte standing before him with his sword drawn.

'We must flee Emeris! Laerte of Uster's troops are at our gates, I cannot—'

The boy's hood had fallen to his shoulders, revealing a face dripping with sweat, and wearing a baleful expression.

'W-who are you?' stammered the Emperor, backing away.

'Your mask!' ordered Laerte. 'Take it off! I want to see your face!'

'Frog!' The Emperor recognised him. 'You're the apprentice ... By the gods!'

'Your mask!' repeated the boy, his sword at the ready.

The glow of the burning city danced across the marble columns. Beyond the balcony, above the tree tops, coils of black smoke rose into a starry sky. The walls shook beneath the rebels' cannon fire. No, it was no longer a mere rebellion, it was a revolution.

'Show me your accursed face!'

'Why? What do you want with me? Where is Logrid? You could not have killed him!' Reyes said in panic as he retreated further, his strange crooked arm slipping beneath his black robe.

Fearing that he would draw Eraëd from its scabbard Laerte charged towards him, letting his rage burst forth. In his haste, Reyes tripped and collapsed on the floor, weeping. His mask fell away, hitting the flagstones with a clatter and acquiring a crack. His face finally revealed, there was nothing imposing or dignified, much less Imperial, about him. He was just a poor frightened figure with his arms held up defensively before him. But the attack he was afraid did not come. Laerte had halted, stupefied.

If one gloved hand opened its fingers wide towards him, the other was a shapeless lump of flesh, covered in white swellings.

'No, no ...' Reyes begged. 'I beg you, no ...'

'You're a monster ...' muttered Laerte, staring at the man he had hated so much for so long.

There was nothing human about the face before him. It was a mass of grooves and hollows, bulges and scars. Some terrible disease was eating away at his ravaged features. His right eyelid drooped hideously. His nose was reduced to two slits between his pockmarked cheeks, above a harelip.

'Don't hurt me!' he cried.

'My father would never have grovelled,' snarled Laerte, before spitting on the ground. 'When you had him hung in the Saltmarsh, he never grovelled!'

Reyes's eyes widened, as if he was starting to understand.

'My mother, did she beg them not to hurt her?' Laerte roared as he advanced towards him. 'Did my sister?'

Reyes lowered his head like a dog afraid of receiving a beating, his body jerking with spasms.

'It wasn't what I wanted ...' he protested. 'It wasn't me, I—'

'You lit the fires of this war, Reyes! You will pay for everything you've done! *You* will pay!'

'It wasn't what I wanted, it wasn't what I wanted!' the Emperor wailed.

'You murdered my family!' Laerte shouted.

As if it were planned, the sound of cannons and loud shouts rang out at that moment, followed by the echo of swords clashing in the streets of Emeris. The rebels had entered; the entire city was aflame.

At Laerte's feet, the Emperor gave him an imploring look.

'Look at me, I'm nothing. I'm just a poor monster who hides behind a golden mask to impress people ...'

Heavy tears ran down his cratered cheeks.

'But I'm not evil! I've always acted for the good of my people. I never ordered your entire family to be ... It was just your father who was to be judged! He was the only one who threatened me!'

Laerte was in no state to excuse anything, or even to comprehend Reyes's motives. His youthful nature favoured impulse over reason. Whatever pity he felt for this monstrosity, he told himself it was his duty to finish the deed here. He swung his sword with a menacing air, suppressing a grimace of pain. His shoulder was bleeding more freely and the hot liquid was leaking from the bandage. The blood was gradually forming a stain beneath his leather jacket.

He hesitated, trembling and feverish, his blade pointed at the cringing man on the floor. Was there any cause for clemency? For mercy towards this deformed thing at his feet? He had waited so long for this moment ...

... and Reyes, his great enemy, was weeping like a lost child.

Laerte had believed that seeing him unmasked would provoke hatred, nothing else. He had imagined a powerful man, a tyrant, who would look Laerte in the face as the young knight ran his sword through his heart.

'No, please, Frog, please … They made me to do it … They told me the Saltmarsh had to be crushed! Don't kill me, Frog … don't kill me—'

'*I am Laerte of Uster!*' the boy shouted.

Another voice, just as loud, filled the throne room.

'Well, there's another mask that has fallen!'

Keeping the point of his sword directed at the prostrate Emperor, Laerte turned slightly to see a squad of ten soldiers filing through the double doors. Four men in armour, barely showing any trace of the fighting, brought up the rear of the procession. He had no trouble recognising Negus and his paunch, Bernevin's proud strut or Rhunstag wearing his bearskin over his shoulders, along with …

'Captain Azdeki! Save me!' ordered the Emperor, stretching out his hand towards the fourth man. 'This madman wants to kill me! Defend me!'

Azdeki stepped forward, examining Reyes's mangled face with contempt. He replied by spitting on the floor.

'How ironic,' he reflected aloud. 'To find Reyes and Uster here together. This started with them, and so it shall end with them …'

The soldiers formed a circle around Laerte and the Emperor, Rhunstag tucking his thumbs in his belt as he walked to the right, Bernevin moving to the left. But Laerte's attention remained fixed on Etienne Azdeki's gaunt face.

'Captain Azdeki! Do something!' Reyes commanded, dragging himself across the floor towards him.

Laerte jabbed his sword at him with an air of intent and the Emperor froze, darting frantic glances at the soldiers. None made any move to come to his aid and his generals ignored him.

'Laerte of Uster, Oratio's younger son …' mused Azdeki. 'I always thought you were older. A clever strategy, making you a myth. Does Meurnau even know that you are here among us? That you've been fighting *against* him all this time?'

Laerte felt the growing symptoms of fever as well as the pain in his shoulder. Sweat beaded his brow.

'Azdeki!' Reyes cried angrily.

Laerte's thoughts wavered like a storm-tossed sea when he most needed to keep his wits about him.

'Don't come any nearer!' he warned with a scowl.

He pointed his sword towards the Emperor at his feet. Azdeki did

338

not react, his face stern, his hand on the pommel of his sword. He remained calm and still. Outside, the cannons continued to boom.

'Do it,' the captain urged, nodding at Reyes. 'End the life of this pitiful ...'

He paused, his lips pinched in disgust.

'... thing,' he finally said, gritting his teeth.

Gasping for breath, Reyes almost collapsed full length on the floor. Tears of blood ran from the eye with the deformed lid. In the other, his panic was plain to see.

'Rhunstag?' he called out in a quaver. 'Bernevin? Negus ... help me ...'

But his distraught calls and pleading gaze met a wall of indifference. The generals stared at him with no sign of emotion, neither pity nor anger. He could expect nothing from them; they disavowed him with their silence and their stillness.

'Mercy ...'

'Why?' asked Azdeki, without even glancing down at Reyes.

For instead, he was looking straight into Laerte's eyes. Responding to the boy's anger with sincere curiosity.

'Why did you join Dun-Cadal Daermon?' he continued. 'Why have you lied for so long?'

'It's time to end this, Etienne,' Negus said impatiently.

Laerte gave him a brief glance and the small man avoided his gaze. His mentor's friend had betrayed him, too. With a tight throat, Laerte spared a thought for Dun-Cadal, worried about his fate. Who could the general turn to now?

'Now,' insisted Bernevin. 'Then we must deal with Meurnau before the fighting in the city ends.'

Reyes was sobbing on the floor, robbed of the capacity to speak.

'It's revenge, isn't it?' Azdeki deduced with a frown. 'Is that the reason you've waited so long?'

'Meurnau and his troops are approaching the palace, nephew!' a heavy rasping voice announced. 'If we don't kill him as planned, he'll claim this victory for himself and rob us of any legitimacy!'

Laerte detected a movement behind him. An obese figure limped into view between the columns, accompanied closely by a small frail man who walked with the help of a cane, and was snickering nervously.

'Azinn,' squealed Reyes. 'You, too ...'

Bernevin acted, taking a bright dagger from his belt. With a firm hand, he seized the back of the Emperor's neck and placed the dagger against his throat. Laerte was paralysed, darting feverish glances about the room. Everyone seemed astonishingly calm, while outside Emeris was falling into the rebels' hands.

'Meurnau's time is up, we need to be quick,' ordered Azinn, giving Laerte an odd look. 'And since Oratio's son has been among us for so long, it will be no lie when we expose him as a traitor to the revolution,' he concluded, running a hand over his smooth skull which boasted a single lock of white hair.

They would survive this war, they would claim victory for themselves; they would become the heroes who brought the Empire down. They surrounded him, eyeing both him and Bernevin's dagger, a few feet away, ready to slit Reyes's throat. Tears flowed freely down the Emperor's pockmarked cheeks, reflecting the glow of the flames consuming his Empire. He was lost. Leaning against a column with a quivering hand resting upon his cane, the Marquis of Enain-Cassart watched the scene with relish.

'We were sure you'd survived, but we thought you were leading the rebellion. How did you manage to fool us?' he asked Laerte with some surprise.

'The registers,' smiled Azdeki, nodding his head smugly as he worked it out. 'That's how. That's why Meurnau burnt the birth registers at Aëd's Watch: to hide your true age from us.'

'Well, that's one thorn in our side we can easily remove,' Azinn remarked with pursed lips. 'The mythical Laerte of Uster is going to lose all his mystery.'

'You've been so useful to us, right to the finish,' conceded Azdeki, staring at the young man. 'Laerte, Frog ... whatever name you use, in the end you are the one who will have destroyed the Empire ... and you alone.'

He seemed sincere, shaking his head slightly, a strange hint of regret in his eyes.

'I am your Emperor,' Reyes suddenly sobbed.

'Times change, Reyes,' Etienne said calmly. 'Times change. The people need another destiny now. A destiny that the gods alone have decided. Yours ends here. What do you make of your existence in this world, Reyes? What do the Fangolin monks say: "There comes a day in every life, a meeting point of what we were, what we are

340

and what we will be. At that moment, as all things draw to a close, we decide our fate. Proud or ashamed of the road travelled …". This is your moment, Reyes. Think about the vile creature you've always been and all the deeds that, in the end, you never accomplished. Are you proud or ashamed of your reign, Reyes? Now your people are massing at the gates of your palace …'

Laerte remained silent, angry, his gaze alternating between the Emperor and the captain. What should he do? Was he going to fail here, once again? He drew in a deep breath, wincing in pain when his torn shoulder rose.

'If there was one hero in the Saltmarsh, just remember his name: Dun-Cadal Daermon.'

Dun-Cadal … he would find a way to escape such an awful situation. Alone, in the middle of all these soldiers, Laerte only had one option.

'Laerte …' the Emperor tried to plead with him, in his wavering voice. 'It was them … they were the ones who decided … about your father. They forced me; now I know that he never betrayed me!'

He raised his eyes as if he were seeking to defy Bernevin.

'Logrid … Logrid warned me about you all, but I never believed him. He saw you all for what you really are: dangerous fools. It's the Book, isn't it? He reckoned that, sooner or later, someone would learn of its existence and you would covet it. So you lied to me about Uster. Who told you about the *Liaber Dest*? Who?!'

'It was Oratio himself,' murmured Bernevin, as if to provoke him.

'Bernevin,' Azdeki said simply, his eyes narrowing.

It did not take more for the nobleman to understand his meaning. The blade slashed the throat. In the distance, an explosion shook the throne room, accompanied by yelling. Blood gushed from the open wound. Without a sound, tears still falling from the corners of his eyes, Asham Ivani Reyes fell face forward against the floor.

Laerte moved backwards and the guards immediately lifted their spears. Etienne Azdeki's raised hand commanded them to remain still.

'The *L-Liaber* …?' stammered Laerte, confused.

'Ah! You did not know!' exulted Azdeki. 'You really had no idea?'

'Etienne, we must—'

'I decide!' Azdeki roared, giving Azinn a glare.

There was no protest. And for the first time Etienne's face was transformed by anger, his expression enough to inspire fear. His features remained tense as he stared at Laerte, one hand tapping the pommel of his sword.

'The first Reyes, the one who overthrew Caglieri, entrusted the Sacred Book to your family. For centuries, the Usters kept it secret. Until your father—'

'You killed them ... you killed them all ...!'

Bam! Bam!

He saw Naïs again ... his sister Naïs ... with her sweet face and delicate fair locks. He recalled his father's firm hand on his shoulder, with the signet ring on his third finger. The dark blue eyes of his brother ... The perfume his mother had worn drowned out the acrid smell of gunpowder that was now drifting up to the palace.

'Do you even know who your father really was?' asked Azdeki.

He was a man who was loved, a good man, a man of letters, a formidable swordsman. Oratio Montague, Count of Uster and lord of the Saltmarsh region. Laerte forgot about his fever, the ache of his shoulder, the irregular throbbing in his temples. Rage gave him an even greater strength than the calm so cherished by his mentor. He only needed to sigh to sense the heartbeats of the soldiers surrounding him. His nose started to bleed; pain compressed his skull as well as his chest, but he was convinced he could keep control for long enough before the *animus* obliterated him.

'We had to do it,' Etienne defended himself. 'We had to recover it. The *Liaber Dest* is too dangerous to—'

Laerte sprang towards the closest soldier, cleaving the air with his sword, carving a gaping wound in the man's neck. Surprised, the other soldiers hesitated for a second before attacking him. He heard the hiss of Azdeki's weapon being drawn from its scabbard, along with the more subtle rustling of his uncle's cloak as Azinn took a step back.

The heat setting his lungs aflame did not deter him. He had to resort to the *animus* to survive, using its power to sense the life around him and take the lives of his enemies. He crouched, parrying a spear thrust before bringing his sword down upon the legs of a second soldier, slicing through his knees.

Each move seemed so obvious to him, so natural, despite the pain every movement inflicted upon him. He lashed out with his fists, dislocated kneecaps with kicks, penetrated armour with his blade without pause. But his muscles seemed to be burning up as his adversaries' hearts ceased beating one after another. The *animus* ... it was going to crush him eventually.

'Azdeki!' Bernevin bellowed.

'Godsfuck!' Negus swore.

'With me!' ordered Etienne, as his uncle and the old man hurried out of the throne room.

Laerte was staggering in the midst of ten dead bodies, wheezing and glassy-eyed but still determined to fight. The cannonades were drawing nearer. The red curtains around the balcony fluttered and the trees beyond were on fire. Laerte came closer to unconciousness with each passing minute. His entire body had become one great painful wound. Only the sight of the four officers helped him hold on, feeding his anger. He watched the men who killed his father now lift their hands against him.

A terrific force ran across the marble, rolling the Emperor's corpse over in its passage. Laerte just had time to throw his arms in front of face, bracing his legs. It was like a storm which broke the flagstones beneath his feet as it pushed him towards the balcony behind him.

'He's a tough one!' bawled Rhunstag.

'How can he keep this up?' Negus wondered.

The fleeting image of his little sister seemed to pass before his eyes.

It was enough to give him the strength to advance a step. Then smoothly, he knelt and hammered the floor with a hard fist.

A circular arc split the marble, sending sparkling shards flying into the air. Negus flew through the air as far as the doors, his head striking the wood with a hard crunch. The three others tumbled backwards, sliding several yards with hoarse cries of alarm. Laerte eased his effort, seeking an exit with befuddled eyes. Each step he took was torture, each movement made him moan. The world spun around him; the balcony, stone parapet, the blazing tree tops.

'Uster!' Azdeki bellowed behind him.

He turned, almost slumping to one side, his sword tip skidding over the floor as his arm dangled.

'Dun-Cadal ...' he said in a murmur, as if calling for help. 'Wader ...'

Azdeki walked briskly towards him, flourishing his sword.

Laerte tried to lift his weapon but it was too heavy. Blood was running over his lips. His legs could barely hold him.

'Why?' he mumbled, before managing to shout. '*Why?!*'

There was a whistling sound; Azdeki was going to strike. Laerte wanted to parry but it was too late. The bright blade streaked towards his face and in the shining metal he saw the vivid image of a cannonball.

The blast of the explosion flung the two men apart. Laerte sank into unconsciousness as his body slipped over the parapet. He fell headlong, striking the pine trees, his body lashed by the flaming branches. His bones cracked as he hit the ground.

How long he remained there, at the feet of the blazing conifers, he never found out. There was nothing but the torment of his battered body. Everything else around him was merely a ghostly presence.

He felt himself lifted up and his cries of pain drowned out the few words he was able to hear.

He was carried off to a secret chamber. His injuries were tended while he howled and screamed senselessly. His tears mixed with his blood. Darkness took him several times, cold and oppressive, until he feared he might be condemned to remain there for eternity.

'He will not survive . . .'

Each time he approached death's door, voices seized his attention and he was dragged back to his suffering.

'Do everything you can for him, Aladzio!'

'I'm an inventor, not a doctor!'

'You're the only chance he has.'

The more it seemed he was returning to life, the more unbearable it became. Life was made of pain, of wounds, and of heartbreak . . .

'So . . . he's Oratio's son . . .'

After a while he was able to attach names to the voices, even though he had only heard one of them once.

'Hold on, my friend. You will not be misfortune's plaything.'

That was Rogant. And the touch of his warm hand on what seemed to be his own.

'I told you it was a bad idea, but no, you didn't listen to me. Straight into the wolf's jaws. And for what? To confront how many men?'

For once Aladzio's voice was like a sweet melody.

'Hold him! Hold him!'

He screamed like a pig being slaughtered. He cried. He only wanted one thing: for all of this to stop, for his heart to cease beating, and for every part of him and his pain to be extinguished.

'You are a great knight, Laerte of Uster. You must not abandon us . . .'

Whenever his mind returned from the mists, he had the impression he was being hammered with an iron taken straight from the forge. His nerves burned. And yet ... he was gradually coming back to life. His journeys in the darkness were now punctuated with memories as sharp as the twang of a bowstring.

'Madog! Madog!'

'Let's see ... you called me Wader, didn't you? Why don't I return the favour? As you seem to like these wriggling beasties ... you will be ... Frog ... I shall call you Frog ...'

'I love you. I'll always love you. Forever. Don't forget me. Don't forget us. Frog! Don't forget who you are ... Frog! Don't ever forget! I love you!'

Esyld ...

When he finally opened his eyes a warm, welcoming beam of sunlight was shining on his face.

A HEART FULL OF RAGE

Thrown into the fire, it does not burn.
Put to the sword, it does not rip.
It is made from the murmur of the gods
And nothing shall ever destroy it.

The book was heavy, made of aging vellum with a riveted metal binding. It was as heavy as the precepts it contained. In the hands of the child, it seemed inordinately big and its cover was graced with two simple words: *Liaber Moralis*.

'Now that you know how to read, you need words to nourish your gift.'

Kneeling before him, a tall man was watching him attentively. With a new beard on his cheeks and recently cut hair, he was wearing a fine white shirt beneath a short black jacket. Custom demanded that he wear a full-length cloak with a fur-lined collar, but Count Oratio of Uster was not fulfilling his public duties right now. In the ray of sunlight framed by the wide window of his study he was offering his younger son a precious birthday present: a copy of the *Liaber Moralis*, the foundation of the whole Imperial society.

'I received this same book from my father when I was your age,' Oratio told him. 'The very heart of men's dealings with one another is revealed in these pages. What it is customary to do, to say and to believe.'

Laerte was eight years old today and had just started to wield a sword under the instruction of the master-at-arms of Aëd's Watch. A great man of letters and an able swordsman, his father deemed it essential that his son receive a balanced education: in no case should the blade take precedence over words, or written works exclude the art of war. For Oratio, the power of pen and blade were fundamentally linked. That was how leaders should be trained, according to the Uster; capable of defending their cause by arms or by words, depending on the situation.

'You remember how we talked to you about this, your mother and me?'

'Yes,' Laerte replied in a shy voice.

He contemplated the book he held in his little hands, hesitating over whether he should open it or not out of fear that he might drop it. The count's firm hand upon his shoulder guided him to the desk where the child was able to put it down with a dull thud. There, he lifted the cover and started to turn the pages, awed by the lines and lines of handwriting punctuated by the occasional illumination.

'The writing is the work of the Fangolin monks,' explained his father as he leaned over him, his hands placed upon the desk.

In a protective gesture, his chin brushed the top of the child's head.

'Why are they the only ones allowed to write?' asked Laerte without taking his eyes off the pages.

The beginning of each paragraph was decorated with a coloured drawing representing mysterious scenes: a man viewed in profile kneeling before a lady; a peasant carrying a lamb in his arms; a knight standing between a frightened family and a band of Nâaga ...

'You're allowed to write,' Oratio corrected him. 'I write plenty of messages and orders for the county guard. And I used to write letters to your mother, before she agreed to marry me. But when it comes to books, which preserve knowledge ... then the monks of Fangol have the sole responsibility for copying them.'

'But ... sometimes, I see you writing books!'

'That's ...' Oratio seemed a little uneasy. '... different,' he said. 'Most books are the work of the monks, because for them books are ... divine. Do you understand?'

'Because the gods invented books?'

'That's right,' he agreed, trying not to laugh. 'Among other things, my son, among other things.'

Laerte pulled a face, disappointed to see sentences which were devoid of meaning for him. The words seemed so complicated, the turns of phrase so heavy, that he was unable to grasp them as a whole.

'I don't understand ...'

Here and there, however, he recognised familiar terms and pieces of dogma he'd heard in sermons at the church in Aëd's Watch.

'That's normal,' his father reassured him. 'But you'll understand it as you grow older and read more of it. The morality of this world, what is good, and what is evil is all here ... The first monks wrote it, based on the words of the *Liaber Dest* ...'

The Lost Book ... the Book of Destiny. A legend that remained very much alive within the House of Uster. His father had often spoken of it emphatically, and would become irritated when Laerte's older brother expressed doubts about the book's reality. No one had ever seen the *Liaber Dest*, and the very idea that a single work, whose origin and authors were uncertain, might hold the destiny of every person who ever lived, from the beginning to the end of the time, seemed like sheer madness to certain sceptical minds.

'One day, I will tell you about the Book. One day you will know, my son.'

Oratio of Uster was an enlightened man, ready to doubt many so-called truths; the *Liaber Dest* always seemed more like myth than actual truth and yet the count would not permit anyone to deny its existence. Whenever someone did in his presence, it prompted the sole, rare occasions when Laerte had seen his father angry. Angry to the point of making the boy fear him. Otherwise, Laerte remembered him as a loving, gentle person.

'Each being ...' murmured Oratio above him, reciting the words on the page the boy was perusing. '... exists in this world to accomplish their work,' he concluded.

The count straightened up, ruffling the child's hair.

'May you accomplish yours, Laerte. A great ...'

'A great ...'

'... mighty ...'

'... mighty ...'

'... and magnificent work.'

'... and magnificent ...'

Pain woke him, sharp and burning, as hot as the noon sunshine pouring down from a skylight into the salon.

'... mighty ...'

He was no longer at Aëd's Watch. He was sitting in a large armchair with one leg stretched out before him, his foot propped on a small stool.

'... *and magnificent work.*'

Upon his knees he had a copy of the *Liaber Moralis*, open to the same page, the same words, with the words spoken by his father years before ringing in his ears. His wounds were healing slowly, each passing day seeming more painful than the preceding one. His body had been broken, shredded. Each movement was intolerable, inflicting fleeting jolts of pain, accompanied by retching to the point of vomiting and fainting. Laerte had come so close to death he had eventually longed for it. Nothingness seemed like an improvement compared to this constant suffering.

Four months after the Empire's fall, he could not remain seated for more than two hours without losing consciousness. This time he had simply fallen asleep, revisiting his memories after glimpsing this copy of the *Liaber Moralis* in the villa's library.

He barely saw the hand that gently took the book from his lap. There, in the large salon with sunlight filtering through the long white curtains, he finally met his host. During these four months he'd had no visitors at all beyond the daily comings and goings of the servants at the Villa de Page. Close to the southern territories, only a few days' ride from the great city of Masalia, the house overlooked a great vineyard which spread before the azure sea.

Dressed in a black doublet with a long slender sword hanging from a leather belt and tall polished boots that rose to his knees, Gregory de Page in no way resembled a nobleman in flight. Pacing tranquilly back and forth as he leafed through the pages of the *Liaber Moralis*, he cut a fine figure. He was one of the victors of this war. He had worked diligently behind the scenes, helping the rebels acquire their cannons and capture the great city of Emeris. But what had become of the man since the fall of the Empire? Laerte had not even attempted to find out, preferring to wall himself up in silence, absorbed by the anger and pain consuming him. In contrast to de Page, Laerte had failed.

'The Book of Morality ... the laws governing the co-existence between men,' murmured de Page in a thoughtful tone. 'Based on the *Liaber Dest,* written by the first monks of the Order of Fangol, and forever lost. Unjust laws, when one considers the place they reserve for the so-called savage tribes ...'

He closed the book with a snap before tossing it on an armchair in one corner of the salon. He walked to the fireplace and leaned against the mantel without saying a word. Outside, the warm noon breeze made its way across the terrace to gently lift the curtains over the open windows.

'Perhaps they're obsolete now,' he mused, rubbing his chin with a black-gloved hand. 'There are so many precepts set down in the *Liabers*, and none express any doubts about their origins. Surprising, isn't it? The wishes of the gods copied out so religiously on paper without anyone knowing who first wrote them down. And no one has ever questioned their validity. Not out of fear of divine punishment, but through fear of other men ... The *Liaber Moralis*. The foundation of the late Empire ...'

Laerte blinked slowly as he struggled against falling unconscious again. His entire face was burning. He had studied it once in the cheval glass that stood in his chamber: his features were still bruised, his eyes swollen half-shut on either side of a broken nose. He could make out the duke's figure but could only fill in the man's features out of memory. His vision was still blurry, and if he had not already experienced so many of these fleeting awakenings he might have believed he was still dreaming.

'Lima tells me that you can manage a few words now,' said de Page.

Lima. One of de Page's servants, beautiful and sweet with an olive complexion and a prettily tattooed face. A Nâaga ...

'So you're aware that it's been four months ... and that the revolution took place ...'

Laerte gave a slow nod.

'And that you are staying in my villa, here in the South,' de Page added.

There was a silence and the duke let it continue, perhaps hoping that his guest would break it. But Laerte refused to speak, instead glaring at the man who'd saved his life, from between puffy eyelids. Gregory de Page looked down, perplexed by his rudeness, before going over to an armchair by one of the windows and dragging it over to the fireplace. He sat down and crossed his legs and his arms before staring insistently at the injured patient.

'You're no longer a hunted beast, Laerte of Uster,' he announced very quietly. 'Meurnau was killed, along with the Laerte who was supposedly leading the rebellion. The people have been told that both Meurnau and Laerte of Uster staged this revolution in order to seize the throne for themselves. Not to establish a Republic. Fortunately, the brave Etienne Azdeki stopped them.'

Laerte looked away. So that was how matters stood ... Yes, he'd truly lost everything. His family's assassin had seized power, and his crimes had all been washed away.

'The Republic was proclaimed a week ago. You see before you one of the councillors charged with ratifying the new laws.'

Laerte bowed his head, his heart filled with rage. Everyone had won something, while he found himself a prisoner, a broken man who hoped for nothing but an early death.

'Come now, Laerte,' de Page said soothingly. 'I'm not your enemy. I saved your life.'

'Why ...?'

His voice was weak and husky, but it was enough to impose silence. De Page's attitude changed, his slight smile of satisfaction replaced with a more serious expression. He uncrossed his arms, placing them on the armrests of his chair. Then he raised his eyes towards the skylight a few feet away from them, savouring the sun's warmth before deciding to reply.

'I don't know. Perhaps I believe that someone like you cannot be allowed to die in such a way ... And then there's Rogant and Aladzio to think of. They care about you.'

'Your servants ...'

'My servants, to be sure. But more importantly, men who deserve respect,' de Page replied sharply. 'And though Aladzio remains in my service, that is a well-guarded secret. It's only thanks to him we saved you. So they're servants, yes. But not slaves.'

For the first time since his fall, Laerte managed a faint smile. But by no means a sincere one ... de Page was hurt by it and looked away, shaking his head.

'Think whatever you please. The fact is your life has been saved and you're in no danger here. No one will come looking for you. Azdeki and his allies believe you are dead. And they have other matters on their mind at present.'

'And Dun-Cadal?' Laerte immediately asked.

The image of his mentor came to him suddenly. And, at the same time, that of a beautiful young woman with curly hair. Another kind of pain afflicted him, even sharper and more devastating than his physical torments, affecting his heart and soul. The pain of guilt. All this while, he had not spared a single thought for them, not even for an instant ... What kind of self-important monster had he become? What sort of pitiful toy had he been in the hands of the Azdeki family, to become nothing but a dismantled puppet?

A tear slid along his eyelid. Had his heart been so numbed by his anger and his own suffering that he had never worried about their fate?

He stifled a sob.

'Esyld Orbey ...?' he managed.

'Dun-Cadal has fled, but I don't know where to,' de Page simply replied. 'As for Esyld ... I will look for her.'

'Find her,' Laerte ordered between two sobs, his mouth twisting in self-loathing. 'Find her and bring her to me.'

Oddly, de Page merely nodded. In other circumstances, in other places, he might have reacted more severely. He was not the sort of man who allowed others to dictate his actions, but he was also sensitive and capable of empathy. He leaned forward, gazing into the young man's half-closed eyes, whose swollen lids were shedding small shining tears.

'I will do what I can,' he promised gravely. 'Until then you need to rest here. Great things are in the making at this very moment; a Republic has been born from the Empire, just as your father wished.'

'But I lost—'

Laerte abandoned himself to his sorrow, his body shaken by spasms. The recollection of his fall continued to hammer his skull, in a dull echo of his deeper wounds. He doubled over with his arms pressed against his aching belly. Hundreds of white-hot blades slid over his skin before they bit into it and he choked back a powerful groan, a thread of spit escaping from his lips.

'—lost everything ...' he repeated over and over. 'They destroyed me, they destroyed everything. Everything ... took everything ... Lost .. I lost ...'

He barely even felt de Page's firm hands holding his quaking shoulders.

'No, no,' murmured. 'You destroyed an Empire. Without you, they could have done nothing. Your existence, your survival, allowed them to overthrow the regime. Your name alone let them justify their deeds.'

'You're—'

Laerte could only breathe in fits and starts, before lifting his head to meet the duke's gaze.

'—you're mistaken. You too, you've already lost. They have it ... they have it. As my father had it.'

'I know ...'

De Page knelt before Laerte and there was cold anger in his eyes.

'The *Liaber Dest*,' he acknowledged

'So you knew,' Laerte scowled.

'Only after your father died, Laerte. When my father's hour came, as he lay dying, he told me everything.'

The duke stared at him without blinking. And then tenderly he placed his hands back on Laerte's shoulders.

'Do you know what it's like to be hated by one's father, Laerte? What it's like to see him, on his deathbed, jeering at you, because you did not turn out as he dreamt? The man was very strange. He openly wished for the death of his only son. And he even proudly told me exactly what he and his friends had done. They always regarded me as a conceited fool, a coward, a wastrel ... an idiot. So I played along. I wore a mask. The one they wanted to see. My father tried to torture me when he revealed the Azdekis' plot. He thought that knowledge of the *Liaber Dest*'s existence would be a constant source of suffering for me. But he was actually giving me the means to survive. He and his fellows would never have believed me capable of acting against them. And yet ...'

Laerte caught his breath, recovering enough to contain his tears.

'Bernevin,' he said.

'Rhunstag, Enain-Cassart ... and several others ...'

'The Azdekis,' Laerte spat.

'The Azdekis,' de Page confirmed.

'Are they now councillors too?' he hissed.

'They're among the founders of the Republic, yes,' de Page said as he stood up.

Then he stepped back slowly, watching Laerte's reaction out of the corner of an eye. No doubt he feared the young man might topple from his armchair in an angry fit, but Laerte was so exhausted that his head merely swayed and his hands gripped the armrests. Grimacing, he dragged his left leg to the edge of the stool and let it fall, almost fainting when his heel hit the marble floor.

'They are the Republic now. Your father's dream.'

'I won't let them get away with it ...' Laerte swore, glaring at the duke.

De Page went over to the closest window and stood with his hands behind his back.

'That is one of the few things which, today, I find I'm certain of,' he avowed. He tilted his head in order to shoot a glance back over his shoulder. 'But right now you cannot do anything.'

'I can do more than you will ever be able to imagine,' Laerte replied defiantly.

'Think before you act,' advised de Page. 'You are still convalescing, and it will still be some time before you are in a fit state to do anything at all. It could be years.'

'You don't— *arrrgh*!'

Laerte had tried to stand up, but from his arms down to his injured leg the pain was too intense for him to rise. He fell heavily back into the chair with a moan.

'They will not act before they have deciphered the *Liaber Dest*. And as long as Aladzio is assigned to that task I have the means of making them wait. They will still be there when you are finally ready to seek your revenge. And that could be perfectly compatible with my own plan of action. For we are seeking the same thing.'

'And what is that?'

'I can't tell you more until I am sure of certain points. And they concern the Azdekis. Rumours and hearsay can be more fatal than a sharp blade. We'll speak again. But for the moment you're here as my guest. And perhaps, in time, you will become ...'

He paused for a moment, letting his eyes drift across the marble floor.

'... my friend,' he concluded, before looking up to meet Laerte's puzzled gaze.

Without saying anything further, de Page nodded his farewell and left by way of a wide door next to the fireplace. Laerte was left alone with the white curtains rippling in a warm breeze that brushed his face. Then silence and darkness returned.

'*The* Liaber Dest, *Laerte* ... the Liaber Dest ...'

'My lord? My lord?'

When he opened his eyes again, he saw the sweet features and fine tattoos of a young woman with a deep olive complexion, her black hair tied into a long braid. Lima was kneeling at his side and had a worried expression on her face.

'You fell asleep again, my lord.'

'De ... de Page?' he asked, his voice hoarse.

'Gone to Emeris, my lord. But he will return soon, he said. And in a month's time, one of your friends should be coming to see you.'

She placed a gentle hand on his wrist, a hand that he lacked the strength to push away although he was quivering from her touch as if it were an assault.

'My lord, it would be better if you lay down. I will call people to carry you to your bed.'

The world outside the villa was by no means welcoming, filled with violence, treachery, lies and rancour. Yet his personal universe was not appealing, either. His own body had become an enemy, reduced to being a constant source of pain. He could barely make out the silhouettes of the three men in blue jackets who came to carry him.

His eyelids had already closed, like the dark doors of a building in ruins, by the time he reached his bed.

The weeks that followed were punctuated by slow awakenings and sudden slumbers. Little by little, the fainting spells brought on by the pain grew less frequent and his sleeping cycle became more natural. The crimson sun of autumn was replaced by the pale shades of winter and frost. Laerte still couldn't walk and barely managed to remain upright for a few seconds before fatigue began to weigh down every movement. As Lima had said, one of his friends moved into the villa to assist him.

It was Rogant, who was thoughtful, calm and sober in speech. Neither man was inclined towards long discussions by the fireside in the evening; they were satisfied with the simple pleasure of sitting side by side, like two friends. Rogant's friendship: it was one of the few things Laerte could be happy he had preserved. Something the Azdekis could not take away from him.

Rogant kept him abreast of news, of de Page's efforts – so far, in

vain – to locate Esyld, of the latest laws passed by the newly established Council … and of the strange behaviour of those the young
man loathed most: neither Azdeki, nor Rhunstag, nor Bernevin,
nor Enain-Cassart made any attempt to accumulate more power.
Councillors they were, councillors they remained. They took part
in debates, represented their electors' interests within the Republic's
legislature and did nothing more.

Oratio of Uster's dream was becoming a reality, embraced by a
people full of admiration for their new institutions and filled with
fresh hope and aspirations. But it was his enemies who were bringing
it all about; the same enemies who had destroyed his life.

One evening, at the end of a meal at the big table in the dining
room, Rogant said some unfortunate words.

'What they're doing is good …'

Laerte pushed his plate away with the back of his hand, looking
flushed, his back hunched. His eyes narrowed, he stared at the breadcrumbs that dotted the great red tablecloth with silver embroidery.
The glow from the candelabra danced over his face, which was still
marked by his wounds.

'Did you hear me?'

Rogant remained calm. Laerte set his cutlery down alongside his
plate, in the middle of which one poor small chicken bone sat on top
of a mishmash of vegetables. When his eyes finally moved away from
the remains of his dinner, he could not meet his friend's gaze. Laerte
was struggling to contain his growing anger. Rogant carried on.

'Whatever crimes they may have committed in the past, the
people support them,' he explained. 'They've given the people a
voice. They've changed things, Laerte. You can't fight against that.
Nobody can.'

Laerte's sole response was a brief movement of his head to one
side. Only the scattered breadcrumbs seemed to interest him.

'Vengeance is not the right path to take … Anger will destroy
you,' Rogant murmured.

At last the young man's bright eyes shifted towards him. Among
the tears filling his eyelids, there shone a beastly light, an anger like a
devouring fire. No words could quench such rage.

'My people are free now,' Rogant said, in a last attempt to reason
with his friend. 'These men will pay for their crimes, but according
to the will of the Republic, not yours … Let de Page take care of this.

Don't ruin your life. You've already suffered more than enough.'

Laerte slowly placed his hands on the edge of the table and, pushing with his palms, he backed away at an angle, grimacing. Rogant immediately rose from his seat.

'It's still too soon for you to stand up, you can't walk yet.'

No words were spoken to contradict him, but Laerte's baleful glare remained fixed upon the Nâaga. Lima appeared at the dining room door, looking hesitant. A very odd scene was being played out before her eyes. Rogant was standing in front of the young man, as if ready to push him back down. Which he did as soon as Laerte sought to rise, pressing his hands on the armrests of his chair to push himself up.

'You're weak,' the Nâaga said bluntly.

There was a moment of silence. Laerte tilted his head forward, gritting his teeth but keeping his eyes fixed upon his friend. The armrests creaked beneath the pressure of his fingers.

'You're weak,' repeated Rogant, pushing him back down again as he tried to rise a second time.

Once more, Laerte, moaning, tried to stand. He thought his legs were about to break as he rose, his eyes still locked with the Nâaga's. An intense jolt of pain ran through his body and his brow beaded with sweat. Yet ... he refused to give up.

'You're weak.'

Neither man was prepared to look away from the other. In her corner, Lima watched them match wills, astonished. Nervously, she rubbed her hands upon her apron. It was a miracle that Laerte had survived as long as he had. But the idea that he might walk again, and so soon, was almost unimaginable. His body was still so tired, so marked by his ordeal, that he might fall to pieces at any moment. Yet, despite every difficulty, he did not bend.

Facing Laerte, the colossus eyed him carefully before taking a step forward. At that point only, Laerte fell back heavily into his armchair. But he had made his point. With Rogant, words weren't necessary. Laerte's determination was too strong for this to be a mere fit of ill temper.

He would see matters through to the end.

And that was how he started to walk again. One step, then two ... and finally three. The days went by, then the weeks and the months.

The pain faded before the sheer strength of his rage. Only his anger was enough to make him forget his suffering, to make him push his limits further every time, until he finally fell from exhaustion.

Spring, then summer ... and at last he could get out into the fresh air by his own means, seeing dry lands dotted with yellowed grass; a broken countryside lulled by the sound of crickets.

Rogant remained by his side.

Laerte took a sword, struck the air with it, and screamed when his shoulder responded as if it had been smashed by a hammer blow. But he repeated the move, and then again. Many times. Slowly. And then more surely.

The tufts of grass eventually wilted. Autumn approached. The heat disappeared, and Rogant was still there, watching him regain his bearings. When Laerte was ready to cross swords again the Nâaga became his sparring partner, placing himself before his friend to parry his blows.

'... a great ...'

Laerte retook possession of his being. He regained control of his movements. Another year passed

'... mighty ...'

De Page returned. Unhappily, he bore no news of Esyld. The Republic was gradually consolidating itself but it remained fragile. Laerte was so focused on his desire for revenge that he brushed away any doubts about the duke's motives. The fact that they shared a common goal was enough.

'... and magnificent work ...'

Thrust ... Parry ... The movements became fluid and controlled once more, until the day came when he felt ready to use the *animus* again.

The effort was exhausting. The first time he tried it he fainted and Rogant had to catch him before his head hit a rocky outcrop in the villa's garden.

'Feel the animus, be the animus.'

Despite the blood running from his – now straightened – nose, despite the burning of his atrophied muscles, he continued to fight both the Nâaga and invisible enemies, from morning till nightfall ... Until, at last, he found himself again.

Nothing had diverted him from his path. Not his thoughts about Esyld; not his questions about Dun-Cadal's fate. Still less Rogant's gentle behaviour towards Lima and their burgeoning romance. Nothing could shake his will. Two years after his fall, two years after the Empire was lost, he left the villa.

II

TO LIVE AGAIN

One day, I will tell you about the Book.
One day you will know, my son.

He had removed his cape and was slowly taking off his jacket, facing away from the door. Opposite him, the dust covering the window shone in the pale moonlight. The young woman watched him silently, one hand pressed against the frame of the half-opened door, contemplating how the moonlight ran over his bare shoulders, highlighting each of the scars that clawed his back. He rubbed a shoulder blade, grimacing.

What combats, how many battles had he fought to bear so many scars? Had his heart emerged intact or, like his skin, was it covered in cracks?

She could have remained where she was, watching him undress. She might even have wanted to. But there were questions she could not leave unanswered. With a timid hand, she knocked on the door.

'Laerte?' she called, her cheeks blushing before lowering her eyes shyly when he turned round. 'Excuse me, I ...'

On his torso he carried the mark of yet another wound. She imagined tracing it with her fingertips while he recounted how he acquired it. But ... Masque Night was tomorrow evening. Perhaps she would never have a chance to confess her attraction to him. The thought made her smile faintly.

'If it's about Dun-Cadal, you're wasting your time. De Page has been warned. He won't be an obstacle,' Laerte assured her briskly. 'As for the Palatio, Azdeki has doubled the number of guards.'

'Good,' she nodded, without daring to meet his gaze.

'Everything is going as planned, Viola.'

'Truly?' she blurted.

He remained still, as if waiting for Viola to finally leave his chamber. But the young woman was determined to make him speak this time. Most of what she knew of him, she had learned from Aladzio, Rogant and, more recently, the old general. The rest she had guessed. She was still waiting for the day when he finally opened up to her. That moment would speak of a connection between them ... or perhaps more. Her heart leapt in her chest, beyond her control. She clasped her damp hands in front of her, feeling nervous.

'Forgive me, but I overheard part of your conversation, and—'

'And what?' murmured Laerte, his voice suddenly stern.

He narrowed his eyes, his expression ominous.

'Who is Esyld?'

'That doesn't concern you,' he replied.

He took his cape and began to fold it.

'She's going to marry Balian Azdeki?' Viola persisted. 'You knew her in the Saltmarsh, is that it?'

Laerte's movements became brusque and he tossed the cape to a chair, annoyed.

'Do you love her?'

There was silence. Viola felt a hollowness deep in her belly, along with an inexpressible sorrow which she quelled as best she could.

'The wedding will take place before the festivities begin ... an overture to the main event,' she declared in a shaky voice. 'If you try anything at that moment then all we've worked for will be for nothing.'

He shot her a black look.

'Don't tell me what I need to do,' he snapped.

'No, of course not,' agreed Viola. 'You're a man. While I'm only a young woman, barely out of childhood ...'

For the first time in her presence, Laerte looked down.

'Laerte?' she said quietly.

He replied with a strangely sad gaze. How she would have liked to go and nestle against him, be with him ... try to make his sorrow evaporate with the heat of her body.

'I'm next door if ever you ... umm, if you want to talk about ... umm, well, whatever you like.'

He neither moved nor uttered a single word. He watched her close the door behind her without calling her back.

'I'm only a young woman, barely out of childhood.'

He sat down on the edge of the bed with a sigh, wondering how he'd come to this. He recalled how powerfully he'd resented those who'd seen him as a *child*, incapable of succeeding at anything. And now he was behaving exactly like them. Although Viola was twenty, he still regarded her as a young girl.

She had been fifteen when he met her for the first time.

'You're a knight?' she had asked, seated at a desk with a pile of open books before her.

She had pretty freckles sprinkled across her still chubby cheeks, over skin as white as snow, and there was a mischievous gleam in her deep green eyes. He had not replied. He was there to meet de Page after years of wandering. He had had no time for a *child*. He had just returned to the villa, stronger than ever, ready to satisfy his desire for revenge. And now, nearly six years later, here he was. Sitting on the edge of a bed, in the gentle night-time warmth of Masalia.

He let himself fall back, his heart an open wound. Esyld, he thought, still loved him. Azdeki was holding her prisoner, that was it. He was threatening her and she had been forced to lie to him. He could not stop repeating her words to himself. Spoken with conviction in her voice ... He struggled to find the slightest doubt, the slightest weakness, the slightest word that would have suggested the opposite. Just a hint ... that actually meant *'I love you'.*

Gradually, he drifted off to sleep.

Quiet reigned within the house. The lamps in the salon slowly consumed their oil. On the divan, Dun-Cadal looked wistfully at the empty pitcher on the low table. Wearily he looked down at his hands. Dark veins bulged beneath his spotted skin. He slowly lifted his right hand and held it out before him. When it shook with tremors, he gritted his teeth. So this was what he had become ... an unsteady body ...

'"Rest assured,"' he muttered, '"that in Masalia you shall find what you seek."'

He had come to Masalia seeking death. Instead he had found what he had been trying to escape. Worse still, the life he'd been so proud of had been nothing but an enormous lie.

When the sun began to rise over the port city, Dun-Cadal was in the kitchen, standing by the table. In the middle lay a sword rolled up in an old blanket. He had never dared seize hold of it. Eraëd had hung from the belts of the greatest Emperors and while he had expressed doubts about its powers, never having witnessed them personally, he had been unable to bring himself to wield it. Out of respect for those he had sworn to serve . . .

With a quick, nervous gesture he unwrapped the cloth, revealing the glittering blade. His fingers hovered a few inches from the golden hilt. Who was he to let himself touch it? The man he'd sworn to protect had destroyed him. So who was he to allow himself to take up his Emperor's sword?

If only it were not a vestige of the Empire . . . and what an Empire it had been: one of betrayals, of hatreds, of massacres and of corruption.

He finally made up his mind and, trembling, went out into the courtyard, his damp hand gripping the rapier's hilt. As soon as he set his foot upon the gravel, he swung it round, almost letting go several times. There was nothing natural about his jerky movements; they were a symptom of his need for alcohol. Frustrated, he sought to parry the blows of imaginary enemies and struck at the empty space before him. But his moves were imprecise and he fell to his knees three times, cursing himself between his teeth. His sword arm twitched involuntarily and tears rose in his eyes. Had he lost all of his skills?

'You're trying to go too fast,' commented a voice from the doorway.

Dun-Cadal glanced briefly over his shoulder. Laerte was leaning against the door frame with his arms crossed. It was possible the younger man had been there for a while, watching him make a fool of himself.

'Your footing's all wrong and you're performing each move too quickly,' Laerte continued in an oddly gentle voice.

Dun-Cadal stood still, watching him approach, and when he drew near, sought to catch his eye. But Laerte was staring at the rapier. He took hold of Dun-Cadal's wrist and helped him keep the sword up, straight in front of him, preventing his arm from trembling.

'Your body should always be straight, the legs very slightly bent to maintain a good balance,' he said in a low voice. 'Your leg is stretched out too far. If a blade doesn't cut it, a club will break it …'

Finally, they exchanged a glance. Laerte could not bear it. How ravaged Dun-Cadal's face looked to him, with sorrow weighing down his features, and huge, dark bags beneath his eyes.

'A great knight once taught me that,' confessed Laerte as he stepped back. 'I don't know if he ever thought I was a good student, or if he was ever proud of the effort I made to improve, day after day.'

He walked slowly towards the house.

'But if I believed I hated him, I have no doubt it was because of what he represented, not what he was. I'm sure of that … today.'

He had just reached the front door step when Dun-Cadal's hoarse voice murmured:

'Frog …?'

It was the first time since they had met again here in Masalia that he had said the nickname without animosity. Laerte turned. His mentor was standing, having set the sword on the ground. Eraëd sparkled on the gravel in the early morning light.

'… is it you?' asked Dun-Cadal, with a lump in his throat.

He seemed so tired, the corner of his eyes wrinkling, and there was a gleam of brimming tears in his eyes.

'So it is you, Frog.'

Laerte did not reply. He understood the meaning of the words and felt their weight in his heart. With heavy, clumsy steps, Dun-Cadal approached. When they found themselves facing one another, the old man seized the back of the boy's neck.

'I thought you were dead all these years …'

'I know.'

'I thought I'd lost you …'

'I know.'

Dun-Cadal was sobbing, his knees threatening to collapse under him.

'Is it really you, Frog?' he asked again.

Laerte tried to remain dignified but found it impossible to be unmoved.

'Yes.'

Dun-Cadal broke down completely, shedding hot tears, for his life, for his fall from grace … for all the lost years when he never stopped thinking about the *lad*. He hugged Laerte fiercely, as if afraid he might lose him again. Laerte had a moment of hesitation and then put his arms around the old man.

This man had taught him everything, given him everything, without ever suspecting Laerte's true intentions. Laerte had judged this man before he came to know him, but over time he had grown used to him and, in the end and despite himself, fond of him. As the sun illuminated Masalia's rooftops below and the city became bathed in a golden glow, he felt as if he saw things clearly at last. Despite all Laerte's insolence and anger, this man had never stopped loving him like a father loves his son.

And here they were, reunited again . . .

'Some moments are not meant to be shared with others,' said Rogant.

Standing at her bedchamber window, on the first floor, Viola gave a guilty start. Behind her, Rogant was giving her an accusing look. She had not heard him enter, too busy spying on the two men in the courtyard.

'I'm just making sure that everything is all right,' she explained cheekily.

'de Page has prepared all the details for Dun-Cadal's departure. On Masque Night. He will not stand in our way. He's nothing but an old ghost.'

'It's not that. I'm worried about Laerte,' she retorted. 'He never should have revealed himself. This story is upsetting him.'

'Believe me,' said Rogant as he walked towards her, 'it's not the old man who is upsetting Laerte most . . .'

She gazed down again at the courtyard. No, to be sure, there were greater dangers than the presence of Dun-Cadal.

'Do you think he'll try to disrupt the wedding?' Viola asked anxiously as she watched the two men draw apart.

'I've known Laerte long enough to tell you that he does not abandon anything . . . or anyone. If she's marrying Balian Azdeki then both De Page and Aladzio knew it. And if they did not tell him then they had good reason. Now that he knows, he'll have to decide where his loyalties reside.'

Neither of them were dupes. Whatever they said to him, Laerte would do as he pleased. He was the one leading this mission, he would decide what they should or should not do.

'He's going to make us miss our chance,' railed Viola, balling her fists.

Rogant looked down at her with an odd smile. Outside in the courtyard Dun-Cadal was alone now, retrieving Eraëd. He hefted the rapier in his hand before vanishing inside the house.

Later that same morning Laerte crept out of the house and, finding a deserted alleyway, climbed up a long drainpipe to the rooftops. He knew the risks he was taking, knew that if he made the slightest mistake then everything could come to an end before he fulfilled his purpose. But the Book could wait for a few hours. Esyld was being coerced into marrying Azdeki's son and that took precedence.

What sort of knight would he be if he did not come to her rescue? Even the possibility that he might fail and wreck their chances of entering the Palatio on the fateful evening would not deter him. He had mastered a dragon, fought at Dun-Cadal's side, and faced four of the Empire's greatest knights singlehandedly before defeating death itself. Nothing was impossible for him. Leaping stealthily from roof to roof he crossed the city undetected. He climbed to the top of a tall building overlooking the square in front of Masalia's biggest cathedral and waited for noon to arrive. In the distance behind the church's great tower he could make out the bulge of the Palatio's dome.

'It's easy to fight with a sword.'

A crowd of officials, councillors, captains of the guard and nobles, all dressed in their finest, were gathered before the sanctuary door. Most of them were already sporting the colourful masks that every inhabitant of Masalia would be wearing during the festivities that evening.

'But to vanquish one's demons, a blade is of no use.'

At the foot of the cathedral's steps, a red carriage decorated with gold trimmings came to a halt. Laerte studied the ground a few yards below him. And leapt.

'If you are on your knees, pride gone, then stand up, even if you tremble, and regain your dignity.

'Regain your dignity.'

'"For it is the only weapon which protects you from the powerful,"' recited de Page.

The coach rocked and swayed, making the duke, seated upon a purple bench, seem to dance to the rhythm of the vehicle's movements. One hand gripping the handle by the window, he glanced out at the misty countryside. The misshapen silhouettes of dead trees loomed out of the fog and, at times, he glimpsed crows perched on their twisted branches.

'The only weapon,' he repeated thoughtfully. 'Dignity ...'

He was wearing a plain black outfit, with no adornment but a golden buckle on his belt, flared black gloves and a pendant that hung from his closed collar. Otherwise he was dressed with a sobriety which Laerte did not recall seeing before. The first time he had met the man had been at Emeris during one of his orgies. The second time, at the villa, Laerte had felt like the plains they were travelling across at present: befogged and forsaken.

Shaken by the jolts, Laerte observed the duke carefully, studying each gesture, each sentence he uttered, in the hope of finding some certainties about the man. De Page was a schemer and, although he had saved Laerte's life, the young knight favoured wariness over blind trust. He did not believe the duke was his friend for a single instant.

'Do you know who wrote that?' asked de Page as he looked out at the mist.

Laerte shook his head. The duke appeared to have expected this response since he continued without even giving his travelling companion a glance.

'Your father,' he said.

The smell of burnt grass filled their compartment, forcing de Page to turn away from the window. Through the opening, Laerte glimpsed a flaming heap being stabbed by the silhouettes of peasants armed with pitchforks. The duke pinched his nose for an instant before sighing and leaning back against the bench. He allowed a moment to pass, observing Laerte.

'I've read his writings. I managed to obtain copies even though they were banned by the Fangolin monks.'

Laerte nodded, his heart suddenly heavy. He'd never had the chance to read anything Oratio had written.

'Do you know what he meant by that?'

'No.'

'That only dignity puts us on equal footing with decision makers. I've seen poor men who were more dignified than their ill-mannered, cowardly barons. I've seen peasant women stand up to tax collectors in order to defend their meagre harvest. I've seen enslaved Nâaga hold their heads high, I've seen—'

He stopped speaking suddenly.

'Swords are not the only way to fight, Laerte.'

He turned back to the window.

'We're arriving.'

The coach slowed, the jolting became less severe, until the vehicle finally shuddered to a halt and the horses snorted.

They had travelled for more than two hours from Garmaret, where they had agreed to meet. Laerte had left the duke's villa nine years ago. He had been roaming the remains of a broken Empire, in a newborn Republic which, day after day, had restored hope in its people. He had been following the course of events from afar and yet he always had the feeling that he was in the heart of Emeris, almost the Azdekis' shadow. De Page had played his part in ensuring that.

For, even separated by great distances, they had remained in close contact all these years, Aladzio having placed a most reliable friend at their disposal, charged with delivering messages. Nine years of travel, comings and goings, farewells and reunions. From the Vershan mountains to the West, to the far North, to the gates of Masalia, Laerte had hunted for Esyld. When his despair grew too strong he returned to de Page's villa to seek out Rogant, and sometimes Aladzio. The inventor also travelled back and forth at the orders of the Azdeki family, searching the Fangolin monasteries in the hopes of finding the key to the Sacred Book. The passage of time might have kept them apart and discouraged them. But the eleven long years since the fall of the Empire had in no way shaken Laerte's resolve. When the councillor sent word that the moment had come to settle their affairs, he had been quick to reply to the invitation.

Aladzio's friend welcomed them with a piercing cry as the coach door opened. Laerte stepped down from the coach's running board, his foot sinking into dense mud. Raising his head, he spotted it in the mist, circling the ruins of a tour, continuing to call. The gods alone knew how the creature had been able to locate him during his travels, but it had always appeared in the sky and landed on his outstretched arm, bearing a capsule containing a letter.

'Don't be fooled by the look of the building,' the nobleman advised him, with a raised eyebrow and a faint smile. 'Its beauty lies inside.'

With a wave of his hand, de Page invited Laerte to approach the heavy wooden door, from which several planks were missing, revealing the flickering flames of torches within. The tower had been built upon a waterlogged hill, where even the grass struggled to grow. A thick, viscous mud clung to Laerte's boots. He took a step forward, then halted, certain he'd seen a similar tower before, despite the gaps in the stonework and mouldy beams jutting from its crown.

'Fangol,' said de Page, detecting his puzzlement. 'A Fangolin monastery, one of the first to be built. It's the same design as the Tower of Fangol, although on a smaller scale, of course.'

Of course. In the *Liaber Moralis,* the most sacred shrine of the Fangolin Order was described as immense, rising from a mountaintop to reach the sky. On some days, according to legend, its summit pierced the clouds. It was strange to see its replica bathed in mist.

De Page pushed the door open and entered first, removing his gloves and slapping them against one another. Dust covered the stones and the air seemed foul despite the embrasures in the walls. In one corner, there was a wretched old table at which sat a man in an even more pitiable state. He lifted his chin, with a blissful smile on his lips and shaggy white hair falling over his round, wrinkled face. At the rear, in a hollow of one sagging wall, a staircase rose and next to it there was a trapdoor set in the ground. Laerte closed the door behind him and was greeted by a snickering laugh.

'So, here they are,' the old man applauded with hands twisted by arthritis. 'Oh yes, the scent, the pleasant scent of the noble lord. And with him ...'

He sniffed the air. Coming closer, Laerte saw that the man's eyes were covered by a white film.

'Cataracts,' de Page explained. 'Don't mind him, he's mad.'

'A man of the sword?' the old man cried cheerfully. 'Wise, wise, yes, oh yes, but not sufficient.'

'Shut up, you stupid old monk,' ordered de Page. 'We're not here to listen to your foolishness.'

Laerte had never heard the duke speak so sternly. When the councillor turned towards him, he saw his face also bore a severe expression.

'Brother Galapa looked after this monastery. The crazy old fool never realised what a treasure he was sitting on.'

'Oh, but I did,' Galapa contradicted him, still wearing a grin. 'Yes, oh yes, but other people never listen to me, ha-ha! Galapa doesn't see? Galapa sees everything! And he hears things too.'

De Page seemed annoyed, but he adopted a more seemly attitude, placing a hand on Laerte's shoulder.

'Come, we'll find Aladzio down below.'

He led the young knight to the trap door and took hold of the rope attached to lift it. There was a flickering glow in the darkness beneath. De Page stooped to enter.

'It's all down below, yes, oh yes, always,' laughed Galapa, rubbing his hands. 'The little knight will find so many things down below. Was it written? Oh yes, surely. Yes, oh yes.'

The old man continued to nod his head, giggling. Laerte gave him a final suspicious glance before entering the hole in his turn. There were stairs and, to his great relief, the passage grew steadily larger. He climbed down, gradually straightening up, and joined de Page who waited for him at the mouth of a tunnel. Torches sputtered on the damp walls. Their light flickered upon the heavy stones, the cracks between them filled with black dust.

They followed the tunnel until de Page caught sight of a small alcove.

'Here.'

He ducked his head and stepped within.

The creaking of the old door was loud in the narrow corridor. Laerte hesitated for a moment before entering the niche, seeing a small opening that led him into a large and strange-looking room filled with the scent of pepper and jasmine. Here and there among the long, heavy wooden tables, candelabra diffused a golden glow over piles of books. The high ceiling featured heavy slotted beams from which giant spider webs hung. A few alembics filled with boiling liquids of various colours fumed away on top of dusty old tomes.

'My lords,' a small voice to their right called out in greeting.

Startled, Laerte instinctively brought his hand to the pommel of his sword. But he relaxed slightly when he saw it was an attractive young woman. Her green eyes shone in the soft light.

'You don't recognise Viola?' the duke laughed. 'Viola Aguirre?'

He patted Laerte's shoulder, amused. The young knight stood looking at her. When he had first met her, during one of his stays at the villa a few years earlier, she'd been a child fresh from the country. Today she was a young and pretty woman with her red hair tied back, a few delicate strands falling upon her milky white nape and dangling in front of her ears. She had timid eyes and freckles sprinkled across her cheeks. Wearing a simple brown dress, there was a certain elegance about her.

He wasn't attracted to her, no, just surprised to see how much she had changed. But had he remained the same? His years of wandering had surely hardened him.

'She's trustworthy. She's a historian now!' de Page informed him proudly, walking between the tables overflowing with manuscripts.

Viola greeting the young man with a clumsy curtsey, blushing. Just as she was about to speak to him he turned away, intrigued by the strange utensils sitting beside the books. As to what purpose these odds and ends might serve, he had no idea. On the other hand, the person making use of them was no great mystery.

'Frog! Ah, ah, ah! Frog!' chortled a jovial voice.

In a corner dimly lit by a few candles, a familiar figure was descending a ladder placed against a tall bookcase. When he walked towards Laerte with his arms opened wide the knight discerned, little by little, a coat with puffed shoulders and a tricorne jammed over a face split by a wide grin.

'So good to see you here! Ha-ha! Fro ... excuse me, Laerte,' Aladzio corrected himself. 'I'll never get used to that.'

'Well, who would have guessed that the cellar of that mouldy old tower was hiding such a library?' Laerte said in wonderment.

'No one,' replied de Page.

Laerte looked around for the duke and found him sitting in a large armchair behind one of the book-laden tables. The nobleman rubbed a hand over his smooth-shaven chin.

'Viola,' he called, while staring at Laerte. 'If you would be kind enough to leave us now, Galapa will be happy to tell you one of his mad stories.'

Near the small door, the young woman gave a brief nod of her head, barely disguising her disappointment. She knew certain things would be kept from her until the end and, despite her curious nature, she was forced to accept the situation. De Page was careful to keep control of everything, both information and the roles of everyone involved.

371

'As usual?' she asked a little wearily. 'I can just pretend to be listening to him?'

'That's it,' de Page smiled.

When the door shut behind her, Aladzio gave the young man a friendly pat on the shoulder.

'It's such a great pleasure to see you, if you only knew. Such a great pleasure,' he repeated cheerily. 'How many years has it been since our last meeting?'

'Three,' Laerte replied simply.

They'd been at the villa, he recalled. A brief conversation before he returned to the road, seeking Esyld. De Page had scarcely had any news to give him on the subject during all this time, but nothing other than his thirst for vengeance could divert him from his quest.

'Three,' Aladzio echoed thoughtfully. 'Yes, three years. You were returning from Polieste. Did you take my advice and go back to the Saltmarsh?'

Laerte let out a sigh. The Saltmarsh. He had been avoiding travelling to the region, it would be his last resort. Returning to the marshes, seeing Aëd's Watch again, walking in the footsteps of the past ... he had baulked at the idea for several reasons. Of all the lands within the Republic, Esyld might well have found refuge in the Saltmarsh after the fall of the Empire. If he couldn't find her there, he would lose all hope of ever being reunited with her. So, perhaps paradoxically, he kept postponing a visit there.

Aware that he had touched on a delicate matter, Aladzio immediately moved on to something else.

'Beakie has often told me about you, you know. I think she's grown fond of you after all this time.'

Laerte relaxed.

'Aladzio,' he smiled, tilting his head towards him. 'It's a bird.'

'A falcon!' protested the inventor, drawing back from him. 'A peregrine falcon who, I may remind you, has always brought you our letters. She's not a ...'

He pinched his lips distastefully before scornfully pronouncing:

'... *bird*, as you put it.' He pointed an accusing finger at Laerte. 'She will be sad when I tell her you said that. Really, really sad.'

Laerte could not hold back his smile. How good it was to have Aladzio for a friend. While Rogant reassured him with his calmness and self-control, Aladzio's lunacy brought some lightness to his heavy heart. Sometimes when he found himself alone by a campfire and felt his anger gnawing at him, he imagined that the inventor was there at his side.

He loved and respected him – all the more because he knew Aladzio was in constant danger, working for the Azdekis since de Page's father had ceded his services to them, but secretly being the duke's accomplice. Although everyone took pains not to raise any suspicion where he was concerned, if a single mistake were made, if a single message mentioning the inventor were to fall into Etienne's hands, it would mean certain death for Aladzio … And for good reason. Theodus de Page, sensing death approach, had transferred him to his partners because the inventor had displayed such astonishing intellectual acuity since his earliest youth.

At the age of fifteen, he had translated a text derived from the ancient Gueyle dialect. At sixteen, he had written an account of the Perthuis dynasty's ascent to power, described the victorious tactics deployed by the Marjoranes during the great battle of Polieste, and even proposed an effective counter-strategy. His only weakness was his instability: a gentle form of madness that he was unable to control and which, at times, distanced him from reality. It was a kind of childlike naivety, and it could always soothe Laerte.

'Beakie has always been sweet with you. She's very fond of you,' Aladzio ruminated, shaking his head in disappointment. 'Very fond.'

'Aladzio,' called de Page quietly.

'There are bonds between men and beasts that must be respected, things that are … beyond the ordinary world, and you should not be scornful of them, Frog. I mean, Laerte.'

'Aladzio!'

De Page raised his voice, and spoke with just enough authority to make the inventor fall silent. But he continued to look annoyed and muttered to himself as he set his tricorne down on the table to his left.

'I don't think Laerte has come all this way to hear you talk about your bi … about your friend Beakie. And we have more important matters to discuss. Am I wrong?'

De Page had no need to insist further, for Aladzio's face lit up with a smile. He hastily pushed away several books lying on the table and dusted off the covers of others before finding the one he was looking for.

'Heeere it is,' he said.

He raised his eyes towards Laerte, looking delighted, and tapped the worn goatskin cover.

'The codex.'

'The codex?' Laerte repeated uncertainly.

'Of Gueyle,' interrupted de Page, eager to get to the point. 'One of the most ancient dialects of the former Kingdoms. And one of the first written scripts. This language was lost over the course of time, and would still be but for—'

'Me!' Aladzio proudly interrupted. 'Ha-ha! Here we are in one of the first libraries of the Fangolin copyists!'

As he spoke, he walked backwards between the tables, with his arms spread wide and the codex held in one hand.

'Books by the hundreds, Laerte! And in each of them, centuries of knowledge: dead languages, glyphs, descriptions, and this codex which establishes the link between the three *Liabers* that we know and ... and ...'

He stopped in the middle of the room, with a graver expression than Laerte had ever seen before.

'I succeeded.'

Laerte's face darkened. He gave de Page a black look and the nobleman met his glare without flinching.

'Succeeded in what?' Laerte asked, feeling a dull anger coming to life inside him.

Between the tables, Aladzio shook his head dreamily and then looked around the room.

'In understanding,' he revealed.

He hurried over to the ladder. The top was hooked to rails and he slid it along the bookcase.

'About the power of the Book,' he explained, running his hand across the spines of the volumes aligned on the shelves. 'The power of those writings ... and what it is the Azdekis are after.'

Once again, Laerte exchanged a glance with the duke and, seeing de Page's contrite headshake, realised that his impatience was visible on his face. Was political power not enough for Etienne Azdeki and his uncle? Were they harbouring some other ambition? They had everything – the Republic, the *Liaber Dest* – what more could they want? He needed clear answers.

'Aladzio,' called de Page. 'The facts. Keep to the facts.'

The inventor paused, looking surprised. But when he opened his mouth to express his dissatisfaction, it was Laerte's voice that rang out.

'What do they hope to do with *Liaber Dest*? That's what this all about, isn't it? Aladzio, you've translated it at last ...'

De Page contented himself with giving Laerte an enigmatic stare without saying a word. The young knight heard Aladzio's quick foot-steps behind him. He turned sharply as the inventor drew close and found him looking somewhat sheepish, lifting a finger to the tip of his nose.

'Not ... exactly,' he murmured, as if sharing a shameful secret. 'It's more—'

'The *Liaber Dest* cannot be translated like an ordinary book,' de Page interrupted quietly. 'It has to be decoded. It is made up of poems, of thoughts written in several languages, and of engravings. They need to be assembled in the right order for their true meaning to become clear.'

'It's the destiny of men, Laerte,' continued Aladzio, suddenly excited. 'The legend of the monk in the Tower of Fangol, who heard the voices of the gods murmuring the destiny of humanity! For thirty days and thirty nights, he wrote it all down. Thirty days and thirty nights without food, without rest, until he died ... I still don't understand it all, but ...'

'But what?' said Laerte angrily, pressing up against the inventor. 'Have you decoded it? What do the Azdekis want? Tell me. Talk about that, and only that, Aladzio.'

'I haven't decoded it yet,' Aladzio immediately replied. 'It's complex. I've seen things in it, yes, that could be related to past events, or could be warnings about things to come. But how to be sure of that? And—'

'They want to overthrow the Republic,' de Page suddenly cut in.

The duke leaned on the armrests of his chair and slowly stood up.

'They created it but they can no longer control it. The Order of Fangol is losing its legitimacy, they're being supplanted by other beliefs. Nothing is turning out as they planned. Azdeki dreamt of being a saviour; the people's chosen one. He has always hoped to find a glorious destiny laid out for him in the Sacred Book. He wants to reveal that he possesses the *Liaber Dest*, and now that Aladzio has started to decode it, it has become a matter of time before he is capable of reading it ... and understanding the gods.'

Without even glancing towards Laerte and Aladzio, he carefully adjusted the sleeves of his shirt.

'Think of the Azdekis, Rhunstag, Enain-Cassart, all those who had lost faith in the Reyes dynasty. When your father revealed the pact between your family and the Reyes Emperors – keeping the *Liaber Dest* secret for so long, and ensuring a Reyes always led the Order of Fangol – they had no doubt what needed to be done. They have always believed that the *Liaber Dest* holds the destiny of humanity and that the Order of Fangol is the sole guarantor of respect for that tradition. But now that they have founded the Republic, they have discovered it is leaning dangerously towards beliefs and ideas that do not suit them at all. They don't simply want the power to make decisions. They want the power to shape a world in their image, as the Reyes and Usters did. Do you see, Laerte?'

De Page gave him an even smile.

'We have common interests. Before we act, I need to be sure I have all the cards in my hand. At this very moment, Azdeki is preparing his advent. I need to know who is ready to follow him and I know where we can find them. To satisfy his pride, he wants to associate this moment with his son's wedding. A great new dynasty will supplant the Republic, with the support of the gods and an Order of Fangol more powerful than ever. Your father's dream will be swept away once the Azdekis have no further use for it.'

'No,' said Laerte in a murmur. 'Never.'

'No. We will prevent this from happening.'

'When?'

Laerte's voice cracked like a whip.

'In a year's time,' announced de Page. 'At Masalia, during Masque Night. After the wedding of his son.'

'During Masque Night.'

'After the wedding ...'

The wedding ... When he had told Laerte this, de Page must have known who the happy bride was. His silence was no doubt intended to prevent Laerte from attending the ceremony. In vain. A year later, the cathedral bells were pealing. And a man advanced slowly through the crowd, his face hidden by the shadow of his hood. Laerte made his way forward without anyone noticing him. His discretion was equal to his rage: they were both complete. He weaved through the costumed guests under the very noses of the guards on duty and entered the cathedral.

The bells pealed, while Laerte's broken heart quivered and jumped in his chest.

The bells pealed and, in the house, they sounded like a death-knell to Viola. If Laerte revealed himself before Masque Night began, all would be lost.

12

THE CHOICE

I did not doubt, no!
I never doubted the *Liaber Dest*,
But it had been thus for centuries.
To the Usters the Book, to us the Sword.

The great stained-glass windows lining the nave split the sunlight into a hundreds of multi-coloured rays. They landed on the tiled floor, caressed the edges of the varnished pews and enhanced the fine fabrics worn by the guests.

From deep purple velvet to the leafy green of their jackets, from azure blue to the pure white of their ceremonial robes, all of Republican high society was on display in Masalia's cathedral. Perched on the wooden beams crossing thirty feet above the floor, and nestled along the cornices, turtledoves fluttered their wings, indifferent to the strange spectacle taking place before their eyes. They might have been the only beings to see the anomalous silhouette with a hood thrown over its slightly bowed head.

Laerte slipped among the crowd so discreetly that his presence barely registered. He insinuated himself between the guests, barely brushing against them and keeping a watchful eye on the soldiers posted by the towering columns.

Against one of the nave walls rose the statue of a woman, with a simple drape covering her breasts, and one hand lifted towards the heavens. She was only the first in a long series of sculptures, all of them the same height, but more importantly the only one Laerte could reach stealthily. Once he had broken clear of the human tide that continued to enter the cathedral, slipped behind the base of the statue. He silently climbed the giant figure's back and, once he arrived upon the woman's shoulder, he checked that no one was looking in his direction. Reassured, he used the *animus* to propel himself to her raised hand with a simple thrust. From there he made an impeccable leap to seize the edge of the cornice, his legs hanging in empty space.

The turtledoves flapped their wings loudly. Some of the spectators even looked up.

But none of them saw the silhouette that was effortlessly hoisting itself onto the ledge. Laerte crouched, one hand on the hilt of his sword. This was an ideal vantage point. A few yards away, in the cathedral's choir, stood a stone altar, partially covered by a red and gold cloth. At its centre two chalices were being filled with clear water by a holy man wearing a long mauve robe and wearing a hat decorated with an oak leaf. Men at arms stood nearby.

Laerte recognised Etienne Azdeki, his shining armour bearing the emblem of his family: an eagle holding a snake in its talons. Not far from him, seated upon one of the first pews, the shapeless mass of his uncle shuddered with each of his snores. A young man came up to whisper something in his ear, rousing him from his sleep.

Live, Laerte thought, *enjoy yourselves and laugh while you still can ... Soon you will receive the punishment you deserve.*

He looked for another knight present who might have Azdeki blood running in his veins: someone with a gaunt face and an aquiline nose, ugly and arrogant-looking. But he found no one who matched the image he'd invented for Balian Azdeki.

Once everyone had found their place within the cathedral and a path had formed from the open doors to the altar, the holy man lifted his arms towards the ceiling. Laerte retreated into the shadow of the cornice, placing one knee upon the ledge.

'High councillors, family members, friends and dignitaries of Masalia, we welcome today the heart of our young and very dear Republic ...' the holy man proclaimed. 'We are gathered here beneath the gaze of the gods to bind the destinies of two fine young people.'

At last Laerte spotted him. The holy man had given one of the young knights standing on the altar steps an obsequious smile. The breastplate of his armour did not bear a family coat-of-arms but nevertheless stood out from the others, being shinier and lighter in colour, and there was silver embroidery on his epaulettes. He had blond hair, cut fairly short, and his face was barely marked by any signs of active duty as a soldier. He must have spent the war years confined to the family castle in the Vershan region. There was a hint of anxiety mixed with excitement in his expression, a joy that lit his face. He stood with a proud bearing, the focus of every gaze here in the temple.

There was something about him that reminded Laerte of Iago, the son of Captain Meurnau in the Saltmarsh ... the one Esyld wouldn't stop speaking about before the war broke out. Laerte tensed as he knelt on the cornice ledge, his hand gripping his sword's hilt.

The cooing of the turtledoves was matched by coughing from several guests as the holy man continued the service. His words rang out through the entire cathedral but Laerte no longer heard them. He stared intently at the blond knight. He noted every detail of his entourage, counted the guards by his side, already imagining pouncing upon his victim while giving him ample opportunity to see his own face. Laerte was determined that the last thing the man who had snatched away his beloved saw before he died should be the very incarnation of wrath. Ah! So he wanted to force her to live with him? He thought she was his slave? His possession? What terrible future did he have in mind for her?

As he envisioned the horror that lay in store for Esyld, he felt an indescribable anger rising; more violent than anything he had known before, a fire that unfurled through his entrails and stirred his entire being to give him an implacable strength.

At that moment he saw her, preceded by four bridesmaids in yellow with long trains gliding behind them. She was wearing a golden gown with a wide ruff rising behind her perfectly curled hair. A diamond sparkled at her neck, just above her corseted bosom, and her face seemed frozen, her eyes avoiding the attention of the crowd. She walked slowly and was followed by a squad of halberdiers, their weapons held upright against their shoulders, wearing conical helmets with leather flaps protecting the back of their necks.

They were forcing her down the aisle, Laerte was certain of it. He must not hesitate, must not let her be subjected to this degrading ceremony. He moved along the cornice, bent over, and then halted, overlooking the altar. How far away was it? Twenty yards or more? When he had been thrown from the Imperial throne room on the evening of the revolution, he had dropped more than forty yards, without using the *animus* to break his fall.

She had reached the altar, and was welcomed there by the usurper.

He offered her his hand, helping her climb the steps to the cushions placed at the feet of the holy man. They both knelt and exchanged a glance.

A single glance.

'Do you love her?'

Of course he loved her. Of course he could not leave her in the hands of these monsters.

'Times have changed. Nothing is the same as it was before.'

'Balian Azdeki, son of Anya Bernevin and of High Councillor Etienne Azdeki, Commander of the Order of the Republic, Count of the Vershan, do you take as your lawfully wedded wife Esyld Orbey, daughter of Alena Angenet and Guy Orbey, here present?

'The wedding will take place before the festivities begin ...'

This would not alter his plan at all. It would not put anything at risk. He was powerful enough to take care of Balian Azdeki without ruining their chances of infiltrating the Palatio. Etienne Azdeki would never postpone the ritual ...

'Yes ... yes, I do,' replied Balian in a voice trembling with emotion.

'I had to forget you, Frog.'

'Tell me you no longer love me!'

'Esyld Orbey, daughter of Alena Angenet and Guy Orbey, do you take as your lawfully wedded husband Balian Azdeki, son of Anya Bernevin and High Councillor Etienne Azdeki ...'

She kept her hand on the knight's. She was squeezing it. Laerte had to act now or never. She loved him, she had said so. Those feelings could never die, they were eternal.

'... Commander of the Order of the Republic ...'

There was a stabbing pain in his heart as a hungry void swelled within him like a famished creature feeding upon his sorrow. It was as if there were nothing else left inside him.

'If you try anything, all we've worked for will be for nothing.'

Viola was just a child, she knew nothing about life, passion, or sacrificing oneself for the sake of another. How could she understand what he was prepared to do for Esyld? He would suddenly appear with his drawn sword, plunge his blade into Balian's throat, get rid of the guards and then melt away into the crowd like a shadow ... just as he had killed the Marquis of Enain-Cassart by the port. As stealthily as the Hand of the Emperor himself. And allow fear to gnaw even more strongly at Etienne Azdeki.

'Tell me you no longer love me!'

He did not believe her answer for a single instant. She had said *'No'* to protect him.

'... Count of the Vershan, here present?'

His heart stopped beating. There was a long silence among the assembly. Not even the turtledoves made a sound. In the sunlight tinted by the stained glass of the cathedral's choir Esyld's face seemed to harden. Her eyes grew misty with tears.

'No ... say no,' murmured Laerte. 'Say no, I beg you.'

He stooped down on the cornice, quietly drawing his sword from its scabbard. By the altar the holy man seemed embarrassed, darting a few worried glances towards Etienne Azdeki and his uncle. He asked again:

'Esyld Orbey, daughter of Alena Angenet and Guy Orbey, do you take as your lawfully wedded husband Balian Azdeki here present?'

'No,' urged Laerte.

Fits of coughing echoed around the choir. Coughing due to the fatigue of aged throats, as well as the awkwardness caused by the silence.

'Say no ... No ...'

She raised her eyes towards the holy man, on the edge of tears. And yet ...

She was smiling, radiant.

No! She was being forced to marry, this couldn't be of her own free will. The Azdekis manipulated the people around them. Why would Balian be any different? How could she possibly love him? Laerte seethed on his ledge.

'Yes,' she replied at last in a low breath. 'Yes, I do.'

And the entire cathedral was swept by an immense sigh of relief, preceding a salvo of applause.

'I hereby declare you united by the bonds of matrimony in the eyes of the gods and the Republic they protect,' the holy man announced proudly. 'Drink from the chalice and seal your union.'

'Things change. People change. This world is no longer at war, Laerte!'

How could she kiss him so tenderly? How could she leave her hand upon his cheek as if she wanted to press him against her? The image of their two naked bodies suddenly sprang into Laerte's head. He retreated to the very rear of the cornice, his heart filled with rage. He could not help seeing the two of them entwined, nestled against one another, caught up in their passion ... her skin against his, her lips against his, and her heart belonging to him ...

'I am at war!'

He sat down, folding his legs against himself and, like a child, hugging them in his arms. He struggled to breathe as he fought his overwhelming urge to leap upon Balian, skin him alive, strike him down, destroy him, slice off the lips that had kissed Esyld's body, sever the hands that had caressed her curves, plunge his fist into the young knight's chest and tear out his heart before reducing it to shreds.

Yet he had seen Esyld looking so beautiful, so happy. She hadn't lied to him. Things changed. After so many years ... she had grown apart from him, however firmly he believed such a thing was impossible. When he could have stayed at her side, he had gone off to war with Dun-Cadal, obsessed by his longing for revenge. He remained where he was, grief-stricken, during the rest of the ceremony. The religious hymns followed one another, and the bells pealed again when the bride and groom presented themselves on the front porch of the cathedral to be greeted by the crowd gathered outside. When Laerte was alone in the nave at last, he let himself slip down the statue and left through a small side door. Skirting around the people cheering beneath a rain of confetti and streamers in a thousand different colours, his gaze sought out the newly married couple. In the bright sunshine, they greeted all of Masalia who had turned out to share their happiness. They were smiling, moved by the crowd's response.

Laerte crept away, leaving part of his life behind him. Here their paths had definitely parted ways. Things had changed indeed.

'We need to finish matters here,' he said, standing on the threshold of the front door.

In the salon, all three looked up at him gravely: Rogant seated on the divan, Viola on the bottom steps of the staircase, and Dun-Cadal by the kitchen, with a tankard of wine in his hand.

'And ... the wedding?' the young woman asked as Laerte passed in front of her.

Laerte did not reply, crossing the salon briskly. He had no wish to speak of the ceremony, it did not matter any more. He concentrated on their plans instead. In just a few hours they would depart for the Palatio and Dun-Cadal would leave the house in his turn, free and perhaps more at peace, after so many years spent weeping for the loss of Frog. Although it was Laerte who had desired peace when he revealed himself. Perhaps he had even hoped for forgiveness.

Without saying a word the old man had followed him out into the courtyard. Side by side they contemplated the city, exchanging a few tense glances. Before them the rooftops of Masalia had taken on an orange glow. In the distance they could see the port where several three-masters lay at anchor, while on the horizon the sun's reflection cut a dazzling track across a calm sea.

Laerte lowered his eyes towards the tankard that Dun-Cadal was bringing to his lips. He shook his head in resignation. The old man did not seem to be drunk, but how much longer before the alcohol rose to his head? The sound of the wine splashing upon the gravel made Laerte look down again. Dun-Cadal was tilting the tankard to let the contents run out with a distracted air.

'I could drink to our farewell, but I don't really feel any desire to, lad ...'

Laerte simply nodded. With a sad smile Dun-Cadal watched the wine spill down. It was as if he were watching his regrets vanish into the gravel too ... down to the very last drop.

'If I've understood rightly, this evening I'm free to go.'

'A carriage will come fetch you just after we leave,' Laerte said at last in a hoarse voice. 'It will take you wherever you want to go. De Page has agreed to give you enough to live on for another few years.'

'So he's buying me off ... Is that how he does things?' said Dun-Cadal with a scornful laugh. 'He hid his game well.'

Laerte would have liked to tell his mentor what awaited him, to reassure him and know that the old man was serene before he left him for good. The recent hatred he had felt towards him had no deeper cause than discovering him here, lost and addicted to drink. He had learned to love Dun-Cadal after all these years. But he had preserved his memory of a proud general, rather than the filthy shadow of a knight at death's door he now saw before him.

He made an effort to clarify his feelings. Although he still wasn't capable of saying so, he knew what they were. He loved the man.

Laerte hesitated over whether to put a hand on the old man's shoulder.

He did not move. His gaze drifted out again to the city spread below.

'Tell me,' Dun-Cadal asked, and then cleared his throat. 'Tell me: everything will play out at the Palatio, won't it?'

Laerte did not reply.

'He has the *Liaber Dest*, lad,' continued the general, letting his tankard drop.

It smashed on the ground. Through the shards of stoneware, he watched the red wine trickling through the gravel like so many tiny rivers that had decided on their course.

'He holds the destiny of men in his hands.'

'That's a possibility,' admitted Laerte, still looking out at Masalia.

'He does not deserve to possess such power ...'

'That's a certainty.'

'So stop him, son.'

Time seemed to slow in the moment when Laerte finally placed his hand on his former teacher's shoulder. For an instant. Then he drew away to go back inside the house.

'Frog,' Dun-Cadal called out in a muffled voice.

When Laerte turned round, the setting sun wreathed a bright halo around the old warrior's hunched silhouette. Slowly the man recovered his stature and from the sound of his voice, his backlit features in silhouette, Laerte finally saw the general as in his time of glory.

'Have you become who you wanted to be, my boy? Are you a knight ... or an assassin?'

His tone was more confident but it still contained a hint of sadness.

'What's the difference?' asked Laerte, seeming disturbed.

Dun-Cadal took a step forward and the light fell upon his wrinkled face. In his expression there was a calmness quite unlike what had been there before, an air of wisdom that now surrounded him.

'There is a difference, for you and me. The oath, do you remember? We took the oath.'

'We were supposed to serve the Empire,' Laerte replied without animosity.

'It goes much further than that,' asserted Dun-Cadal. 'It's about the path you chose to take. What if you come across Esyld this evening? Will you give in to your anger?'

Laerte grew tense. He did not want to think about that, he did not want to imagine it. He needed to concentrate on his goal. But the mention of her name unleashed a storm within him that he feared he could not master.

'That's what the oath is about, that's the promise you made. Remember it. The path of anger leads to an abyss, for to continue walking it you must constantly feed your anger, and always be looking behind you. Vengeance only calls forth vengeance.'

Dun-Cadal slowly approached him.

'The choice belongs to you ... Laerte of Uster. My son ...'

He made no gesture, he merely looked Laerte straight in the eye.

'I have always been so proud of you.'

He did not wait for any reaction, passing Laerte without adding anything further. In the end it wasn't knowing which choice the boy would make that mattered to him, it was reminding him that a decision was inevitable. Once the general entered the house, Laerte advanced to the edge of the courtyard, admiring the sunset.

'Thrown into the fire, it does not burn ...'

Everything would be decided this evening, everything he had been fighting for, whether it was worth all the sacrifices he had made, deliberately or not ... including losing Esyld to Balian Azdeki.

'Put to the sword, it does not rip.'

'It is made from the murmur of the gods and nothing shall ever destroy it.'

The Sacred Book was unique in that it was indestructible. Aladzio had been able to verify that, it was one of the first things his new master had demonstrated, by throwing the book into a hearth. The flames had licked the cover without blackening the leather, and when Azdeki had removed it, still hot, he had told Aladzio to stab it with a dagger.

The blade had broken.

So it was absolute incontestable truth: the *Liaber Dest* was far more than a mere book. But did that mean, as legend claimed, that it contained the destiny of humanity? de Page, hostile to the Order of Fangol, doubted it. The Azdekis were certain of it. As for Aladzio ...

The inventor was torn between his critical perspective as a scientist and the hope that something greater than mere human reason existed. Although he tried to analyse the world, he would have liked to believe in something superior, something ... *divine* ... and perhaps to find therein something greater than his own intelligence.

In the tangled labyrinth of legends he was exploring he had come to recognise certain myths were true: such as the existence of an ancient tower filled with ancient manuscripts. Based on some enigmatic inscriptions on the very earliest maps of the former Kingdoms, he had managed to narrow down the building's approximate location. But when he had finally been able to go there, full of anticipation, he found nothing but ruins guarded by a disgraced monk called Galapa.

Long ago, Galapa had lived in the Tower of Fangol, the Order's first monastery. But he'd been banished shortly before the Saltmarsh rebellion, sentenced to the thankless task of caring for some ruins that no one in the world cared about. Yet here, beneath its wobbling stones, slumbered the immense storehouse of knowledge Aladzio was searching for, including the first great works produced by the Fangolins – tomes which had later been forgotten when they lost their most eminent representatives. For one aspect of the Fangolin Order had survived Kingdoms and Emperors alike: the art of secrecy.

Aladzio had stayed in the ruined tower to decipher and translate these texts, thereby coming to understand how the Fangolins had recounted history in their own fashion; copying and recopying vague legends until they became accepted as indisputable fact. But it had taken centuries for their official version to outlive dissident voices. And the very earliest written works that Aladzio had discovered preserved liturgies that were markedly different from those practised during the Reyes dynasty.

Throughout the numerous ancient texts dealing with the *Liaber Dest*, Aladzio observed a curious correlation with references to a holy blade. Over the centuries, as references to the blade dwindled, one sentence had been preserved and its meaning was discussed repeatedly: *'In my left hand the Book, in my right hand the Sword, and at my feet the World.'* Over time the Fangolin monks and the more educated members of the nobility all came to agreement about the symbolic nature of this sentence. As the centuries passed, the hypothesis that it might have a more literal sense was dismissed.

'At my feet the World.'

But if it was a real blade, what sword could it be, if not Eraëd? What other blade was as old as the Emperors?

For Aladzio, it became a certainty: one could not exist without the other. If the book was real, so was the sword, and the repetition of an unknown symbol – a rectangle crossed by a straight line – became a reference point for him in every document he consulted. It had taken his discovery of a codex, written in the ancient Gueyle script, to make the meaning of this drawing clear to him.

The codex allowed Aladzio read between the lines. To learn the origins of the Book and the Sword. To uncover the truth: that the sole purpose of the blade was the destruction of the book.

Driven by their obsession with finding their destiny in the pages of the *Liaber Dest*, and ignorant of the Fangolian's lost knowledge, the Azdekis had forgotten about the sword of the Emperors. All that mattered to them was having proof that they were indispensable to the smooth running of the world. If they had founded the Republic, if they had sought to improve the lot of the common people, it was because something dark and mysterious had been feeding their ambitions since the Empire fell. Something mystical. Faith.

The Book might not give the Azdekis the key to the destiny of men, but it would at least instil respect for them in believers, as well as fear in those who doubted. For the Azdekis would be in possession of the mythical *Liaber Dest* itself, once thought lost for eternity. They had already earned admiration for overthrowing a tyrant and creating a more just Republic. Henceforth they would also have the gods' support. But there was a flaw in their plans. A pact whose significance they had overlooked, a secret known only to a few and quietly passed down through the ages, one designed to preserve the balance of power: to the Usters the Book, to the Reyes the Sword.

The Book and the Sword were linked. True power required possessing them both.

'It's ironic, don't you think?'

The torches in the tower's cellar created a curious interplay of shadows and light that ran across the councillor's smooth face. De Page leaned on the long wooden table with both hands, his eyes sweeping over the open books.

'That he should be in Masalia ...'

'The sword is with him,' said Laerte, leaning against the wall near the alcove.

De Page lifted his chin.

'I think so too,' he agreed with a nod. 'This ... Dun ...'

He could not help smiling and raising an eyebrow, but he ran aground on Laerte's expressionless face.

'He wouldn't have hidden it anywhere but close by him. He's having a laugh, sending people off to the cold Vershan mountains while he enjoys Masalia's sunshine.'

De Page paused.

'"The city of all possible things" . . . It hasn't usurped its nickname. What are your feelings for him?'

'He doesn't mean anything to me, de Page. He won't be an obstacle. He'll talk, I know him.'

The duke straightened up with a sigh, abandoning his cordial manner.

'We won't have any margin for error. Not even once. Aladzio is en route for Masalia to prepare for Masque Night, upon the Azdekis' orders. He has obtained powder for the fireworks in rather greater quantities than necessary. Certain councillors are about to set sail. At the port, you—'

'I shall satisfy myself with Enain-Cassart,' Laerte interrupted him coldly.

'Leave Etienne Azdeki for last, that's important.'

'I drew this plan up with you, de Page. Are you having doubts about me now?'

For the first time, the duke was unable to conceal his anxiety. His usual serenity and self-control had vanished. Where Laerte was concerned, he was no longer in command. They were going ahead with this mission side by side, as equals.

'No, I have no doubts about you.'

'Why?' Laerte asked suddenly.

'Wh-why what?' stammered de Page.

'I want to know your motives before leaving for Masalia. You know what drives me. Are you really acting for the sake of the Republic as you claim? Is that what you're fighting for?'

'I've already told you. They plan to—'

'Why?' Laerte asked again quietly.

Since the fall of the Empire, de Page had treated Laerte with kid gloves, providing him with information, deductions and the premises of their plan, but only as the duke saw fit. Now that Masque Night was only a few months away and the warmth of spring was bringing the land back to life, Laerte wanted to be certain he was not simply a weapon in the duke's hands. De Page's mistrust of the Azdekis was matched by Laerte's own anger, to be sure, but what would happen when their mission was completed?

'It is essential that neither you nor I are seen as having any part in the forthcoming events—'

'You haven't answered my question,' Laerte cut him short.

'If I can't find out who Azdeki has rallied to his cause, I won't be able to distinguish our enemies from simple councillors. We need to identify those who are prepared to destroy your father's dream out of religious piety, and give the Order of Fangol power it does not deserve. They believe the gods have everything. It goes against the very idea of a Republic where men choose which path to take. They will proclaim themselves as the elect, not of the people, but of the gods. And since the people are fearful, and have doubts, they will listen to our opponents and make them new—'

'Why?' Laerte repeated in a murmur.

'Because destiny isn't written!' cried de Page. 'Anyone who disagrees with them will end up hung or burnt at the stake. It will be done in the names of the gods, without any regard for humanity.'

The duke pounded his fist upon the table and then, bewildered by his own anger, ran his hands through his hair, his jaws clenched. Laerte was still, studying him with a suspicious gaze. De Page came round the table to confront him.

'What do you want to hear? That my father used to beat me because he saw in me the degeneration of his entire lineage? How he called me to his deathbed so he could mock me? He laughed at me, Laerte.'

He spoke coldly, keeping his eyes fixed on the young knight.

'Or I could take of my shirt to show you the scars of the lash upon my back when he sought to drive a demon out of my body,' de Page proposed. 'We've all suffered, Laerte, all of us. We all bear our wounds and they remind us how necessary it is to act. The Order of Fangol used to hang people like me and if Azdeki achieves his ends, the monks will make their presence felt once again, believe me. There will be no more freedom to choose, they will claim that everything is already written, that everything is immutable, that nothing they don't accept can be permitted to survive. I'm not just fighting for the Republic or to satisfy your vengeance, no ...'

He took another step forward and, nose to nose, he seized the back of Laerte's neck. The young man felt the duke's breath upon his face but did not make the slightest movement.

'Everything is a question of faith, Laerte. Everything is a question of the meaning that one gives to one's acts, of their symbolic importance. I do not believe that the destiny of men is to be found in the Book. One day we will learn how and for whom it was written, why the sword was forged along with it, and what gives them this ... indestructibility. But, we have this chance, Laerte, this magnificent chance Aladzio has offered us, and to us alone, to reveal the power of the sword. I shall seize this chance. And we will take care of the Book, ensure no ever claims it is divine again. We are only on the first step, my friend. My faith lies in democracy. In mankind, not in the tyranny of gods who set our fates and then wandered away.'

Laerte lowered his eyes.

'Is that what you wanted to hear?'

'Wherever he is, your father must be kicking himself for revealing the secret to you,' whispered Laerte.

De Page hesitated for a moment before a chuckle escaped from his pinched lips. Then he moved away, still laughing.

'Indeed,' he admitted. 'He never suspected that I might be one of his most dangerous opponents. Just as Azdeki—'

He reached a half-open trunk and lifted the lid with a yank.

'—has no idea about the ghost which is going to haunt him,' he concluded in a murmur.

Laerte slowly walked over to his side, one hand on the pommel of his sword. De Page had not forgotten his request; he had found it and brought it back. It had passed from hand to hand, like a vestige of the Empire saved by nostalgic servants, until the duke had paid a fortune for it in an antique shop. At the bottom of the trunk lay a green cape and, on top of it, the broken mask of the last Emperor.

Laerte looked at it with tightened jaw and his stomach in knots. He would wear it. He had to wear it, whatever it might cost him. His vengeance required it, for it could not be satisfied with simple assassinations. He wanted each traitor who had destroyed his family to feel fear grip and then choke them. They would each be forced to confront their past, their vile acts, and not one would know peace when Laerte ended their lives. He would hunt them down, just as he had been hunted in the Saltmarsh. He would play on their nerves and goad their consciences.

'Don't get carried away. Just Enain-Cassart and Negus,' de Page reminded him as he reached down to pick up the mask. 'Azdeki will not postpone his great moment, your goal is to scare him so that he acts accordingly. Keep them guessing ...'

The glow of the torches drew forth golden reflections from the mask de Page held out to him.

'We're all set now, Laerte.'

He would humiliate Etienne Azdeki in front of his supporters and then he would kill him. For the Book was not indestructible, not against this rapier forged from some unknown metal.

'And when the moment comes, plant the sword in the *Liaber Dest* so that no one will ever see it as anything more than a book. Just an ordinary book. Everthing is in place.'

And so there he was, in place, just a few feet from the big square in front of the Palatio, hidden in the shadow of an alley.

There was a big crowd on the streets as the evening began, men and women in carnival costumes wearing a wide variety of masks: smiling faces or expressionless, plain or multi-coloured, decorated with peacock feathers or golden trimmings ... All of it shiny, superficial and self-satisfied. Fire-eaters breathed tall flames, jugglers entertained bystanders, and musicians tapped their feet, their fingers plucking the strings of mandolins. Pennants and ribbons fluttered over the heads of laughing children. Couples exchanged a kiss and the stars appeared in the dark blue of dusk. And behind the bulging Palatio roof a pale moon was rising.

Laerte pulled the hood over his head, hiding the top of his golden mask in shadow and then left his position. He knew the Palatio doors would be heavily guarded on all sides. There was only one that interested him, located at the foot of the gardens where he was certain there would be no onlookers. Everyone preferred to stroll up and down the big avenues in their colourful outfits, playing drums, drinking and laughing. And the echo of their revelling could be heard all around the palace.

There were five soldiers, two of them posted to either side of the small door leading to a stairway lit by torches. Behind them rose the tall wall surrounding the garden, but the street was enveloped in darkness. They heard his footsteps before they saw the gleam of the mask or the crack running across it.

When one of them ordered Laerte to halt, he obeyed, placing a hand on the pommel of his sword. Gripping his halberd, the guard who had spoken approached him, quickly followed by another member of his team. Behind them, coming down the steps, other soldiers arrived. Soon there were ten in total.

'Don't move!'

'The mask ... it's him!'

'It's the assassin!'

Laerte gripped his sword but did not draw it. He didn't move an inch as he heard blades piercing the coats of mail, the death rattle of the soldiers smothered by the hands of men they believed were their team-mates.

'We're all set, Laerte.'

One by one they fell. And then there were only four soldiers, all of whom accompanied Laerte into the heart of the Palatio.

13

THE MURMUR OF THE GODS

For you, I will be more than a murmur.
I will be a cry.

Tugging on the leather reins, Rogant slowed the horses pulling the barrel-laden cart. He walked over the dimly lit bridge. Before him rose the Palatio's imposing dome and, at the foot of the building, he saw some halberdiers supervising the unloading of other carts bearing produce, with a great deal of shouting. As he drove up, several guards eyed him but none showed signs of any particular wariness. Other Nâaga were carrying cases of drink inside.

'What's this?' bawled a soldier approaching his cart.

'Wine,' replied Rogant curtly.

If his manner was off-putting it was meant to avoid attention. The Nâaga were not known for being sociable and the soldier responded to his surly attitude with a weary headshake. Giving him a thumbs-up he directed Rogant towards the wide-open doors of a warehouse filled with victuals. Inside, servants were busy sorting the supplies before carrying them through a swinging door. Flicking his wrist, Rogant slapped the horses' croups with the reins. Although a few of the domestic staff on duty were of other origins, Rogant noted with a certain sadness that most belonged to his own people, who were given the most arduous tasks despite the obvious frailness of some. Not all Nâaga were as massively built as Rogant.

Once he entered the warehouse they started to unload the barrels without waiting for Rogant to descend from the cart. But two guards were quick to interrupt the operation.

'What's in this load?' asked one with a red cross upon his breastplate.

Climbing down, Rogant stared at him in silence. The Nâaga was more than a head taller, but the soldier, senior in rank by the look of him, was not intimidated. His partner, on the other hand, avoided Rogant's gaze and seemed uneasy, keeping a hand close to the sword hanging from his belt.

'I said: what's in this load?' insisted the first soldier, stressing each word.

'Everything has been delivered already,' noted his partner.

'The caterers are already setting up the buffets and nobody said anything about more wine!' the first said angrily. 'Who sent you?'

Around them the Nâaga were setting the barrels on the ground, not knowing whether they should carry on or turn to some other task.

'Who sent you?' repeated the soldier, becoming more and more aggressive. 'Are you on the list?'

'An oversight on my part,' said a breathless voice.

Aladzio's tricorne appeared behind the two soldiers.

They did not require any further convincing. The inventor was a well-known figure here and moreover had a sizeable escort. Rogant accompanied him without having to justify himself and the cart was unloaded. The silent Nâaga followed them, supporting the barrels on their shoulders with bare arms covered in strange tattoos.

'You weren't going to answer him … too forcefully, I trust?' asked Aladzio in a hushed tone, looking worried.

Rogant gave him a mean-looking smile in reply. The clichés about his people lingered, even with an enlightened man like the inventor. Weary of being constantly offended, Rogant preferred to make light of them.

'Where do you want them, exactly?' he asked when they arrived at a large inner courtyard surrounded by balconies bedecked with flowers.

Here and there colourful festoons decorated the hedges standing in the middle of the grass bed, running between the balconies and twisting around the marble columns from which awnings had been stretched. On either side of the courtyard, double doors gave access to the Palatio's interior where staff in blue-and-black livery were coming and going. Workers laid out trestles and tables, plates and cutlery, and barrels of wine equipped with wooden spigots.

Aladzio nodded towards a platform where servants were already hoisting some reserve barrels into place.

'Pile them up over there.'

Rogant clapped his hands and his people hastened towards the platform to deposit their barrels. Aladzio advanced into the courtyard and then, lifting the tip of his hat and turning slowly around, he looked up at the balconies.

'I filled them correctly,' he assured Rogant when the Nâaga joined him. He offered an embarrassed smile, rubbing his hands nervously.

'I don't doubt that for a second,' Rogant replied calmly.

'Ah? Because I do, a little, when all is said and done,' Aladzio declared suddenly.

He raised his eyes towards the nearest balcony, imagining Laerte's silhouette lurking behind one of the columns.

'We'll know for sure soon enough,' he said, resigned to it. 'Either there's just enough to create a diversion or we'll all go up in smoke. Nothing to worry about!'

He patted the Nâaga's shoulder before moving away.

'Wonderful . . .' sighed Rogant.

The guards' boots clattered across the corridor. The four soldiers advanced in a mechanical fashion, as though they were so used to taking this route that they no longer marvelled at the magnificent red wall hangings brightly lit by the oil lamps. On this festive evening they bore their frustration silently as they marched back and forth, mentally cursing their patrol leader for assigning them to this part of the Palatio and denying them the possibility of seeing all the costumed guests. They kept their hands on the pommels of their swords, but did not expect any call to draw them forth. Although two murders had been committed during the course of the preceding days, it was unlikely another crime would be perpetrated in this place. Especially when their own numbers had been doubled at the last minute.

The three men coming towards them were part of these reinforcements, wearing leather chest protectors and armed with plain swords, plus bows slung over their shoulders. Their kit seemed rather dull next to the bright armour sported by the Palatio's regular soldiers, but the extra troops reassured the dignitaries. They'd been assigned to watch only areas forbidden to the public, where no one except the regular guards would look askance at their appearance.

They saluted with wordless nods of the head, when a caped figure appeared at the end of the corridor. A golden mask shone beneath its hood and its left hand gripped the hilt of a sword.

The regular guards had no time to react, blades piercing their backs and punching out through their breastplates. With firm hands the mercenaries slit their victims' throats before assisting their fall and depositing them gently upon the tiled floor. Laerte stepped over the dead bodies silently. He beckoned the soldiers of fortune to follow him.

'Did you have a pleasant journey?' asked Viola.

Taking her outstretched hand, the duke descended nimbly from the running board, leaving the quiet of the coach for the hubbub of the big square before the Palatio. The disgust he felt when he saw a rivulet of urine running between the cobblestones remained hidden behind the wild boar's mask covering his face. Not far from them a squad of guards were berating a man who struggled to raise his trousers, his balance unsteady, in front of a bed of flowers.

'The festivities have already begun, it seems,' remarked de Page.

People thronged to the square, merry and colourful, all of them dressed in strange costumes which varied from the most refined to the most patched together, wearing masks that were elaborate or made of mere paper. Only eyes could be seen, only words counted, appearance meant nothing. Masque Night had always been thus, an ancient celebration which the Republic had adopted as a national event. Feigning equality for a single evening, it allowed the citizens to forget their origins; the most exalted noble sitting beside the humble artisan, the wealthy man drinking with the pauper, their differences hidden. This year, at the invitation of Councillor Azdeki, most of the dignitaries in Emeris had made the trip to Masalia and the southern port city thus found itself hosting a Masque Night of unusual significance.

Flutes and mandolins accompanied singers offering a one-night performance. Roars of laughter ran through the crowd. Bodies entwined without any sense of modesty, exchanging kisses and caresses beneath the amused gaze of onlookers.

'We left the house just as you asked,' Viola told the duke, tucking her hand into the crook of his elbow.

De Page gave her a smile that she only saw in the crinkling of his eyes. He seemed to be devouring her with his gaze and she could not disguise the blush that spread across her cheeks. A mask hid the upper part of her face, with plumes rising along her brow to curve back over her braided hair. Her low-cut dress the same blue as the sky at twilight and the gauzy fabric revealed her thighs with every step she took.

'Although it cost me some,' muttered de Page, 'Dun will give us no cause for concern. He is taken care of. That matter is closed.'

'The main thing was the item he held. I don't think Laer—'

'Don't defend him,' the duke replied brusquely. 'Choosing to reveal himself to the old man, without warning me, is something we will settle later. For now, let's look happy, Viola Aguirre.'

They traversed the crowd, presented their invitations to the guards and were then escorted to the front steps of the Palatio, whose domed roof was illuminated by a thousand torches. Overhead, the moon grew brighter and brighter and the stars began to twinkle shyly. They entered the palace, discovering its sumptuous décor of marble and ancient tapestries whose beauty was enhanced in the warm light shed by torches and oil lamps. They were led to an immense ballroom decorated with wall hangings and crystal chandeliers, imposing statues and paintings by master artists. Two wide stairways descended from the floor above, each of them forming a perfect curve. And above it all, rising from a height of thirty feet, the Palatio's dome covered the room with a martial painting, including the depiction of a semi-nude woman planting a spear in the heart of a misshapen Emperor.

There they all were, in their finest attire, with masks subtly fitted to their faces, as they laughed, chatted, bellowed and drank blood-red wine from silver goblets. They stuffed themselves at the gargantuan buffet set up around the edge of a great indoor fountain from which rose a statue of a bearded colossus. De Page had no trouble recognising the councillors he had grown accustomed to debating with in the assembly, but which of them stood ready to join Etienne Azdeki's cause? There was Rhunstag with his wife, both of them wearing bear masks. He had proudly draped one of his ever-present animal hides across his shoulders. Not far from them, conversing with four other councillors, Bernevin had chosen a simple domino mask combined with his usual statesman's toga. But the person who drew de Page's closest attention wore an eagle's head, its sharp beak casting a slight shadow over his thin lips and clean shaven chin. A black mantle with a silver belt fell to his mid-thighs and from his waist hung a slender sword in a scabbard set with precious stones.

He felt Viola lean against him when Azdeki caught sight of them and made his way through the crowd to greet them.

'What a surprise to see you here,' said Azdeki in a grating tone.

'You recognise me? Have I chosen my camouflage so poorly?' the duke replied playfully.

'On the contrary, your mask is a near-perfect reflection of yourself ... But I would have thought you preferred the capital's climate to our stifling southern heat.'

'I thought accepting your invitation was the polite thing to do, dear Councillor Azdeki. Your son's wedding is a major event in our fair Republic.'

Azdeki nodded, his eyes narrowing behind the eagle mask. Finally he turned his head to look at Viola.

'And this must be the first time I've seen you with a woman.'

'Oooh, let's not be fooled by appearances,' murmured de Page with unfeigned pleasure. 'On Masque Night we are all free to adopt the image we choose. Even a weak man can pretend to be powerful, don't you think? It's only the following morning we realise what an illusion it all was. But perhaps I'm being rude; you're not the type to let yourself be deluded by illusions.'

'No,' replied Azdeki shortly. 'But you, perhaps?'

'Me?' asked de Page in surprise, pressing a hand against his chest. 'No, let's forget our disagreements in the assembly. We both serve the Republic, which is at least one point we have in common. Let us respect one another this evening; it might be our last upon this earth. I was sorry to hear a killer has struck in Masalia ... Poor Enain-Cassart, poor Negus.'

'The work of a madman who will do no more harm,' Azdeki assured him firmly.

'You have doubled the guard, I'm told. I'm not worried, but ... wasn't it difficult to find trustworthy men to ensure our safety here?'

'Are you calling my competence into question in such matters, honourable councillor?' Azdeki asked with a menacing smile.

'Not in the least. I simply don't dare imagine the difficulties involved, to requisition additional guards for the Palatio without stripping the city of its protection. So I concluded that you must have done some ... recruiting.'

'I did what was needed, de Page. Have no fear for our security. Whatever you may have heard about this assassin ... or on any other subject,' Azdeki said slowly, tilting his head towards the duke in a threatening fashion.

'Oh, there are always rumours flying about, and you know me. Sometimes, I worry over trifles.'

'You are cleverer than you let on,' Azdeki admitted grudgingly. 'Is there something you would like to say to me, de Page? Any questions about something you might have heard in the corridors of Emeris? Fears for your own safety, perhaps?'

'No, no, no. Nothing like that. I don't imagine for a single instant that you're hiding anything from us. And of course you'll be able to protect us from this assassin. Accept my apologies; I had no intention of offending you. This evening, above all.'

'Then, if you will excuse me, I have other guests I must attend to.'

'Of course, of course,' de Page agreed. 'I will go and do what I do best, then, in the company of my lady. Get drunk and indulge in pleasure.'

'To the first, I don't doubt it for a second,' Azdeki said mockingly, turning to Viola. 'But as for the second, my lady, I fear you may be disappointed.'

'Ho-ho, what wit,' de Page acknowledged as Azdeki gave a bow.

The councillor disappeared into the crowd with a hurried step and the pressure on de Page's arm immediately lessened. Looking at Viola, he could see she was as pale as snow beneath her mask.

'You had to defy him, you just couldn't help yourself,' she accused.

'So what?' he replied, looking amused. 'Azdeki isn't an idiot. It's taken him some time, but he's realised this is not the only evening when I wear a mask. We who work in the shadows recognise one another. He won't back down because of a few veiled threats. Relax.'

'I am relaxed!' she protested, sounding hurt. 'Although if you enjoyed your verbal duels a little less, I would be more so.'

The buzzing of the crowd covered the councillor's quiet chuckle. The festivities were fully underway now. At the Palatio gates, a line of halberdiers kept the curious onlookers back, while in the square the people laughed and danced to the rhythm of flute players.

Everything was dark and silent near the staircase. Only the floorboards creaking beneath his feet proved that he was still alive.

Moonlight passed through the dirty windows looking out on the alley, casting long rectangles on the dusty wood. He was alone, he was weary, and he sat down on the stairs. Then he joined his hands upon his knees, trembling. He awaited death, certain that neither Laerte nor de Page would honour their promise to let him leave.

He might have fled. He could have left this house.

But he had come to terms with his situation. Wherever he went he would take his pain with him. So when he heard the wheels of the coach and the sound of hooves on the cobblestones he felt at peace. Soon it would all be over. The snap of the reins was followed by the snorting of the horses and footsteps. He balled his fists when the door handle turned.

The front door slowly opened, letting the light from oil lamps enter. He closed his eyes and straightened up. There in the doorway was the silhouette of a woman wearing a long violet dress with an ample hood over her head.

'Dun-Cadal,' she said.

He had already recognised her from her lavender scent. His hand placed upon the railing, he descended the stairs, feeling both surprised and disappointed. He had been waiting for death, but it was Mildrel who came to find him.

She lowered her hood before entering, revealing her calm face. Her eyes, outlined in black, inspected him without her saying a word and, imagining what she might be thinking of his state, he remained silent too. How wrong he had been ... Laerte had kept his word. The lad still cared about him after all.

'So, how do I look?' he asked weakly.

She hesitated ... then gave him a sad smile.

'Still as old as ever, despite all the news?'

He let out a wheezing laugh, nodding nervously. His eyes caught the dark patches dotting his hand on the railing. He let it fall to his side.

'You know then,' he realised.

'I know. Frog ...'

'Yes?'

'He survived. That he's here. And that he asked me to take care of you. That's all. That's more than enough for me. They gave me money, enough for both of us to leave Masalia—'

'Who did?'

'de Page.'

He nodded gloomily.

'This doesn't concern us any more, Dun-Cadal,' she argued as she came closer to him. 'The affairs of the Republic are none of our business. We're from a different time.'

Her black-gloved hands slid over his and, instinctively, he looked down. How slender her fingers were, how lost they looked resting upon his wide, age-marked hands. It seemed so long ago, the days when he went to find her in a richly furnished chamber within the Imperial palace, having just returned from battle, his body still dirty from a long ride on horseback. Their past life seemed to have only existed in a dream.

'I wandered for a long time before coming to Masalia,' he confessed, his throat dry, his eyes fixed on their hands as their fingers intertwined. 'I didn't know where to go, I was looking for something. Looking for answers. And then, here, I gave up . . .'

'Answers to what?'

'About who I am, why I failed,' he answered in a low breath. 'A meaning to it all. Why did the gods write such a destiny for us? Am I merely a murmur? And now that . . .'

He was about to mention the *Liaber Dest*, explain to her his fear that his whole life was reduced there to a single sentence, but de Page had surely refrained from telling her anything about the Book. Dun-Cadal stifled a nervous laugh.

'You had settled down here,' he said, 'you took me in, you tried to protect me from myself. Without much success, but you were always there for me.'

At last he dared to look her straight in the eye and saw something he'd thought he'd never wanted to see again: the blaze of love when she looked at him, an unstinting, unending love, capable of bending without ever breaking. So what now? She deserved to have him take care of her for once. They could flee, leave all this behind. As she said: these affairs of the Republic did not concern them.

'He's grown up, you know? He's a man . . .'

His thin smile faded.

'And he still has scores to settle with Azdeki—'

'The less we know, the better off we'll be, Dun-Cadal,' she said. She was begging him not to continue.

'Mildrel . . .'

He held her gaze, lifting their hands to shoulder height, then drew closer to her. He could smell her lavender scent, but this time it did not soothe him. He nestled against her, hoping to drive away the sadness that weighed down his heart.

'We should leave. Come with me,' Mildred urged. 'Let's forget all this. Forget the Republic and its business, forget the Empire, and just live, the two of us. That's what you want, isn't it?'

'Yes ...' he murmured.

Mildrel drew away from him, retreating before him, stretching her arms out before letting go of his hands. She was smiling too, but it was a knowing smile, grave and bitter. It was as if she were resigning herself to the inevitable.

'Will you come with me?'

'Yes,' he repeated, disconcerted.

He looked away from her, seeking something in the darkness of house that might remove the thoughts going through his mind. But there was nothing that could help dispel this awful feeling that he was giving up.

'No,' he corrected himself.

He paused, hoping Mildrel would get angry and force him to leave the house, climb into the carriage and leave Masalia with her. She remained mute.

'He's going to the Palatio,' he said in an oddly calm voice, 'he plans to assassinate Azdeki.'

'And you're afraid he won't succeed,' she said simply.

'I'm afraid that someone will stop him, will make him lose his nerve, will ...'

He did not dare draw closer to Mildrel but at least he was brave enough to meet her gaze.

'He needs me.'

There was no reproach in her eyes, nor any trace of anger, barely even a hint of sadness. She nodded.

'I don't know if I've always feared it ... or if I've always known it,' she acknowledged before tilting her head to look back over her shoulder. 'Coachman! The trunk!'

Out in the street he could see a man's hunched silhouette. There was the sound of ropes being released and then some panting accompanied by a dull thump. Finally he appeared on the doorstep, dragging a worn-looking trunk closed with a brass hasp behind him.

He was wearing a tailcoat that was filthy with dust and had bushy ash-coloured hair and an expressionless face. He slid the trunk between Mildrel and the general.

'Thank you,' she said without giving the man a glance.

With a wave of his hand the coachman gave Dun-Cadal a timid salute, then returned to his carriage.

'Your things?' asked Dun-Cadal.

'I didn't pack them,' she confessed.

Hesitantly, he approached the trunk. So she never had any intention of leaving Masalia. But what then had she brought? He lifted the hasp with a trembling hand.

'I've always kept it with me,' Mildrel said from behind him. 'I knew that sooner or later you would put it back on. You're a man of the West, a general of the Imperial Army. You are Dun-Cadal Daermon.'

He opened the trunk and the gleam of an old suit of polished armour made him squint. Or was it the tears brimming in his eyes? With his fingertips, he brushed the blade that lay upon the breastplate. This sword had served in the Saltmarsh, in the Vershan, at Kapernevic ...

'There's a horse waiting for you ...'

He stood up slowly, feeling Mildrel leaning against his shoulder. He raised his hand to caress her cheek and then slid it along her nape, savouring the smoothness of her skin. And without a word they held each other in their arms, for one last embrace, one last time.

They knew they would never see one another again.

Azdeki would summon the councillors who were sworn to secrecy to the inner courtyard. He'd bring them to the gods' chapel on the opposite side of the courtyard to the ballroom, the doors would be shut behind them, and the most loyal guards would be posted in front of the entrance. And then he would achieve his goal.

No, thought Laerte.

He would give a long speech about the history of the Sacred Book, about the decision of Aogustus Reyes to place it in the safekeeping of the Uster family, about the deliberate decline of the Order of Fangol and about the dangers of a corrupt Republic. Azdeki would condemn the councillors as too lax, too inclined towards change; he would evoke the loss of values, of the Order's morality, of the teachings of the Holy Scriptures. And then he would show them the *Liaber Dest*, would brandish it like a standard so that all would follow his lead. He would allow the monks of Fangol to decide the fate of the former Bishop of Emeris, as proof of his faith and devotion. And a new regime, more just, more respectful, less permissive, would be born from his words. He would rely on the *Liaber Dest* to legitimise his seizure of power, translating the enigmatic verses and the strange engravings in his own fashion. He would give them whatever meaning he wanted, thanks to Aladzio's work. It was what Azdeki was hoping for, that's what he'd been preparing for all these years.

A thousand times no, Laerte swore to himself. The future of the Republic was not his primary concern. But the idea that his father's assassin might also pervert his dream was unbearable. As he advanced towards the balconies that surrounded the inner courtyard he recalled his years of suffering, hiding behind the identity of Frog, denying what he had been. He was ready at last.

His hand on Eraëd's pommel, he walked with a resolute step. The men at his side opened the way for him, quietly suppressing the guards. Not once did he unsheathe the Emperors' sword. Soon an entire section of the palace would be under the control of de Page's men. The very men that Azdeki had been pushed and manipulated into recruiting, thinking to fortify the place. How ironic ...

'Take your positions,' Laerte ordered in a low voice.

Standing in a doorway, he designated each corner of the balconies and then walked out onto one of them, letting his gaze drift over the crowd conversing below. Men in livery were doing their best to provide service, filling glasses of wine at the barrel, bringing out platters of grilled meat, making their way as deftly as possible among the prestigious guests. All those present were councillors, dignitaries, wealthy men. This gathering was far from the spirit of Masque Night. More ordinary people were restricted to the great ballroom and under close guard.

The mercenaries concealed themselves behind the columns and, armed with their bows, knelt down as close as possible to the balustrades. Laerte looked at the barrels, piled up to form an odd-looking stairway. With a firm hand, he grasped the shoulder of a kneeling man before him.

'The range?'

'Perfect,' the mercenary smiled as he set down an oil lamp.

'Only on my signal,' Laerte reminded him, as he sought to spot familiar figures among the crowd.

There were masks by the dozens and costumes made of silk and linen, all of them different, all of them unique. Colours danced, laughter rose, mouths opened to enjoy pieces of meat and joyfully try the poured wine. The courtyard resembled a fairground show of monstrous freaks.

And within the throng, he spied an eagle's head.

'That's Bernevin over there, and this one here is Daguaret,' de Page whispered in Viola's ear.

The duke was observing the slightest movements, the most subtle gestures, that might indicate any associations between the chatting councillors. It was second nature to him, first at the Imperial court and more recently in the Republican assembly, to pay close attention to such tiny details. From the glances and nods of heads he perceived, he could work out the links between those sending and receiving them. The opinions of each person, the political manoeuvres and the friendships they valued, all this information served him to envisage the web being woven by Azdeki.

On his arm, Viola was helping him analyse the comings-and-goings of the dignitaries as they walked up a great hallway lined with mirrors, towards an inner courtyard and a delicious aroma of grilled pork.

'Daguaret defended your law on education,' noted Viola.

'Yes. But I bought his support,' smiled de Page as he scrutinised the crowd advancing ahead of them. 'That man has always put a price on ideas.'

'What about El Chaval?' wondered the young woman, looking away.

They passed in front of three men in yellow masks who were involved in a quiet discussion, glasses of wine in their hands. With his hair tied back in a ponytail, an affable air and a well-built body, El Chaval was nodding nervously.

'He's conceited and vulgar but there's no denying his passion,' said de Page. 'Although he is a believer, he's not in favour of a Republic under the thumb of the Order of Fangol. He has an honest position, even if it's not one I share. They haven't approached him.'

His father had told him; he had screamed it at him, propped up on his elbows, before his heart gave out.

'You'll have no place in this world, Gregory! You and your vices will be judged in the eyes of the gods, because no one can be freed from what was written. The Liaber Dest *has been found again!'*

The image of that face twisted in hatred, the lips quivering with rage, and the spittle at their corners, had haunted him ever since. It wasn't simply a question of *power* that had prompted his father and the Azdekis to murder Oratio and co-opt his cherished Republic. It had always been their religious creed. Perhaps some had seen all this as progress – giving people a say in their lives – but that wasn't what mattered to the conspirators. The only thing that counted for them was the word of the gods and that dwelled in the Sacred Book which the Reyes dynasty had taken such care to hide away.

'To your right,' murmured Viola.

De Page tilted his head slightly as a group of Fangolin monks passed by. With their hoods drawn over their heads and their hands joined before them, they were heading towards a door on the opposite side of the courtyard, flanked by four halberdiers.

On the threshold, councillors were gathering without exchanging a single word. As de Page had been expecting, Daguaret accompanied Rhunstag and Bernevin. Under the cover of the uproarious celebrations, no one noticed the group forming in front of Etienne Azdeki. The latter was standing on the porch looking out across the inner courtyard with a steely gaze, his hands behind his back. It was a calm, dignified pose. The monks joined his group.

Not one statesman present had escaped de Page's attention, not a single one. He knew exactly who the enemies of the Republic were and any who survived this evening would not emerge unscathed. He would make certain none of them ever exercised power again.

'This is the moment, isn't it?' whispered Viola, gripping his arm more tightly.

De Page nodded briefly. The courtyard was swarming with guests, many already drunk. If a tragedy occurred the ensuing panic would be total and, more importantly, impossible to control. De Page raised his head towards the balconies, where he could make out a familiar silhouette behind a column. Laerte was ready, the golden mask sparkling in the torchlight. Out of the corner of his eye the duke glimpsed Rogant between a buffet table and the doors leading to the ballroom. As for Aladzio … the inventor was nervously threading a path through the guests, face hidden behind a fox mask, his tricorne jammed on his head. Everything was coming together perfectly.

'This evening, my friends, this evening!' called a voice.

De Page stiffened.

Within the crowd the tricorne seemed to slip between the tall head-dresses and baroque masks. Laerte tracked it until Aladzio extricated himself from the mob. After exchanging a few words with Azdeki he entered the Palatio, but not without giving a brief glance over his shoulder. At Laerte's feet the mercenary was dipping the point of an arrow towards the oil lamp.

'This evening, my friends, this evening!'

He nocked the arrow and raised his eyes towards the man in the golden mask, waiting for him to drop his hand.

'It's a wonderful evening!'

But Laerte was still, as if paralysed. His heart seemed to stop beating as a man in the courtyard helped a young woman to climb onto the barrels.

'For to the joy of this Republican night has been added the sublime happiness of my marriage. My wife—'

Her purple gown hugged her full curves, a star-like medallion hung on her bosom, and her carmine lips enhanced the whiteness of her smile. Behind her mask beaded with gold and silver, her almond eyes shone with tears which finally spilled, taking with them a little of the black kohl lining her eyes. She laughed as she took her place on top of the barrels as if upon a stage, one hand holding her husband's.

'Esyld Azdeki, show yourself to the world!' shouted Balian Azdeki.

'Sir?' murmured a voice at Laerte's feet.

Balian took off his wolf mask to look out at the crowd before him, spreading his arms. Intoxicated by alcohol, he was relishing this moment.

'Thank you all for being here on this day. Long live the Republic!'

The applause boomed like massed war drums. Laerte felt his hand tremble.

'Sir, I'm ready,' hissed the mercenary.

Beneath his eagle's head, Azdeki watch the scene from the porch with satisfaction. His son, so happy, was bowing to Esyld to the sound of cheers from the guests. No one was paying attention to the councillors passing through the doorway or to the monks who followed, disappearing within the Palatio.

Upon the barrels, Esyld was thanking the crowd, bowing to the left, bowing to the right, laughter bursting from her lips, her cheeks flushed with embarrassment ... or with joy. Laerte felt the weight of his mask, his breathing becoming laboured, his muscles rigid and his stomach tied in knots as he watched. Although she was walking across the barrels of wine, the ones stacked behind her were filled with powder. A single spark and ...

De Page was darting worried glances towards Rogant, standing by the doors to the corridor, and towards the balconies where he could still see the motionless silhouette. *The attack, Laerte,* he thought. *Give the signal! Go on!*

Clinging to his arm, Viola tugged the duke forward slightly as if she were about to intervene. But what could she do? Soldiers had pushed back the Nâaga guarding the wine barrels and were flanking Balian and his wife. Viola had no means of drawing them away. The idea that everything they'd worked for might come to a halt right then and there crept in to his mind, leaving him despondent. He raised his eyes again to the balcony where Laerte waited, hoping to see a movement there.

'We're running out of time, sir,' the mercenary said anxiously.

Laerte heard his voice as if from a great distance. His hand was still raised. His heart ...

The councillors had all filed through the double doors.

'Bravo! Bravo!' cried the crowd. 'Long live the newlyweds! Bravo!'

The halberdiers posted themselves before the doors as Azdeki stepped back. One of the guards climbed the steps and closed one of the panels. Azdeki vanished and the soldier approached the second panel.

Still standing on the barrels, Esyld was looking at her husband with such tenderness, her hands folded over her chest.

Laerte's hand remained raised.

The soldier pulled the second door panel shut.

'Sir!'

'It goes much further than that.'

409

With his right hand, Laerte gripped Eraëd. Everything seemed confusing to him. And in the din of clapping hands, he heard a hammering noise, like drumming. Muffled at first ... then more and more distinct, until he could finally identify it as the clattering of hooves on marble. Even in the thunder of applause, a few masks had turned towards the hall of mirrors, intrigued by the ringing of iron on stone. The staccato rhythm continued to rise in volume, accompanied by the barking of orders in its wake. At the opposite side of the courtyard, the double doors were shut. Even if Laerte unleashed the attack now the conspirators, alerted by the sound of fighting, would have plenty of time to flee before he could find them in the Palatio's maze of hallways.

'It's about the path you chose to take.'

Most of the crowd was still applauding the bride and groom. Esyld looked radiant. Balian Azdeki approached the barrels, catching hold of his lady love's hand to bring it to his lips. The sound of hooves drew closer, a continuous drum roll now, stronger, more menacing. And with it, the bawling of angry orders.

'And what if you come across Esyld this evening? Will you give in to your anger?'

Hooves against marble, screaming ... and a voice, stern and hoarse, filled the courtyard like a clap of thunder.

'Azdeki!'

14

THE PATH OF ANGER

Dun-Cadal had forced Laerte to kneel before him, a firm hand on his apprentice's shoulder. The pain of the impact stabbed Laerte's knees but, gritting his teeth, he did not cry out. He knew he was being observed, judged, and not for anything in the world would he betray any sign of weakness. His face must not reveal anything. His heart was pounding and sweat beaded at his temples. He would hold out. The knights were assembled in a semi-circle about him, wearing polished armour that gleamed in the morning sunshine. Behind them stood the tall, pure-white statues of the divinities, their expressionless gazes directed down at the altar.

Across the stained-glass windows, colourful representations of knights fought monsters and demons, rouargs and dragons, protecting frightened families with drawn swords.

'For faults committed,' said Dun-Cadal.

He slapped Laerte so hard that the young man felt his neck crack.

'And so that you shall commit no more, Frog.'

His other cheek burned beneath another powerful blow, so hard his head seemed ready to detach itself from the rest of his body. He could taste blood where his teeth had bitten down on his lip. Tears formed at the corners of his eyes. He inhaled deeply, his jaws tightly clenched.

'Repeat after me,' ordered Dun-Cadal. 'I am the sword, I am the shield.'

'I am the sword,' mumbled Laerte.

'Louder!'

'I am the sword!' he began again, raising his eyes towards his mentor. 'I am the shield.'

'I am he who does not weaken,' Dun-Cadal continued, beneath the stern gazes of his brothers-in-arms.

'I am he who does not weaken.'

'I am the sword against the mighty. The shield for the meek. My word is gold. I shall not renege on it. I am he who marches into combat. My path is that of the just. I shall not falter. I am he who marches into combat.'

Laerte repeated the words aloud while Dun-Cadal drew his sword and placed it briskly upon his apprentice's shoulder.

'I am the sword and the shield, that is my sole path. Nothing shall ever restrain my arm.'

'... nothing shall ever restrain my arm,' Laerte finished in one breath.

He could not stop himself from closing his eyelids when Dun-Cadal lifted the sword before bringing the flat of the blade smashing down on his right shoulder. Laerte gritted his teeth.

'I free you from who you once were. He no longer matters.'

He sensed the sword passing over his head. Then the pain from the blow to his left shoulder made him open his eyes.

'Repeat after me,' his mentor demanded again. 'I hereby pledge my oath ...'

'I hereby pledge my oath ...

'To never take the path of anger, to always serve justice with honour and righteousness. To be a knight, among knights, and in good faith.'

'... and in good faith,' concluded Laerte, with a lump in his throat.

In the shadows and light of the chapel, Dun-Cadal's face bent down towards his, grave and proud.

'I name thee: Sir Frog.'

'I name thee: Sir ...'

'Azdeki! You scum!'

The horse reared as it burst into the courtyard, its hide bristling with spears and dripping rivers of blood. Men and women, terrorised, scattered screaming when the knight was thrown into the air and fell heavily to the ground, wheezing mightily. His mount's hooves fell back to the ground. It was, snorting frantically, and then convulsed and collapsed onto its flank, tongue hanging from its open mouth. Behind it soldiers came running, caught short by the sudden charge. They had seen the rider come tearing through the crowd in the square outside and leap the palace steps, sweeping the air with his sword. Some of them had tried to stand in his way, but the panicked horse had reared and kicked repeatedly. The spears had only maddened it further. And its rider had led it to its death, here in the courtyard.

Dun-Cadal struggled to pick himself up from the ground, still dazed, and bellowing, he sought to find the pommel of the sword lying beside him.

'Azdeki! By the gods! Show yourself!'

Drawing his own sword, Balian Azdeki helped Esyld climb down from the barrels and she was immediately encircled by soldiers. Guards were now pouring into the courtyard, ready to pounce on the intruder, while the crowd, still reeling in surprise, wavered between fear and curiosity. An old man urging a councillor to come out and face him, wearing worn-out armour held together by aging leather straps, seemed more like theatrics than a real threat.

In one corner of the courtyard, de Page was finding the situation not to his liking. Rogant joined him in the pandemonium caused by the general's impromptu arrival and the Nâaga begged him to leave the scene, grasping his arm to push de Page and Viola towards the hall of mirrors.

Out in the middle of the open space, Dun-Cadal faced his opponents, gathering his wits, a strange smile playing across his lips. He felt himself being restored to life. Although his bones ached from the fall and reminded him of his age, he hoped to show the world what sort of warrior he really was. To do it one last time. The guards surrounded him, their spears pointed in a menacing fashion. He had a sensation of déjà vu, and his smile faltered.

'*Your Imperial Majesty, he's still just a child! You have no right!*'

The torches sputtered. There was no more laughter, no more music, nothing but a charged silence. Balian passed through the circle of guards, his weapon in his fist.

'Arrest this man!' he commanded.

'You, blondie, should wait until your voice deepens before giving orders like that,' sneered Dun-Cadal, before raising his own voice. 'It's Etienne Azdeki – *Captain* Azdeki – I've come for! Azdeki! Show yourself!'

The guards hesitated as the shadow of a man emerged from

between the double doors. On the threshold of the hall of mirrors, on the other side of the courtyard, de Page paused. Beside him, Viola seemed lost, glancing at the barrels piled on the platform before meeting Rogant's determined gaze.

'Leave now,' he muttered.

'Don't interfere,' ordered de Page, giving him a black look.

'I won't need to,' the Nâaga assured him, his face grim.

De Page could not be associated with what was about to happen. Whether it succeeded or failed, no one could learn of the duke's role in this operation. Not simply for his own protection, but because of what would ensue from this night. Rogant followed the duke and Viola with his eyes and when they disappeared at the end of the hallway he slipped behind one of the door panels at the entrance.

'Azdeki!' Dun-Cadal yelled again.

He swung his sword, almost dropping it. This would not be easy. The gesture no longer came naturally to him and it had been a long time since he last fought in combat.

'Do you hear me?' exploded Balian. 'I order you to arrest this man. He—'

'Daermon ...'

The voice had dragged slightly as if savouring the name. Standing on the threshold of the double doors, his eyes blazing behind his eagle mask, Etienne Azdeki tilted his head to the side, looking intrigued. At his back the shapeless mass of his uncle could be seen, wallowing in his large white toga.

'Arrest him!' repeated Balian.

The soldiers were ready to obey this time, but they had barely taken a step when Etienne Azdeki called out:

'Wait!'

He came down the steps, one hand on the pommel of his sword, showing no sign of any emotion but curiosity. Feeling more self-assured, Dun-Cadal flashed him the grim smile of a man looking for a fight.

'You weren't expecting me, were you?' he jeered. 'Worried?'

'I'm worried that an old wreck like you got through my doors so easily,' replied Azdeki without losing his unruffled demeanour.

Murmurs of excitement ran through the assembled crowd, few of whom were deciding to leave the courtyard and miss the spectacle being played out there. But although the knight in armour was ready for battle, the councillor remained indifferent to him. Still staring at Dun-Cadal he raised his voice:

'How is this for a touch of Masque Night whimsy? A knight of the Empire has forced his way into the Palatio and ended up here! There's nothing to fear from him. Look, he's as rusty as his armour!'

'Come and test that, Azdeki,' proposed Dun-Cadal. 'Come and pay for your crimes. You betrayed the Empire and now you're planning to betray the Republic.'

He swung his sword again, but this time the movement was slow and precise, his hand gripping the hilt firmly.

'So the old dog still has some teeth,' murmured Azdeki, his lips twisted in disdain, before he addressed the crowd again. 'Please accept my apologies for this incident, it is more spectacular than dangerous! Amuse yourselves, there's no need for concern!'

'Let the celebration continue!' Rhunstag called from behind him.

The guards approached the general cautiously under the supervision of Balian, standing by the platform. Only a few feet away from him, dwarfed between two massive halberdiers, Esyld watched the scene, her face completely white. The councillor spun round and was about to pass back through the double doors when Dun-Cadal rumbled:

'The *Liaber Dest*, Azdeki! Have you told them? Is Anvelin Evgueni Reyes still your prisoner? So explain to them, your guests, what awaits them all!'

Dun-Cadal pointed to the people gathered in the courtyard with the tip of his sword, noting the stir that his words caused with satisfaction. The murmurs grew louder and with them a strange uneasiness, fraught and oppressive. Azdeki had halted on the steps, his shoulders hunched and his body stiff. A word, just one, could be heard in all the whispers: the *Liaber* . . .

'Let them try to stop me, nothing will prevent me from reaching you,' Dun-Cadal promised.

Azdeki turned around, losing his haughty air. Furious, he pointed at Dun-Cadal and snarled at the soldiers, no more than a few feet away from the general.

'Get this rubbish out of the courtyard! Chain him up!'

'Come on, Azdeki, show me what you're capable of,' scowled Dun-Cadal as he slashed the air with his sword, darting a glance right and the left in anticipation of an attack by the soldiers.

The crowd was becoming agitated. The halberdiers urged Esyld to make her way towards the hall of mirrors and Balian was walking around the circle of soldiers.

'Throw him in a gaol cell!'

'Draw your sword! Be a knight!'

Their shouts covered the whistle of the arrow above their heads. Some caught a fleeting glimpse of the wavering flame and a trail of flying sparks.

'You're nothing, Daermon, you're a dea—'

The steel tip split the wooden barrel. And everything exploded.

The fire took hold of the platform with a loud crackling as a thick black smoke rose from the debris. The power of the explosion had caused havoc, throwing Dun-Cadal to the ground and blasting the closest guests, while forcing the others to rush away from the blaze and into the extremities of the courtyard.

Laerte had leapt from the balustrade at the very moment the arrow had lodged itself in the barrel. Using the *animus*, he had landed noiselessly on the ground, feeling his body vibrate from the impact. He sensed the heartbeats of the general lying at his feet and, reassured, swept his gaze around the courtyard. Dun-Cadal slowly regained his wits, his fingers digging furrows in the gravel. As planned, the explosion has just been enough to sow confusion. In front of the doors Azdeki was waving at the smoke, trying to dissipate the thick acrid veil that was obscuring his vision. He didn't see the arrows which sliced through the smoke to plant themselves in the throats of the halberdiers at his side.

And then a rain of steel fell on the courtyard, mowing down the men in arms. The panicked guests rushed towards the hall of mirrors, elbowing one another aside, trampling the poor wretches who still lay stunned on the ground and overturning tables. On the steps Azdeki seemed to be paralysed. The cries, the smell of the powder, the trickles of blood, the smoke rising in coils, all of it was sheer chaos ... in the middle of which stood a man in a green cape.

Laerte waited, his hand on Eraëd's pommel, the rapier's point brushing the gravel. When he caught Azdeki's gaze behind his eagle mask, he was triumphant. For the very first time he saw fear there.

'You ...' he saw the man say. 'It's you ...'

'Oh buggering hell ...' grumbled Dun-Cadal as he stood up.

The courtyard was rapidly emptying. Among the wreaths of smoke and burnt, floating shreds of the awnings, a starry sky appeared. In the torchlight and glow of the flames still consuming the platform, the sword of the Emperors sparkled. Inert bodies, bristling with arrows, were strewn across the ground. All of them were wearing armour or studded leather vests, all of them were still gripping their sword or their halberd. None of them had detected the mercenaries on the balconies, who were now rising before the stupefied eyes of Etienne Azdeki.

Near the hall of mirrors, a few yards from the blasted platform, Esyld was kneeling on the ground, horror-struck, running a hand through Balian Azdeki's dusty, dirt-streaked hair. An arrow jutted from his shoulder at the junction between his spaulder and the breastplate that slowly rose and fell in time with his breathing. He might have been asleep and suffering a nightmare, his mouth twisted in pain. The crackling of the flames covered the words his bride was murmuring to him. She raised her eyes to meet those behind the golden mask and her distraught expression suddenly vanished as anger tightened her features. Laerte eluded her gaze, his heart pierced.

'So that's how it is,' said Azdeki as he watched the mercenaries abandon their positions.

'The *Liaber Dest*, Azdeki,' shouted Dun-Cadal. 'Where is it?'

Slowly, the councillor lifted his hand towards his face to remove his mask. The fear was gone from his eyes and there was a sad, almost mocking, smile on his lips.

'Are there still any soldiers in the gardens? Or did your mercenaries finish them off as well?' he asked, looking up at the now deserted balconies.

Dun-Cadal wanted to take a step forward but almost tripped over a body. Laerte's arm restrained him.

'I can still stand,' the old man growled.

In his reddened eyes Laerte saw a curious spark and, almost involuntarily, he nodded.

Slowly, Dun-Cadal straightened up, tilting his head to the left and right to remove the kink in his neck. There was no need for words; they were still linked by the bond that had formed when they first met. Both of them recalled their shared moments, from the Saltmarsh to Kapernevic, battling side by side, looking out for one

417

another like father and son. Without consulting one another both of them lifted their swords towards Azdeki in a gesture of challenge.

From the distant ballroom, coming down the hall of mirrors, the enraged voices of soldiers could be heard approaching. Perhaps he believed he would be saved? Azdeki drew his sword. But his face hardened when he saw the Nâaga at the entrance opposite. Rogant had appeared around the edge of a panel and, after a quick glance at the soldiers running down the hall towards them, he closed the double doors. Azdeki retreated up the steps on his side of the court-yard, breathing heavily. The trap was closing around him. There were no soldiers at his back to defend him; this private part of the Pala-tio had been mostly entrusted to the mercenaries. All that remained were those assigned to guarding the Book. When the door opposite was barred and Rogant had turned round, Azdeki spied the kneeling form of his daughter-in-law through the thick smoke. Lying before her, Balian raised a shaking hand towards the arrow poking out of his shoulder.

'This it between us, isn't it?' asked Azdeki between two strained sighs. 'Let them live.'

'I am a knight, Etienne,' replied Dun-Cadal, before adding almost scornfully: 'I always have been.'

The old general lowered his sword and stepped to one side without taking his eyes off the councillor. But Laerte turned his eyes towards the wounded man Esyld was helping to prop up as he took hold of the arrow, preparing to yank it out. He imagined himself leaping upon Balian and preventing him from removing it, striking him with all his might until he cried for mercy, and then, ignoring his pleas, plunging Eraëd into his heart. Tears traced dotted lines through the dust that covered Esyld's face and the glow from the flames danced in her pupils. Even dirty and with her hair in disarray, she was beau-tiful; the same beauty he had always admired in the marshes of their birthplace.

'I have your word, Daermon,' declared Azdeki.

His breathing. It was heavy, irregular, and had taken on a whistling quality as he retreated. He had already passed through the double doors and was backing down the hallway, keeping his sword hand slightly behind him. But his free hand was visibly lifting.

'Laerte,' murmured Dun-Cadal.

Laerte tightened his hand around Eraëd's hilt, his belly knotted and his throat dry behind the golden mask. Esyld occupied his thoughts, only her, nothing else could have freed him from his malaise. Not even the annihilation of Etienne Azdeki. Esyld had locked eyes with him and was standing, dignified despite her tears, one hand still holding that of her husband. White-faced, Balian remained on his knees.

'The—'

Dun-Cadal did not finish his sentence. Azdeki stretched out his free hand and the doors immediately slammed shut. The *animus*.

'You son of a dog!' bellowed the general as he charged towards the double doors.

'No!' Balian screamed, almost collapsing as he pulled the arrow from his shoulder with a sudden jerk.

The father could wait; he wouldn't leave the Palatio. Instead Laerte advanced resolutely towards the young man, who was now drawing his sword as he stood up, grimacing from the effort.

With a violent kick, Dun-Cadal separated the two door panels, biting down a curse at the sharp pain in his knee, and stumbled into the hallway beyond before halting. Laerte wasn't following him. Out in the courtyard there was a clatter of swords. When he turned round, he saw Balian and his former apprentice confronting one another, while Rogant struggled to keep hold of Esyld, burning sparks fluttering down all around them.

'Laerte!' he called.

But the only reply he received was the clash of blades.

'No, I'm begging you!' implored Esyld.

Sweat beaded Balian's brow, only the force of will keeping him on his feet. He sought to find the right angle of attack but his adversary parried with far too much ease. Although Laerte knew that time was running short, he enjoyed this brief proof of his superiority. He turned his rapier with a brusque flick of the wrist which disarmed Balian, before punching him in the face.

'No!' cried Esyld, weeping.

Eraëd sped towards the wounded groom's throat.

'Laerte!' she sobbed, falling limp in the arms of the Nâaga.

'Frog!'

The voice was like thunder, so loud, so commanding, carrying with it so many memories. The point of the rapier scored just a drop of blood from Balian's neck. Exhausted, a red, sticky stream running over his armour from his shoulder wound, the young scion of the Azdeki family fell back to his knees.

'You haven't waited all your life for this!' protested the general coming up behind Laerte. 'You are a knight! *A knight!*'

Rogant pushed Esyld behind him and threw himself between Balian and Laerte before his friend finally took a step back. The Nâaga and the young knight glared at one another, neither willing to bend.

'It's not necessary,' Rogant said. 'Not him.'

And as if trying to escape from the condemnation of his most faithful companion, Laerte spun round, stiffened by his bottled-up anger. His mentor waited for him on the threshold of the broken double doors. Behind him, a wide hallway extended into the building, lit by dozens of torches whose light danced beneath the caress of a night breeze. Laerte felt himself torn between two worlds, two eras, two desires, each as burning and as disturbing as the other. Who was he? Laerte ... Or Frog ...?

Everything was suddenly unbearable to him: Esyld's sobs as she threw herself upon Balian and folded him in her arms, the crackle of the flames around them, the smell of burnt wood, the bitter taste of the stagnant smoke, even his own breathing.

'Frog,' repeated Dun-Cadal, sorrowfully. 'Are you a knight or an assassin?'

Laerte inhaled deeply before taking a step towards the general.

'I am a knight, Wader, the best there is,' he assured him. 'The greatest one of all. I promised you that.'

'Then keep your promise.'

There was a chapel undergoing restoration at the heart of the Palatio. At its rear rose an altar and the walls were lined with imposing statues of men and women in long robes. They had suffered with the passage of time: cracks ran over the stone, from the bases to their heads. Sitting against the altar a gaunt old man was moaning, his body bruised and his arms spread wide by heavy chains. A few strands of stringy white hair fell from a skull covered in brown spots. His half-closed eyes moved slowly from the right to the left as if he were seeing his surroundings for the first time. Between the divine statues hung bright yellow drapes and flames danced in broad bowls at the gods' feet. Wide supporting beams crisscrossed the ceiling, masking a vault painted with a damaged fresco.

Anvelin Evgueni Reyes, the last Bishop of Emeris and master of the Order of Fangol during the Imperial era, had known he was a condemned man for years. But far from resigning himself to the idea he was hoping, in these last instants, that someone would rescue him. He had seen him, he had spoken to him on so many occasions these past months. The man in the golden mask. He had told him all about the pact of the Book and the Sword, the importance of their separation, and the link between Uster and Reyes. No one, on this earth, deserved to possess both pillars of civilisation.

'In my left hand the Book, in my right hand the Sword, and at my feet the World.'

Reyes was deaf to the councillors' panic. He simply waited. The sound of a distant explosion had made him smile. The storm that would save him was approaching. And the murmurs of the gods would be fulfilled. It was not his destiny to die here, like some poor wretch. Not when he had governed the Order of Fangol for so many years. Of all the men present only the one wearing the tricorne, who was huddled against a statue, showed any sign of compassion towards him. And of them all, he was the one who did not seem worried.

'Is it an attack?'

'Who would dare?'

'It's the assassin, I'm certain of it! He killed Enain-Cassart and Negus, and now he's coming for us!

'Where is Azdeki?'

'Gentlemen! Please be calm!' demanded Azinn, near the altar.

Draped in his large white toga, he had lifted his falcon mask to the top of his skull and made a soothing gesture with his hands. The twenty or so councillors around him were darting frightened gazes towards the entrance to the chapel, despite the presence of the Azdekis' personal bodyguards in front of the altar. Silent in one corner of the room, the Fangolin monks seemed aloof from the commotion, almost serene. All that mattered to them was the half-naked prisoner.

'What is going on?' shouted Daguaret, pointing at Azinn. 'Is this some sort of trap?'

He was immediately shoved by Rhunstag's massive figure.

'No trap! There's no trickery from the Azdekis,' he swore, looking grim. 'So watch yourselves.'

There was an anxious rumble of voices. All of them were wondering if they should leave rather than risk finding themselves held prisoner. What they had been promised was evidently not going to be found here and the suspicion that they had been deceived was becoming a certainty. Finally, the one person who might calm their panic, the person who had lured them here, came through the door and bellowed:

'Guards! Up here, to the sides!'

He walked with a determined step, sword in hand, his face tense. His mere presence brought silence and the guards obeyed at once, leaving the edge of the altar to position themselves to either side of the entrance.

'Make way!' ordered Azdeki, sweeping the air with his free hand. 'Gentlemen! Make way! Form a guard of honour for our illustrious guests!'

He walked straight through the group of councillors without giving them a glance, his piercing eyes fixed on the man attached to the altar. When he reached the former bishop's side, he knelt down.

'It's time, Anvelin,' he murmured.

The old man barely raised his head, looking weary. Out of the corner of his eye, Azdeki caught sight of the Fangolin monks and beckoned to them.

'Nephew,' whispered Azinn behind his back, 'what's going on? Is it the assassin?'

Azdeki ignored him, standing proudly, his gloved hand gripping the hilt of his sword. Had he lost his able right hand or would he finally prove to the old general that he had always been a skilful swordsman? In a minute, perhaps less, they would be here. So he faced the assembled councillors, still in a muddle and visibly debating whether or not to follow his order. Among them, Bernevin removed his mask, revealing a grave face. After exchanging a glance with Azdeki he nodded tersely and proceeded to divide the group into two, positioning them between the bowls to either side of the chapel.

'Aladzio, bring it here,' commanded Azdeki.

The man in the tricorne joined him, flanked by two halberdiers, reverently carrying a box of varnished wood edged in gold. Azdeki opened it delicately, measuring the importance of the moment.

'Gentlemen,' he proclaimed as he withdrew an old leather book from the box. Its cover seemed to scintillate in the light from the flaming bowls. 'This is why you are here; chosen by the gods so that order may be restored after centuries of chaos and tyranny. This is what Aogustus Reyes hid from men. This is what the Order of Fangol lost.'

His hands trembled; the volume was heavy. But it was the information it held that made him shake. Aladzio watched him lift it above his head like a standard to which one should rally, raising his voice.

'The *Liaber Dest* has returned to the hands of men, as was foreseen. And with its return comes our duty, our responsibility, however difficult it may be, to restore its splendour to the world.'

If they had been forewarned they might have reacted more calmly, but while all those present shared an unwavering faith, this announcement out of the blue came as complete shock. The Sacred Book was no longer a legend. Azdeki placed his sword upon the altar and with his free hand seized hold of the dagger at his belt.

'The murmur of the gods was transcribed in this work, setting out the destiny of mankind, and the heavy task of leading the flock falls to the great lords of this world! See the book that cannot be destroyed. Do not doubt its writings!'

With a violent jab, he tried to plant the dagger in the book's leather. A gasp of horror – and then amazement – ran through the councillors when the blade broke in two against the cover, leaving not a trace, not a scratch behind. The dagger pieces fell to the floor at Azdeki's feet with a ringing sound.

'I have brought you here for the *Liaber Dest*, and what it has revealed to us. The reason why the gods have chosen us.'

He then spoke to the halberdiers flanking Aladzio.

'Unchain the bishop. Deliver him to the monks and let him be judged by them.'

As the soldiers carried out his order without much regard for the injured old man, Azdeki placed the Book upon the altar and took up his sword, his eyes turned towards the Fangolin monks who remained entirely silent and still.

'Accept this gesture as evidence of my good will. The Reyes dynasty weakened the Order of Fangol the better to keep you on a leash. Be free but recognise us. Recognise our destiny as it is written in the Book.'

Supported by the halberdiers, Anvelin moaned, his bare feet trailing on the floor, with dried blood visible along his legs covered in filth.

'No …' he mumbled, short of breath. 'You only see … what … you want to see … you don't understand … *I* am the Order of Fangol. Not them … not them … they're heretics, they're—'

His words died with a gasp when he was thrown to the floor in front of the impassive monks. Azdeki needed their support. If he was recognised by the last upholders of the faith, he would have legitimacy. Enough to seize power? To overthrow the Republic? He couldn't hide his apprehension, clenching his jaws. Footsteps, quick and determined, were approaching the chapel.

'I have freed the people from the yoke of the Reyes dynasty,' insisted Azdeki.

At the monks' feet Anvelin sought to rise, leaning on the palms of his hands with difficulty, the muscles in his thin arms straining from the effort.

'This madman spoke in your name, but he knew the *Liaber* was in the hands of the Usters. He hid the danger from us; he denied the word of the gods. Recognise me! What is happening this evening is not the result of chance.'

Two shadows grew at the entrance, sliding to the feet of the soldiers posted by the first statues and then shrinking back under the footsteps of Laerte and Dun-Cadal as they passed the threshold, swords in hand. There were signs of fresh panic among the councillors, which died down as the soldiers placed themselves behind the newcomers, cutting off their retreat. Some began to believe Azdeki had planned this all along, while a greater number persuaded themselves that this event must have been written too. As if to encourage the idea, Azdeki concluded in a quiet, icy tone:

'The gods do not play at dice.'

Although Dun-Cadal had turned at the rattling of spaulders against breastplates behind him, Laerte only had eyes for the councillor standing before the altar. The sputtering flames in the bowls froze the moment for what seemed an eternity, barely broken by the footsteps of Rhunstag and Bernevin. They joined Azdeki, who was placing the Book upon the holy table. A few yards away Azinn shrank into the group of Fangolin monks as if hoping to find protection there. Most of those present recognised the figure in the green cape who had created such a stir since the murder of Enain-Cassart by the port. Few, on the other hand, could put a name to the old man in armour who accompanied him.

'Oh, joy ...' grumbled Dun-Cadal, before drawing alongside his former apprentice, who had come to a halt in the middle of the guard of honour that had awaited them.

The general was surprised and disgusted when he caught sight of the gaunt Anvelin Evgueni Reyes at the monks' feet. He had never forgiven the bishop for his betrayal years before, but did the man deserve such a cruel fate? Anvelin had helped him many times when Dun-Cadal had been a young cadet, aspiring to the Knighthood. Whatever crimes he had have committed, in the general's eyes he remained the Bishop of Emeris.

To either side of the chapel, the statesmen observed the two intruders with thinly disguised fear. Only one relatively young councillor, bearing a scar beneath his right eye, seemed more curious than afraid. He tilted his head to one side as if trying to see something of the face hidden beneath the golden mask.

'Arrest them!' his neighbour shouted angrily.

The young man gave him a strangely amused look.

'This was not what was planned, Azdeki!' added another, standing in the opposite row.

The councillors all started to speak at once, urging the soldiers to attack the assassin and his companion. At the feet of the first monk, Anvelin had turned around upon his elbows, a blissful smile stretching his wrinkles slightly.

'You're here ... you came,' he whispered, delighted

'Councillor?' called Rhunstag, drawing his sword.

Azdeki did not respond. Nothing mattered to him at this moment but the golden mask and Dun-Cadal's weary face. They glared unspoken challenges, measuring one another, evaluating their respective strengths, certain that their blades were going to cross. Everything had to end here, it was written. The tension in the air was so palpable that silence returned of its own accord, the councillors losing hope of obtaining any answers from their leader. He had no need to raise his voice in order to be heard.

'I know who you are,' declared Azdeki. 'I know what anger drives you. I understand it. Worse still for you, I respect it. But I can't let you stand in the way of my responsibilities. The truth lies within the Book, Laerte of Uster.'

Astonishment ran through the ranks of the councillors. The name had been spoken aloud. It was a myth returned to life, a terrible legend for all those involved in founding the Republic. Hadn't Laerte of Uster tried to seize power, according to Azdeki, just after the Emperor had been overthrown?

'No, the truth is you're frightened, Azdeki. And you have reason to be!' said Dun-Cadal.

Azdeki could not contain his laughter.

'Of what? Of you, Daermon? Of your spectacular entrance, worthy of the boor you have always been? You will die here, you know, along with the Uster boy. I know my destiny, and I can deduce yours. You won't be able to prevent anything.'

Although he was trying to sound confident, fear tightened his features. Bernevin and Rhunstag hesitated briefly before coming down from the altar. The master and his pupil were reunited and, although time had passed, these two men at least knew what they had represented during the revolution. Azdeki also took a step forward, glancing briefly at the Fangolins.

'Brothers? I need your benediction.'

The monks remained mute beneath their hoods. Before them, Anvelin struggled to remain propped on his elbows, his eyes now filled with tears. Laerte brought his hand to his mask and removed it before letting it slip from his fingertips.

Near the altar, Aladzio retreated slowly, trying to catch Laerte's gaze. But Oratio's son kept his eyes on the three councillors before him who, despite their age, seemed ready to fight.

'There will be no benediction,' Laerte promised. 'No vote of confidence from your councillors. Your book is not so eternal as you claim, Azdeki. Nor does it contain the destiny of men. The Republic shall not fall beneath your yoke.'

'I am not seeking the fall of the Republic,' retorted Azdeki with the poise of one who has no doubts. 'I seek to defend it!'

He took a deep breath.

'Your benediction?' he asked again of the monks.

One of them tilted his head slightly to the side, and then a muffled voice said coldly:

'You have it.'

426

'Now arrest them,' Azdeki ordered in a weary tone.

Azdeki knew that it would not be easy, that he would have a part to play in the combat about to ensue, that both Dun-Cadal and Laerte knew how to employ the *animus* and would not bend before the soldiers. But he would gain some time.

While Azdeki's men launched their assault, Aladzio huddled against the last statue at the rear of the chapel. Things were not going according to plan: Laerte should have attacked the *Liaber Dest* immediately. He should have run it through with his sword and everyone would have fled, losing all faith in Azdeki's claims. Fear gripped the inventor's heart.

And pain seized Dun-Cadal's heart when he crouched, knees creaking, to avoid a spear thrust. He threw himself forward, rolling across the floor, from where he lifted his sword to parry Azdeki's stroke which swooped down on him. Their blades clashed but his chest was on fire. He thrust the palm of his free hand towards three councillors who were charging at him. The *animus* only pushed them back a few feet; but that was enough to allow the old general to regain his feet.

Behind him, Laerte allowed his intuition to guide him, confronted by ten soldiers and the dumbstruck faces of the remaining councillors, who were starting to panic again. Each time he parried he followed up with a slashing stroke, each time he dodged a spear he grabbed the shaft, drew the soldier towards him and pierced him with his blade. Never before had he used a sword as light as Eraëd, as easy to wield, like an extension of his arm. It did not merely block thrusts, it broke steel; it cleaved through armour and bone, sparkling in its lethal dance. Not for one moment was he in any difficulty, not for one instant did he feel overwhelmed. But time was running short. He drew a breath.

His entire body seemed to plunge into flames.

Surrounded by the five soldiers still standing, he dropped to one knee, striking the marble floor with his fist.

The *animus* threw the soldiers into the air like bits of chaff. One flew so high that he crashed into the torso of a statue. The watching councillors rushed for the doors without further ado. When Laerte stood up and turned towards the altar, he saw Dun-Cadal fending off, as best he could, his former companions in arms. His belly full of rage he ran towards his winded mentor, evening the odds with their enemies. Dun-Cadal sidestepped, so that he was left facing Bernevin alone.

'No! No!' screamed Anvelin, only a few feet away.

Forgetting his fatigue, overcoming his pain, he was wrestling with one of the monks. When the Fangolin had placed his hand upon the *Liaber Dest* resting on the altar, the bishop had wrapped his arm around the man's neck and tried to drag him away. Beneath the gaze of Azinn Azdeki, who remained at a safe distance from the fighting, the monk bent backwards, almost toppling on the former bishop. Then, wrenching himself from Anvelin's embrace, he gave the old man a vicious elbow blow to the ribs. The bones cracked. His face turning purple and glassy-eyed, the old man fell into one of the huge fire bowls by the wall. The hungry flames enveloped him as the freed monk returned to the altar. He seized the Book without a glance at the bishop who had been set alight.

The swords continued to clatter and screech as blow followed blow. Parry, thrust, cut. Azdeki and Rhunstag were hard-pressed by Laerte's fury. He was steadily gaining the upper hand over his two opponents. He plunged Eraëd deep into Rhunstag's chest, grabbing the man by the back of his neck to pull him onto the blade completely.

Completely engulfed by the flames, Anvelin let out a harrowing cry. The pain shook him like a loose puppet and it endowed him with enough force to stand up suddenly. But then his legs started to fold beneath his weight and he reeled against a hanging drape. The flames promptly raced up the cloth to reach the wooden beams that crossed the vaulted ceiling.

Bernevin's blade stabbed towards Dun-Cadal's knee, penetrated the gap in his armour below his thigh and tore through his trouser leg to strike muscle. With a moan, the general staggered. His heart labouring painfully, he managed to lift his sword before him with a delicate twist of his arm and deflect his enemy's killing blow.

Standing in the shadow of a statue, Aladzio saw the bishop throw his flaming body, with a last gasp, into the midst of the Fangolin monks who were seeking to flee. The fire spread to their homespun habits. Frightened, Azinn had taken refuge behind the altar. All around the room, fire was running across the beams to propagate itself upon the hangings. The chapel quickly became filled with a thick acrid smoke accompanied by the pungent odour of burning flesh. Two Fangolin monks were rolling on the floor, trying to remove their tunics. The one who held the Book in his hands hurried towards the exit.

A beam gave way above him with a terrific crash.

The monk was crushed beneath it, the *Liaber Dest* falling open near his hand. Flames started to lick the exposed pages.

Amidst the chaos, Dun-Cadal was still holding Bernevin off, while Laerte confronted Azdeki. Each passage of arms was accompanied by wheezing breaths. But it was Laerte's voice that carried furthest, and it was Azdeki's silhouette that retreated first into the smoke. Laerte could make out his adversary's eyes, reddened by the fire and his lean, slender body. At times he saw the gleam of the councillor's blade crossing Eraëd before bending. The image of his father hanging at the end of a rope sprang into his mind.

Laerte struck so powerfully that he heard steel break. Azdeki let out a yell of dismay. Immediately Laerte lunged and swept the air with his sword. He felt Azdeki's knees resist the blow, before they were breached by the ancient blade. Straightening up, he tore the veil of smoke with his arm to seize his fallen enemy by the hair.

He met Azdeki's gaze, and saw fear and disbelief in them, followed by stark terror when Laerte lifted Eraëd.

He brought the sword down upon the man's neck and, one fist retaining its grip upon the grey locks, felt the weight of Azdeki's body disappear. The councillor's head dangled from his fist, its eyes eternally open.

He let it drop. He did not even hear it roll across the floor. His belly was burning. Laerte wanted to vomit, to die, to disappear. His anger still tortured him, and he was short of breath. And then he saw it lying on the ground a few feet away, fallen by an open hand. The *Liaber Dest*. Flames were dancing on its pages without consuming them. Any of them. It remained intact, protected by an unknown magic. But it was something else that made him kneel, his heart pounding fit to burst. Something besides the Book's astonishing invulnerability.

Beneath the flames he saw an ancient engraving, surrounded by strange glyphs. It showed a knight in plain armour sitting beneath a tree. At his feet a child dressed in rags, similar to the ones he had worn in the Saltmarsh, watched him sleep, with a sword in his right hand. And in his left hand ...

429

'Frog—'

Dun-Cadal had crawled to a statue and turned over on his back, his head resting against the base. He was smiling, but there was a strange sadness in his eye as he stretched his arm towards Laerte. Crossing the caustic smoke, the young man joined him and knelt at his side to take his hand. The old general had a gash in one knee and a trickle of blood ran from his lips but no other wounds were apparent. Laerte understood: it was not a sword that had felled him. They exchanged a glance in silence. Not for from them lay Bernevin, his throat slit.

'Laerte …' Dun-Cadal said with difficulty.

His chest rose in fits and starts. His heart was betraying him. Laerte felt the old man's hand in his, but in the midst of the blaze all around them, it was icy cold. They looked at one another. Simply looked. Hand in hand. They were together.

One last time.

A final breath passed through the chapped lips of Dun-Cadal Daermon.

'Laerte … the Book,' he heard.

Through the thick smoke he could see Aladzio's silhouette, his tricorne jammed on his head. He seemed lost and distraught.

'It's not here. It could not have burned, it—'

The inventor fell silent when he saw Dun-Cadal's inert body. Laerte slowly placed the general's hand on his breastplate, and released it. The sound of footsteps and cries could be heard in the distance. He stood without saying a word. His anger had not left him. His fingers contracted around the hilt of his sword as they heard the soldiers approaching. They had broken down the door and occupied the inner courtyard, but had surely been delayed by the panicked councillors. So he wasn't surprised when he heard Rogant's deep voice behind him.

'We have to go.'

The Nâaga tried to hand him the golden mask but Laerte continued gazing upon his mentor's calm and peaceful face.

'I cannot leave him here. Carry him,' he demanded in a terribly cold voice.

Everything around them was on fire. And in a few more minutes, the corridors in this part of the Palatio would be swarming with soldiers hunting for them. They had to leave the chapel and find the passage Laerte had used to enter the building.

'Carry him,' Laerte insisted.

He snatched the mask from his friend's hand.

It had not disappeared.

His anger . . .

EPILOGUE

The destiny of men
Has never been anything
But the murmur of the gods.

Dun-Cadal was buried by the sea without any great ceremony. Only Mildrel stood before the holy man who performed the service, wearing a long black dress with a veil covering her face. No one knew what had really happened at the Palatio. But the rumours spread like burning powder: lies and half-truths, revelations and denials. One name was on everyone's lips, a name that had been reviled since the fall of Asham Ivani Reyes.

Laerte of Uster.

Etienne Azdeki's body had been pulled from the fire in time. But not his head. An investigation had been promptly initiated by the High Council in Emeris, disturbing questions had been raised, and dubious answers were given by way of explanation. The atmosphere in the capital was tense, the councillors looked daggers at one another, and there was widespread speculation that a coup d'état had been narrowly averted. But some whispers in the corridors of the former Imperial palace said the plotter was perhaps not who most people suspected. There had been no news of Azinn Azdeki since Masque Night.

The *Liaber Dest* was mentioned repeatedly. The *Liaber Dest* had supposedly been found.

Balian Azdeki had taken pains to give impassioned testimony before the High Council, swearing upon his honour that his words were true. His father was above any suspicion, he had founded the Republic and fought the tyrant Reyes.

Only after serving him, some objected.

Esyld, devastated, was even summoned to support her husband's claims. Timidly, with tears in her eyes, she faced the councillors and swore she had recognised the son of Oratio during Masque Night. She confessed she had known him and tacitly conceded that he had planned to assassinate the Republic's founding fathers that evening. It was accepted that, as Etienne Azdeki had always claimed, Laerte of Uster had sought to overthrow the Republic and seize power, like the Reyes family before him.

So the truth was deformed, shredded and sculpted by rumours, convictions and political interests. The councillors argued over numerous points, concerning both the nature of these events and their consequences. The only thing upon which they agreed was regarding Laerte of Uster. He had returned and he represented a danger to the Republic. A price had to be placed on his head.

And everyone, from peasant to tavern keeper, from soldier to councillor, told their own version of the tale, imagining the shadowy motives of the Uster heir, his perfidy, his cruelty ... his vendetta. Without anyone, ever, knowing the truth or hearing the tale of the heroic return of a broken glory. Without anyone ever saying the name Dun-Cadal Daermon, laid in the ground beneath the pouring rain in a cemetery at Masalia, by the edge of the ocean.

From far behind the cemetery gates Laerte watched Mildrel grieve for the man who had left them with dignity.

'Vengeance only calls forth vengeance.'

With his fists balled, he looked at her, so beautiful and calm. He wondered for a moment if he should join her to pay his respects to the man who had taught him everything ... but he resigned himself to retreating back into the city's alleyways.

'They're tearing one another to pieces,' shouted Aladzio. 'They've designated you the guilty party, but in truth they're just tearing one another apart. What happened in Masalia has just exacerbated the disagreements among the people's councillors.'

He was nervously piling books up on the long table, coming and going between it and the shelves. Winter was approaching and although the library in the tower lay below ground, a cold draught found a way down and caused the candle flames to flicker.

433

'They're all talking about the *Liaber Dest*. The Fangolin Order is insisting the councillors who were in Masalia account for the disappearance of their envoys. And worse still, particularly for de Page, they are now demanding seats in the assembly.'

He sorted through the volumes distractedly, throwing those he deemed unworthy of interest over his shoulder. He placed the others in big bags made of worn leather.

'They're coming here, Laerte. The Republic's soldiers.'

He stopped suddenly, wearing a serious expression.

'The Order of Fangol wants to recover what it considers to be its rightful place. They will inevitably come here, so I'm saving what I can.'

Leaning against a wall with his arms crossed, Laerte held the inventor's gaze.

'You can't imagine de Page's anger,' sighed Aladzio, reluctantly deciding to abandon three thick codices. 'But that said, he's come out of all this rather well, compared to you. There's been no mention of his name; he's pure as snow, and his mercenaries all had time to leave the Palatio by way of the gardens. He talks about you, you know. He asked me if I knew where you'd gone.'

'You gave me your word,' said Laerte.

'I gave you my word,' acknowledged Aladzio. 'But you should contact him. Perhaps he could protect you.'

'He knows where Azinn went, doesn't he? That's who took the *Liaber Dest* ...'

Aladzio gave him a dark look, bit his lip, and then struggled to close his bulging bags.

'That's what he thinks, yes. But you're not looking for Azinn because of the Book, are you?

With an effort, he placed the bags around his shoulders.

'Rogant is on his trail. He's expecting to see you soon.'

He smiled, but the expression faded as he looked around the library with a resigned gaze.

'They keep knowledge secret,' he said sadly. 'The Fangolins. All of this left to ... it breaks my heart.'

With a limp hand, he patted the leather of one of the bags hanging in front of his chest.

'I'm taking my due,' he smiled grimly.

*

Galapa greeted them with a snigger, sitting on his chair by the door to the ruined tower. Aladzio placed the bags over the croup of his horse, raising his eyes towards Laerte, who was climbing onto his own mount.

'I fear for this old monk,' confessed Aladzio contritely. 'He's a madman, certainly, but I'm going to miss him.'

The inventor seated himself in his own saddle. In the distance, upon the horizon, a cloud of dust was rising. Riders were approaching. Aladzio lifted his tricorne with one hand before placing it again snugly upon his head.

'We're all set,' he said.

'Aladzio ... the Book ... you've read it ... you've seen every page.'

The inventor did not look at Laerte, not even for a second, as if he were embarrassed. He knew what his friend was asking and he was not at all eager to reply.

'Everyone sees what they want to in it, you know,' he said evasively.

'Truly? I don't believe in a destiny written by the gods, but I saw ... At the Palatio, I saw Dun-Cadal in the Book.'

'Ah?' Aladzio smiled with a little hesitation. 'I don't remember seeing that.'

He was still avoiding Laerte's gaze. Galapa's sniggering continued.

'Aladzio, look at me.'

The inventor studied the horizon, seeking to make out the horsemen's silhouettes in the cloud of the dust.

'Look at me,' repeated Laerte.

At last, Aladzio deigned to turn his eyes towards his friend. But his face had lost any trace of embarrassment. A gravity he had never shown before had come over his features.

'Do you truly believe that?' asked Laerte.

'I still have my doubts, Laerte. Certainties are what are really killing the Republic, and I have doubts. And yet, I should like to be *certain* this book is nothing but a fable written thousands of years ago. Upon my life, I wish I could tell you that it was.'

He licked his lips, tugging slightly on the reins to direct his horse towards the muddy path.

'Because I've seen the end of the Book. It's an engraving, a simple image that still keeps its secrets but ... but I'm certain of it. We're approaching that end, my friend.'

'And?'

'And for nothing in the world would I wish to live this particular ending.'

There was a flash of fear in his eyes, just for an instant, that had never been there before.

'You should go and find her,' he advised, with a serious air.

'Who?'

'Viola. Viola Aguirre. She spoke of you, you know. You would have to be blind not to realise how much she cares about her mysterious Laerte of Uster. So you should find her. She left Emeris two days ago for the County of Daermon, in the West. She claimed it was to do some research, but we know that's not the only reason, don't we? It's her way of honouring him. I think ...'

He paused, sniffing the air.

'Yes, you should go and find her. And enjoy a peaceful life, my friend.'

He made his horse join the path and then urged it into a trot.

'Beakie will follow you! Use her to contact me and take care of yourself, Laerte!'

Galapa's chortling had stopped. Laerte remained for a few minutes longer, silently contemplating the view, looking thoughtful. Where should he go now? What path should he follow? He had the feeling that he had lost everything, that he was no longer anything.

'He came, you know, son of Uster, he came to see me,' Galapa announced, with a beaming smile.

His voice was almost whistling as he lifted his milky-white eyes towards Laerte as if he could see him clearly. Disinclined to begin a conversation with a madman, and seeing the riders drawing nearer, Laerte nudged his own horse onto the path that descended from the tower. But Galapa called out again:

'He told me that you sliced off Azdeki's head! That he stood on the threshold to watch you fight!'

Laerte pulled on the reins so sharply that his horse whinnied. He forced it around on the path.

'Who are you talking about?' he demanded. 'Who?'

The only answer he received was a long and exasperating snicker. The old monk slowly unbuttoned his tunic. His head swaying, he spread the lapels of his collar, then proudly exposed his chest.

'The one who left me this handsome present, of course. The one who knows the Book and the Sword must be united!'

436

On his pale skin was an old ridged scar in the form of a rectangle crossed by a straight line. No, not a line. It resembled a slender blade, topped by a twisted hilt.

'The fat Azdeki, he knows him. He heard him murmuring in his ear,' continued Galapa, sounding amused. 'What news of the West? What news from beyond the great sea?'

Time was running out, the riders had become more distinct and one of them bore the banner of the Republic's soldiers. Laerte would have liked to question the monk longer, but he had no desire to fight.

'Who's there?' asked Galapa suddenly.

He ran a brown-spotted hand over his lips, looking confused. Then he snickered again.

In the distance, on a dirt track, dust was rising behind a column of travellers. An obese man with an absent gaze was hiding in the back of a shaking cart beneath a dirty blanket full of holes, clutching a book against him. At times he took little glances around, making sure no one recognised him. In a few hours they would arrive at Eole. At the very end of the track, beyond a wide, dark forest, a city of stone surrounded by strong fortifications rose from the top of a cliff. Here, Azinn Azdeki would be safe. At least he hoped he would be . . . Perhaps he would have thought quite differently if he had noticed the man stroking the flank of his horse on the hill overlooking the track.

'Vengeance only calls forth vengeance. It's about the path you chose to take.'

Laerte watched the column straggling its way along the road. Then he climbed back into his saddle, resolute.

'The path of anger only leads to the abyss, for to continue walking it you must constantly feed that anger, and always be looking behind you. Always. The choice belongs to you . . . Laerte of Uster. My son . . .'

He kicked the horse with his heels and they set off at a gallop . . .

ACKNOWLEDGEMENTS

To Barbara Bessat-Lelarge and Quentin Daniel who were the first to believe in this book.

To the entire team at Bragelonne who have shown great kindness and exemplary professionalism towards me.

To Claire Deslandes for her precious work and advice in revising the work. To Tom Clegg for his suggestions.

A very special thanks to Gillian Redfearn at Gollancz and Stéphane Marsan at Bragelonne for their confidence in me.